P9-BZJ-744

TWICE BORN

Also available in English from Margaret Mazzantini:

Don't Move

Margaret Mazzantini

TWICE BORN

Translated by Ann Gagliardi

Viking

VIKING

Published by the Penguin Group

Penguin Group (USA) Inc., 375 Hudson Street,
New York, New York 10014, U.S.A.
Penguin Group (Canada), 90 Eglinton Avenue East, Suite 700,
Toronto, Ontario, Canada M4P 2Y3 (a division of Pearson Penguin Canada Inc.)
Penguin Books Ltd, 80 Strand, London WC2R 0RL, England
Penguin Ireland, 25 St Stephen's Green, Dublin 2, Ireland
(a division of Penguin Books Ltd)
Penguin Books Australia Ltd, 250 Camberwell Road, Camberwell,
Victoria 3124, Australia (a division of Pearson Australia Group Pty Ltd)
Penguin Books India Pvt Ltd, 11 Community Centre,
Panchsheel Park, New Delhi–110 017, India
Penguin Group (NZ), 67 Apollo Drive, Rosedale, North Shore 0632,
New Zealand (a division of Pearson New Zealand Ltd)
Penguin Books (South Africa) (Pty) Ltd, 24 Sturdee Avenue,
Rosebank, Johannesburg 2196, South Africa

Penguin Books Ltd, Registered Offices: 80 Strand, London WC2R 0RL, England

First published in 2011 by Viking Penguin, a member of Penguin Group (USA) Inc.

10 9 8 7 6 5 4 3 2 1

Copyright © Arnoldo Mondadori Editore S.p.A., 2008
Translation copyright © Ann Gagliardi, 2011
All rights reserved

Originally published in Italian as *Venuto al mondo* by Arnoldo
Mondadori Editore S.p.A., Milan.

Publisher's Note: This is a work of fiction. Names, characters, places,
and incidents either are the product of the author's imagination or are
used fictitiously, and any resemblance to actual persons, living or dead,
business establishments, events, or locales is entirely coincidental.

LIBRARY OF CONGRESS CATALOGING-IN-PUBLICATION DATA
Mazzantini, Margaret.
[Venuto al mondo. English]
Twice born : a novel / Margaret Mazzantini
p. cm
ISBN 978-0-670-02268-7
I. Title.
PQ4873.A9532V4613 2011
853'.914—dc22   2010045258

Printed in the United States of America
Set in Warnock Pro
Designed by Francesca Belanger

Without limiting the rights under copyright reserved above, no part of
this publication may be reproduced, stored in or introduced into a retrieval
system, or transmitted, in any form or by any means (electronic, mechanical,
photocopying, recording, or otherwise), without the prior written permission
of both the copyright owner and the above publisher of this book.

The scanning, uploading, and distribution of this book via the Internet or
via any other means without the permission of the publisher is illegal and
punishable by law. Please purchase only authorized electronic editions and
do not participate in or encourage electronic piracy of copyrightable
materials. Your support of the author's rights is appreciated.

To Sergio

To our children

Oh human tenderness,
where are you to be found?
Perhaps in books alone?

IZET SARAJLIĆ

TWICE BORN

A journey of hope. Leftover words among the many that remain at day's end. I saw them on a jar beside the drugstore cash register. There was a slot on top for donations and a photo of a child who must travel a long way for an operation. A journey of hope. I turn my head on the pillow. Giuliano's heavy body is still. He sleeps as always, bare-chested and on his back. Every so often he lets out a little grunt, like a placid animal shaking off flies.

Hope. As it takes shape in the dark, the word has the face of a bewildered woman dragging her failures along but still moving forward with dignity. It could be my face, the face of a girl grown old but frozen in time out of loyalty, out of fear.

I step onto the balcony and rest my eyes on the familiar surroundings. The shutters are closed on the building across the way. The electric sign in front of the café has yet to be turned on. I hear the silence of the city, the dust of distant noises. Rome—its celebration, its stagnation—is asleep. The outskirts are asleep. So is the Pope. His red shoes are empty.

The phone call comes early one morning. I wake with a start and trip down the hall. I yell, probably to seem like I'm awake. "Who is it?"

There is a noise in the receiver like wind rustling through branches. "May I speak to Gemma?" The Italian is good, but the words are enunciated with excessive care.

"This is Gemma."

"Gemma? You're Gemma?"

"Yes."

"Gemma . . ." He repeats my name and now he's laughing. It only takes me a second to recognize the sharp, hoarse laugh.

"Gojko . . ."

He pauses. "Yes, it's your Gojko."

It's like a motionless explosion, a long void full of detritus.

"My Gojko," I stammer.

"Gojko himself."

His smell. His face. All these years.

"I've been trying to track you down for months."

Out of nowhere, he came to my mind a couple of days ago. I was taking a walk. A boy on the street made me think of him.

We talk. He's fine. He lived for a while in Paris. Now he's back home.

"There's going to be an exhibit to commemorate the siege. Some of Diego's photos will be in the show." I feel the cold of the floor climb up my legs and come to a stop in my gut. "It's an opportunity." He laughs again, just like always, without real cheer, as if trying to console a slight but perennial sadness. "Come."

"I'll think about it . . ."

"Don't think about it. Come."

"Why?"

"Because life passes and we with her . . . do you remember?"

Of course I remember.

". . . and laughs at us, like a toothless old whore awaiting her last client."

Gojko's poetry, life transformed into one long ballad. I recall his habit of touching his nose as he recited the poems he scribbled on match covers, on his hands. I suddenly wonder how I've managed without Gojko for all this time. Why do we insist on depriving ourselves of the best people in life? Why do we spend so much time with people who don't interest us, who don't do us any good—people who simply happen along to corrupt us with their lies and train us to keep our heads down? "Okay. I'll come."

And now the still mud of life is flying toward me like dust.

Gojko shouts with joy.

When I left Sarajevo there was dust everywhere, displaced by the gelid wind to rise up in the air and whirl through the streets, blotting things out as it went, covering minarets and buildings and the dead in the marketplace who lay buried beneath vegetables and knickknacks and pieces of blown-apart stalls.

I ask Gojko why he waited all this time to look for me, why he didn't miss me before now.

"I've been missing you for years."

His voice disappears behind a sigh and again there's that sound of wind, of kilometers of distance.

Suddenly I'm afraid the line will be disconnected and the silence that lasted all those years will return. I ask for his phone number. It's a cell phone. I scratch the numbers onto a piece of paper with a pen that doesn't write. I'm scared to put the phone down to go look for another. The noise grows louder. I picture a telephone wire snapping and letting out sparks as it falls to the ground. How many dangling wires did I see in that isolated city? I press the pen into the paper and grab hold of the past. I'm afraid I'll lose it once again.

"I'll call to let you know when my flight will get in."

I go to Pietro's room and rummage through his pens so I can trace over the white number. Pietro is sleeping, his long feet sticking out of the sheets. I think what I think every time I see him lying down, which is that his bed is too short and we should get him a new one. I pick up his guitar from beside his slippers. It's not going to be easy to convince him to come with me.

I shower and join Giuliano in the kitchen, where he's already made coffee. "Who was that?"

I don't answer right away. My eyes are glazed. In the shower, my skin seemed tougher, like long ago, when I'd soap up quickly and leave the house without drying my hair. I tell Giuliano about Gojko, tell him I want to go.

"All of a sudden, just like that?" But he doesn't seem surprised. "Have you told Pietro?"

"He's sleeping."

"Maybe you should wake him."

Giuliano needs a shave. His mussed hair falls over his forehead, making the balder part in the center of his head more visible. By day, a creature of the city, he's always tidy, at home in carabinieri stations and state archives. This untidiness is for my eyes only. To my mind, it's the best, most pungent and secret part of us. It goes way back to the beginning, when we'd make love and then sit looking at each other, naked and disheveled. We're husband and wife. He came to my aid in a military airport sixteen years ago. Yet when I tell him he saved my life he shakes his head and blushes and says it's not true, says, *It was the two of you, you and Pietro, who saved my life.*

He's got a sweet tooth. Taking advantage of my distraction, he eats another piece of pastry.

"Don't come complaining to me if your belly gets any bigger."

"You're the one who complains. I accept myself as I am."

It's true, he does, and that's why he was able to welcome us, why it's so comfortable to be with him. He stands and puts his hand on my shoulder. "You're doing the right thing."

He's read second thoughts in my look. Suddenly I'm scared. I've fallen backward in time too quickly into the ardor of youth. Now it all seems like nothing but regret. My neck is cold beneath my damp hair. I'd better go back to the bathroom to dry it. I'm myself again, a vanquished girl on the threshold of old age.

"I've got to get ready. I'll have to stop by the office. I don't know . . ."

"You know."

He says he'll call me from the office after he's checked the Internet for cheap tickets. He smiles. "I doubt people are lining up to go to Sarajevo."

I go back to Pietro's room and open the shutters. He pulls the sheet over his head.

This year he shed his childhood skin, abandoned his little-boy bones and became a big limping heron incapable of controlling its own movements, always staring down at the ground, coming in and out without saying good-bye, standing in front of the fridge to stuff his face. Without even trying to, hiding behind an absurd insolence, he managed, with disarming foolishness, to fail the year at school. His loud, surly voice is a constant irritation. He seeks me out only to demand things, to scold. Whatever happened to the plaintive little voice that accompanied me for years and seemed to be in perfect harmony with my own?

Now I feel sorry for him—when he's sleeping, when his face is relaxed. He must miss that graceful little body just like I do. Perhaps he looks for it in his sleep and that's why he never wants to wake up.

I touch his newly bristly hair as I pull down the sheet. He pushes me away.

Now that it's summer, he regrets having failed the year. He leaves the house with his tennis racket and his huge shoes and comes back angry at his friends, grumbling that he doesn't want to see them because next year they won't be in the same class anymore. In his mind, they're the ones who betrayed him.

"I need to talk to you."

He sits up with a jolt. "I'm hungry."

In the kitchen, he spreads Nutella on cookies, making little sandwiches that he swallows in a single bite. His mouth is dirty and the table is full of crumbs. He opened the cookies the wrong way. The package is ripped down the side.

I don't say anything. I can't always be scolding him about everything. In silence I watch him eat. Then I tell him about the trip.

He shakes his head. "No way, Mom. You'll have to go without me."

"Sarajevo is a beautiful city."

He smiles and looks at me with an appealing, cunning expression on his face. "What are you talking about? That's pathetic. Everyone knows Yugoslavia's horrible."

I bristle. "It's not Yugoslavia anymore."

He crams another Nutella-sodden bundle into his mouth, wipes a droplet off the table and sucks it off his finger. "Same difference."

"It is not." I lower my voice, practically begging him. "A week. Pietro. Just the two of us. It will be fun."

He looks at me sincerely this time. "Come on, Mom. How could it be fun?"

"We'll go to the coast. The sea there is gorgeous."

"Why don't we just go to Sardinia?"

I'm doing all I can to hold myself together and this fool starts in about Sardinia. He stands up and stretches, then turns, and I look at his back, the down along his neck. "You really don't care about the place where your father died?"

He puts his cup down in the sink. "Give me a break, Mom."

I'm begging him. My voice is weak, uncertain, just like his when he was a little boy. "Pietro!"

"What do you want?"

I stand abruptly, accidentally spilling the milk.

"What do you mean, what do I want? He was your father!"

He shakes his head and studies the floor. "I'm so sick of this story."

This story is his story, our story, but he doesn't want to hear it anymore. When he was little he was braver and more curious. He'd ask questions and hug me, lean against me, as he looked at the yellowed photo of Diego that I kept on the fridge. But then, as he grew older, he stopped asking questions.

His universe shrank to fit his needs, his selfishness. He doesn't want complications. To him it's enough to know that Giuliano is his father, Giuliano who brought him to school and to the pediatrician's, Giuliano who slapped him once when he dove into shallow water at the beach.

I brush my teeth, put on my jacket and go back to his room. He's still in his underpants, playing the guitar with his eyes closed, the pick brushing against the strings. *A journey of hope.* Those words, which caught my attention by chance, come once again to mind and make me think of Pietro. Hope belongs to children. We adults have already hoped, and almost always we've lost.

"Pack a small bag, a carry-on."

He doesn't reply.

We're in the car. Rome at this hour is wan, colorless. Pietro is sitting in the back with his Ray-Bans on, his hair shiny with gel.

You can't do this to your mother, Giuliano said to him last night at dinner. Pietro called his friend Davide to tell him he wouldn't be going to sailing lessons because he had to go away with me. His friend must have asked him when we'd be back. He pulled his cell phone away from his mouth and asked, *When will we be back?*

I looked at Giuliano. *Soon.*

Soon, Pietro said to his friend.

"Come back soon," Giuliano says as we kiss goodbye in the airport. Then he hugs Pietro, puts his hand behind his neck and pulls him close. Pietro lowers his head and rubs it against Giuliano's. They stand that way for a few moments.

"Be good."

"Yes, Dad."

I put my bag on the conveyor belt and we go through to the other side. We walk alongside luminous ads for Lancôme, for Prada eyewear. The wheels of my little bag roll along behind us. I stop and turn around. Giuliano is still standing there, looking after us, his legs wide apart, his hands in his pockets, like a waiting driver, an anonymous figure in the bustle of the crowd, as if he's lost his identity now that we're gone. His face is different, inert, as if his muscles had given way. For a moment I'm conscious of the solitude I'm leaving him with. Then he sees me and all of a sudden springs back to life, waving his arms and smiling. He gestures to me to hurry, to go, and blows lots of kisses, his mouth curling in the empty air.

We're on the plane. Pietro's guitar takes up an entire overhead compartment. The flight attendant didn't complain. Economy class is relatively empty. Business class, on the other hand, is full of businessmen in designer ties rather than the dark, synthetic ones they might have worn years ago—nouveaux riches from the East grown fat on the sorrows of their people. They read the financial papers, eat hot meals and drink champagne.

Our trays arrive, cold and meager. Two slices of smoked ham, a salad of pickled vegetables, a plastic-wrapped dessert. Pietro devours his food. I pass him my tray as well. He calls the flight attendant and asks for more bread, in English, with a decent accent. I'm surprised. He smiles at her. My son is very handsome this morning. His eyes shine like two bits of sea.

We're flying over the Adriatic. He chews and looks down at the blue below. I look at him. The light coming in the window limns the contours of his profile.

The flight attendant comes back with the bread and when Pietro thanks her there's something downright charming about his rocky voice. His friends' mothers always compliment me on his politeness. My son is a terrible hypocrite. He shows his worst side only to me.

He bites into the dessert, a buttery little rectangle covered with frosting. He doesn't like it. "Do you want it?"

"No, thanks."

He sits there with the buttery thing melting in his hand. "I don't want it."

"Then don't eat it."

He takes the empty containers from the meals he's just eaten and puts them on my tray table. Then he puts his own tray table up and rests his knees against it. He puts on his earphones and settles into his seat. He glances at me. "You seem kind of out of it."

It's true. I am out of it. Before we boarded the plane I fretted like a novice traveler, even thought I'd lost our boarding passes. Pietro stood there looking around him with his lynxlike face, scrutinizing the world and leaving me to worry, to empty out my bag. He didn't care if I lost the boarding passes. *Let's go back home,* he said, before I found the two pieces of paper and told him to get moving.

When we went through security, he didn't like the security man putting his hand inside his guitar. I told him the man was just doing his job. He said, for the umpteenth time, *Give me a break.* Then, as we walked to the breeze-way, he said it would be a cinch to go through security armed to the teeth and drove me crazy hypothesizing hiding places for box cutters and forks from one of the airport restaurants.

I asked him if he'd brought a book. He said no, he didn't have books to read over the summer because he'd been held back. *I'm going to rest,* he said.

When we got on the plane, he said it was old and that Eastern European airlines bought the airplanes other companies threw away, airplanes that crash. *We'll end up on YouTube,* he said. I asked myself, *Why did I bring him? He'll drive me crazy.*

Now his eyes are closed and he's moving his head to the music on his iPod. He's happy. He's stopped complaining about our destination. When all is said and done, he can still get excited about things. He's got plenty of faults, but at least he isn't apathetic like so many kids his age.

He falls asleep, mouth open, head bent, iPod droning on. The sky outside the plane is white with clouds, motionless and unreal.

I force myself to think about something else, about the summer to come. We've made plans to spend time with friends in Liguria. There will be adults and kids Pietro's age. We'll go to barefooted parties, read, take walks along the rocks with the crabs in their pools. Giuliano will go to the hardware shop to buy the hooks and screws he needs to fix one of the shutters. We'll make love in the middle of the night, in the velvety coolness when the wind comes up off the sea and the dark allows us to forget our age.

Pietro wakes up, looks my way and yawns.

"What do you know about Sarajevo?"

"Isn't it where they killed the Archduke?"

I nod. Better than I expected. "What else do you know?"

"It's where the First World War began."

"What else?"

"Don't ask me."

"And all the things I told you?"

He doesn't answer, just stares out the window.

The plane begins its descent. I feel the landing gear move beneath us. My arms and legs are stiff with tension. The wheels, readying themselves to land, could be coming straight out of my gut.

I look down at the black flank of Mount Igman. It's still there, long, horizontal, a sleeping giant, a slain bison covered by a wild dark overgrowth. And yet I recall having seen it once covered with flowers, or perhaps they were flags, little white flags like lilies marking the trails for the Olympic athletes and greeting from above all those who descended upon this golden valley, this Jerusalem of Europe, where the snow fell on the black spires of the Orthodox churches, the lead domes of the mosques, the crooked stones of the old Jewish cemetery.

There's no bus to take us to the terminal. We walk across the tarmac. The air is white. There's no sun. It's at least ten degrees colder than in Italy.

Pietro is wearing a T-shirt with a cannabis leaf.

"Are you cold?"

"No."

The façade of the airport looks the same, impermanent as an industrial warehouse. I thought they would have torn it down, but all they did was refinish it.

There's only one little plane on the tarmac. It has a red cross on the side, like an ambulance. It could be a medevac craft, but it's just a Swissair plane, a tourist plane for times of peace.

People jumped down from the military planes with their eyes lowered and ran across that wide-open space toward a blurry wall of camouflage uniforms. Everyone was yelling; it felt like anyone might take a shot at you. The airport was the only way out of the besieged city. Every so often some wretch would attempt a nighttime crossing, a stupid idea. Out in the open like that, even a crummy marksman could get you.

The entrance hall is quiet, almost empty. Fluorescent lights, plywood walls, the sad lighting of a provincial train station.

The boy at the passport desk wears a fixed smile on his colorless face. "Italians."

I nod. He hands the passports back.

IZLAZ, exit. We follow the sign. Pietro's guitar is slung over his shoulder. He's looking at the people around us. A Muslim girl wearing a lot of makeup and a flesh-colored veil is hugging a desk attendant. They kiss in the middle of the crowd, blocking the way.

It's chaos in the arrivals hall. I scan the people leaning up against the metal barriers, look over the heads of those nearest me toward the people in the distance. There's cigarette smoke everywhere, a fog that blurs and dirties the colors.

I put on lipstick and fluffed up my hair in the airplane bathroom shortly before we landed, hoping it would make me look better.

To the right there's a bar with a curved counter and high tables where people are eating and drinking and smoking standing up. A man steps away from the counter and comes toward me. I'd wondered if I would recognize him; I know him right away. He's gained a few pounds. His black linen shirt is wrinkled. He's got a red beard, and his hair's not so thick. His walk is unmistakable: legs apart, relaxed even as he hurries, gangly arms slightly akimbo. He hugs me without hesitation, holds me tight as if I were a parcel of things belonging to him. Then he plants his eyes on my face and takes everything in, my lips, my chin, my forehead. He doesn't leave my eyes but lingers, penetrating, like seawater that's taken separate paths and then crashes back together. He digs thirstily back through lost time with this shameless, lacerating, joyful gaze.

I'm the first to give in. I lower my eyes and pull back from that pathos out of shyness, discomfort. Back in Italy, no one looks at you like that. I scratch at my arm as if I had scabies. Two damp hands, fleshy and perhaps not all that clean, surround my face.

"Beautiful woman!"

"Old woman," I mock myself.

"Fuck you, Gemma," Gojko says.

I smile, recognizing his derisive humor, the kind that comes to chase off deep feeling after a bout of drinking, bringing on laughter instead. He kisses me, hugs me again, enclosing my breath in a cage. I breathe in the linen smell of his shirt, his excitement, the warmth of his body. I feel him pass his hand over my back, feeling my bones like a blind man, counting my vertebrae with those boiling hands. I recognize the smell of neck, of sweaty hair, of houses with oilcloth on the tables and jars of white cherries in brandy, of offices where laden ashtrays burst into flames and the photocopy machines keep breaking down.

The knot in my throat rises but pride makes me push it back down. I promised myself not to give in; at fifty-three it's easy to piss out incontinent tears. I pat Gojko's arm. "You're a little chubby."

"Yes, well, I've started eating again."

He looks at Pietro and steps forward on his swaying legs, stumbling without falling as he raises a hand. Pietro immediately raises his own. Their palms slap against each other. Gojko points to the guitar.

"Musician?"

Pietro looks at him and smiles. "Amateur."

Gojko is sitting up front with the taxi driver, his arm out the open window; they're talking.

"Mom, can you understand them?"

"A little."

"What are they saying?"

"That it's going to rain."

"Fuck you, Gemma," Pietro whispers.

I sit still on the gray upholstered seat. Beyond the dusty window lies that long, unforgettable boulevard. If I can make it through this moment, maybe I'll manage to make it through the rest. I refuse to let this city get to me. I let the first things glide by without really taking them in, furtive little glances, scraps, like burnt stamps.

The trick is to slide through without absorbing what I see. I've learned that anything can be banished. Even horror can lose its shape, dissolve into something too ridiculous, too absurd to ever have been true, like the black carcasses of cars, exploded windows, a child's heart burst alive from his chest to splatter against a white wall.

I fiddle with an earring.

I'm calm. It helps to have Pietro here, to feel his jeans-clad knee against mine. He's unfazed, unaware of all that happened here, if anything bored by the urban dreariness.

The old gray social-realist buildings are still here, balconies piled one atop the next like shabby filing cabinets in a public office. The shell marks have been covered over with cement.

All it takes is a rut in the pavement and I have to resist the impulse to duck my head. Those mad dashes; you had to cross the sniper boulevard at 120 miles an hour, head bent between the seats, breath down between your knees, the red carcasses of trams leaning against each other as a defense against the line of fire. I turn toward Pietro. *He's not wearing a bulletproof vest*, I catch myself thinking. I clench my inner cheek between my teeth. *Stay calm.*

Gojko is silent. He turned once, then left me to myself.

I look at him, alive, safe along this long road, a man of today in the forward-moving world.

The lights at the intersection seem strange, the pauses at regular intervals, the people calmly crossing in front of us. Gardens climb the hills that rise above us, calm little white houses among the fir trees. They used to fire from up there. Every opening between two buildings, every bit of green, of light, meant a sniper who might have a bullet for you.

The seat of the legendary *Oslobodjenje* newspaper has replanted itself upon its own ruins, squashed into a low, orderly building. Next to it stands an immense skyscraper, looking unperturbed through its mirrored glass windows upon the ruins of the old city hospice. Red letters on top say AVAZ.

"It's the most widely read paper, the owner has become a very rich man . . ." Gojko rubs his head. "It doesn't even have a cultural page."

A man waits near a flower bed of freshly tilled dirt for a dog to finish doing his business. A girl crosses the boulevard on her bicycle. A family with blond children smiles in an ad for Sarajevo-osiguranje. Near them, two EUFOR soldiers, a chubby man and woman, arms folded over their camouflage jackets, smile out of a billboard. People walk along the sidewalks, flesh moving along in an orderly routine.

Birds cross overhead, flying above the pedestrians as they move from tree to tree, descending to earth now and then to gather a morsel.

One morning I woke up and saw a huge black swath in the sky. The birds were all flying away, frightened by the constant explosions, the smoke from the fires, the unbearable odor of half-buried bodies. They flew up the Miljacka to take refuge in the most distant woods, where people used to picnic in the cool areas beside little waterfalls that glittered like silver knots. There wasn't an inhabitant of Sarajevo who didn't envy the birds their freedom to rise up from the ground and leave the city, undisturbed.

I turn and there it is, the Holiday Inn, a yellow slap in the face, a motionless cube made up of so many smaller, mobile-looking cubes. Throughout the siege it was the haven of the foreign press. The front faced the Grbavica snipers. You had to enter through the back, car slipping along the ramp to the parking garage. And yet, once you'd made it inside, it was a sort of paradise beyond the reach of those who in the meantime were dying. There were satellite telephones and hot food and journalists who recorded news clips from their rooms, lucky people who could come and go.

We're in the center. In the geometric seraglio of the old Austro-Hungarian buildings the traffic flows with difficulty. People cross where they can, grazing the slow-moving cars. The trees have grown back, youthful trunks with no past. I look at the stores, new windows next to tidy, sad old-fashioned ones with far fewer wares than those back home. Consumerism has taken root only here and there in this city still in need of reconstruction, her face corroded by war as if by acid. We pass a mosque with little domes like a basket of dark eggs and then we're pulling to a stop in front of our hotel in a side street behind the old Ottoman market in the Baščaršija.

Gojko won't hear of my paying for the taxi. He carries in my bag for me. Inside, it's cozy and welcoming like the entry to a house. There's a light-colored, almost silvery curtain over the door and a red carpet with little black diamonds. A big vase of stiff, patently artificial flowers stands in a corner. Pietro touches them to see if they are real, then rubs his hands on his jeans. He observes the girl at the reception desk, walled in behind a dark wood counter, as she looks up our reservation on the computer. Men's voices come from an adjacent lounge. I notice shoddy shoes, too-short socks. They're smoking; the air is terribly foul. The smoke accompanies us up the stairs, insinuates itself into the little elevator. Pietro says, "If we stay here more than one night we'll go back to Rome with cancer."

The room is decent-sized, with a blue synthetic bedspread and two brand-new bedside tables. I open the window and look down onto the street. It's a dead-end street, with a few parked cars, a tree with red foliage, a tin shed spotted with pigeon turds.

Pietro laughs in the bathroom. "Look, Mom."

"What?"

I turn. He comes out with a glass in his hands and shows me the bag it's in, which says HYGIENIC CLEANING.

"So?"

"The bag isn't sealed and the glass is an old Nutella jar."

I smile and tell him to put the glass back where he found it.

I wash my hands, sit on the bed and start organizing my purse. Pietro throws his backpack in the wardrobe without even pulling out his pajamas.

"Let's go, Mom. What are we doing in here?"

If it were up to me I'd stay in the room. I have a travel-worn banana in my bag, all I really need. I want to stretch out my legs and lie here until tomorrow. Last night I couldn't sleep for thinking about this trip. Now, from the taste of blood in my mouth, I realize that I must have bit the inside of my cheek in the taxi. I have to put my slippers under the bed, check to make sure the blinds close and that the shower has a decent spray. That's all I want to do. But Gojko's waiting for us downstairs.

"Okay. Let's go."

It's seven in the evening and night is falling; all of a sudden I feel cold. I listen to the noise of the feet around us. They sound like horseshoes on ancient flagstones. We're on the road that leads to the Gazi Husrev-beg Mosque. Crowds of girls wearing veils joke among themselves and push each other. There's an exhibition of local crafts in a courtyard full of little arches behind the madrassa. A long series of tunics with embroidered plastrons hang off a clothesline to form a multicolored curtain. A pale woman dressed in white gestures delicately, an invitation to look inside her little embroidery shop. She brings her hands to her chest and bows as I leave.

Pietro takes pictures with his cell phone of bags of spices and copper utensils that fill the shops floor to ceiling.

We wander over the fluvial stones of the narrow little streets. The stores begin to close, their lights buried behind their wooden doors. Pietro stops at a stall selling shell fragments and shiny shell cases—souvenirs. He lifts a shell case, sets it back down, laughs and lifts another, heavier one. "How many people could this one kill?"

I want to kick him.

Gojko doesn't seem to mind, even seems amused.

"Recycled war materials, our green energy."

"Were you in the war?"

Gojko nods, lights a cigarette and lowers his voice. Maybe he doesn't want to say more. "Like everyone."

"Were you a soldier?"

"No, a poet."

Pietro is disappointed. Poets, in his mind, are an order of pathetic cripples steeped in misfortune, responsible for poisoning the lives of millions of normal, carefree kids. "I'm hungry," he says.

We leave Baščaršija and stop to eat at a little wooden stand, a squalid hut with aluminum tables and fluorescent lights. The smell of onions and roasting meat wafts out, the unmistakable odor of food that will give you heartburn. Gojko says their ćevapčići is good. The girl who serves us has three careless fingers stuck inside our glasses. Pietro orders a Coke and asks Gojko how to say "straw."

We eat. The meat in the ćevapčići is savory and delicious. It fills our mouths with blood and life. The pepper burns the cut inside my mouth but it doesn't matter. I'm feeling a little less tired and have an appetite now, thanks to this aroma that doesn't seem to have changed over the years. And perhaps the alcohol helps, as well, a bottle of red Montenegrin wine. "It's not Brunello," Gojko says, "but it's muddy." He probably meant to say "mellow." Every so often he makes a mistake, despite his nearly perfect Italian, but his mistakes are fitting. This is a muddy wine. It takes us back in time, protects us with a sort of muddy slowness.

We ate ćevapčići the day we first met. We bought them from a kiosk and ate them standing. It was an icy-cold day. The woman roasting them wore a woolen jacket and a cook's cap. She observed our hunger, watched our every bite, delighted in our appreciation of her ćevapčići. They were the pride of her life as a purveyor of street fare. I see her as if it were yesterday, with her proletarian face, worn but infinitely sweet. She was one of those beneficent people you meet by chance and want to hug because they smile at you from the depths of their human experience and just like that make up for the other half of the world, the disheartening half of humanity closed inside its dark well. How many happy people I met during that first time in Sarajevo. All of them had red cheeks from the cold, of course, but it was from shyness, as well, because they dared to hope.

The Winter Olympics were going on. The imposing Moorish-revival National Library looked like a city unto itself. I met Gojko there, in one of those giant rooms with columns fleeing upward toward the light of distant windows like something you'd see in a cathedral. I was sitting on a little office chair beneath an overhang of ancient volumes that made me feel insignificant. In came a redheaded boy wrapped in a leather jacket lined with crushed wool. He moved in bursts like a big mechanical doll.

"Are you Gemma?"

"Yes."

"I'm your guide."

We shook hands. I smiled. He was enormous.

"You speak Italian well."

"I go to Trieste at least once a month."

"Are you studying there?"

"No, I sell yo-yos." He pulled one out of his pocket. "They're all the rage here. They relieve tension. People are really agitated. Thanks to the Olympics we've had to work really hard, and we don't like working hard. But the city had to be spiffed up, you see?" He laughed. I didn't understand why. "Is your hotel okay?"

I shook my head. I was staying in a guesthouse full of tourists.

"Do you appreciate the glories of a star-studded sky?"

"Why?"

"If you want, you can sleep beneath one of the countless bridges along the Miljacka. No one will bother you. All the drunks and purse snatchers have disappeared. A Communist cleanup. For the first time, we're showing our ass to the world."

I had to finish my doctoral thesis on Andrić. I'd requested a decent guide and instead here I was with a yo-yo salesman.

He pulled his yo-yo out of his pocket again and started doing tricks. Maybe I wanted to buy one? "Now, that would be something to be proud of, selling a yo-yo I bought in Trieste to an Italian. My friends would buy me a drink for that."

I'd been in Sarajevo for a few days. The enchantment of the snow and of the festive city did not match my mood. I was unhappy. I couldn't get used to the place. I had decided on my research project at my professor's urging; his ulterior motive was for me to gather information for something he was writing on the literature of the Balkans. To top it off, I'd had dysentery for two days, and the smells of the robust cooking, the unbearable cold and the breath of this pathetic show-off of a hick with his ridiculous black leather jacket that looked like it was lined with Siamese cat fur were enough to sour my mood.

I look with distaste at his greasy ponytail. I can't decide if his pointy-toed boots make him look more like a parody of a rocker or of a wolf hunter. I say, "Listen, maybe you're not the right person to bring me to Andrić's places in Sarajevo and to Višegrad, to Travnik."

"Why not?"

"You hardly strike me as an intellectual."

"No problem. I have a car."

I expected a goddamn Yugo, its exhaust pipe spitting out black smoke like most of the cars around the city, but instead he has a Golf, not the cleanest car I've ever seen, but decent.

"They assemble them here," he says. "You know why the Germans trust us?"

"No, I don't." I look out the window. It's early in the morning. He'd arrived punctually, but it's clear he didn't get much sleep.

"Because we're so precise about what we do, even though we're expensive."

He laughs, too hard. Alone. Then a sort of hiccup—perhaps the consequence of a drunken night—swallows up the fringes of his laugh. "Did you believe me?"

I want to tell him to shut up, that I'm not paying him for all this chatter. He stinks like a wet dog, his hiccups smell like putrid slivovitz and, I now discover, he's got a terrible disposition. It seems that my lack of interest in what he has to say has angered him.

"Maybe we're not all that precise, but we're cheap, that's for sure." He says it in a rough tone of voice, almost as if he were angry with me.

"I'm paying you well."

He looks at me instead of the road.

"You must be a real bitch."

I don't look at him. My neck goes rigid. I'm scared, but I'm too proud to give in to my fear. I'm the perfect victim for a maniac. I can picture him delightedly wringing my neck. He's a big Slav made even bigger by his lined jacket. He must be messed up, just like Communism since the death of Tito. I am a reluctant bourgeois, part of the backlash, the new wave of young women who in the aftermath of feminism put on high heels to enjoy the opulence of the new decade, the opposite of those raving ragamuffins in clogs.

Politely I ask him to pull over. I want to get out. He yells in his language. I yell, too. "Shut your mouth. Your breath stinks."

He looks as if he'd like to kill me, but instead he stops the car.

I get out and walk for a while on the edge of the terrifying road that leads out of the city. Dirty trucks brush past me.

He drives off but waits for me around a curve, where I find him leaning against the open door and smoking. "Get in. This is ridiculous."

I don't get in. He drives at a walking pace, the door open. "It's a friend's car. I have to bring it back by this evening." Then he thrusts a book out at me. I take it. It's a collection of Andrić's poetry in Serbo-Croatian. "Poetry cannot be translated!" he proclaims.

Imbecile, I think. But I'm tired, the dirty snow on the sides of the road is piled high, my calves are freezing. And the faces looking out at me from the trucks aren't any more reassuring than his.

I don't speak to him while he drives. After a while he starts speaking in Bosnian, his voice deeply moved. I think he's completely crazy.

I say I don't understand a single word. He tells me to listen to the sound, blathers something about poetry being like a musical score, with the sound of invisible elements: night, the wind, nostalgia. "Close your eyes."

I shouldn't close my eyes because he might strangle me. He's turned on the heat for me because I'm freezing, and he's sweating in his leather jacket. I almost feel bad for him. I close my eyes.

After a while I really hear something, dirt falling in the dusk. "What's this poem about?"

"The gravedigger, burying a poet and swearing while he does it, smoking over the grave."

"And spitting?"

"Yes, he spits."

"You know," I whisper, "I understood some of it."

He nods and hands the book over. "It's a phonetic language, you pronounce it as it's written." He watches me as I stumble over the verses. "It's full of sweet sounds, without many vowels. The words infect each other, each harmonizing with the ones around it. If there's a feminine term, everything becomes feminine. We're very gallant."

He brought me to Travnik, to the house where Andrić was born. We looked at the manuscripts and photographs. We stopped in front of the crib where the writer slept as an infant. I fell asleep on the way back. Gojko woke me by blowing air over my eyes. "Does my breath still smell?"

"No."

We were hungry after all those miles on those rough roads. We found the kiosk with the ćevapčići, the best I've ever had, tightly packed into bread stuffed with onions. The woman's smile blessed our hunger, our youth. "What a lovely couple."

"We're just friends."

Who knows what became of her, of her saucepan full of grease, her woolen sweater, her face? I still see her on the corner in front of the Bezistan market, smiling at us while she satisfies our hunger, encouraging us to eat and believe in what's good.

Even if a bomb carried her away and a burst of flames scattered her poor belongings, she's alive tonight in the street vendor and in our damp eyes as they meet over the muddy red from Montenegro.

Gojko loved the poet Mak Dizdar, Bruce Springsteen and Levi's 501 jeans. He longed for a black pair to impress everyone in the bars where he went to get drunk and draw satirical vignettes on the walls. Over the next few days he took me by the hand and showed me Sarajevo through his eyes. The old public baths, the Marijin Dvor tobacco factory, the little Magribija Mosque, the Bogumil stećci. He knew every nook, every legend. He dragged me up long,

pungent-smelling stairways to garrets with wooden ceilings where tough artists carved out canvases full of dramatic tension, to Sevdah-rock and New
Primitives clubs where barefoot girls danced in each other's arms beside
piles of boots dirtied with snow, to shops where women rolled out white pita
dough on pans as big as shields and old men in red fezzes played dice on the
threshold. He knew almost everyone and was loved by them all. I followed his
ponytail, like the crooked tail of a tomcat.

One night he recited one of his poems for me.

Keep your mouth closed, boy
until someone tells you to keep it closed.
Then, rebel, and speak.
Speak of your youth and impatience,
of the moon, yellow like the sun.
Your mother is a good woman,
But she's gone away
and your dog hasn't eaten for two days.
Speak of the empty streets,
they've all gone home to bed
and you want to sing,
before your old Anela wakes
to wring the neck of a crazy hen
who no longer lays eggs
but sings like a rooster.

"What do you think?"
I play with his yo-yo. I'm determined to learn how to do it.
"Who is the crazy hen?"
"Sarajevo."
"Interesting."
He takes back his yo-yo. He needs it. He's agitated, and anyway, I don't know
how to do it. He can't stand watching me mess it up. He says that I should just
tell him if I don't like his poems. He says I'm an asshole, that all I care about is
my career, that I'll become one of those literary critics who squashes fresh tal-
ent because I'm a stupid frigid schoolmarm, a leech who sucks others' blood.

We're walking along the Miljacka. Gojko waves his hand in the air toward a miserable winter branch. "Any one of these leaves throbs with more life than you."

"Leaves fall," I say with a snicker.

"Like poets. They fertilize the earth too young." He has the yellow eyes of a rebellious bear and his usual alcoholic breath.

I can't take it anymore. I tell him he has to take a shower and stop stinking of slivovitz, because the world is full of great poets who live, sober and clean, to a ripe old age. He stares at me like an offended child. He says he's never been drunk in his life, that his hair looks dirty because of the styling cream he uses and that if I want to have children I had better learn to use the yo-yo because it's something little children love.

He teaches me, his hand on mine so I can feel the way my wrist is supposed to move, the rustling of the string, the silent click as the magic spool starts its upward journey.

And that night, before he said good night, he said, *Volim te iskreno.*

"What's that mean?"

"I love you truly."

I took a small step backward. Gojko squashed his nose with his thumb as if it were clay. He stopped on the threshold. "That's what I say to my mother before I leave at night."

He skidded across a frozen puddle, then disappeared.

Now he's here, on this warm night, elbows resting on a plastic tablecloth in this city compromised by sorrow and now silent, with litter on the ground, cigarette butts, the footsteps of people heading for home. We've finished the wine, and enjoyed it, and the miracle is the charitable normality of it all, this baklava we're sharing, a sweet supple mixture of nuts and phyllo dough. Our spoons touch on the plate.

"You can have the last cherry."

Pietro loudly slurps up his Coke. He's not misbehaving. He talked about tennis with Gojko and stood to show him Federer's forehand. Now he wants an ice cream, but all they have here are Bosnian desserts. Gojko points through the dark to an ice-cream shop.

"How do you say 'ice cream'?"

"*Sladoled.*"

"And the flavors?"

"*Čokolada, vanila, pistaci, limun . . .*"

"If I just say 'ice cream,' will they understand?"

Gojko nods, smiles at him, watches him as he goes. "He's a nice kid."

I study the road where Pietro's gone and already I feel the empty space I feel every time he leaves my sight. "He's just like his father."

A rustling noise comes from Gojko's narrowed mouth.

"What?" I ask him.

"Nothing. I'm just looking at you." He takes my hand, asks if I'm okay.

I tell him yes, though my voice is shrill, as if I want to defend myself.

"Call me whenever you want, for whatever reason. I sleep sitting up."

"Don't you have a bed?"

"I don't like to sleep lying down. I can feel my heart in my eyes."

I look at him, at the eyes his heart climbs into at night. He crinkles them slightly, as if he wanted to smile but without actually managing to do it. It's as if the two of us were stuck back in that time, as if nothing had happened in between, not even an hour's peace.

His hand is slightly puffy, with freckles and a too-tight wedding ring. "You're married?"

He nods.

"What's she like?"

"I got lucky."

He tells me about the years he spent as a refugee, the odd jobs working in gas stations and parking garages and as a watchman in a campground. "It was an advantage to be Bosnian, everyone felt so sorry for us at first." He smiles and orders two glasses of rakija. "It didn't last very long. Europe tired early of feeling guilty. We don't have a good reputation and we waste time because we're always lost in contemplation."

A crooked, stick-thin woman dragging along a leg like a broom handle passes next to me and lays an open hand on the table without saying a word. Gojko gives her five convertible marks. She's so weak she doesn't even have the strength to close her hand. I watch her walk away, her dirty jeans over an ass that's all bones.

"Do you remember her? She used to sell lottery tickets."

I have a vague recollection of a hand, a silly good-luck doll.

"She was one of the most beautiful girls in Sarajevo. Now she's a junkie." He gulps down his rakija and crinkles his eyes again. "It was easier to run from the bombs beforehand than to walk on the ruins later."

Pietro comes back with his ice cream. He watches the woman who is holding on to the wall, bent over like a dog that needs to piss.

"Why is she limping like that?"

"One of those baubles you saw at the market today went into her hip."

My son is agitated. He fiddles in his chair. "And there's nothing anyone can do to help her?"

"No. How's the ice cream?"

For a while the only sound is the noise of Pietro finishing his ice cream. Then he rests his sleepy face in the palm of his hand.

"Let's go," he says. "I'm beat."

I, on the other hand, could walk for hours now. Cross the city, go all the way to Ilidža through this summer fog that cancels out some of this reality, dive into a steaming jumble of memories.

I look up at Mount Trebević. I ask Gojko about the refuge where they served tangy cheese and warm brandy. He doesn't answer right away as he turns over the flavor of those memories in his closed mouth.

"You're the one who brings it all back. You." Then, brusquely, he says there's nothing left. The forgotten cabins of the ski lift hang in the sky like rotten teeth. "It's full of mines. It took no time to plant them, but finding them will take years and years and mountains of money. But if you want, we can go. We can risk our hide to go back." There's a flash in his eyes, as if he expects some sort of challenge from me, a folly.

"Good night."

We take the stairs because Pietro doesn't trust the elevator.

"Is your friend crazy?"

"For Bosnians, being crazy is a matter of pride." I stagger from one step to the next.

"Are you drunk?"

"A little."

"That's disgusting."

I sit on the bed to wait while he finishes brushing his teeth. He's in his underpants, bent over the sink, his wide-open mouth full of foam while he brushes, elbow held high. He's a maniac about oral hygiene. He's already had two cavities and can't figure out why. Once, he asked me to open my mouth. He wanted to see the state of my teeth because the dentist told him cavities are hereditary. I opened and closed my mouth quickly. *Leave me alone*, I said. *I'm not a horse.* Then he asked me about his father, just to know what kind of teeth he had.

Now he's sleeping. A hiss comes out of his half-open mouth. He's not wearing a shirt. His nipples are a little swollen. Pubertal mastitis, the doctor said.

"I'm not going to get boobs, am I?"

The doctor laughed. *This boy puts you in a good mood. It's hard to find funny kids nowadays.* Yes, everyone likes him. He's got a nice sense of humor, ready to make fun of himself before mocking others. He's only a jerk with his mother.

Pietro.

Maybe it's the rakija, but tonight his name is enough to make me cry.

Tonight it's easy to be lacerated by a name.

The window has a wide sill with space to sit and stretch my legs. I lean against the glass. Giuliano calls, his voice hoarse as if he'd been thinking in silence. "I left you so many messages." His voice is worn with tiredness and worry. "You sound far away."

"I am far away."

I picture our house, the carabinieri calendar hanging in the entry, the salad I left for him in the fridge, the list for the cleaning lady, the sponge I use to clean my face at night.

Tonight I haven't taken off my makeup. The creases around my eyes are full of eyeliner.

Pietro sleeps. The closed lashes in the white of his lids are a row of bare trees in the snow, earth cut in two by a trench.

I leave the window and go down to the lobby in my bare feet. Men are drinking and smoking. Men are always drinking and smoking in this hotel. They look at me, offer me a drink. I ask for a cigarette. They give me two. Drina cigarettes, good old Drina cigarettes, I haven't had a cigarette in years, but tonight I smoke barefoot on the sidewalk because I need something that burns when it goes down into my belly.

Someone walks by, a man who hovers over a dumpster, a poor beggar looking for something, a leftover that still holds its flavor, some scrap that's worth the bother. Like me, in the end.

Chapter 2

It was Gojko who brought me there.

We'd spent the whole day walking, from Bistrik to Nedžarići, but all the same I let him drag me out with him that night. Fog swirled around us. The Miljacka was milky pale, like colostrum. It was my last night in Sarajevo.

Italy won the gold in the luge race and there was a celebration. Sports journalists and athletes who should already have been sleeping in the Mojmilo Olympic Village were dancing on the tables and downing slivovitz.

"Come on, I'll introduce you to the Italians."

I end up squashed in between strangers with smoke-bleared eyes and sunburned faces. The bar is a warren. Stuffed heads of brown bears and chamois decorate its low archways. Flags dangle from the vaulted ceilings. I'm sitting below East Germany.

He isn't there. He's already said goodbye and gone for his coat, but he can't find it among all the snow-covered parkas and overcoats in the coat check and the coat-check girl is off getting a beer. He comes back to look for her.

I see a long thin back in a colorful Peruvian wool sweater. Gojko calls out, "Hey, Diego!"

Diego lifts his hand to the nape of his neck as he turns. He has a wispy beard and hollow cheeks like a thin little boy's. Later he'll tell me that his head was pounding, his eyes burning after a day in the path of fast-moving sprays of snow. He walks toward us. Later he'll say that he came over to speak to Gojko even though his eyes hurt, even though he was tired, because he saw me and was attracted like a bull to a red flag. I watch him come toward us. One can never say what it is, exactly, that connects two people—some kind of membrane, a prison from the start. Another life has traveled a great distance toward our own. We've felt the wind as it moved, breathed in the scent when it paused. The sweat and toil of that life have always been inside us. Its every effort has been for us.

We're still for a moment, listening to that simultaneous rhythm of so many things. My cheeks are red. There's too much smoke, there're too many elbows, too many voices. Then there's nothing else, only the colored splotch of that sweater moving toward me. In a second my eyes burn the contours of his flesh; it seems I can feel his soul. That's it.

He reaches our table. In the meantime, the coat-check girl has given him his stiff blue jacket. He puts it on and stands there all bundled up and sweating. Gojko leans forward to hug him across the table of dancing revelers. "Are you leaving?"

The pom-pom on the woolen cap dances as he nods.

"This is my friend Diego. Remember? I told you about him."

I don't remember.

Diego puts out his bony hand. It burns as it lingers in mine. Already, it's Pietro's hand. Time rends time. A body stands before you, young and strong, and yet another body is already taking its place, the son already in the father, the boy within the boy.

The son will be the memory, the child who will carry the flame.

I slide over to make room for him, a couple of inches for him to fit himself into on the bench. We laugh because we're sitting so close. I don't remember what we talked about. There's a strange singsong to his voice that makes me think of the sea.

"Where are you from?"

"Genoa."

He hasn't even taken off his cap. Drops of sweat roll off his forehead and fall into his eyes.

"You're sweating."

"Let's go outside."

We get up and leave, just like that, the two of us together out past the tables and the dirty glasses, the bear heads, the people pushing their way into the restrooms. Gojko doesn't say a word, just lifts his hand like a traffic cop ordering a car to stop. Later he'll say he saw it right away, that a blind man would have known what was happening. He'll say that lightning strikes and kills the poor cat as it lies in wait for its prey.

Diego walks beside me in his blue jacket that looks like part of a navy uniform. He seems very young. I wonder how old he is.

"My plane tomorrow morning will probably be crammed full like the one coming over." He's here for work, he says.

"What do you do?"

"I'm a photographer. It was hot in there." He smiles. It's a gentle smile.

I tell him about my thesis and about Gojko, who's been so generous, who's made me fall in love with the city.

"Why are you up so late?"

"I was waiting to hear the bells ring and the muezzin's call to prayer."

He tells me we can wait together. We'll climb up to the old railway station; the minarets down below look like lances piercing the sky.

How far will we walk tonight? A sanitation truck follows us for a while. When it stops the street cleaners pick up empty beer bottles and sodden leaflets. Long black brooms rustle over the pavement. The chilled and weary men sweep and gather, climb back up on the truck, stop to sweep and gather again. We wouldn't have noticed the mess if we'd been left alone. We're used to dirty cities. Instead, it's as if we were in a spell; the streets are being cleaned for us as we go along.

"Are you here with a newspaper?"

"No, I'm freelance."

He spent days lying on the ground with his chin in the snow at Bjelašnica and Malo Polje while bobsleds and ski jumpers splattered him with snow. He says he's fucked up his eyes.

"Why didn't you wear sunglasses?"

He laughs and says that would be like making love with your clothes on; nothing should come between the eye and the lens. He looks at me.

"Do you think I'm photogenic?" I tilt my head, showing him my best side, like a teenager.

"Are you with someone?"

I'm about to get married. I don't say so. I say I've got a long-term boyfriend. "And you?"

He spreads his arms and smiles. "I'm free."

We sit on the edge of the frozen Sebilj Fountain. There's a half-frozen bird walking on the ice. It lets Diego approach. He picks it up and shelters it in his two hands and lowers his mouth to blow in warm air.

"Come with me."

"Where?"

"To Brazil. I'm going to photograph the children in the red mines of Cumaru."

Lit cigarette in hand, Gojko appears from behind a market stall in his fur jacket, as if he'd been waiting for us. "I promised the young lady I'd take her up into the hills to see Sarajevo from Andrić's window."

"Who's this Andrić?"

"A poet, but don't worry. Gemma doesn't like Bosnian poets. They're smelly and they drink too much."

His presence protects me from the embarrassing torment of emotions I feel. We can pretend to be three friends, three innocent siblings out for a walk.

The gelid wind moves the gaunt trees. Gusts of sleet burn our faces and settle in our hair.

We look down on the city, the bony points of the minarets among the snow-laden roofs. Sarajevo looks like a supine woman. The streets are the lines of a wedding gown.

My own wedding gown awaits me back home, a stiff satin swirl like a calla lily, a motionless flower.

Night is departing. The electric lights below us dance in the dawn like candles on the sea. Gojko stretches his arms wide and yells in German, *"Das ist Walter!"*

"Who's Walter?"

"He's the main character in a propaganda film they showed us at school, a partisan hero. The Germans spend the whole film trying to find him, without any success. At the end, the SS officer looks down on the city and says, 'Now I know who Walter is. This is Walter. It's the whole city, it's the spirit of Sarajevo.' It was a crappy film, but it made us cry."

We sit on the ground beneath a canopy at the old station. Gojko pulls a bottle of rakija out of his jacket.

"Ladies first."

It's like lava going down. Diego takes a sip after me. He looks at me as he puts his mouth where my own had just rested. It's our first erotic exchange. Sweat pours down my back despite the cold.

"Damn."

"What?"

"I wish I had my camera." He wants to take a picture of my reflection in a frozen puddle between the tracks.

Gojko drains the rest of the bottle as if it were water and then throws it into the snow. He blathers on in his crumbling voice about the future, the poems he'll write, the new toy he wants to import, a magic cube, a puzzle that'll make him rich. We let him drone on. It's like nighttime radio. Every once in a while Diego says something, anything, so it's like we're a trio of friends enjoying the night. When Gojko lights another cigarette, Diego elbows him. "Careful with that lighter. You're so full of rakija that we'll explode if you burp."

"I see you've learned something about Bosnian humor."

I laugh even though my jaws are paralyzed with cold. Gojko looks at me and I can tell he's angry. He shakes his head, gestures that we should go to hell and turns over on his side in the snow. "Let me know when you're done making out."

He's completely wasted, but he doesn't want to leave us alone. He stays there like a guard dog pretending to sleep. Diego takes my hand.

"And so . . ."

I wait for him to finish. His breath is white in the air.

". . . you're you."

"What does that mean?"

His voice goes hoarse. "Don't go. Don't leave."

He lowers his head, buries his eyes in my hand and breathes there like the frozen bird at the fountain. I run my fingers through his hair.

"Do that some more."

"I'm getting married in forty days."

He looks up brusquely. "Who to? The old flame?"

I pull myself together, stand up and brush the snow off my rear end. I say it's freezing and that I have to go finish packing. I prod Gojko with my foot. "Get moving, Walter!"

We go back toward the hotel. No one talks and none of us mind. We've gone too far and now we're tired. Now I don't like this thin, intense boy walking beside me. His mood is defeated like Gojko's, black like the night. All of a sudden I can't stand either of them. I'm surrounded by stupid men, gloomy admirers. Dawn curls itself around the furtive city like a big gray cat. I scold myself. Why did I stay up all night, drink so much, get so cold? Taking advantage of Gojko's bulk, I squeeze his arm. Diego slinks along ahead of us, close to the wall like a dog. Gojko runs his hand up and down my back, glad to warm me. He senses the change in Diego's mood, can tell something happened while he was sleeping. Now it's his turn again. He doesn't mind my fickleness. He picks up a piece of wood and tosses it at Diego. "Hey, photographer!"

Diego starts, slips on the sleet and falls. Gojko didn't mean to hurt him. He didn't think he was so floppy.

"Are you okay, my friend?"

Diego pulls himself up, brushes the snow off his pants and says he's fine. All of a sudden I feel sorry for him. All of a sudden I realize I've hurt him.

"See you in the airport." Waving listlessly, he limps off without turning around.

It takes Gojko's full weight on my suitcase for me to zip it closed. I bought too many trifles, piles of embroidered tablecloths for my new home. We drive past the Eternal Flame. For the last time I look at the boulevard, the brand-new buildings and Vucko the wolf, the mascot of the 1984 Sarajevo Olympics, beside an enormous image of Tito. The sky is white. My stomach is upset from not sleeping. I ask Gojko to put out his cigarette.

At the check-in counters there's a crowd, journalists, television crews, tourists. A group of Finnish fans follow a girl in a gold parka and leather miniskirt. She's waving an inflatable snowman.

He's not there. My head doesn't move a fraction of an inch as my eyes scan the crowd. I buy an English tabloid. Princess Diana, her firstborn on her lap, is on the cover with her heavy blond hair and red cheeks.

His plane was supposed to leave an hour before mine, so he should be here. Maybe he slept through his alarm. I bet he's one of those boys who sleeps too much and wastes time.

I'm wearing a cowl-necked angora sweater with a straight skirt that falls just below my knees and camel-colored boots. My big sunglasses are pushed back on my head. I look slightly older than my age. I started dressing like a grown-up when I finished college. I open the first button of my jacket and breathe beneath my composed chest, cross my legs, set my purse down beside me. In a sense, I'm playing a role, like we all do when we're in public. It's like a dress rehearsal for the woman I'd like to be. To be honest, the only thing I know about myself is that I don't like to suffer. The world I grew up in was comfortingly horizontal, with no highs or lows.

In the end, it seems, Sarajevo will leave me with a trace of sadness. Even the opening ceremony of the Olympics, impeccable and sumptuous as it was, was cloaked in metallic sadness that the graceful movements of the baton twirlers and the jumps and twirls of the skaters did little to dispel. There was a military gloom, shared by all the Eastern Bloc athletes. You got the feeling they had never once had fun during a training session. I remember a little boy I bought toasted hazelnuts from outside the Zetra Stadium. His eyes could have belonged to a mouse. I caressed his cheek, gave him a tip. He didn't move a muscle, a child of stone.

Gojko's still here, though I told him he could go. He's shuffling around the airport, making deals. He comes over and blows smoke on me, then spots my magazine.

"Who's that?"

"The wife of Prince Charles of England."

"Is she Bosnian?"

"Of course not. She's English."

"She looks just like my mother."

I stuff the magazine into my bag.

"Actually, my mother's more beautiful."

I'm so sick of this presumptuous Bosnian who thinks that this armpit of a place is the center of the universe. He never gives it a rest. *The border between Orient and Occident. The Jerusalem of Europe. A crossroads of ancient cultures and vanguard movements.* Now his mother is more beautiful than Lady Diana. Go to hell.

The city is freezing cold in the winter, sweltering in the summer. The people who live here are depressing, arrogant, ridiculous. The women are either covered in makeup or utterly faded, while the men stink of onions, rakija and sweaty feet in cheap shoes. I'm sick of pita bread and ćevapčići, I want salad and grilled fish. I'm sick of you, Gojko. Your jokes aren't funny. Your poems leave me cold. I think of Andrić and smile to myself. *If I had to tell you in a single word what drives me to leave Bosnia it would be: hatred.*

"My mother's in the hospital."

"Really? What's wrong?"

"She's having a baby. She's been there a week. The baby is taking its own sweet time."

"How old is your mother?"

"Forty-four. She had me when she was seventeen. Now there's going to be another baby after all this time."

"That's a wonderful thing."

"That's life."

Why aren't they announcing any flights? The departures boards haven't changed for ages. "Is there a strike?"

Gojko bursts out laughing. He can't believe I've said such a stupid thing.

The airport is starting to feel like a station at rush hour. The smell of cigarette smoke is unbearable. I stand up and walk toward the windows at the end of the terminal. I want to see the runway, see whether or not any planes are taking off. I press my nose against the glass and can't see a thing. Everything's white. It's snowing.

I hear a sound, the vibrating chords of a guitar. I turn. Diego is sitting on the floor, leaning against the wall in a corner between the window and a service entry. Head bent, he strums his guitar.

"It's snowing."

"Yup."

"A lot."

I lean against the white blizzard, my destiny. Now I realize that all I wanted was for someone else to make the decision for me. I run a finger over the glass, drawing a wavy line, a thought, in the condensation left by my breath.

"You hurt my feelings."

What's he going on about? Why does he talk about us with such intimacy?

"Come sit here."

I sit next to him on a bench. Not on the floor. That would be too much in this skirt. I'm a good girl resigned to a benign life without highs and lows, without sorrows, without desires.

"Do you like Bruce Springsteen?" He starts singing. *You never smile, girl, you never speak ... Must be a lonely life for a working girl ... I wanna marry you* ... "I'm in love with you." He smiles at me, pushes his hair behind his ears.

Once again my attraction wanes. He's either scary or an utter dolt. "Are you always like this?"

"Like what?"

"Racing ahead, imagining things all on your own."

"I want to do everything with you."

"I don't even know you."

He tells me his entire life story in bursts. His father was a port worker and died young. His mother is a cook at the Gaslini Hospital, she's always brought him food in aluminum tins. The building he lives in looks like social-realist architecture even though it was the Christian Democrats who built it. On the ground floor there's a photo studio and that's where he got started, by going down and busting their balls every day.

The snow keeps falling. A scratchy voice says that all flights have been canceled for the moment.

Diego stands and grabs his guitar.

"It couldn't be better! We won't lose our tickets and they'll pay for the hotel. Shall we get connecting rooms?"

"I'm waiting in the airport."

"Didn't you hear? They're closing the airport. You'll be here all by yourself."

I think about my bags, about Fabio, who's planning to get me at Fiumicino Airport, about my mother, who will have bought fresh tagliolini. I see my life covered with snow, erased by the snow. *Come on*, I think, *there's nothing to be afraid of. This goofball will become another little brother, just like Gojko. That's how it goes.* I was quite the success on my trip. I picked up two losers, a Bosnian poet and a photographer from Genoa. Fabio will laugh. He'll say the world is full of crazies and that I'm a little crazy, too, which is why he likes me. He'll look at me in that way he has when he's about to jump on me, happy like a dog about to rub himself over a turd in a field. Why am I saying this? Why am I spitting on my life? Who is this boy beside me?

"I'd be fine staying here in the airport, just the two of us inside and all the snow outside. Anything is fine with me."

He jumps around with his hands in his pockets. "I'm a lucky guy."

"Oh, really?"

"Very lucky."

"How old are you?"

"Twenty-four. How about you?"

"Twenty-nine."

He smiles and says he'd thought worse, that I look thirty. He curls up his whole face and shows all his teeth. I look at that smile, too big for his little face.

I'm finding you again on this first night in Sarajevo after all these years, shovelfuls of life one after the next. My white skin is more than fifty years old now. More than fifty years of thoughts and actions. Would you still want me, Diego? Would you like the loose skin on my arms? Would you still love me with such a carnal passion, such joy? Once you told me you'd want to lick me all over even when I was old. You said it and I believed you. What does it matter that time didn't let us try? Somewhere, the two of us did grow old together. Somewhere, the two of us are still rolling around and laughing. The window is dark. I can't see Sarajevo. I see nothing but a street, an anonymous view. This city is a pita bread stuffed full of the dead, innocents torn away from innocence. Your son Pietro is sleeping, Diego.

There's a long line for the pay phones. Gojko cuts in front of everyone, hollering that there's an emergency. He glues one ear to the receiver and sticks a finger in the other. He speaks in a loud voice, then hangs up the phone and yells, "My mother had the baby! It's a girl! It's Sebina!"

He throws his arms around our shoulders and drags us along. We must get to the hospital as quickly as possible to see the baby. So what if the snow is as high as the doors? He has chains for the tires. We have to toast to his mother and Sebina! He's glad it's a girl because there are only ever boy babies in their family. What luck she was born today—those born during a snowfall have a long and sweet life. He hopes she takes after his mother, who is so beautiful and cooks the best meat soup in all of Bosnia. He kisses and hugs us. He's so happy he's almost crying. Before you know it we are, too; six damp eyes looking at each other like stupid fish.

In the car we sing along to the songs on the radio without knowing what we're singing. The snow is deep, the sky dense as plaster. Cars creep forward with their headlights on. A snowplow leads the procession. Once again, someone is cleaning the road for us.

Everything is white and deep. Gojko stops to buy something for our toast. Sinking into the snow one step after another, he walks toward a neon sign. Diego turns to me. "Are you happy?"

"Yes. I've never been in a blizzard before."

He extracts my hand from my pocket and holds it. "I want to take your picture. I'm going to take your picture all day long."

Gojko comes back as snowy as a sled dog and opens a bottle of bubbly wine. "It's Austrian. It costs a fortune."

My life is buried in a distant garden beneath a slab of ice. The headlights move through the white. Those long fingers weave themselves through my own. They speak to me, vowing everything, and that's enough, right now, the hand of this boy I don't know tearing me from the stagnant solidity of my body. It's like a child's hand, a hand from a long time ago, the hand of a little friend at nursery school, a little boy who wanted to be with me all the time. I wipe a tear from my eye, the gesture so small it's invisible.

It's cozy warm inside the hospital, almost too warm. The maternity ward has a homey smell of pans on the stove, clothes hung to dry. The room is big but almost all the beds are empty. Gojko's mother is sitting, her back against the pillows, looking out the window at the falling snow. Gojko bends over her and hugs her tight. We hang back a few steps. He gestures for us to move forward. Mirna says, "*Hvala vam.*"

"My mother thanks you."

We ask what she's thanking us for. Gojko shrugs. "For giving me work."

I'm astonished. With her stately neck and fragile face that stretches across her cheekbones like cloth over a loom, his mother really does look like a more beautiful version of Lady Diana. Her eyes are indigo, her hair golden.

So there we stand beside the bed of a new mother as beautiful as a queen. A long shiver runs through me. Maybe the photographer from Genoa is feeling the same thing. He's taken his cap off as if he were in church. Life is mixing up the cards and crowing, like a rooster, the dawn of day.

The baby appears, swaddled in a scrap of white cloth. She's homely, with slightly square cheeks and a pointy chin. She doesn't cry. Her eyes are open as if she already knew everything. Mirna's mouth opens when she sees her, as if it were the mother who sought food from the baby. Tears as big as seeds roll down Gojko's cheeks. He takes the baby's hand in his own and studies her. *Allow me to introduce myself, young lady. I'm your brother Gojko. I will be a father to you.*

Gojko's father died of cancer a few months earlier. Fortunately, his mother has a good job teaching in an elementary school. She's a Croat from Hvar, very Catholic, and she never once thought of aborting the baby.

Now she's yelling in a cracked voice that clashes with her beauty. She doesn't want her son to touch the baby before washing his hands. Gojko goes to the little sink hanging from the wall and returns with dripping hands. He jumps around with his little sister in his arms, kisses and smells her. He stays next to the bed while his mother nurses her, resting his head beside theirs on the pillow. He stays there almost without breathing, like a dog afraid of being chased away.

Diego loads his camera and snaps a picture of the nativity scene. Embarrassed, Mirna shields her breast with her hand. The woman in the next bed, who hasn't given birth yet, makes dark, bitter-tasting raspberry tea on a little electric burner and offers it to us in glazed iron cups. When Mirna pulls up her leg to scratch one of her feet, I see that her legs are covered with red spots. She notices my gaze and smiles, embarrassed. It's eczema. She got it while she was pregnant.

I rummage in my bag for the arnica lotion I always carry for my constantly chapped elbows. I ask her if I can put some on her legs for her.

She shakes her head but I insist. Her legs stiffen. She lowers her head and sniffs as if she were worried she might smell. She has the solid calves of a woman who spends a lot of time on her feet. Her dry skin drinks in the lotion. I smile up at her and she smiles back at me. She makes it clear that she already feels better, that the lotion is miraculous. I tell her she can keep it if she wants, though I'm sorry that it's half empty.

Mirna says something. *"Hoćeš li je?"*

"What did she say?" I ask Gojko.

"She wants to know if you want to hold the baby."

Mirna holds out the newborn still warm from her womb.

The woman who made the tea is telling a funny story and everyone is laughing. For a moment, they forget about me.

The newborn wears the smell of her voyage, a smell from the bottom of a well or a lake. I walk to the mirror beside the sink to see what I look like with a newborn in my arms.

Diego joins me and takes a picture of my reflection in the mirror.

"Do you want kids?"

"What about you?"

"All I want is kids."

He's serious, almost sad. He knows I don't believe him.

It stopped snowing for a while and then started up again. In the Baščaršija there's a sort of white trench along the side of the little streets where the shop-keepers have shoveled in front of their stores. At six in the evening, when darkness swallows up the snow and the smell of wood smoke comes down from the hills, the muezzin climbs the stairs of the minaret to pray. We're already tipsy.

Gojko drags us along to a designer friend's fashion show. The lighting is miserable. The models look like multicolored birds with their raptorlike hairstyles and sequin-covered clothes. They move forward half naked to a soundtrack of Slavic disco music, their skin spotted with cold in the freezing room that looks like a provincial dance hall. The members of the audience seem to have been dragged in off the street. Their shoes are covered with snow, their umbrellas dripping. Gojko's friend is plump and hairless. He's wearing a black wide-knit T-shirt with big holes like a spider web. When he comes out at the end to thank the audience, he bows to the ground like Maria Callas.

Out on the street we laugh like kids on a school trip. Imitating the frozen models, I sway in the snow. Diego throws himself at my feet to take my picture as if I were a star and yells that he wants a spider shirt, too. Gojko says we are two *krastavci*, drunken pickles. He's angry. We're acting too complicit, too stupid. He's getting upset again. He walks ahead of us, tough and ill tempered in his cat-fur jacket.

We glide into a club frequented by the Sarajevo underground, and if it weren't for the slivovitz, it could be London. Artists with long white hair tinged yellow by nicotine circulate alongside spectral swaying girls with closed eyes and black-shadowed eyelids that shine like mussels. The lights come and go. The music seems to come from the bowels of the earth. Like an earthquake, it makes the tables tremble, the ashtrays, the empty glasses no one takes away. Gojko introduces us to Dragana, who works for the state television, and knows how to do voices—she does a Smurf voice for us—and to her boyfriend Bojan, a mime and actor, and then to Zoran, a lawyer whose pockmarked face wears a serious expression, and to Mladjo, a painter who studied at the Brera Academy in Milan. We lose Gojko. He's swallowed up by his friends.

Diego kneels beside me. "What do you want, little one?"

"I don't know. What should we get?"

I'm in a daze. I haven't been in a club in ages. Everyone's half dressed. They're all dancing. I'm wearing an angora sweater and a stiff skirt. I feel clumsy and out of place.

I manage to grab a seat on a slippery couch. Diego comes back with a big cup of ice cream, just one for the two of us. "There wasn't anything else."

Ice cream, with all that snow outside? But it's just the thing. It melts as it slides down into my flaming body. We eat from the same spoon. He puts a spoonful in my mouth and watches me. Then instead of the spoon he brings his mouth to my mouth and lingers there without kissing me right away, his breath on my cold lips as if he were waiting for final approval. He moves into the kiss very slowly. He may be cleverer than I thought. Maybe he's one of those sensual boys with a lot of experience. It's a long soft kiss. Our tongues are snails crossing a city square.

What if he hadn't trusted me that night? Instead, it's all he wanted to do. Our mouths were like a single mouth. Pietro turns over in bed, mutters something, moves all of a sudden toward wakefulness and then dives down again, like a devil ray coming up to the surface and then returning to the dark depths. It's been years since we last slept in the same bed. I'd forgotten about his loose nerves like guitar chords that snap all of a sudden. He's never wanted to hear about his father. *Pietro puts up defenses*, Giuliano said. *He's a kid, and kids are always afraid of getting hurt.*

I always talked to Pietro about his father with levity. I told him about how funny Diego was, told him about his stork legs and the wispy beard he grew so he'd seem older. I told him about the time his father came home saying he'd done the best photo shoot of his life only to realize he hadn't loaded the camera and about how Diego's pants fell when he walked because he was too thin, *like you*, I told him, and he didn't remember to put on his belt, *because he was absentminded, like you*. Every time, I swallowed my tears and laughed.

Giuliano didn't say anything for a long time. Then he said, *Your pain is what he's perceived.*

It's true. I've looked anxiously for signs of his father every day of his life.

One night at dinner Pietro got angry with me because there was no ice cream in the fridge. I told him to sit back down because we weren't finished eating. I said he was spoiled and selfish. Giuliano laid his hand on mine and said he'd get some ice cream from the café downstairs. I told him that it wasn't any help for him to let Pietro treat him like a doormat. He went out and left us alone. Pietro was standing in front of Diego's picture on the fridge. He turned toward me. *What in the hell are you talking about? I'm nothing like him.* He looked at me with the eyes of an adult, a stranger. *I'm not like anyone.*

That night there were kisses, one within the next. Diego sat on me on the leather couch among the fluttering colored lights in that den of smoke and voices.

"Am I heavy?"

"No, you're fine."

Curved over me with his smell, his breath, the sweetest words. Like a snake devouring a little beast, swallowing it slowly. I'm suffocating down here.

I get up and dance. I need to move, to go wild. I raise my arms and legs, pick them up off the ground and move back and forth like seaweed. Who cares that my skirt is stiff, or that I don't know how to dance? I dance like I used to dance in high school. Diego watches me, his eyes half closed in the dark. I've already made my wedding list. Fabio and I spent an entire afternoon in a store downtown with the saleslady beside us making lists. A crystal salt-shaker with a silver cap, its companion pepper shaker. What will I do with them? Where will I scatter the salt? On the salad, or under the bed to get rid of the ghost of this bonehead who's watching me as if I were Bo Derek?

Nothing will happen, nothing will come of it. I tell him it's late. We have to go. He studies me as I put my scarf on. I don't look at him anymore. I look at my feet.

The hotel for the passengers on the canceled flights is on the outskirts of town. The last tram left some time ago. Gojko invites us to sleep at his house. There's room because his mother's in the hospital. It's a big housing block with a courtyard that makes me think of a prison, but inside it's nice. The overhead light shines on a welcoming home with an upright piano, a Turkish carpet, two rows of books on the wall, puffy curtains like little white sausages. Gojko gives Diego his room. "The sheets are clean. I've only slept on them a few times."

I'm to sleep in his mother's room. Gojko shows me how to turn on the light on the bedside table and clears some stuff off a chair so I can put my things there. Beside the bed stands a little crib, all ready, half an egg made of wicker.

"It was mine. Now Sebina will sleep there. My mother made a new mattress and embroidered the sheets."

I'm enchanted by the lace, by a bit of hanging ribbon.

We stay up talking for a while in the living room. Gojko doles out the remains of a bottle of his mother's homemade pear kruškovača. A framed picture of Tito hangs among the others in the kitchen as if he were a member of the family.

Gojko starts talking about his father, who managed to save himself on the Neretva when the Marshal blew up the bridge to trick the Germans.

I stand and say good night. Diego stands, too, and follows me for a few footsteps. "Can I come visit when the partisan is asleep?" His face is like a beggar child's. I shake my head like an angry mother.

I hear them talking for a while, then the buzz of the television. I hear Diego say, *I'm going to bed, I don't understand a fucking thing.* Gojko says, *It's true, you don't understand a fucking thing.*

I'm calm. I read. Tonight Andrić's woman from Sarajevo doesn't leave the Hotel Europa. The words don't sink in. They hang in the air, useless as clothespins on an empty clothesline. There's something gracious about this bed, about this room with its gauze curtains and beige cotton rug. It's clean, the room of a humble woman. I get up and look in the closet: a flowered dress, a suit, two men's jackets and below piles of blankets, sheets and towels. Two neckties and a red patent leather belt hang from a wire on the inside of the door. I go to the bathroom and wash my face and under my arms.

The toothpaste gets rid of the taste of those kisses. Gojko is sleeping on the couch, his arms abandoned, his hands swollen like a child's. The room smells of feet and of lingering cigarette smoke.

Diego calls me, *Psst, ciao.* He's standing in the doorway to his room in a yellow terry-cloth jumpsuit. He smiles. "I found it under Gojko's pillow."

I smile and say good night again.

"Are you sleepy?" he asks.

"Yes."

"You're such a liar."

We're shy in this intimacy that doesn't belong to us, and Gojko asleep is more formidable than Gojko awake.

Diego stands there in those pajamas like a duck suit, his hair long and wavy like an angel's. He twists his mouth like a cartoon. "I'll close my door, so you won't hear me cry."

I tell him to go to hell.

Then something happens. Gojko lets out a long full-bodied fart, a sort of little anal symphony. Diego makes a very intense face and nods. "Nice poem, Gojko. Congratulations."

I cover my mouth and laugh.

Diego laughs, too. I turn and take a few steps toward the room where I'm destined to sleep if I can manage. Diego picks me up off the ground as if he'd never done anything else, like a mover with a rolled carpet.

We fall onto the bed, next to that empty crib. In a second Diego's shucked off Gojko's pajamas and there he is in nothing but a pair of absurd red underpants. I laugh. He doesn't. He has thin legs and a frail body like a child's.

"Do you think I'm ugly?"

"No."

I see pieces of us, my limp hand hanging out of the bed, one of his ears, dark like a well, the point where our two torsos stick together. Before he enters me he stops and asks permission, like a child. "May I?"

It's a root going into the ground. He stays there, looking at me, looking at the miracle of the two of us together. He puts his hands around my head like a crown, looks at my hair while he rubs it. "Now you're mine."

Afterward there was that bed and the empty crib where Gojko slept when he was a baby and where his little sister would now sleep.

I lie with one arm under Diego's head. I feel calm, sated. I think about the phenomenon I've just witnessed, this boy who sensed instinctively what I wanted as if he hadn't done anything else his entire life.

The blizzard has been over for a while. Voices rise up off the street, drunk kids. We get up to watch them from the window. Diego hugs me. I cover myself with a piece of the curtain. They're big guys who speak English, athletes who've lost their way. They stay there for a while throwing snowballs, then go.

We go back to bed. This night will pass drop by drop.

Diego touches one of my nipples, small and dark like a nail. He touches the sadness that will come when he thinks of me. I feel no fear, no regret, no embarrassment. No recognizable feeling intrudes. Regret is a tired old man who can't climb over the gates we build.

Diego picks up his guitar and starts playing, his legs bent, his chest bare, his eyes lowered over the chords.

"What song is that?"

"'I Wanna Marry You.' Our song."

We sleep for a while, a deep blind sleep. I open my eyes to the smell of his body. His nose is stuck in my hair as if he stayed there to breathe in my smell. Day is dawning, small and livid. There's time to make love one more time. His elbow pulls out some of my hair. It hardly matters. I get up, and it's the hardest thing I've done all night long. He watches me while I bend to put on my underpants and gather things here and there.

"I'll miss you my whole life long."

We meet in the kitchen. Gojko's made coffee and bought milk and sweet pitas. He must have passed his room, must have seen the unused bed. He watches us have breakfast together in that kitchen with its dove-gray cupboards, the lamp that looks like an upside-down mushroom. He plays with the crumbs on the table, watches my hands on the cup handle. He doesn't make jokes. We're neither happy nor sad, only lost.

I get my bag and open my wallet. I want to pay Gojko for the hospitality, the food, the sheets that need washing. He looks at the money, all I have left. He's broke, as usual, but he brushes me away with a decisive gesture.

I tell him he'll have to come visit Rome. He can stay with me.

He watches us, breathes in that air of agony. "Why do you have to leave?" I go to brush my teeth. I cry. My mouth is a cesspool of white foam that I can't close. I rub off the makeup beneath my eyes. I go back to the kitchen with my bag. Diego is playing with a yo-yo. Gojko turns, bends over the little sink and throws the cups into it. There are tears in his voice. "You're just a couple of *bakalars*, two cods."

Twenty-four years later I'm having breakfast with my son in a low-ceilinged basement breakfast room lit with fluorescent lights. A few of the tables around us are already dirty. Others are occupied by some of the men who were talking in the lobby last night. Many of them are already smoking. Pietro complains about the smell of smoke and about the food.

"Don't they have anything normal here?"

"What do you mean by 'normal'?"

"Like a pastry, Mom."

I stand up to get him some butter for his bread. I peek into the sad metal containers and find a yogurt and a piece of cherry cake for me. All things considered, I'm hungry. I butter Pietro's bread and tell him the honey here is very good. The girl from the kitchen comes over to the table. She's wearing a uniform: white shirt, black skirt and little apron. Pietro looks at her. She's young, barely more than a child. She has an oval-shaped face, almost transparent, and big yellowish eyes. She asks if we want a hot drink. I ask for tea. Pietro wants to know if they have cappuccino. The girl comes back with my tea and a big mug of darkened milk for Pietro. She smiles as she sets it down in front of him. She has little pimples on her forehead. Pietro looks at the watery liquid without a trace of foam and tries to say something but stops partway through because he doesn't know how to say "foam" in English. The girl smiles at him and in a second—maybe the tray is wet—the teapot slides onto the ground. It doesn't break. It's made of metal. But the spurting tea hits Pietro's white jeans.

He jumps to his feet like a crazed man because his leg is burning. He jumps in the air and pulls the boiling cloth away from his skin. The girl is shocked. She says she's sorry, that she's only been working there a few days. She speaks English with a slight Slavic accent. Pietro unzips his jeans and slides them down to his ankles. He sits there in his underpants, blowing on his thigh. He grumbles in Italian, *Moron, klutz*. But because he's a coward, he says in English, *Don't worry, it's okay.*

The girl continues apologizing. She bends to pick up the teapot. In the meantime a hefty woman in an apron has come out of the kitchen. She speaks quickly to the girl. We don't understand a word of what's being said but it's clear she's being taken to task. Her cheeks are flaming red. Pietro has pulled his jeans back up. He taps the fury on the shoulder and says, "It's my fault. The girl is very good, very much good." He adds a pointless "indeed" for good measure.

The woman leaves. Pietro sits back down.

"You don't say 'very much good.'"

He complains that I'm always on his case, always, even when he's being good.

I smile. This time he's right.

I watch his white crooked teeth tear at the bread. The little Sarajevo waitress thanks him with a tiny bow.

We said goodbye at the airport. We leaned against the wall, close together. Diego put his hands under my coat, seeking the heat of my flesh. I let him. Everyone had already boarded. We stood without moving beside the row of empty seats. Then I turned and went away. I saw him knocking like a little bird with its beak against the glass. I had been crying but he was yelling to me that I should smile, that I should be happy no matter what, even without him.

Chapter 3

I slipped right back into my life. When the charity for the blind came around collecting old clothes, I donated the long parka I'd worn every day in Sarajevo and went back to wearing my tailored city coat. At the university, student voices floated along the halls, echoes of lives that were still carefree, unlike my own. With Fabio it was easy enough. I told him the truth: that I felt tired and a little depressed. He didn't ask for more. He was quite a boy. He found his own reasons for my malaise. Of course I was tired. I'd studied too hard. I always asked too much of myself. We never seemed to have time to make love. When we saw each other it was so that we could deliver wedding invitations to his relatives. Our relationship was pleasant, docile. I watched Fabio as he drove the car with his thoughtful gaze. He worked for the family engineering firm; his father was gradually handing it over to him. They were always competing for public contracts, multifunctional spaces, green areas, social centers. The first time Fabio and I ever made love it was in their office, among the drafting tables and the transparencies. I was a virgin. Fabio muttered about something that had happened before he met me but he was so clumsy I had trouble believing him. Now I couldn't remember anything about the two of us there in that empty office that served as our Saturday night refuge for years. Fabio was the boss's son. He would wash himself off in the little bathroom with its toilet freshener that turned the water blue when you flushed. *The bathroom is free*, he would say, and then watch me as I walked, naked: *You have long legs*, or *You have a sculpted torso*, the same appraising eye as when he calculated cement quantities.

I watched his face as he studied the traffic, his thoughts stuck in some problem, a construction site, equipment, drainage. I liked the way his car smelled, the little packet of chocolate cookies we always ate after making love. I didn't ask myself why it was so important to sweeten our mouths afterward, why he was in such a hurry to wash, to rinse the humors of my body off his dick. We were more comfortable with our clothes on, when we went out to eat and he would help me off with my coat and study the wine list. He was thirty-four, stable and sensible. I was almost thirty, and I dressed up because he liked me to. We shared a silent, solid harmony and the knowledge that our future together would never leave us exposed.

Now we went to see the priest almost every evening. Neither of us was particularly religious, but we liked those premarital interviews, the smell of the sacristy, the priest's footsteps as he came toward the little door where we waited after ringing the bell, his voice: *Come in, come in.* He was a hearty, upbeat boy squeezed into an ill-fitting cassock. He was still studying theology at the Università Cattolica. He spoke to us as a friend, illuminating us on the sacraments we were about to celebrate with passion. He always begged our pardon before asking an indiscreet question. I felt safe there. It was a clean room made for waiting and for purification. In its tidiness and humility it reminded me of rooms I'd seen in Sarajevo. I didn't feel guilty. It was as if I had no obligation toward my future husband, at least not in that sense. The knife was stuck in my gut, but it didn't hurt. I had no intention of confessing to our friend the priest. Sarajevo belonged to me and cradled a remote part of my existence.

I missed Diego but never thought of changing my life and told him so during a long, nocturnal phone call. His voice sobbed out impossible requests. He was in rough shape, unable to think about anything else, unable to eat or take pictures. He'd called off the trip to Brazil. He was dying. He talked about that night, our bodies, our mud.

I don't trust his voice. I pull back. It's impossible for something like this to go on, impossible for it to last. Diego says his love will last his entire life because he's crazy, but I won't give him a chance. He didn't wash for days just to keep the smell of my skin on his. He laughs but it dies on his lips. He wants to know if I still smell the same. I'm crying. I tell him to shut up.

"I'm waiting," he says. "I'm here."

He's just a child. He's out of his mind.

He doesn't ask about Fabio, about the wedding. He asks about my feet, my belly button, the little wells behind my ears. He's developed the pictures he shot in Sarajevo, pictures of the snow, pictures of athletes relaxing at Mojmilo and especially the last ones he shot, pictures of me. He laughs. His mother has been asking him about all the shots hanging in his room of the girl surrounded by snow snapped from so close that she seems to be moving. He lowers his voice when he tells me about the one he keeps hidden away, the one of me standing naked beside the window.

"When did you take it?"

"When you didn't notice."

He takes it out at night, looks at it during our phone calls and when he's alone, holds it against his stomach, sleeps with it and, he hints, does other things with it, as well.

I picture him in the room he's described, the banner of the Genoa soccer team, the spartan bed he made himself with a few boards and some nails, the photographs of Native American children on the reservation and of his hard-core soccer-fan friends—the ultras—from Marassi Stadium. He turns on the stereo, tells me to be quiet and puts the receiver to the speaker so we can listen together to our song . . . *To say I'll make your dreams come true would be wrong . . . But maybe, darlin', I could help them along . . .* He's skinny, naked himself. He closes his eyes and looks for me.

Whenever I saw Fabio I felt better. If I'd been truly unhappy, I told myself, I'd have left him. I had the courage to do it. Instead, he calmed me. The personification of calm. That was my boyfriend. How many winter afternoons had we spent with our books open on the table of the little tearoom where we used to study and eat pastries? We'd grown up together. He liked to come shopping with me. He sat and waited, he had patience and taste. I would cross my legs and admire my nylons, my delicate woolens, the bag I wore over my shoulder and all the other layers that kept me far away from my nakedness, from the vulnerable childish pit that was my body. I didn't want to suffer. As a teenager I had swooned over the sad sagas of tragic literary characters, but I didn't see it as my destiny to chase after empty dreams or harvest tears. The world was overflowing with every possible thing. Love stories, like everything else, could eat away at you with nostalgia but then they were over in a flash. It was foolish to believe in them. I began to feel serene again, blessed with normalcy, with moderation.

That night in Sarajevo had been my last goodbye to another woman, a crooked beggar who dwelled inside me.

I'd been back for two weeks. It felt like years and like no time at all. My mother noticed the long nocturnal phone calls but didn't say anything. The people around you don't want to know you. They take your lies as truth. She did what she always did: she hid. She'd taught me to fear suffering, taught me that a good life does not require truth at all costs. You could always pull back, turn your gaze to a flower pot or a passing car, sacrifice what was authentic for the sake of unhindered forward progress. She would have been the perfect wife for a monster. I know this must sound horrible, but who knows? If my father had been a pedophile, she might well have studied her hands and removed her wedding ring, but then, certain she'd manage once again, she'd have put it right back on with a sad smile because that naked hand would have been too much to bear. But life didn't give Annamaria a chance to take the measure of her fear. My father would never have raped his daughter. He was an upstanding gentleman and a bit too vague, too distant, for there to be room for him in my agitated life, which was why his words struck me so, coming out of nowhere as they did, out of the hallway, where he stood, as usual a book in hand, the same after-dinner expression as always.

"Are you sure you're doing the right thing?"

I turn. Fabio is waiting for me down in the car. Tonight's our last meeting with the priest. "What are you talking about, Dad?"

He gestures toward the table in the dark living room, a funeral bier of gifts, boxes of plates, silverware, silver pitchers, objects for wardrobes, for dinners, for fucking weddings. "You don't have to worry about that jumble of pots and pans. We can send it all back."

He teaches shop and his hands smell of sawdust and glue, but in the evening he reads Homer and Yeats. He's blushing. He felt that he had to do it, that he had to speak to me. He may or may not have thought in advance about what to say, but he realized that our days together were coming to an end and that there wasn't going to be another chance to say something, so out it popped, here in the darkened hallway. My mother's sitting in the den, her face tilted toward the blue light of the television. I resemble her, but I'm shrewder. I know how to strew lies like nuggets of truth.

"I'm happy, Dad. This is what I've always wanted."

"And the other guy?"

For a moment, I think Diego would be grateful to this honest man who dares to speak through the fog of this house. Then, without blushing, I write him off without giving him a chance.

"He doesn't exist, Dad. He's nobody."

He nods. "Well, then. Good. On with the pots and pans." He smiles and mutters something. He's shy. He took a chance. He threw me a rope and I let it drop.

He goes off, shrugging. He believes me because I'm his daughter. He believes me, although not entirely. He believes in the plan in my head, the compartments I've opened and closed. He's willing to bet on the chess match of my life. He doesn't try to put himself in my shoes, in my underpants; he must have barely managed to get into my mother's. Women are little ogres, tidbits for bolder palates. He's a great admirer of reasoned thought, which is why he kisses me now on the forehead. He doesn't know about the rest. It's none of his business. He may have an inkling, which is why he trembles.

The next day I figure it out, and as I'm realizing it I walk toward a drugstore on wild legs, like a dog who's escaped from the pound. I buy a test, fumbling for words, *the thing . . . the pregnancy thingie.* An eternity passes as the woman wraps it in paper and tape.

I slip into a snack bar. It's midday. The place is full of teenagers. Grease oozes out of the floors. Trays dance up and down the stairs. The place stinks of meat, of frying. I wait alone in the restroom with a bunch of girls putting on makeup and chattering. Finally I enter a stall that stinks of warm piss. I read the instructions, flood the little wand, close the cap and wait.

That's how I found out, my back against the filthy door with its graffitied tales of love and obscenity, standing with one foot on the toilet seat and my eyes on the little wand. At first the little blue line was very light, and then it darkened. I stuck it in my coat pocket. When I'd walked as far as the Ara Pacis, I stopped and checked again. The line was still there, as blue as the sea.

The low, nocturnal ring of the phone came just as I was thinking of calling Diego. We didn't say much. It was raining in Genoa. You could hear the rain below our words. I told him that he wouldn't be able to call me anymore after I was married. He said he knew and that he wanted to get the most out of these last days. Then I asked him if it was true.

"What?"

"That you're about to board the train for Rome."

He was whooping, probably jumping for joy. He'd take the first night train. He had a present to bring me. He said he would take off all my clothes and lick me from head to toe until his tongue fell off.

That's not how it went. That very night I lost the child who'd only just begun. Physically, it was nothing. I was sleeping when it happened and I went right on sleeping. I saw the blood in the morning. I washed myself and stared at my petrified face in the mirror. Not even then was I willing to suffer. I went out first thing. It wasn't really necessary but I went to the hospital all the same. The gynecologist was an ancient woman. She gave me a pelvic exam and said not to worry, that I didn't need to do anything, that sometimes women don't even notice they're pregnant before their bodies eliminate what she called a *blighted ovum, a pregnancy sac in which the embryo does not develop.* I thanked her and probably shook her hand a bit more energetically than necessary. I wanted to ask her something else but I didn't know what.

The Easter eggs I used to make with my mother came to mind as I waited at an intersection on my scooter. She emptied them through a little hole so they wouldn't stink.

Diego would be arriving soon. I stopped to have breakfast at a café, a big ear-shaped pastry with jam that looked like earwax. I didn't feel ill. The pelvic exam and the gynecologist's calm tone had restored my equilibrium. I even thought it was probably better this way. The very last remains of that boy had left me. There was nothing believable about our story, just absurd twists and turns, one after the next, like in a puppet theater.

I watched him arrive. He had his neck out the window, his long hair in the wind like a torn flag. He was right up front, ready to launch himself out of the train. He sought me in the crowd like a man returning from the wars. He jumped around on his thin legs. What on earth was he wearing? A strange aviator jacket and red, narrow-legged pants that made his legs look even thinner. He looked like a sixteen-year-old, like one of those kids who go to soccer matches and demonstrations. I watched him from my hiding place behind a big marble column down the platform. I wanted to throw my arms around his neck like a teenager. Instead, I waited, still as a gecko. Sometimes we act older at thirty than at fifty.

He stood looking around, mouth gaping like a fool. The platform was nearly empty. I'd leave, that's what I'd do. Did he stink of his journey or smell of himself? I stayed there, spying on him, a sad game like something in one of those artsy movies full of sad gazes in stations, the main characters brushing past each other and never meeting because the director is a constipated son of a bitch whose sole goal is to send you home empty-handed, a finale without the kisses you'd find in an American film.

I'm leaving, I said to myself, in the meantime not moving an inch. I was sitting now on the bench at the bottom of the column. Diego was walking back and forth and turning around continuously as if I might come out from anywhere. He looked toward the great hall at the end of the platform but didn't move. I could read his thoughts, predict his moves. He had a leather bag over his shoulder and a chair in his hand, a little green plastic chair. What was it for? Every once in a while he jumped to find his flair, the spring in his legs. Now the platform was filling with people getting off another train.

He boarded the train. *He's leaving*, I thought. But he was just helping a woman with her bags, a big fat woman dressed in white. She must have been one of those American tourists who travel with a ton of bags, convinced they'll find a porter, boys from another era. Diego was explaining something with her map. Then the platform emptied again. The sky was dark; the rain had come south with him from Genoa overnight. Now Diego was lying on a marble bench, his backpack as a pillow. He lifted the chair, looked at it, set it back down. I walked over to him.

"Hey!" He leaps to his feet like a gymnast and takes my hand without a word about how late I am. He studies my face, moves a lock of hair. "You're even more beautiful than I remembered. What have you been eating, Heaven?"

How does he come up with the things he says? He jumps around me. "What about me? How do I look?"

I take in the torero pants, the rail-thin body. "You look good."

"I've lost a little weight." He gives me the chair. "Here."

"What's this?"

"Your present. Don't you like it?"

"Yes . . ."

"It was my chair when I was a little boy. It's the only thing I didn't break, because it's made of super-strong plastic. I wanted you to have it."

He sits down in the chair, in the middle of the station. "I still fit in it. My butt's the same size."

He comes close, seeks my eyes. He opens his mouth to kiss me and I move aside so his kiss lands on my cheek. He lifts my chin. "How are you?"

"Okay."

He's too close. I smell his breath, his relentless love. We're out in the open, in the chaos of Termini Station.

"Come on. Let's go."

I walk beside him without giving him my hand. He carries his chair. What a dumb idea to bring that chair.

My scooter is parked near Via Marsala. In front of us there's a sign for one of the many no-star pensions near the station. He pulls my arm and says he'd like to go into one of them. I say they're ugly and squalid, full of poor foreigners and shady couples.

He says he adores making love in squalid places.

"I'm indisposed."

"I can't believe it. You called me after all this time and . . . good timing!" He makes a worm face. "As far as I'm concerned, there's no problem. I have red pants on."

I slap him hard across the face.

He laughs. "What's wrong with you?"

I push forward with the scooter to pull up the kickstand. He grabs on behind me, his long bent legs, his bony knees. He holds me tight around the waist, tickles me. I tell him to be careful or we'll fall, have an accident. He says I'm a disaster on a scooter, that I ride the brakes. When we're waiting for the lights to change, he kisses my neck, my ears. We look like high school kids.

Later, sitting in a café, I tell him. I tell him about the pregnancy wand at the snack bar and all the rest. I'm calm. I'm wearing my sunglasses. I watch a passerby. He doesn't say anything. His beer sits there untouched.

"Are you sorry?"

He nods and smiles but his mouth is sad like a rusty hook. He drains his beer. "What about you?"

I shrug. There hadn't been time to be sad, it all happened so quickly. I tell him it was a blighted ovum.

He tells me about his grandmother, who is blind. "She was twelve years older than my grandfather. He always saw her go by on her bike. One day she fell in the water. She hadn't seen the sea. My grandfather fished her and her bicycle out. They stayed together as long as he lived. Now she's on her own. She doesn't need help, she manages to cook and do everything. When I go see her she makes handmade pasta. She can get the pasta into the pan of boiling water better than I can."

"What's your grandmother got to do with it?"

"Nothing. Just an example. Love stories that seem ridiculous can work out. I'm only five years younger than you, and I'm reliable like my grandfather. I'll die before you because women live longer. Don't get married, baby. Choose me. I'm your blighted ovum."

He's got the sky in his eyes. He puts a hand on the nape of his neck and waits. It's a gesture of surrender, maybe even of defeat, as if he were putting all the weight of his body there. It's the same gesture I noticed the first time I saw him, when he turned toward me in that bar and brought his hand to the nape of his neck and stayed there that way, without moving. There will come a time when I'll miss that gesture to the point of agony.

I tell him it's the last time we'll see each other, and that when I'm married he's not to call me.

He asked me if he could take my picture, so I stood on the stairs of San Crispino and let him. A crowd of pigeons hovered around me like little undertakers. I shooed them away with my hand. We wandered around, ate some pizza, looked at a window full of camera lenses. I ran into a friend and said hi without stopping. In the meantime it began to get dark. For a moment the cobblestones downtown turned a grayish blue, then dark filtered through the alleys like smoke. When I went with him back to the station, he drove, racing like a maniac among the first lights of evening. He said he always drove like that, that for him it was normal because it was practical. He'd had lots of scooters, had spent his teenage years with oily black hands and spare parts. Now, he said, he had an amazing motorcycle. He'd ride down on it the next time he came to see me.

There won't be a next time. We walk toward the platform. He asks for a kiss. It's a strange kiss that already tastes of train, of the lonely journey he's about to take, with his red pants, his bony knees, his Genoa soccer team scarf. He'll lean his head against the window, go to the bathroom, go back to his seat. In the pitch-dark he'll get off the train at Brignole and make his way toward the port, the alleyways and the little darkroom where he'll develop the picture of the pigeons and my hand shooing them off the same way I shooed him.

Enough. Let's get going. Life is in a hurry, but yes, there's time for one last thing. Before the door of the train closes, I say, "Be careful. Don't do anything stupid."

He looks like a child going off to summer camp.

I get married. I walk down the aisle toward Fabio, who turns to watch me. He's wearing a shiny gray morning suit with tails and a starched shirtfront. He looks like a big pigeon in the embellished dusk of the church. I see the altar, the friendly priest, the white roses and calla lilies. My father's arm is stiff, tense, like a wooden arm held up by a string. He's not used to being at the center of attention. He moves forward slowly without knowing whether or not to greet people or look ahead and in the end compromises by greeting them with his eyes and trembling. He'll be more at ease in a couple of decades, when his coffin travels down the same aisle, between the same pews, and I'll remember this absurd day, his wooden arm ferrying me along into the depths of my haze as if I were made of crystal. If I'd leaned over to whisper, *Let's get out of here*, he wouldn't have thought twice. His arm would have softened and he'd have taken me by the hand. I'd have thrown off my high heels and we would have fled the church, leaving behind all those starched shirts. My father liked a little restaurant in San Giovanni where they made *spaghetti con cacio* with lots of pepper. We would have had a glass of wine, too, my wedding dress crumpled beneath me on the chair, wedding banquet be damned, his eyes shiny and crazy like mine. He'd have gotten a kick out of it. But this has nothing to do with what actually happened. My father took his place in the pew, my mother moved to make room for him. He coughed. My mother with her tense face, her too-tight shoes, my mother-in-law all freckles and evanescence, puffed up like her son in dove-colored silk, her hair like powder, my father-in-law the engineer, white-haired and robust, elegant and irritated at being in church.

And so I married my groom. I read the vows. We exchanged rings without dropping them. The rice hailed down on us. A photographer took our pictures. We went from table to table with a basket of Jordan almonds. There were songs and jokes. I laughed all the time, even when I went into the bathroom and freshened up without regrets. The bodice fit me well, like a stiff petal, a little shell. The old guests left and the young ones stayed, our friends. We danced barefoot on the grass, Fabio shirtless, wearing only his pants and top hat. It was a jitterbug. He pulled me toward him like a spring. He was drunk.

We took our places inside our house. White walls, parquet floors, an "eco" bed that smelled like bird feed, a refrigerator that was far too big.

Scenes from a marriage.

Fabio comes home from work. I hear the keys, hear him moving around. I don't move from the couch. "How are you?"

He moves past me. "I have to go to the bathroom."

Fabio watching television, his face pale in the dark. Fabio opening the fridge and asking what we should eat for dinner. Fabio watching the street from a window. Fabio at the movies, glasses on, mouth closed, his breath changing when he opens it again, more like his father's.

Fabio's things are in the washing machine. He's been running and now he's taking a shower. He comes out naked and dripping. I look at the drops of water on the wood floor, at his blond body.

"What's wrong?" he asks.

"Nothing."

Dinner at his parents' house, the polished oval table, the long paneled curtains. Fabio is wearing a blue knit tie; he and his father are discussing calculations for a landfill. His mother serves us chicken galantine. I smile at the Filipina maid who clears the plates.

Dinner at my parents' house. My father doesn't speak. My mother jumps up constantly to get things. When we leave I offer to bring the garbage down for my mother. In the elevator Fabio complains about the stink, says I make absurd gestures and treat him disrespectfully.

"What, because of a garbage bag?" I ask as I pull the lever that opens the dumpster.

"Not only . . . it's everything."

I tell him I don't want to argue, I'm tired, I worked all day, I was at the university until late.

"That's not work."

"So what is it?"

"They don't pay you."

We don't make love. We lie beside each other in bed talking about our friends, the lamps we need to install, a three-day weekend on the Argentario.

I can't say it was an unhappy marriage. It was like stepping into a furniture showroom, looking at the kitchens that haven't been hooked up, trying out the sofas and the beds, no dirty sheets, nothing broken or worn, no scratches on the floor, no fights. It was something I'd decided to do to obey a blind desire. I wanted to honor that promise even if only for a few days.

Fabio comes back at night and sits next to me on the sofa. Sometimes he takes my hand. Sometimes he's tired and rests his hands on the crotch of his pants. I don't know what he's thinking and don't wonder. I don't know what I think. I don't mind taking refuge between these walls, in this fashionably furnished barracks. We don't lack a thing. We're young, reasonably attractive. We have the most expensive shower stall possible, a single slab of curved crystal. We walk barefoot on the wood floors, a young couple without any constraints. The fridge is frequently empty. Every so often we fill up a cart at the supermarket. Fabio isn't picky. On Saturdays he cooks, wearing the long white professional chef's apron that he asked for in a hotel. We frequently have dinner guests. We like cooking for our friends, opening the wine, lighting candles.

Do I miss the boy from the alleyways? I don't think about him. There's no space for him in this white house. I know he's gone. He finally worked up his courage and went to that red region at the edge of Amazonia. It was what he'd always wanted to do, a backpack full of film, his camera around his neck, hitchhiking and riding stinking trains and trucks full of leaves and children to photograph. All's well that ends well, everyone on their own edge of the world, in their own scrap of life. At the university they don't pay me. I'm not earning a thing. I think about leaving. I'm sick of the smell. My research grant hasn't been renewed. I'm not interested in Andrić anymore. He's part of the past like all the rest.

Fabio and I stand in front of the refrigerator.

"What's wrong?"

"I'm not happy with myself."

"You're never happy with yourself."

I fall riding my scooter, slip beneath the rain. I'm not hurt, but I stay there like a mummy, unable to move, to get out of the way of traffic. A boy helps me, a high school kid. He has a bandanna around his neck and his face is wet.

"Thank you."

"You're welcome, ma'am."

Ma'am. I'm a poor old lady. I drag my scooter along beneath the rain. I stop to have a beer in a café. A beer, alone, at four in the afternoon. I go back to my parents' house, dry my hair and put it up in a ponytail and put on jeans and an old sweater like when I was in high school.

My father meets me in the hallway with my white face. "What are you doing here at this time of day?"

I want the green plastic chair. I've lost some weight and it fits me better now. I sit on the balcony at my parents'. It becomes a habit, sitting out there squashed into that little chair, my knees up near my mouth, the sleeves of my sweater pulled over my hands when it's cold. I can see a bit of the riverbank. I watch the seagulls coming up from the sea, people out jogging. I take up smoking again. I'd stopped a few years earlier and now I start again. I don't go to the university anymore.

"What are you doing?" my mother asks.

"Not a damn thing."

Fabio plays soccer in the evenings. I go with him. I stand at the railing and smoke. A group of wives cheer, their high heels in the spaces between the bleachers. Floodlights light up the nocturnal pack of fools sweating in their shiny socks.

"I'm not coming anymore. It's damp."

Fabio nods as he fills his duffel. He shows me the new shoes he's bought, full of transparent rubber bubbles to diminish the shocks. He's become fixated with sports. He likes the way it makes him feel, likes to be in shape. I smoke, I'm short of breath. He says nothing, just asks me not to smoke in the house.

One late afternoon I go into a record store and listen to music with headphones alongside all the kids. I buy a few cassettes, including our song. *You never smile, girl, you never speak.* I listen to it as I wander around the center on my scooter. I go fast now, like him. Tears slide down my face. It's as if I were fourteen all over again. I'm a poor fool. I stop in Piazza Farnese. In the depths of night, even the junkies have gone away. I lie down on the marble and smoke a cigarette. I like drawing in the smoke. It tastes like something that I lack, fills my body.

Frequently I stay at my parents'. "It's closer to the university," I tell Fabio. He doesn't know that I don't go to the university anymore. I have my own set of keys. Sometimes my parents are already asleep when I arrive. They know something isn't right but they pretend everything is normal and don't ask me anything. "Are you eating here tonight?" My mother fries my favorite meatballs. My father opens some wine and we talk about politics, Reagan, Margaret Thatcher, our own Christian Democrats. Dad says I'm becoming a subversive. He doesn't mind. He asks me for a cigarette. My mother doesn't complain. We smoke where we like.

At night I play the stereo low with the lights off. I dance in front of the mirror in the open door of the wardrobe where the light coming in through the shutters is reflected. I look at my breasts, my belly. This is my childhood bedroom where I cried and studied and listened to the radio. My posters are still here, my books, my old clothes in dry-cleaning bags, the white helmet from when I did fencing, the poncho with the fringe I used to suck on when I was riding the bus to school. This room contains my entire life up to the age of thirty. I look at it, look at what always greeted me. I acted alone, hostage to my own desire. In the end, I was never good enough for anything. I dance in the dark. Incompleteness and illusion are my malady.

"I found a job."

"Doing what?"

"Tending bar. I like making cocktails. I'm a quick learner."

My husband shakes his head and looks at me differently. He says I'm crazy but it's a craziness he likes. I tell him I'm young, we don't have kids, I can afford an unconventional job. One night he comes to the bar with a couple of guys from his soccer team, a lawyer and another engineer. He watches me move from table to table in my miniskirt and black apron. I only look at him once. My tray is always full. I see a fuzzy blond head in the midst of the hubbub. He can't stand the noise and the smoke but he stays until closing time. We get in the car. He stops at the Janiculum and wants to make out. He mutters about how much he likes me, says we should go back to being boyfriend and girlfriend, says I didn't seem like his wife tonight but like someone else. The way his friends were looking at me made him jealous. He's sorry we don't make love anymore, but now . . . he's floppy, drunk.

I tell him I don't love him. "And you don't love me, either."

I tell him it was a mistake for us to get married. He gets out of the car to pee. I hear his urine splashing into the grass. He says I'm exaggerating, that I'm too dramatic, that being with me isn't easy.

Gojko calls one night. "Hey, beautiful!"

I'd been missing his dirty hair, his voice.

"You didn't come to Italy!"

"Yes, I did. I went to Diego's. I was there for almost a month."

"Why didn't you call me?"

"Diego said you were an old married woman who didn't want to hear from old admirers."

"Fuck you."

"He was in pretty bad shape."

"I know."

"It wasn't easy to pull him out of the hole. I helped. We emptied lots of bottles."

"Oh, I see."

He tells me he's discovered limoncello, that it's delicious, that Diego's gone.

"I know."

"It's Sebina's baptism next week."

"So late?"

"We had to wait until after the mourning period for my father."

"How's Mirna?"

"Good, but she didn't have enough milk, so Sebina's on formula."

I smile. "Give her a big kiss."

"Would you be the godmother?"

He's insistent. He calls me the next night, too. Mirna would be so happy, and after all that snow I have to see the green hills and smell the heather and cyclamen that take root in the crevices and descend into the alleyways of the Baščaršija.

I buy a little cross on a chain for Sebina. Fabio says nothing except that he can't bring me to the airport because they've got a sealed construction site. Once more they've unearthed Roman remains while digging.

And so there we are once again, sitting at an open-air café, the pigeons jumping on the tables. Gojko is drinking Sarajevsko pivo and I've got a dense, dreggy bosanska kafa. I brought him a carton of Marlboros and two bottles of limoncello. He offers me one of his foul Drinas. "I'm glad you took up smoking again."

He studies me. He comments on my haircut. He says I look younger, that marriage agrees with me. He asks me about the university. I say I'm waiting tables in a bar.

"Do you get good tips?"

"No."

"You've got to learn to wiggle your ass."

He stands to show me. When he sits back down he reads me one of his poems.

Why is it that your body no longer floats over mine?
Like that barge we saw on the Neretva
the pink fog like your breast
my legs impudent like floodwaters.
Along came the scorching sun to drink everything, even the mud.
Like a lazy cow, you rubbed your tongue
in the holes where the flies were moaning.
You turned me over like a carcass
and I waited for your mouth
on my bones.

"Did you fall in love?"

"She left me. To marry someone else." He laughs.

I cry and tell him that my marriage is a joke. He asks me if I'm in love with Diego. I tell him no.

"Well in that case, I have a chance."

The city had dismantled the Olympics. Away with the flags and the big billboards for an audience of foreigners. The city looked like a house after the guests leave, even more beautiful than before in its silence and frugality.

The baptism, simple and moving, took place the next day in the Cathedral of the Sacred Heart. The priest sought our eyes as he spoke and emphasized terrestrial things.

Sebina wore a cap with a big white flounce that circled her face like a halo. She looked like a little abbess with her red cheeks and her dark, deep-set eyes.

My dear Sebina, I picture you in the light of the cathedral on that funny day when the sacrament that liberated you from the original sin of the Christians was celebrated in the presence of your Muslim relatives. Your peace brought peace. Someone passed your body into my arms. You were surrounded by a halo of goodness, of wisdom made flesh. You would grow to become a great eater of pitas and to have a fish named Bijeli, "White." You would adore watching *The Simpsons* on TV. You would have the most disorganized notebook in your class and your legs would be the fastest in your Novo Sarajevo neighborhood.

I feel a presence beside me. I don't turn my head but I know it's him and it's such a shock I worry I'll drop the baby. My legs go weak. The blood drains from my head. That's his elbow, his smell. I clutch Sebina. She weighs very little but I'm worried I'll lose my grip. It's him. This is just the way he would appear, out of the blue, foolish, without even thinking that I might faint.

He whispers in my ear, "I'm the godfather."

Now I understand everything, the meaning of the day and the place and of Gojko's sly expression. Later, when I punch him in the gut, he'll say, "It was hard not to tell you, but I'd promised!" I understand that it's what I'd been waiting for, what I'd been asking of God, asking of each body that entered the church.

Some blood returns to my face and I'm able to turn and take in a bit of him, his hand, a lock of hair, his jeans.

But it's not true that he's the godfather. Later Gojko will explain that he couldn't have us both because of family obligations and that Diego said to choose me. *That way she's sure to come.* He wasn't sure he could get there on time. He smells of two days and nights of travel, airports, layovers.

So I move toward the baptismal font alongside Mirna's brother, a man with a big black mustache. But the baptism is ours. When the water bathes Sebina's body, I seek Diego's eyes with my own.

We eat trout and bosanski lonac at a long table before a mountain chalet with a gigantic stuffed bear over the entrance. I talk, emptying my throat and my heart. We hold hands beneath the table. They burn and tremble. He's surprised, almost incredulous, to find me so willing to give in. Maybe he doesn't believe me. He sweats and he drinks. He couldn't have imagined me like this. He looks at my hair and my face without makeup.

"You've gotten younger. I've aged." He shows me a white hair in the sideburns he's grown. He's mangy and sun-baked and thinner than before. It's true, he does seem a bit older. A couple of months. He raises his arm and sticks his nose in his armpit. He apologizes; he had a quick rinse-off in the airport bathroom. He's been wearing the same T-shirt for three days.

"Where were you?"

"At the other end of the world."

He was immersed in an enormous swampy river, risking his legs and his life beside a placid colony of caimans. He took pictures of an old ferryman on his bamboo boat laden with sun-dried skins. He felt better. He even tried to make love to a German girl in a bungalow beneath a fan that twirled mosquitoes. She got up to close the door because she was scared that snakes might come in. He watched her. Those few steps were enough; he knew he wouldn't be able to go through with it.

"Liar. What did you tell her?"

"That I had diarrhea. I closed myself in the bathroom until she left."

He laughs. He thought he was cured. He got up at dawn and caught the red sun rising over the plateau, *bright red, like a lollipop.* He loaded his camera and walked through the forest toward the little villages of the rubber tappers. And in the end, he even started to think he might stay there like a hermit, like a monk. He looks at me, smiles his little smile and shakes his head. "I'm no monk, baby."

When he got Gojko's telegram he threw his things into his backpack and started running beneath a torrential rain, his thumb in the air, waiting for a passing truck or car. In the end a Policia Civil jeep picked him up. He traveled across the forest, soaking wet, between two big dark men who seemed more like two devils than guardian angels. *If she comes to Sarajevo*, he kept telling himself, *it will mean that she misses us, too.*

He moves his head toward me. "Look at me! Don't move your eyes away. This time I'll kidnap you if I have to."

Suffering has made him bolder. He pulls me up to dance with the others in the field. He holds me tight like a groom. His arms are stronger. He pulls me by the hair as if I were an ear of corn, pulls me to his mouth, breathes into mine. There's menace in the way he seeks me, like a caiman on the surface of the water.

"Look at me."

I'm looking at him.

"I love you."

He dances divinely. I'm a rag in his arms. His shoulders are straight like a flamenco dancer's, his pelvis sinuous, his legs crazy like Michael Jackson's. Where will this madman take me? Into what paradise, what hell? For now, I can't tear myself away from his lips.

"It will be a party, a party every day. I'll give you everything, I swear."

It's dusk. The sun is leaving the field. Sebina's dress is wrinkled, her flounces limp. She looks like a little goat, dirtied with milk. She's sleeping in my arms, sweating onto my shirt. She smells like tiny flesh, crumpled in a sky bigger than our own. She's like warm glue, honey in the sponge of a beehive. The impalpable moves before me, dragged along by the buzz of an insect, the feeling that life will take its course, like links in a chain.

Diego and Gojko arm wrestle on the table covered with empty glasses. The women divide up the leftover food, wrapping kitchen towels around red terra-cotta pans.

Sarajevo lies down below in her bed between the mountains. The sun's last rays rustle as it dies. It looks as if it has been immersed in water. It looks as if everything, the houses, the minarets, were there by chance, by magic,

and that all of it could disappear from one moment to the next. Like us, like
Sebina, like anything too alive to last.

We take a room at the Holiday Inn, deserted now that the Olympics are over.
We go up the stairs in the long galleries that surround the lobby. The monumental chandelier looks like a huge jellyfish trapped in a net. The waiters
down below move like seaweed in an empty sea. The room smells of newness,
furniture fresh from the factory. There's a big bed and a big window overlooking the boulevard. Diego says he has to take a shower because he stinks like a
pig. While I wait I look out the window at the Zemaljski Muzej with its botan-
ical garden beside the brand-new monolith of the Parliament. He kisses me
from behind. His hair is wet. The water drips onto me. We make love almost
without moving, holding tight to one another. It's different from the other
time. We're shyer. We've suffered. We're scared. We don't dare risk a thing.
We're a husband and wife who've been reunited and fear failure. Diego's lost
his verve. His eyes are closed. He missed me so much, he says, too much, and
now he's too drunk to be happy.

Afterward he lifts my damp hair and kisses the back of my sweaty neck.
"This is the place, you know. It's here in the nape of the neck where life is
born. The nape of your neck is the river, your destiny."

"How do you know?"

We sleep flesh against flesh. From above we look like two people who've
fallen into a ravine. We wake at dawn because the window is already full of
light. We have breakfast in the room. A waiter knocks and pushes the cart
inside. Later the tray lies on the floor alongside the crumpled towels. We're
on the bed again. I'm on my back, my breasts falling to either side. Diego
photographs my belly, focuses on my belly button. We don't get dressed until
afternoon. I can't find my socks. He looks under the bed. I look under the
other side. We stay like that for a while, studying each other. At the airport he
asks, "What am I supposed to do?"

"Wait for me."

He's listless, his backpack full of dirty things on the ground. He fiddles
with a rusty buckle. "You'll dump me this time, too. It's written in the cards."

"Where?"

He goes to the bathroom and comes back right away. He's holding a hand over his forehead. "Here's where it's written." He moves his hand and I read LOSER. I spit on my finger and rub. His forehead is still a little blue.

"Don't be such a chump."

"I'm desperate."

I go back home. It's a time when I know Fabio won't be there. I gather my things and pack them into old mineral-water boxes. I don't want to take one of Fabio's suitcases. I sit on the couch and smoke a cigarette while I watch the news. The newscaster has thick glasses and narrow, squared shoulders. It looks as if his head's been set into a box. He reads the news, an image of the Sapienza University behind him. Next comes a lifeless corpse in a car and then the typewritten notice from the Red Brigades. After that, the domes of Red Square; Chernenko died a few days ago. There's an image of the new leader of the Communist Party of the Soviet Union. He looks like a nice man in the black overcoat that opens before him in the wind. He smiles. He has a round baker's face and a stain on his forehead that looks like a geographical region. Fabio comes in and throws his gym bag on the floor. He's surprised to see me. I speak. After a silence he says, "Let me get my head around this."

He looks around. It's his house. It's in order. He appraises it in a glance, and without asking much, quickly comes up with some sort of explanation for what's happened. But he cries. He comes back from the shower with red, swollen eyes and grabs the milk carton from the fridge. "Damn," he says. It's gone sour. He looks at me, worried, and asks if it will hurt him. I shake my head. "Don't worry. It's like yogurt."

"I'll miss you," he says. He's not crying anymore. He's already got his head around it.

He helps me to carry my things downstairs, including my books. He sweats, gets stuck in the elevator door. In the mirror as we go down, he admires his arms, big now from the gym. I thank him and give him a hug. It's like hugging the doorman, someone who says hello when you come in and gives you your mail.

I didn't think about him again. I ran into him last summer. We were boarding the ferry to Corsica. I was in the iron belly of the boat, in that stink of sea and diesel, stuck between the already parked cars. As usual, Giuliano had put us in the slowest line, and I stood clutching the door with anxiety as I looked at the cars down at the end. We were cut off by a line coming from another wharf. Giuliano was calmly reading the paper. We argued. Pietro as usual took Giuliano's side. He took his iPod from his ear to say how nice he thought it was to fight on vacation. In the end I brought the car into the boat while they boarded with the other foot passengers, and then Pietro came back down to get his guitar. So there I was, all sweaty, rummaging around in the trunk that I couldn't get to open all the way. Fabio was getting down out of a well-maintained older-model SUV in the next aisle. He still had a full head of blond hair. He was wearing a vest full of pockets, and from the look of his arms it was clear he'd never stopped doing sports. We came face-to-face. There was no way to pretend I hadn't seen him. He hugged me and began speaking in his booming voice that echoed throughout the car hold. He looked at me and I saw myself with his eyes. I was wearing a tank top ruined from the long ride in the car. It revealed the same skin under my arms I'd seen so many times in the mirror. I stiffened and closed my arms. I thought of my hair, the white regrowth on my temples. I hadn't bothered going to the hairdresser's before leaving. It hadn't seemed worth it, we'd be at the seaside, I'd have my straw hat on all day. I felt ill at ease. I was white from having spent so much time in the office. I didn't have any makeup on. He was tan, the sort who's already in the water in May. He told me about his wife and his three children. The youngest was still quite small. "But he's already windsurfing." He patted the trunk on his Jeep, where their windsurf boards were all lined up, perfectly arranged.

"How are your parents?"

"They're dead."

He smiled and nodded. "Of course. We're getting old."

He wasn't old at all. He looked better than before. The years had roughened his veneer and brought along a bit of disorder, improving his simpleton face.

I introduced my son. "He's fifteen."

Pietro was peering into the trunk of the Jeep, the fishing rifles, the scuba gear. Then he asked about a bag with a spout that looked to me like a limp set of bagpipes. Fabio explained that it was a portable shower. It was made of a special thermal material. In the morning they filled it and left it in the sun. In the evening, when they emerged from the already cold water after a day of scuba diving, all of them could take a warm shower right on the beach.

"If you're careful not to waste anything, there's enough for four people."

Fabio's ass went up the stairs ahead of us, his floating key chain hanging from his pocket. Pietro said, "There's a guy who knows how to have a vacation, Mom. Did you see how organized they are?"

I was hot and discouraged. Rivulets of sweat darkened my top, and the money Giuliano was about to spend wouldn't be worth anything, nor would the beach, nor the hotel. At the very most Giuliano could put worms on a hook, but Pietro wanted to go surfing and underwater fishing and fly over the sea on one of those dangerous kites. He would gladly have jumped from our car to Fabio's Jeep. Giuliano was already at the cafeteria. He'd saved places for us and filled trays with food. He waved me over. He wasn't mad anymore. It was time to eat. He was happy. He was scared I'd be angry about the laden trays.

"So we don't have to stand on line twice," he justified himself. He put a spoonful of potato salad into my mouth. "It's divine." His belly was resting on his belt. I was slightly embarrassed. Fabio came over to introduce his wife, a blonde my age, athletic like him.

"She's had a boob job," I said to Giuliano when we went up on deck.

He pointed through the night toward a barely visible spray. "Look. Dolphins!"

He rested one hand on my shoulder. I put my arms around his waist, his generous flesh. We stood on the deck of that boat, which was taking us toward what would be a so-so vacation. My son would do what he could to ruin it. It was already in the air. But now he was walking around to scope out what other kids were on the ferry and we were free, momentarily in peace. Moonbeams were reflected off the big black sea. We were a middle-aged couple, not beautiful, not ugly. Nice, for certain. If someone had called us we would have turned with inviting smiles. Frequently we don't realize what we have. We aren't grateful to life. I touched Giuliano's hip, smelled his aftershave and the sea air and thanked life for having given me this good man.

I think my mother asked about the wedding gifts out of agitation, so as not to talk about the important things that might have caused her to suffer. "I

left everything with Fabio," I said, without even stopping beside her immobile body in the door frame. My father wore a gloomy expression. He was
pretending to be saddened, adopting the demeanor he imagined appropriate
for a father whose daughter married a young engineer bursting with public
contracts only to return home after a few months of marriage.

"What? You left him the pots and pans?" he said, and started laughing,
while my mother looked daggers at him. I was packing a little bag.

"Where are you going?" he asked, pretending to be offended. Scamp.

"I'm taking a little trip."

"Destination?"

I didn't answer. As he said goodbye on the doorstep, he asked me to bring
him Genovese *trofie* and pesto. He smiled. He knew everything.

I get off the train at Brignole. I walk beneath the rain in a vain search for a
taxi among the headlights. I have his address but I don't even know if he'll be
home. He doesn't know I'm coming. I cross the little border that separates
the rich part of the city from the casbah. It's as easy as following the smell
of the sea and the narrow little alleys with their shuttered windows. Faded
light embroiders its way through the harbor street. Junkies lying across the
hoods of cars, the smell of burnt chickpeas and marine detritus. His house
is in a block of public apartment buildings in a crooked ravine. Somewhere,
a closed-in dog barks. It's no longer raining, but it's damp. A thin, hoarse
female voice comes out of the intercom.

"Who is it?"

"I'm a friend of Diego's."

The voice disappears and a head emerges from a first-floor window. Neat,
yellowish hair, a turquoise bathrobe. She looks at me. "Are you the girl from
Rome?" she hollers.

"Yes."

She lets me in. Diego's not in but he'll be back. He went to take pictures of
a friend's band in a garage. She's short, thin like her son, with different eyes,
sky-blue, and the same slightly wide nose. I apologize for having bothered
her at this time. *It's no bother*, she says. *It's a pleasure.* She apologizes for the
disorder that looks perfectly orderly to me, with the kind of varnished furniture and pleasant smell you find in modest homes. She invites me to sit in the

little living room, where it's clear no one ever goes. She offers me something to eat and drink. I go to the bathroom to wash my hands and she follows with a clean towel. I accept something warm, a chamomile tea. She looks at me. I stand and she stands, too, in a flash, as if she were worried I might leave. The reason I got up is to give her the little gift I've brought, a bedside clock set inside a porcelain mask. She leans over to kiss me. "You shouldn't have troubled yourself."

She kisses me again. I feel her body tremble against mine.

"Diego's told me so much about you."

She has a strong Genovese accent like a little lament. Her name is Rosa.

Now she notices that my hair is wet and insists I go to the bathroom to dry it. She gives me another clean towel.

She brings me to Diego's room. I see a poster of the Genoa soccer team, his stereo, the bed he made by nailing some boards together, its blue sheets in a tangle. I'm everywhere, my belly button at the foot of his bed, beside the window. There's a pair of boots upside down on the floor. His mother bends to pick up a rag, underpants perhaps.

"I'm not authorized to come in here."

I hear the sound of keys, a door banging shut. I turn. We meet in the hall. He stops still. "No!"

He falls to his knees at my feet. He flips over like a dog, rubs his head against the floor, kisses my shoes, my jeans. "It's not true! It can't be true!"

He leaps to his feet like a spring. I throw my arms around him, my legs around his hips, and he drags me around the house like that. His mother crushes herself against the walls, stands in the bathroom doorway.

"Mama, this is my woman! My woman! The mother of my children. This is my dream!"

Rosa dries her eyes on her bathrobe and applauds. I tell Diego not to yell like that, he'll wake the whole building. But his mother yells that of course we should yell. The others always make noise. Tonight it's our turn. She's crazy, too. It's a family of mental cases.

We eat some fruit and cookies in the kitchen. Then we slip into that bed with its blue sheets and slowly, slowly make love like two kids who don't want anyone to hear them. The music comes out of the stereo with its little lights in the dark. A luminescent glow comes in from the street. There's a full moon. We look at the giant image of my stomach. The belly button looks like a crater.

"What happened?"

"I threw darts at it."

I stayed until almost the end of the summer. Every day I said I should leave, and every day I stayed. Diego's habits and schedule were completely different from mine. He slept until lunchtime. Then he made his way to the kitchen and, still in his underpants, opened the fridge and pulled out one of the containers of food his mother brought him from the hospital. He'd gobble down a hardened piece of lasagna or a cold, watery bit of fish. That's how he was used to eating. His mother was never there. She had a boyfriend, an old-fashioned man with silk scarves and two-toned shoes.

If it was sunny we'd go to the sea. He kept a little boat, which had sails as small as napkins, in a run-down sailing club. We'd stay out until late at night, without eating, our windbreakers drenched. At night we wandered from one club to another in the caves in the alleyways. He was euphoric to have me there in his world. He introduced me to his weird band of friends, their young faces already worn. He translated from dialect into Italian and peered at me to see if I was happy. He passed me a filthy joint that had been in many mouths. I shook my head. I didn't want him to smoke, either. He brought me to the Ethiopia wharf, where his father had died, crushed by a container. We sat on a mooring bit and looked out at the dark sea.

He confessed that for a while he'd used heroin. *A few squirts and then I quit; in Genoa it's hard not to use drugs.* He said he'd been in jail for a while with the Marassi ultras.

"Are you disappointed in me?"

"No."

I tell him I can't live like this, from day to day, completely uprooted from everything. Even his mother seems different to me as I leave, defeated, a squashed lizard.

"I'm sorry," she says.

"Whatever for?"

Chapter 4

Pietro and I are waiting in the lobby. It's raining. Pietro lolls on the low couch, legs spread wide, shoulders hunched, sweatshirt hood pulled up over his head. He's looking out the windows at the water sliding down, his blue gaze darkening like the sky. There's an Internet café across from the hotel and he'd like to be there, chatting with his friends. I told him no, which is why he pulled up his hood and why he's sitting there dejected and insolent like a soccer player who's just been ejected from a match. The girl from breakfast is vacuuming the stairs. The extension cord wraps itself around her legs. Pietro smiles and says, "She's totally incompetent."

I say, "She's the same age as you and she already has a job."

Infuriated, he speaks in a rush, swallowing his words. He wanted to get a job and I said no. It's true. He was offered a job putting advertisements on car windshields for twenty euros a day. I didn't want him to spend hours in the disgusting traffic with his smart-ass friend Bifo whose eyes are always shiny from smoking joints. I could say that it wasn't a real job anyway, that in order to be considered work a job must be a response to a real need, and instead he has a moped and a guitar and sunglasses and a savings account. But I hold my tongue because I don't feel like arguing.

I go to the reception desk and ask for an umbrella. They give me a floppy, half-broken yellow stick. In the meantime, the girl on the stairs trips for real. She stands up immediately and peers around, terrified someone's seen. We're the only ones there. Pietro plants his fists on his temples and shakes his covered head back and forth. He laughs like a madman, guffawing in his blue sweatshirt. The girl looks at him with a serious expression, so Pietro feigns nausea by clutching his stomach and pretending to throw up. He points to the full ashtray on the coffee table. The girl comes over and takes it. Pietro says, *Thank you.* He tries not to laugh but keeps guffawing like a cretin. The girl simulates a little bow and her breath moves some of the ashes as she bends her legs. Pietro shakes his head and brushes the ashes off his jeans. Then he raises his hands and laughs, this time with tenderness.

"I surrender."

The girl crinkles her face, a firm and fair-skinned face like a freshly peeled potato, and says, "What?"

Pietro shakes his head. He doesn't know how to translate *I surrender*. He says, "Sorry."

The girl steps away and returns with the clean ashtray. She's red in the face. "You're great," she says in a feeble voice as she moves away.

Pietro coughs and looks at me. "What did she say, Ma?"

"You heard as well as me. She said you're *great*."

"Really?"

He perks up and watches the body of the little Sarajevan as she walks away. He pulls his hood off his head and runs his fingers through his hair.

"Do you like her?"

He turns on me like a snake. "Are you out of your mind? She's pathetic! I like Italian girls."

"Why?"

"Because I understand them."

There's Gojko in the entrance. He doesn't have an umbrella. The shoulders of his jacket are dark with rain. He shakes the damp off his hair like a dog. Then he seeks me with his eyes, crosses the lobby and kisses me hello. His wet body is warm this morning. He smells nice, like hay in the rain. He sits, orders a coffee and crosses his legs. He's late because he was helping set up the photo exhibit at the gallery. He's in an excellent mood. He asks how we slept. Do we want to go around the city, continue the sad tour of war landmarks? He's used to doing it because it's what all the tourists want. We can go see the Jewish cemetery where the snipers did their work or hang out downtown until the exhibit opens.

First Pietro says it's all the same to him. Then he says he'd rather stay downtown. This morning I did something stupid. I was only half awake and by mistake I reached my hand out and called him Diego. That little Genovese ghost had haunted me all night.

Pietro moved away from my hand. "Mom!"

"Oh." I was still half asleep.

"What did you just call me?"

"I don't know. What did I call you?" I was trembling, because I hadn't even noticed. "I'm sorry."

"You're out of it."

He stormed into the bathroom to get away from me and from my body and its ancient torments. When he came out I saw him bend over the bed to see if there was any possibility of dividing it in two. I said, "If you want to change rooms, we can get one with separate beds. You move around too much. I'm not sleeping well."

But I wanted to cry.

It's raining but there are a lot of people out and about, lots of kids. We're in the street that leads to the madrassa. Groups of Muslim students pass with full backpacks like students from any school in the world. The umbrella they gave me in the hotel is totally useless and I have to take care not to blind passersby. I stop to buy one for Pietro. Gojko says no, thanks, they just get in the way. I tell him that at his age it's bad for his health to get soaked to the bone. He grumbles that at his age so many things cause harm it's not even worth thinking about. I take his arm. "Do you still write?"

I'd like to hear him recite some of his poems in a voice thick with feeling and intentions. He lowers his head and says that for a little while now, mostly at night, he's been working again with words.

I ask him why it took so long. "There was no other way," he says. "There had to be a white space in between, like a bandage. God has to help, without any reservations about your tattered soul. Without your even noticing it, he has to help you fix the balance between good and evil."

He opens his hand and—I don't know why—spits into his palm.

"One day I happened by a field that was red with poppies. For the first time, I didn't think of blood. Instead, I was mesmerized by their fragility, their beauty. It would have taken a lot less than an ax, a *maljutka*; a gust of wind would have destroyed them in an instant. That field was waiting for us behind a curve. It was immense and dotted with red tongues like hearts that had dropped into the grass from the sky. I was driving with my wife. We stopped the car. First I started to cry, and then she followed. The tears we cried slowly emptied and restored us. I started breathing with a full chest again that night. I could finally bear it. For years our breath had been stuck in our throats. It couldn't go any farther. Two months later my wife was pregnant."

We're walking again. My arm is safely tucked under his. After a while it feels like old times, when we walked aimlessly, when our lives felt protected beneath the umbrella of a friendship that gave us courage.

The woman who passes us with her net shopping bag is like a woman anywhere, hurried, worried she'll be late getting home . . . but she walks with the strange gait of a broken insect. Beneath her jacket, which is too light for the season, her hips move in disarray like mismatched wheels on the same vehicle. Her stiff legs are like the pendulums on a wall clock. After a while I notice that the streets are full of people like her, with old shell fragments lodged in their bones. They're all skilled at concealing their infirmity, at losing themselves in the crowd.

"It's the first thing we learned."

I observe people, calculate how old they would have been then and whether or not they would have been adults or children, calculate how much the war devoured by adding up the circles beneath their eyes, the still-as-glass gazes, the wet cigarettes that tremble in their hands. I count the faces, gray beneath the rain, which are like dead rising up from the sea.

"We ate too much uranium, too many of those damned humanitarian packets full of leftovers from the Korean War."

I tell myself that the children we see are safe. They don't know, they didn't see, so they can't remember. But it's not entirely true. From the way they follow warily in the footsteps of the adults, it's as if they knew. These are the children who were born. Upon their shoulders rests the invisible universe of the others, who didn't have a chance to come into the world and experience their earthly destiny.

I look at Pietro's neck beneath the rain. Every so often he stops in front of a shop window. He's not interested in the merchandise, he's curious about the prices in convertible marks and how they translate into euros. He says stuff is *pretty cheap*. Then he thinks again and says, *But not super-cheap*. He asks Gojko about average salaries. I didn't know my son was interested in economics.

"How much does a hotel maid make?"

"A hundred fifty, two hundred euros."

I smile. Pietro wrinkles his nose. He's irked. "What do you want?"

Water drips off gutters, balconies, roofs.

We go by the Latin Bridge, where Franz Ferdinand was killed.

"They removed the commemorative plaque and kept it off for a long time because Princip was a Serb. Now they've put it back up for tourists, but they've taken away the word *hero*."

In the square with the giant chessboard, all the old men carry umbrellas. They play unperturbed beneath the falling water, bending every so often to move the giant horses and pawns over the squares on the pavement. Pietro takes some pictures with his cell phone. He's amazed by the determination of these old players.

"Most of them are farm folk, people who came afterwards. The city's become more rural. For years I didn't recognize a soul."

We walk a while longer. The rain becomes lighter and then stops. Water runs through the drains. The sky is still laden, but for a moment there's a break from the downpour. Pietro is soaked. He likes to get wet, likes to get sick, likes to burn with fever for a night and then burst with health again the next day. All this water's made him thirsty. He stops at a stand and downs an icy Coca-Cola. He looks down and asks about the splotches of red paint on the ground.

They're Sarajevo roses, a testimony to the dead and the bombs. We walk over the rose that commemorates the first massacre, when people were killed while waiting in a breadline. Gojko looks at me for a moment. I open my mouth and close it again.

We cross the street and round a corner. More roses, more splotches of fading red paint in the bustle of people coming and going at the Markale Market.

"At one point they said we were firing on ourselves to guarantee attention from the television cameras, so we would stay in the public eye."

The stalls are full of colors and much more orderly than I remembered. The list of dead on a gray stone wall at the back is staggering. It's a list of people torn from life in a single instant, carried off in the time it took a single devil to bat his wings. I ask myself where that devil has gone. Is he still limping along somewhere near here?

Earlier this morning Gojko made a comment that sent shivers up my spine.

"There are a lot of people in Sarajevo who think we're just living through a pause in an unfinished war."

We climb the stairs to a little restaurant right above the market. It's a sort of balcony with tables and wooden benches overlooking the stalls below. It's like being in a turn-of-the-century train station. I look down at the chalk-white cheeses in the display cases. Gojko shows me the only stall that still sells pork, way down at the end, separate from the others.

Pietro wants to know why people from Sarajevo don't like pork. Gojko explains that nowadays most people are Bosniaks—Bosnian Muslims, that is. Muslims don't eat pork. Pietro says he learned about that when he did a paper on the three monotheistic religions. He laughs and says you can't tell people here are Muslims. "They're too white," he says.

Gojko tells him about how, when he was little, he celebrated Christmas at home like a good Catholic and then went out to collect alms with his friends for the end of Ramadan. "It was completely normal then. Now they teach three different languages in the schools, and when you register a child, you have to declare which ethnic group he or she belongs to."

We order a Bosnian soup. They bring us a kettle full of dense broth with bits of meat and vegetables floating side by side. Pietro eats pljeskavica, the closest thing to a hamburger.

"What was the reason for the war?"

Gojko laughs wildly and rests a hand on Pietro's head.

"It would take a great comedian to answer your question, someone mute and desperate. Someone like us. Through it all, we never stopped laughing. It would take someone like Buster Keaton. Have you ever seen *Film*?"

Pietro shakes his head. He doesn't like black-and-white movies.

Gojko puts out his cigarette. "What do you want to be when you grow up, Pietro?"

"I don't know. A musician, maybe."

Of course he doesn't dare look at me. Ages ago I rented a piano for him and it rotted for years in the house. Pietro rarely practiced because, he said, he didn't need to. Then, two years ago, he picked up the guitar, all on his own. He goes to a jazz club to take lessons. Every time he's felt the slightest pressure from me, he's done whatever he could do to resist.

We're back on the street. The rain cleaned the asphalt. The streets glitter like polished iron.

Pietro walks ahead of us with his indolent gait, stomping through the puddles and treading upon the roses marking the bombs as if they were cobblestones in a Roman alley, as if he were indifferent. He's being boisterous, almost offensive, on purpose. He's been avoiding me since we arrived. These spiteful little actions are for my benefit because he senses I have an unexpressed goal for this trip. I'd like to grab him and hug him close but I don't dare go near him. If there's something for him to understand here, something for him to sniff out like a dog, he'll have to do it on his own. I can't help him. In any case, he resembles his father. He's got a little radar that senses lost frequencies.

"He takes after him, doesn't he?"

Gojko doesn't look at Pietro. He looks at me.

"Do you want me to tell you the truth?"

"Yes."

"He takes after you. He walks like you and smiles like you. He's moody just like you, too."

He hugs me tight, enclosing me in his bulk. I feel his breath in my hair.

"You must have gotten under his skin, Gemma. You've always had this talent for slipping in beneath other people's skin and conquering them without even trying. Did I ever tell you how much I was in love with you?"

"No, you never told me."

"You were so in love with him. The two of you were so in love."

We step into a courtyard of low Ottoman archways beside the mosque. The photo exhibit will take place in two long rooms with walls of glass punctuated by white metal frames, like big bay windows or a greenhouse. A diaphanous girl with a thick pair of black knit stockings hanging off her otherwise bare legs is making final adjustments to her works, which hang from thin steel wires. She comes over to greet us, punches Gojko on the arm, steals a cigarette from his jacket pocket, smiles and kisses him on the mouth.

I ask him if she's his wife. She laughs because she understands my question even though she doesn't speak Italian. She shakes her head. She's a well-known artist, mad as a hatter and very talented.

I stop to look at her photos, images of men and women who were interned in the Omarska concentration camp, snapshots of elderly people, their skeletal faces hollowed out by hunger and fear, close-ups taken from so near that their hair isn't even in the picture and all that's left are the eyes, the tortuous routes of their wrinkles, their worn mouths. Not a single one wears a meek expression. They all seem to be focusing on the same point in some dark zone, as if they were asking the camera lens for some clue to their history as human beings, seeking an answer that no one as yet has been able to provide.

Diego's photos are in the second room. I sit on a chair to look at them. The show isn't open to the public yet. A woman is busy arranging food on a table covered with a paper tablecloth. There was no need to come all this way to see these shots I know so well. There aren't many. They occupy a little wall behind a column. There's the woman running from the snipers, her hair made ragged by her flight and one leg raised like a broken wing. There's the bathtub in the rubble, a bottle of shampoo on the edge and a dead body shrouded in a green Muslim cloth inside. There's the old woman taking down the washing as the snow falls, her arms reaching through a glassless window frame. There's the cat sleeping on the seat of a burnt bus. There's the baby carriage full of tanks of water and a smiling Sebina pulling it along.

Pietro wanders about and studies the shots on this wall or that. I wait for him and, gradually, start to feel a sort of peace.

I have scads of Diego's photos, hidden in the house, in the loft. For a long time they kept me alive. Euphoric and agitated, I would wait for the baby to fall asleep as if I were waiting to get away to my lover. I could go days or months without thinking about them, like sex—for which I've always had an on-again, off-again interest, sudden bursts and then nothing. In the late afternoon I'd find myself saddened by the doors in our house, the hall door, the door to the dark living room. There was mud everywhere, things moving, things being dragged along. Giuliano frequently had to work the night shift and I'd be alone. Out of nowhere, the dark of the windows, the depths of the baby's slumber, thoughts of Diego would come at me with such insistence they'd leave me feeling ill.

I'd close myself in my room and open the boxes. The light would be low enough to erase my surroundings as I scattered the photos over the bed and onto the carpet. I'd weep and smile as I crawled over the path of shiny paper.

One morning Giuliano found one of the photos beneath the bedspread. It was crumpled from the night. He tried to flatten it out with his hands and handed it back to me. *Here, love. This must be yours. It's very beautiful.*

He was sitting on the bed, his shoulders hunched, his stomach like a little pouch. I moved toward him, took his orphaned hand from the bed and cried into it. After a while he started crying, too, small solitary sobs. It struck me that he was far more alone than I was, that men are always more alone than women no matter what. Crying together, for a couple, is a tiny emblematic event. It's the other's breath dying in your throat. It's the sorrow that you carry inside you for the world and for yourself, useless sack of flesh. Your stomach dances with your tears. Rise up, miserable creature. Move away from there into the depths of the house or throw yourself out the window. If you stay, say something that might console us.

Giuliano said, "I'm so sorry he died. You can't know how sorry I am."

I smiled. "You probably would have arrested him. He was the type of guy the police would arrest."

Pietro moves closer. He's wary like a mouse approaching a trap, risking its head because it's hungry.

"Are these his?"

"Yes."

He quickly scans the photos from top to bottom and then again, two quick parries and that's it.

"Do you like them?"

"The one with the cat is great. Were you there with him?"

"Not always."

There are no other chairs, so he slides down the column and sits on his heels like a big bird.

"Where was I?"

"Waiting to be born."

"Weren't you scared?"

"Of what?"

"Wasn't it scary to be pregnant during a war?"

I nod and sniff and say maybe I'm getting sick. The rain made me cold. My shoes are wet. Pietro glances at my feet and moves away. I see him nibbling at the snacks. In the meantime, people have started arriving in little groups of two or three. Wine glasses in hand, they stop in front of the panels of photos and talk. I'm the only one down here in this corner. I know these photos, but it still feels strange to be seeing them here on this wall.

I study the details—a hand, a bird in the sky, the bumper of a car that's been hurled by a blast to one side. I look at Sebina, her round button eyes, that funny mouth: delicate at the edges, puffy in the center, red like a tongue.

I smile because I know that expression so well, the leader of the pack, a little neighborhood tyrant.

"Come here for a second, Bijeli Biber." That's what I called her, White Pepper.

She'd move toward me with her deep-set eyes and the dimple in her chin, the perfect hiding place for a pearl. I'd hold a candy in my fist so she could guess which hand held it. She always guessed right.

"Bijeli Biber, you need to do well in school, okay?"

She would nod, in a hurry to move away. I told Gojko to keep an eye on her, to make sure she didn't spend too much time out in the streets.

"What will Sebina do if she doesn't study?'

Gojko loved his mischievous little sister as if she were a gift. He was enchanted.

"Maybe she'll be an artist. She knows how to ice-skate and walk on a tightrope. And she's a great liar."

Sometimes she acted downright rude, not bothering to say hello, or playing insistently with the noisy little balls Gojko had imported for a while but which had never met with the same success as his yo-yos. No one could figure out where the bad mood came from, but I knew how to get to the bottom of her malaise. It was always some unthinkable little nonsense thing, but I understood. I'd been a crazy perfectionist as a child, exactly like Sebina, defeating myself many times over in the course of a day.

She would become stubborn, even disagreeable as she sat there on the wall in the courtyard sucking her hair and speaking unpleasantly to anyone who came near. *Hey, Bijeli Biber*, I'd say, and hug her close. It was like hugging an outsized pride, the least attractive part of myself, the obstacle that would forever make it impossible for anyone to love me to the core. Sebina could penetrate my solitude. We were the same, presumptuous and stupid. She threw her arms around my neck, her legs dangling around me as I climbed, and let me carry her back up the stairs to her mother. It was okay now. The darkness had passed. I've never been particularly good with children. I'm impatient. I can't talk in funny little voices. But Sebina was different, a gift from God, a foretaste of love. I can still see the landing where I'd stop to catch my breath between flights of stairs because she was so heavy. The gray of the courtyard came in through the long frosted-glass window as dusk neared and Sebina hung off my neck with her breath and her mystery.

Pietro calls from behind a column. "What about this one, Ma?" He points to a photo I hadn't noticed beside the exit, above the umbrella stand. "Is it one of Diego's?"

I tell him I'm not sure.

"There's his name, underneath."

It's grainy and out of focus, maybe a piece of wall with a deep dark stain surrounded by gaping red petals, some sort of rose.

"What's that?"

"I don't know."

Pietro likes it. He stands there and looks at it. "It doesn't mean anything, but it says something."

He says it looks like a cool CD cover.

I see a tangible sadness in this strange material image. There's more war in this red image than in all the other war photos.

I reach out to touch that grainy hole in the center and shake my head. "I don't think it's your father's. They must have made a mistake."

Diego showed up in Rome on his motorcycle at dawn after five hundred kilometers of nighttime highway. With his tiny mosquito body he'd passed truck after truck, headlights by the thousands, without ever stopping. He rang the bell at my parents' house. In his hand he held a bunch of sunflowers from an all-night florist's. I went downstairs in my nightgown. Dawn's first light floated through the dark. The café's metal shutters were still closed.

"I've got everything worked out!"

I take the sunflowers. They hang from my folded arms. I've been back from

Genoa for less than a day. I haven't even unpacked my suitcase and he's already here, his hair flattened by his helmet, his cheeks hollowed out by the cold.

"You can't stay here. I just separated from my husband a few months ago. I can't bring another guy to my parents' house."

He looks around. "Who's this other guy?" Then he smiles. "I have a place to stay. It's all set." He says it didn't feel right to leave me alone at such a delicate moment in my life. He's meek as a lamb. I kick him. He laughs because I end up hurting myself. I'm wearing flip-flops and he's wearing hard leather shin guards like a real motorcyclist.

He looks up and waves. My father's leaning against the balcony railing in his pajamas, smoking. Dad waves the hand holding the cigarette.

The way Diego's waving, his hand will come off.

"Hello."

"Hello."

"It's me. I'm Diego."

"I'm Armando, Gemma's father. How was the trip?"

"It was a smooth ride."

I nod at my father. He can go back inside now. Instead, he comes down in his pajamas, the ones I gave him for his birthday. He throws his cigarette butt into the dawn and comes toward us. They shake hands. Dad walks around the motorcycle.

"Triumph Bonneville Silver Jubilee. Great choice!"

Later I would learn that they'd spoken on the phone many times during my marriage. They talked about me, about photography, about travel, and they hit it off. You can tell now from their expressions that they like each other. This dawn is giving birth to another great love. Maybe it's easy because Diego's father died when he was a child and my father never had a son. All he had was that son-in-law who never fully entered his heart.

Diego asks Dad if he'd like to take a spin on the motorcycle. Dad's tempted. He's wearing his overcoat over his pajamas. He starts buttoning it up. I send him a withering glance. He says, *Never mind*. He'll do it another time, when he's properly dressed.

The café is opening. Dad insists on treating us to breakfast. We wait while the coffee machine warms up and the girl arranges the pastries on a tray.

Diego eats; he's hungry. Dad has a coffee and smokes another cigarette. We look out at the street, the day's first movements. My father says, "It's so nice."

"What, Dad?"

"It's so nice when something is born."

"So where is it?"

"Down there, beside the river."

We're wandering around behind a market. Diego is carrying a crumpled bit of paper and a bunch of keys in an envelope a musician friend gave him. We go down the travertine stone stairs among moss stains and bottles left over from nighttime parties. When we get to the embankment it's colder and slippery. The yellowish river water wraps itself greedily around the little overgrown islands that rise up from the bottom and catch the trash. The city din is up above us, back near the market. Down here we hear only the noise of the water and, every so often, the rusty shriek of a seagull. I look around. I don't see anything.

"Are you sure this is the place?"

"No."

We walk along the embankment and turn back. We pass beneath a bridge with fire marks on the walls. There's an upside-down box on the ground.

"God exists."

I turn. He read it on the wall, in the middle of other graffiti. It's red. GOD EXISTS.

"Do you believe it?"

"What?"

"That God's down here under this bridge?"

I shake my hands and sigh. "I bet it's a code for organized crime."

Diego doesn't believe in God. In one of our nighttime conversations he raved about a big energy that surrounds the universe, a sort of fluid hat. There are souls that never make it there because they are too old, dirtied by too many terrestrial journeys. Instead, they turn to dust and get sucked up by the cosmic darkness. Beautiful souls go straight there like rockets to regenerate themselves after life's travails. They send little benevolent shocks down to earth. He probably smoked a joint that night. As for me, I'm like most people. I believe in God now and then, when I'm afraid.

Beyond the bridge the embankment is tidier. There's a deserted sports center with two tennis courts and a little playground hidden behind the reeds. Diego points to a barge moored on the river.

"There it is."

It's a club. It belongs to one of his friends, a guy he met on a trip. It's been closed for a few months. *Someone was selling pot. My friend had some trouble with the cops.* It will open again in the spring but now it's the end of September and Diego's friend is glad to let him use it as a pied-à-terre for as long as he can stand it, until the river damp gets to him. I'm speechless, incredulous. The key fits into a rusty old lock. Diego has to push the wooden door open with his shoulder. Inside it's darker than outside. The windows are dusty and green with mold. It's a big room with a fake wood floor that's actually linoleum. There's a long bar in the center beneath a big dangling rudder-shaped light and a jumble of metal tables, benches and chairs at one end. I rub my arms. I'm already cold. Diego is enthusiastic. He pulls the little iron hooks to open one of the portholes and we see two guys go by in a canoe.

"Are you really going to stay here?"

"Don't you like it?"

I look at the bar fridge with its transparent door and nothing inside and the vinyl sofa covered with ballpoint graffiti. Diego leans over to read an obscenity and laughs.

"This is such a cool place." He's excited. There's a mad gleam in his tired eyes.

"Are you back on drugs?"

He isn't offended. He says yes, he's high on me. I'm better than heroin because the effect never wears off. It stays in his blood. I could never be cut with strychnine. He wants to make love right away. I tell him not to touch me, to stay away. This place is debilitating. I don't know where to sit. It's damp and dirty.

He unpacks his bag—a few books, a tape player and some crumpled clothes among his cameras. He has another present for me, a jar of walnut pesto wrapped in a pair of oily underpants.

He hums while he finds places for his things. He puts his clothes up in the glass rack. He walks barefoot over the dirt-encrusted linoleum, then goes down the stairs into the hold and comes back with a broom and a bucket full of water that he dumps on the floor. I lift my feet and he cleans. I sink into the sofa with its obscene graffiti and think we'll never go anywhere as a couple. It will last a few months. He's out of his mind, a vagabond. He's slept all over the place, even sitting on a toilet once in some African airport.

I'm wearing freshly laundered white sneakers. I picture Fabio's face, wonder what he would think if he saw me here. Diego's fiddling around with a gas tank in a little niche with a couple of burners behind a curtain, checking to see if there's any cooking fuel left. "Would you be my guest for dinner?"

I go back for dinner. It's nine o'clock. He insisted I dress up, so I held my breath and zipped myself into a tight black dress I'd worn once to a New Year's party. Then I opened my mouth in the mirror and gave myself over to the soft gesture of putting on lipstick. I'd asked if I should bring something, a bit of salmon, some mozzarella, but he said there was gas for the cooker and he had everything under control. I went to get some wine. The stores were closing. I ducked under the half-closed metal shutter of a lingerie shop to get a pair of stockings. As I rode in the taxi I crossed my legs, sheathed in dark new thigh-highs. The lights of the cars on the road along the Tiber danced across my face. I felt small and insignificant.

The tennis courts are lit up. Someone must be playing a night match. One of the barges across the river is putting on a light show. The boat vibrates with deafening music. It must be some private party, a wedding or a birthday.

A weak little light pulsates like a firefly inside Diego's barge, making it look like a parchment lantern sitting on the water. The river makes noises in the dark and emanates a sad, silent fog.

He comes out. I can't see his face, just the white blur of his shirt, and I hear his light footsteps.

"Welcome."

He gives me his hand and pulls me toward him. I smell a scent I've never smelled on him before.

"What's that?"

"Juniper shower gel." He laughs.

I laugh, too. We both feel a little shy. It's a special evening, a celebration of the fact that we're together.

He stops on the threshold and turns to run his eyes over me, taking in my legs, the low-cut black dress, the lipstick. "Wow."

He's dressed up, too, in his way. He's wearing tight black pants with stripes and a skinny tie over a T-shirt.

"I forgot to pack my shirts."

He studies me with his sweet, insolent face. Light filters around his shoulders. There's the smell of good things cooking.

"Come in, my love."

I look around. He's completely transformed the place. The chairs and tables are spread around in an orderly fashion, like a restaurant waiting for clients. A little candle burns on every table and here and there, on the floor, there's a little island of beer glasses full of bouquets of flowers. I raise my eyes and see the photos of the two of us from Sarajevo and Genoa pinned with clothespins to two clotheslines that cross the barge like streamers along with photos of my eyes and my stomach. Music comes murmuring out of the little stereo and loses itself in the big room. At the end, near the window, there's a table set with a white cloth and long-stemmed wine glasses. In the shadowy light even the vinyl sofa has its elegance.

He laughs. "So, what do you think?"

"It's like you."

I feel like crying. No one has ever done anything like this for me and no one will ever do it again. I look at the expanse of candles and tables, and smile. "Those are cemetery candles!" Now we both laugh.

He brings me champagne with peach juice. He bought it at the supermarket along with the shower gel, the colander, the radicchio and the candles.

The walnut pesto is delicious. He also made a little pot roast on one of the stove burners because the oven was wrecked.

He watches me eat and raises his glass again for another toast. I've lost count of how many times we've clinked our glasses.

I ask him if he's rested at all. He says he can't sleep. He's too happy, too excited, because our life together is starting and he feels euphoric, full of dynamite. I tell him to calm down because he's scaring me. In any case, it can't go on long. One day he'll wake up and see me for what I am, ordinary and not all that nice.

He says that's impossible because he loves me. "I'll give you so many children."

I smile and shake my head. I tell him we don't have a dime. We couldn't even afford a dog. "How do you plan to make a living in Rome?"

He'll go around to the photo agencies and see about shooting weddings. Or knock on old women's doors. He's done it before in lean times. "They all need a picture for their gravestone. They put on their earrings and pose and then they offer me coffee."

I look at him with that little tie hanging off his neck like a leash. He's excited like a dog who's escaped from his owner. He could be a high school kid. There's no way the two of us will go anywhere. We'll sink together in this barge.

"How do you manage to stay so happy all the time?"

"Easy. Being sad is disgusting." Then he yells. "Ahhh!" It's as if he's been shot. When I moved my leg he caught a glimpse of the bare skin above the lace edge of my stocking. He bows his head and says I must have it in for him. A vision like that is too much for a man in his condition. He crawls over to me, takes off my shoe, massages my foot, kisses me through the nylon. He whispers that if we want to have all those kids we'd better get started because he needs time, lots of time, and it's going to take more work than putting in a subway in Genoa.

We stretch out on the vinyl couch with all its graffiti, hearts with arrows and ejaculating penises.

Later I look up at Diego from below. I'm still lying on the couch and now I'm wearing one of his sweaters because I'm cold. My legs are curled up, my knees beneath the wool. He walks barefoot across the barge, which now strikes me as the most beautiful place in the universe. He's cleared the table and put the dishes to soak. He's naked except for the tie that hangs forgotten around his neck. For the first time he looks like a man. I trust him when we make love, when we stop talking, when I feel his soul and only his soul.

I close my eyes. I know he's taking my picture, that he's bent over me to steal an eye, a hand, a piece of mouth, an ear.

It's almost dark. The candles have melted into mushy little pools one after another. It's time to leave. I think about gathering up my stockings and my shoes but stay right where I am and watch those dimming lights. Time is no longer breathing down my neck. It's spreading placidly through my stomach. This is bliss.

Early the next morning I go back home and leave again almost right away. My mother is waiting for me with a tense, defeated expression.

"Are you sure you're doing the right thing?"

"No, Mom. I'm not sure of anything."

I'd climb down those slippery damp stairs among the linden trees and find Diego down on the river. It began to seem perfectly normal that he lived there. The city up above us felt so far away. Little groups of dark ducks floated by on the currents. When it rained the windows drowned in water; it was like being in a submarine. I liked it down there. I grew accustomed to the clumps of reeds and the harsh screeches of the seagulls. Sometimes Diego would steal away at dawn. After the rain he liked to go out to look for puddles. He could spend hours on his knees taking pictures of things reflected in them—a building, a tree branch, a streetlight. Sometimes I'd go along. I'd open his film for him and put the used rolls in my pocket. Hours would pass. Passing cars would splash him and he'd barely notice, though he liked the way the spray looked in his pictures, the dismembered images like explosions. He never brought the film to be developed. Instead, he let it pile up on the bar in the barge and forgot about it. Once in a while I'd do it for him. Then I'd show up at the barge with yellow Kodak envelopes and throw a pebble at the window to let him know I was there. He'd thank me and scatter the photos over the floor. Then he'd walk around them, barefoot, move one aside with a toe to see the one lying below. Frequently he didn't recognize his own work. Looking at it tired him out. It was as if he needed to maintain a distance from himself. He'd fish two or three pictures out of the mess and clip them to the clothesline with clothespins. Then he'd put the rest back in the envelope and abandon them on the bar with the rolls of film.

We were such an odd couple. No one would have bet a fingernail on us. The best we could hope for was a handful of wonderful months together. Then we'd collapse and flatten out like Diego's curls after the rain. We were so different. He was loose-limbed. I was rigid, with under-eye circles and a tailored overcoat. But the months passed and we still walked down the street with our hands entwined and slept at night curled together like two fetuses in the same amniotic sac. Neither of us got bored.

Another year, another round. I started to pick up freelance writing assignments with various newspapers.

Diego stayed on the barge all winter. He always had a red nose and a cold. It became too cold to take off our clothes. We'd make love inside a sleeping bag. I wouldn't even take off my sweater. He bought a case of whiskey and we started drinking a little too much, warming ourselves like two bums, one drop after the next.

Destiny gave us a hand when we found that apartment. A religious charity was renting it out at an affordable price. We went one night to see it, passing back and forth beneath the barred windows. We counted windows in the dark and could hardly believe there were so many—six big windows on the second floor of a lovely Umbertine building. We climbed the stairs for the first time one March morning with the guy from the agency. What else is there to say? It really felt like that house had been waiting for us, because houses wait for their inhabitants, surviving without them for years before opening their doors and shutters like arms held wide to a young couple, two fools trembling with happiness. I can't help but think of the heart. It had been carved with a nail into the plaster on the landing. An arrow next to it pointed toward our door. The doorman said the apartment had been inhabited for decades by a childless old couple. Who carved that heart? A nephew? A child who lived in the building? A beggar the two old people had been generous to? I don't know. It doesn't matter. What matters is that the heart was there and that it stayed there for years until they redid the plaster. I was so angry; I wasn't there the day the construction workers did our landing.

Diego pulled out his checkbook and paid the deposit and three months' rent. He leaned against the wall to write the check with a pen that barely wrote. He was sweaty and red in the face.

"Do you have all that money?" I asked, as we went down the stairs.

"Let's hope so."

It was a good apartment. It had borne witness to reserved and thrifty lives, lights turned off so as not to waste electricity. When we got the keys and went in on our own for the first time it was like entering a sanctuary. We ran our hands over the walls, rested our cheeks against them, kissed them as if they were alive. Now those bricks and that plaster would defend our lives.

The only piece of furniture remaining in the empty apartment was an old upright piano. It was a lady's piano, cream-colored, with a flower motif. The antique dealer who emptied the apartment was supposed to come back to get it. Diego lifted the cover and started to move his fingers over the keys.

He'd never had lessons. He was playing by ear. The piano was completely out of tune, but it sounded like the most beautiful music in the world.

"What is that?"

"Bits of this and that. Debussy. Leonard Cohen."

His shoulder blades moved beneath his T-shirt. A ray of sunlight bathed the floor. The traffic sounds stayed down in the street. Diego's hands brought the little cream-colored piano to life. The notes floated through the empty rooms, baptizing our future.

When the antique dealer came back, we struck a deal and managed to keep the piano.

We changed the bathtub, painted the walls, filled the gaps in the wood floors, spent hours drying putty with the blow dryer. At midday we'd collapse to the ground to eat workmen's sandwiches with bologna and sausage and eggplants, the best sandwiches of our entire lives. One night we made love on the newspapers spread out on the floor. The ink came off on our warm bodies. A piece of a Soviet soldier in Afghanistan was tattooed on Diego's back.

I gave him a poster he liked, Man Ray's portrait of Braque in his studio, and had frames put on some of his own pictures, my favorites—the Marassi ultras, some disconsolate Arctic penguins on the march, a raft with a palm-roof leaf going down the Mekong in a cloud of flying blue hummingbirds, the sleeping baby in the wooden box at the Sarajevo fruit and vegetable market.

The phone company installed a gray phone. It sat for ages in a corner on the floor.

"How are you, poet?"

"How are you, pigeons?"

Gojko's smoke-ravaged voice came to us down the wire.

"You sound happy."

"We are!"

"Out in the world, there's someone working hard on your behalf."

"Who?"

"A poet."

"Does he send us good wishes?"

"My thoughts. I don't know how good they are."

He laughed the big laugh that made it sound as if his throat were a sanctuary or a scrap metal dump.

We bought a couch covered with white cotton upholstery. It had little wheels so we could move it around the living room. Diego signed another check. He wanted to pay for everything himself. Later I found out that he ran out of money; his mother had to run to the bank and deposit the pension she got as the widow of a port worker into his overdrawn account. My mother brought us a long copper umbrella stand. She looked at me from her gaunt face and explained, almost as if she were justifying herself, "At least it's something useful."

Diego planted two long sticky kisses on her cheeks. She turned beet-red and stood there like a rag doll while he hugged her.

"Is he even old enough to vote?" she whispered.

My father stuck his head out the window. He liked the view, the tram tracks that cut the street in half, the market stalls among the plane trees, even the flocks of shitting birds. It was the kind of old building he liked, though he'd lived his whole life in a little building from the 1960s because my mother insisted on having a garage.

The apartment still stank of paint. My mother coughed and looked around like a prisoner. She wouldn't let my father leave her side and forbade him from looking in our bedroom. Diego padded back and forth on bare feet with canapés and bowls of olives and lupini beans from the kitchen. My mother watched him like a wild animal, as if she were fascinated and scared at once. There was too much sauce on the pasta. My father splattered his shirt. My mother shook her head and rubbed her napkin over that terribly red stain.

"What do you do?" she asked Diego.

"I'm a photographer."

She nodded. "Aha." She ate another mouthful. "What kind of photographer? Advertisements? Weddings?"

Diego smiled and pointed with his rigatoni-laden fork at one of his photographs on the wall. "Puddles."

I burst out laughing. I'd already had two glasses of wine and I was happy. I'd fixed the wood floor, painted the walls. My mother tried to laugh, too. I almost felt sorry for her. I knew how much effort it took, how wooden she really was.

My father put on his glasses and went to look at Diego's photos hanging on the wall. He called my mother. "Annamaria, come see."

And Annamaria went. They stood together, noses glued to the wall, and tried to find something of me in Diego's photos, something that had escaped them.

Then my mother softened. She started inviting us to dinner almost too frequently, and when we got there she'd hold her cheek out expectantly for Diego's sticky, childlike kisses. It was true, my father and I had always left her to her own devices. We were both solitary, a little arrogant, smarter than she was. She felt a special tenderness for this skinny boy who spoke in bursts and constantly rose to help her. She heaped gigantic portions on his plate.

She bought him a sweater and stuffed it in my bag one night when we were saying goodbye on the doorstep. She was too shy to give it to him herself.

"What is it, Mom?"

"Nothing, just a sweater. If you don't like it you can give it away."

Diego put it on right away. It was lovely, a thick wool turtleneck sweater.

"This will last for ten years!"

My mother was flushed with pleasure at having got the right color and size. Diego was so easy, nothing like me.

"Let's go home, love."

"'Bye, Dad! 'Bye, Mom!" I waited in the elevator while he bestowed kisses on their aged cheeks.

"'Bye, kids! See you next time!" Yes, he called them kids.

That was the start of our normalcy. I worried that sooner or later the rehashing of the same things, day after day, would be the end of us, and that one dismal smoggy day disenchantment would make its way through the slats of the shutters. We'd begin thinking selfishly again and worry separately about our own problems. We, too, would find ourselves enveloped in the opaque veil that eventually descends upon all couples, when illusion dies along with the benign blindness that obscures the other's defects. That's how it would happen. It had happened to my parents. My father was happy to leave the house in the morning, and my mother drew in a deep breath and savored the smell of her solitude. And yet they loved and respected each other.

But we were part of another life that was bolder and more casual. We were made of more malleable stuff. We were the children of comfort brandished as life's only necessary conquest.

I'd lost touch with a lot of my old friends. They'd shrunk away like poorly washed sweaters after my split with Fabio. We hung out with just a few couples my age, and they were depressing. In a short amount of time they'd been broken in, tamed. In restaurants and changing rooms they talked in loud voices about money and sex. They didn't say *make love*, they said *fuck* and boasted about what was intimate. Irony seemed to have devoured all modesty.

I dragged Diego along to sit through those depressing evenings.

"We can't isolate ourselves," I said.

He'd get a glass of wine and sit in a corner. He didn't participate in the conversations because he had nothing to say. But he was never hostile. What did he have in common with those young arrivistes? You could tell from the smiles on their faces how they would end up, flesh that would quietly pickle in the brine of prosperity, oblivious to everyone and everything. At the time, I saw them as friends. Later, over the years, I saw them for what they were, sailors of high and low seas. I'd see some of them on television with trendy glasses and transgressive striped stockings beneath their austere black dresses. A foot in each camp, a mouthful of holy water, a mouthful of sin. Full pockets, prestigious apartments, long couches to fit everyone in.

I dragged Diego along to a world that seemed more sophisticated than my own. I was the daughter of a shop teacher, a man who went into the classroom with a jigsaw and pieces of plywood. He smelled of books and honesty. I laughed at the jokes, played games that struck me as intellectual—guessed the opening words of a book or the words of a philosopher, mimed scenes from the most obscure films.

Then one night I saw him standing by the window, the farthest from the couch where we were yakking.

"What are you thinking about?" I asked.

"My father."

"Your father?"

"It's raining. When it rains I think of Genoa and of my father walking beneath the rain."

I was distracted, one ear on the conversation on the couch, the game that was continuing. I went back to my friends. I was everyone's darling because I knew the answer. It was too easy, the opening lines of a book that was in vogue that year. The Chernobyl cloud was floating over Europe. A nutritionist was listing the most contaminated foods. We couldn't even trust bread.

Diego was still looking out at the rain. I remembered that his father died during a torrential rainstorm, when a container came free of the steel wire holding it down.

I returned to his side and put a hand on his shoulder. I stayed there beside him, silent, and in silence I heard the sound of his heart, the sound of his childhood footsteps. He had run to the port with his mother. They found his father lying in a puddle of blood mixed with water.

That's the first photograph I imagined, he had told me one day in Genoa. *The first puddle. It's always with me at the bottom of every roll of film.*

We left even though it was raining, even though it was still early.

"We're going."

"Are you sure?"

"I'm tired."

The motorcycle seat was wet. We were soaked when we got home. We made love on the floor, on top of our wet clothes. We made love on that never-taken photograph, on that dead father, drenched with rain and flat as a stingray. Diego said, *Thank you.* I pulled up his head and licked his tears away with my tongue.

"I want a child," I said. "A child like the boy you were, like you. I want to give you back your father. I want to give you back everything, my love."

He burst into sobs, just like that day when, a desperate grimy kid, he sobbed beneath the rain that killed his father.

One hazy July day I went with him to the welcome center where the first children from Chernobyl were coming in. I was his assistant. I loaded his cameras. I was amazed as I watched him. I was tense and ill at ease with those children. They were indelibly marked. I worried about the radiation. They looked phosphorescent to me, like glow-in-the-dark dolls. My movements were wary and detached. Diego, on the other hand, picked them up in his arms and pulled out a few words of Russian. He wasn't interested in taking their pictures at all costs. After the first few shots, he put down his camera and started to play. I realized he'd never make a cent as a photojournalist. His eye wouldn't stay behind the camera, morbid and blind. I watched him give up the best shots in favor of others that amused the children. He even put his camera around the neck of one of them and let the kid waste an entire roll of film. It would have been impossible to sell the miserable set of photos we brought back home. We managed to get by with what I earned. We couldn't afford to have a child. Without saying anything to Diego, I continued taking the pill.

Every day, even on the worst days, he'd get up full of energy and thank me for still being there beside him. It was like living with a cat, the type that follows you around the house and as soon as possible jumps on you and licks you with its rough tongue. He stayed in the darkroom until late at night and came out with red eyes and worn hands. In the morning I did my best to be quiet, holding my breath when I opened the closet. But he wanted to be with me, and he'd get up to make my coffee and write little notes to put in my coat pockets. It was hard to leave him there in the kitchen. I'd unlock my scooter and look up to wave at him hanging out the window. He wouldn't eat lunch. He wouldn't do anything without me. He'd leave the house, too, and try to sell some of those photos that no one wanted. He'd walk trustingly around the city on his skeletal legs, his bag hanging over his shoulder, and he never got depressed.

There are little things I'll never forget, little nothing details that say more to me than anything else. The stairs in the building where we lived, the black-and-white marble curves around the landings, the banister I held as I ran. I came in from work with my bag hanging off my shoulder, my scarf dangling, bags of groceries in hand. I didn't bother waiting for the elevator but ran up the stairs, lungs bursting. Without even taking off my coat I'd empty the bags onto the table and start cooking. I'd pull out the place mats and the good wine glasses. I wanted every night to be a celebration.

I got a job as an editor for a monthly scientific magazine. There were five of us and I did a bit of everything. I translated articles from English, took care of layout, looked after the archive. I spent hours on the phone promoting annual subscriptions. I spoke with teachers and school principals, secretaries of public and private concerns. The magazine could have closed at any time. Though there were few prospects for the future, I killed myself for my small paycheck. I wasn't all that interested in molecular medicine, radial vector fields, submarine energy or the wave theory of light, but at the same time I didn't dislike the marginal little world of this minor magazine. I liked the offices, in the city center, a big room in the basement of a historical building, formerly the stables. The smell of saltpeter still rose up off the terra-cotta floors and the archways still bore the hollows of the horses' backs. I liked the metal shelves full of files, the electric teakettle in the corner beside the basket of tea bags, the conversations with colleagues, each holding a hot mug of tea.

Sometimes Diego came to get me. He'd knock on the low window to let me know he was there and come down the stairs to peer around the door with his lively pale face, his prominent eyes and that smile, so big it rent his thin cheeks. It was winter, and he had his woolen cap on. His head looked smaller than usual in that dark wool.

"You're so beautiful."

I wasn't beautiful. I was normal. I had circles under my eyes, a stale office smell and a hoarse voice from having spent hours inside. My body in the city was any old body, bundled up in its coat and its thoughts. We went toward home with our arms around each other as the lights went off in the window displays and people walked quickly on the sidewalks. My arm around Diego's bony body, I felt at peace.

Rome was full of stores and restaurants that were always crowded. In the city center, double-parked cars sat waiting in front of the revolving doors of the big hotels for high-end tourists, politicians and women in fur coats despite the mild climate. We walked alongside that ostentation. It seemed like there might be room for everyone, but was it true? People moved forward on the quicksand of illusion. Sometimes I thought of Gojko in his leather jacket as hard as cardboard. I missed Sarajevo, all those humble, dignified people, the flavor of pita, the smell of pine resin burning in the chimneys.

Then Gojko came to visit. He liked the apartment. He liked the two bottles of wine we shared. Diego was wearing a thin wool tie. Gojko laughed at it. We may have seemed a little dusty to him. He'd probably imagined the life we led as shinier. He watched me as I donned my apron to wash the dishes. He seemed older, too, more taciturn, mired in life's swampiness. He wasn't selling yo-yos and counterfeit Levi's anymore. He talked about poetry on the radio and wrote a column for a cultural magazine. He only had time to work as a tour guide on weekends. He slept in the only extra bed we had, which opened out of an armchair in a room that otherwise had no furniture.

One night he pulled a newspaper clipping from his wallet, something he'd saved in a rage. He translated bits for us. A poet friend of his in Belgrade had written it. The dead of centuries before were being exhumed, battles against the Turks. The epic spirit was almost risible.

Diego listened thoughtfully. Our world was soft and untraceable, immersed in a greedy present. But he'd spent time in the Marassi Stadium and maybe he heard in those ravings about ethnic groups and open wounds the primitive code that all ultras are sensitive to.

"Are you worried?"

Gojko shrugged.

"No. It's stupid, fascist shit."

He crumpled up his friend's article, set it on fire and used it to light himself a cigarette.

Diego made friends with a gallery owner and finally had an exhibition of his photos of the ultras. I noticed that he'd managed to capture solitude even on the stadium steps in a neck, a pair of cold ears, a scarf brandished like an axe. The photographs from the stadium were among his best, black-and-white and grainy, mouths that looked like holes, eyes that looked like planets seen from close up.

The show went well. It was moved from the gallery to the halls of one high school, then another. He even managed to sell a few prints.

He spent it all. He came home with some white truffle that he grated onto my plate like a waiter.

No one wanted the shots of feet waiting for the subway. Diego spent three days down there and shot scads of photos of people waiting for trains. Then he mounted them next to each other. It was a slice of urban life, a long garden of solitude that held the entire range, from the narrow feet of morning to the tired dusty feet of evening. It was my idea to hang them in our house. The long row of unknown people's shoes filled the corridor, curved around the living room and reached the kitchen. It kept us company.

He was terrified that I might tire of his invasiveness, of his physical need for me, the way he touched me constantly, like a child. Even at night he slept glued to my back. When I woke up I was covered in sweat, his drool in my hair. I figured that sooner or later he'd naturally start sleeping on his own side of the bed. But no, if he moved away it was by accident or because I pushed him away on a hot muggy night. As soon as he noticed, even in his sleep, he'd move back toward me. He slept sideways, his head on my stomach like a child in his parents' bed, delighting in that soft pillow. Every so often I kicked him. Three years had passed.

There were some rough moments. Diego looked around for odd jobs. For a while he worked at the counter in an electronics store. Then he started to take pictures of tourists at the Spanish Steps and the Trevi Fountain. He'd run to have the pictures developed in a shop around the corner but as often as not the tourists wouldn't wait for him and he'd come home with his pockets full of pictures of unknown smiling people. Laughing, he'd spread them out on the table for me to look at while he told me about the funny things that had happened to him that day. I worried that sadness was beginning to deposit itself at the root of his vitality.

"Why don't you go somewhere?" I said. "Go on one of your trips."

"I'm the happiest man on earth."

My father tried to give me money a few times but I stubbornly refused.

He'd bought himself a Nikon, too, and he was always asking Diego for advice, questions about lenses and light. Diego got into the habit of taking my father along now and then. Dad helped him, changing rolls of film, numbering the spent rolls. When he didn't have anything to do, he'd come to our house. He was never intrusive. He sat in a corner and didn't even ask for a glass of water. He helped put things in order. He threw out photos Diego discarded, bought binders and catalogued all of Diego's work. He gathered up all the negatives scattered haphazardly around the house and had contact sheets made. He spent days with the magnifying glass identifying the best shots.

Thanks to my father, Diego was finally signed on by an agency. Dad put on a nice tweed jacket and took the train to Milan with a binder of photos under his arm. He convinced a woman more or less his age and all dressed in black, with close-cropped, ice-colored hair, to take Diego on, harness his talent.

Diego didn't seem very happy. He read and reread the clauses of the contract as if he were looking for a reason not to sign. Then he took up the pen and scribbled his name because it was a good contract and because my father was standing there, arms folded, like a police commissioner.

"Sign it!"

And that's how Diego got his first real, regularly paid job. He photographed a new line of shoes for a downtown showroom, sandals like Greek buskins with silvery, crystal-covered straps that Diego put on the feet of a Pina Bausch dancer. He took her to an abandoned factory and had her dance completely naked in those sandals among the broken glass and weeds. He rolled on the ground as that dramatic body flew over him like a dying bird. The contrast between the baroque sandals and the skeletal figure, ribs arched backward, one leg bent like an animal's paw, was disorienting. The shots—out of focus, deformed by the wide-angle lens—were like splotches in motion, as if a bucket of water had been dumped over them. You could barely see the object being advertised, a dangling strap here, a metallic sole there. Yet there was something outrageous in those pictures, the luxurious sandals and the dirty factory floor, the tormented body. The young owner of the shoe company liked them.

The photos were put on display in a long gallery in the showroom, one after the next, the many frames of a single leap. Diego got a nice check and I received a pair of those unwearable sandals as a gift.

He took me out to dinner in a two-star Michelin restaurant. I wore my black dress. He wore a vintage American tuxedo he'd got at the market in Via Sannio. It was two sizes too big; he rolled up the sleeves, a bit of lining showed at the bottom. We sat in that restaurant like a royal couple and ate luxurious tidbits—savory puddings, meat stuffed with ice cream. We drank to everything.

Chapter 5

Whan do I remember about that day? It rained all night the night before. Violent downpours pelted the windows and thunder woke us more than once. In the morning the city lay sodden beneath a gray and menacing sky.

"Are you going out to take pictures of puddles?" I asked Diego. He shook his head. No water games for him today. He had a deadline. He'd spend the day in the darkroom. My father had come over to help and brought kiwis, which he was peeling in the kitchen. Kiwis were a novelty, fuzzy like monkeys on the outside, bright green on the inside. Dad said they were a concentrated source of vitamin C and insisted they would give us strength.

I threw mine up. A bile-green clot filled my mouth on its way into the wastebasket beside my desk at work.

During my lunch break I left the office. I felt better and the rain had stopped. I wasn't hungry, so I went into a record shop. I wanted to get a present for Diego, an old Doors compilation he liked. In line I realized I had exactly enough for the album. That's when I made the decision, though I can't say why. I grew restless as I waited for the people ahead of me to pay. A wave of heat rose up out of my jacket and burned my cheeks. An elbow accidentally brushed against my breast and I brought up both hands to shield myself. If I bought the album, I wouldn't have money for anything else. I wasn't quite conscious of what I was deciding. The thought was taking form in that precise moment, a sensation rising up out of the depths of my body. I looked at the poster of Joan Baez hanging on the wall above the cash register next to another of Jimi Hendrix wreathed in a cloud of smoke. I dumped the album and left. A few doors down, I stepped into a pharmacy. I waited for the customer in front of me to move away and then made my request quickly, in a hoarse whisper.

A pregnancy test, please.

The pharmacist gave me a pale blue oblong package. I dropped my money and had to bend down to pick it up. I smiled a joyless, desperate smile, desperate that it might not be true.

I did the test in the bathroom of a nearby McDonald's. I squinted to read the instructions, held the stick under the flow and waited.

The urine spread over the strip at the center of the stick. It had been raining for two days. The city was drenched to its core.

The confirmation stripe appeared next to the other one, faint at first, then a distinct blue line. I was pregnant.

We hadn't bothered with birth control for more than a year but nothing had happened. I was almost thirty-four. With each day I discovered further signs of time's passing. I pulled back my hair, put on makeup. I still looked fine, perhaps even better than before. But I was moving forward like a tightrope walker, trembling on the inside and showing a confident face to the world. The uncertainty made me more human. A few months earlier, on a day just like any other, I'd noticed in an elevator mirror the thousand tiny paths that would one day be traced by wrinkles—for the moment barely visible—as they recast the features of my face. I'd understood that the root of this explosion is a worry that starts deep down and whittles away at us from within. That's where the little lines start, like a pane of glass that shatters yet doesn't fall. Old age does not come gradually, but with a single blow, a bitter knot, a spark that strikes us, stains us and casts bitterness across our faces.

An unmoving, unacknowledged desire melted over me as I looked at the blue line on the white stick. Now time was free to descend, to age me, because the root of aging wouldn't be regret but a gift, softening everything. My face would be a mother's face, creased with time by fertility and by the love that would come to rest in a witness, a child.

I put the cover back on the stick and dropped it in my pocket. Outside, the sky was forbidding, full of dark low clouds like dense smoke. I stopped to call Diego from a phone booth.

"What are you doing?"

He said he had to meet a gallery owner to talk about a job. He heard the traffic and asked why I wasn't at work.

"I felt like taking a walk."

"Is it still raining?"

"No . . ." I decided not to tell him yet, not over the phone, surrounded by all that buzzing traffic. I'd wait until I got home, when we could hug each other and cry tears of joy in private, away from everything else. Back at work I stared at the computer without accomplishing anything. I couldn't concentrate.

Diego was playing the piano in his bare feet. I turned the key and found him there, his long hands sticking out of his tattered sweater.

This was our music! A love song that we'd been rewriting over the years, note after note incessantly shattering against the walls in the echo chamber of that gentle home. I slowly sank into the armchair behind him and listened until he stopped to stick a finger in his nostril, like a child.

I continued the symphony, whistling despite my leaden ear. He turned to look at me.

"My love. You're home."

We were tired. We'd been tired for months, worn out by the constant comings and goings, by the ever more despotic city.

I moved toward him.

His eyes continued to study me, aware, perhaps, of my dense thoughts.

I handed him the stick.

Here, father. The first picture of your child. I'm sorry you weren't the one to take it.

He tore off his sweater, tore off sorrow to make space for joy. He began to race bare-chested about the house, beating on his chest like a victorious chimpanzee. Then he transformed into a nagging husband. I'd really taken a chance by coming home on my scooter. The roads were in such bad shape. I should have been more careful. I had to look after myself. I should have called him to come get me. He went into the kitchen and came back with a bottle of dark wine and two glasses. I didn't want alcohol. I took a couple sips and watched him while he got drunk. He cradled the empty bottle like a newborn.

"Pietro," he said. Pietro, the name we'd always thought of for a boy.

"What if it's a girl?"

"Pietra."

I laughed. I was worn out by that joy that illuminated everything. It was a mild evening, a cozy evening in a city apartment. The radiators were on. Diego smelled of wine.

I told him I wanted to take a bath. He held one hand in the water as it filled the tub. His other hand clutched the stick.

"Are you sure this thing works?"

I called my gynecologist. She said I should go for a blood test the next day to check the levels of hCG in my blood.

Diego slipped into the tub with me, sending water over the sides. I drew back my legs.

"You don't want me?"

"Of course I do."

We turned out the lights. The soft light of a candle dripping on the edge of the tub blurred the little diamond-shaped tiles. We were immersed in utter well-being. Life had been gently dragging us to this point. This was where it all converged, this calm pond, our little underwater movements. We sought each other's hands and wove our fingers together, like those defenseless little cells clumping together down inside.

"I love him already."

He stuck his head underwater and came back up. His wet curls were flattened to his head, his big ears like stingrays.

I was sure the baby would look just like him.

We fell asleep, warmed by the bath. Still half wet, we buried ourselves in the covers. Music woke me. It was Diego playing the piano.

My mind drifted to the photo gallery in the hall, all those strangers' feet on the wall. Now it seemed to me that they were on the march, walking toward us through the hallway still submerged in darkness. I imagined them throwing off shoes, boots and sadness and dancing to the notes as they celebrated along with us.

I smelled coffee. Diego was in the kitchen. I reached for his hand, touched his chest. We dressed and went out. We wanted to take advantage of that silence, of that night as it stretched out like a long vigil.

Dawn emerged with its blue light and the night withdrew. The café rolled up its metal shutter. Vendors began bustling around the counters at the market. It felt like we were on vacation. We waited in a café for the lab to open. The coffee machine had to warm up before they could serve us.

I pulled up my sweater sleeve. They tightened the rubber strip around my arm. I looked away so as not to see the needle as it withdrew my blood.

The first women were making their way through the market with their shopping trolleys. We walked, arms around each other, our secret within us.

"Should we buy something? How about some broccoli?"

There was a green crateful of freshly harvested bunches, speckled with dew.

"Yes, let's get broccoli."

And some bananas. And radishes. We closed ourselves in the apartment. At lunchtime Diego cooked the broccoli and we ate it straight out of the pan, a forkful for me and one for him, dipping in bits of bread that came out bright green.

Then Diego went back to the lab to pick up the test results.

I waited for him at the window in a pair of underpants and one of his sweaters. He looked up, waving the envelope. He smiled with his mouthful of young teeth.

I called my gynecologist. She said everything was okay. The hCG was still low but within the norm, given that the pregnancy had just started.

The days that followed were peaceful and satisfied. Diego called me constantly at work to ask how I was doing, whether or not I'd eaten, whether or not there were too many people smoking in the room. I stuck to my old habits, riding my scooter and eating my lunch standing at the counter in a café.

Diego laid his ear on my belly, only his ear, because he didn't want to press too hard. He rested there in that uncomfortable position, listening, the expression on his face so dreamy he looked dull-witted.

My parents were speechless when we told them. I saw their eyes become soft and moist. Instinctively my father sought my mother's hand, a gesture I hadn't seen in years. My mother said, "We thought you didn't want to, that you, Gemma, didn't want . . ."

"Why?"

"Because I was always so apprehensive."

My father quit smoking and started going jogging in the morning. He'd come by in his tracksuit to get Diego, who followed him, sluggish and drowsy, in old Superga sneakers without any laces.

It seemed like a miracle that I could be harboring that tempest of cells in the stillness of my body, as if I'd swallowed the entire world. I walked slowly, immersed in a soft wet forest where life was branching, submerged like albino roots in the silence of a swamp. At work noises bothered me, the constant ringing of the telephone, colleagues whose chatter suddenly struck me as far too excited. I sat quietly at my desk, huddled behind a barrier of files and stacks of paper, calm in the stillness that separated me from the rest of the world like a little mole in its underground hole. When Diego came to get me I hugged his thin body. He held my hand in the warmth of his pocket. We stopped to look in the windows of a baby store. I was curious, sluggish and out of breath. I studied that world of minutiae I'd never known existed, but then a strange anxiety rose within me and I told Diego I wanted to move on. He brought me to a window full of rice balls browned in oil.

"Shall we have an *arancino*?"

I took two bites and felt my stomach turn. He ate mine, too, his mouth swollen with rice, with joy.

It was a white time of waiting, of dreams that lengthened into a long vigil. When I closed my eyes I could see those evanescent circles that come when the sun's rays weigh upon your eyelids and you're struck by an intense drowsiness, like on an idle summer's day.

Then the snake came. It crossed the white in its shedding cloak, leaving a greasy trail in its wake.

One day we took a walk in a park. Our feet moved along through red leaves beneath leafy branches that seemed to dirty the sky. We were surrounded by the smells of vegetation and dog piss. It was a beautiful day. A snake, an innocuous water snake, slithered over one of my shoes. It was very odd for there to be a snake in a city park full of dogs. In a split second it slipped away into the green beneath the bushes.

"Did you see that?"

No, he hadn't seen it. He picked up a piece of wood off the ground and rummaged in the bushes, but the snake was no longer there. We left it behind us. I pretended not to think about it.

It was our first ultrasound exam. We were in a dark little room at the clinic. The gel on my stomach was cold and unpleasant, like a snail's trail. The doctor slid his instrument through the slime. The snake came to mind, the disgusting little creature that had slithered over my foot. The doctor's face was immobile. He pushed his instrument lower, all the way to the edge of my pubic hair. The embryo was there, a little black dot in the magma of my uterus, but the white intermittence of the heartbeat was missing, along with the noise my book said should sound like a galloping horse. The doctor looked at me and asked if I wanted to do a transvaginal scan. I nodded without knowing exactly what I was agreeing to. I wanted just one thing: to hear the heart. Diego's waiting eyes were like a wild goat's, glued to the monitor, to the doctor's stingy mouth. The probe entered my body. Then it came back out, covered with its plastic glove and gobs of gel, like a simple instrument of medical investigation, of exhaustion, of torture.

There was no heartbeat.

"It may be early," the doctor said. "You could have made a mistake with the dates." He filled out the chart and told us to let at least a week pass before coming back for another ultrasound. The woman after us had a big stomach at least six months along.

We took refuge in a café. We ordered two cups of tea, two paper labels hanging out of a metal teapot. There was a smell of dirty grills and cold grease and a bunch of kids celebrating something. Diego was trying to smile to console me but he could barely console himself. A bitter flash crossed his kind eyes. He held my hand on the dirty table, covering it with his own, like a curtain, almost as if he wished he could suffocate my thoughts beneath it.

"That snake," I said. "That fucking snake."

We swallowed the unpleasant tea. It was made with coffeemaker water and it had a chemical aftertaste. Diego stood up and came back to the table with a pastry, confectioner's sugar on his chin. He tickled me and slid the pastry into my mouth for a bite.

"You'll see. Everything's going to turn out just fine."

The next day we redid the hCG test. They stuck a needle in my arm. I looked away, at the wall, the jar of alcohol next to the cotton balls on the metal trolley. We left the clinic. People were arguing, poor people who stank of crowded buses, their mouths full of bitterness. We had breakfast standing up in a better café than the day before. A guy came in, an advertising executive Diego knew, someone who gave him work. He was robust and loquacious. He threw his arm around Diego and started talking about a project. He was in-your-face, noisy, croaking with life. Diego and I were like a pair of lemurs, two poor spirits set down upon the earth by mistake. I saw Diego laughing excessively as if bracing himself. He introduced me and I extended my bony hand. We went back home. Later, Diego went to pick up the results. I watched from the window as he approached, his face tense, envelope in hand. We opened it together on the sofa. I called the gynecologist. The hCG levels were too low.

I lost the baby two days later. I was at work when I felt the flood between my legs. I stood, terrified, and raced to the tiny bathroom with its shelves stacked with reams of paper and boxes of pens. I pulled down my stockings and the rest and saw a swamp of blood and clots that kept coming. I patted myself with paper towels and held myself up, dazed and shaky. I could see myself in the little scrap of mirror on the wall, my face completely altered. I was scared and lucid like a first-time killer after a homicidal frenzy. I tried to clean up the proof. Red water went down the drains in the sink and bidet.

I put a bundle of paper towels between my legs and rested against the door as I waited for the hemorrhage to stop. The blood soaked through the paper towels in a second. They were an unbelievable bright red when I changed them. I'd never seen so much blood in my entire life.

"Come get me."

"Is something wrong?"

"Come get me."

I waited for him, sitting on a step. The homeless man who usually sat there had already left for the day. I could hear Diego's running feet on the pavement. I threw myself upon him with my mouth open and drowned in his jacket.

I lost the baby. I lost the baby. I lost the baby.

The atmosphere in the hospital was calm. A group of nurses huddled with their cigarettes around a radio transmitting a soccer match. It was an old, softly lit building in the center of the city, with wide marble stairways darkened by footsteps. It was almost Christmas. People were out shopping. The hospital seemed half empty. I had stopped crying. I dripped like a weary sky.

They did a pelvic exam and an ultrasound. Someone handed me a long piece of paper towel so I could clean off the gel. The doctor on duty smiled. He was a hefty man with a loud voice like a street vendor's.

He said I was lucky because the hemorrhage had saved me from a D&C.

As for the rest, it wasn't even a real miscarriage. "It was a blighted ovum," he said. "Your body expels them naturally." I was young. I could try again right away.

"You'd be surprised how often this happens."

We went back home with empty hands and an empty belly, comforted by the doctor's words. There was no reason to be dramatic. We needed to look to the future. We turned on the lights and faced the evening before us. Diego opened yet another bottle of wine, the best we had in the house. He wanted to chase away the mud. He sniffed the cork. *This is a fucking good wine.* We comforted ourselves with a glass of dark red. You win some, you lose some. What was there to do? The good wine warmed us. Our little nothing of a baby had gone away among the clots, a wretched discharge with no visible body, a death without a coffin, without a funeral, a sense of mourning we shouldn't even be feeling.

We looked vainly for the phrase "blighted ovum" in the little glossary at the back of the pregnancy book. We closed the book and chucked it in a corner. Diego horsed around and tried to make me laugh but in the lamplight I could see his sorrow.

"All this means is that it wasn't our child. The children who are meant to come will come. Don't worry."

We didn't say anything more about it. I joined a gym. There, my thinness was a privilege, a prerequisite. I wasn't at all sure I wanted to try again.

We were sad for a while. Then we got used to the idea and went back to our old routine. The mist of unpleasant thoughts dissipated. Days passed in our apartment, over the marble stairs and the closed piano and my scarf hanging in the entryway beside Diego's motorcycle jacket. Once again we were caught up in our pleasant life of little things and miracles, like one day when we ran into each other by chance.

I was waiting on my scooter at a set of lights on the road along the Tiber when I saw him. My face was tense in the traffic and hubbub of ordinary life. He was walking across the street with his heavy bag, his shoulder bent. I honked my horn and he turned but didn't see me. He quickened his pace on the crosswalk. I pulled up beside him, letting the river of traffic pass me by. I followed him for a moment at a walking pace, at his pace. Then I called to him.

"Diego . . ."

He turned, recognized me and dropped his bag to come hug me.

"I was just thinking about you!" he yelled. "I was thinking about you and there you are!"

He hugged me tight as if we hadn't seen each other for months, though we'd said our morning goodbye just a few hours before. It was a surprise, a gift.

We walk for a while along the river, hand in hand, like tourists. The last few days haven't been good. His thoughtfulness hasn't been enough. There's a permanent wrinkle of perplexity on my forehead. I'm not satisfied at work. My temperament remains unchanged, a lukewarm tyrant. I float through the world without optimism, my eyes full of questions. That lost child is far away, banished in haste, though it may be that he dwells in that wrinkle.

It's so nice to run into each other by chance on a day like any other. I squeeze Diego's hands in mine. I don't want him to go away. His eyes make up for everything.

"Where were you going?" I ask.

"Nowhere. I was going back home, to you."

"My love."

"My love."

"I don't ever want you to be sad."

"I only live for you."

A passing car skids and just misses us. It could end like that, by mistake, in an instant.

We go down onto the riverside promenade, that filthy riverbank we like so much, where we were young and stupid, where we embraced and danced naked to R.E.M.

Where is our houseboat? Where are the tardy little swallows that used to stop for a sip of water? Down here you can walk without a care alongside the black brick wall. The city is up above. Down here there's just this deep rut of rough water, carrying things away.

That night, we make love. We climb back up to the city, leaving behind the sunset over the river and the smell of memories and damp. We dwell in the city now, in the metropolis that sometimes robs us, skins us alive, reduces our lives to fragile threads. We climb back up, arm in arm. We could have made love down there, thrown ourselves into that mud, that cesspit. But I don't dare. I'm cold. Maybe I'm getting old.

Do you still love my heart?

Always. You, always, forever.

Don't you think I've changed? For the worse? Cowardly, crude, curling into my cashmere sweaters and my stunted steps?

I think I'll always love your smell.

We make love in our bed. For the first time in months, hope returns to us, with its languor and a wriggling tongue, licking and cleaning.

I see the child again and again, always the same child, always him. But I can never remember his face. I never see it fully. He's sitting still in a train station, little legs dangling over the wooden legs of an old bench like a little railway man with his lantern in the fog telling the trains to go, to hurry.

We left, too. We went to Paris. Diego wanted to see a Josef Koudelka exhibit at the Centre National de la Photographie. We saw the bird hanging upside down from a wire, the angel on a donkey. We came out stunned and silent. We stopped to eat *oeufs à la neige* outside the Beaubourg and stared at the Millennium Clock counting down the minutes until the end of the century. The photos of gypsies, the wind—they made us want to leave Rome and everything behind. Every so often thoughts like this would take hold of us. What sense did it make to live in a city where we didn't have any real friends and where we had to take a walk beside a dirty river that seemed like the city's last living muscle in order to feel like ourselves?

I bought a pregnancy test on the way back, in the airport, without saying anything to Diego. I went off and came back with a pack of gum and a tube of French aspirin. At home, punishing the very thought, I opened my suitcase and put the dirty clothes in the washing machine. I left the test in my purse until evening, until I really did forget about it.

I waited until the house and the empty streets were filled with a nocturnal silence interrupted only by distant voices of people coming out of a restaurant and stopping to chat beside a parked car. I went to the bathroom and held the stick beneath a flow of urine. I closed the cover and left it on the edge of the tub. I waited without looking. I took off my makeup and brushed my teeth. I turned to look. I was pregnant again.

It was a cold joy. Now I was an expert, I knew which tests to take, the various hormone levels. I could observe my state from a scientific standpoint. I didn't want to sink deep inside myself. The voice of need was growing a bit too loud.

We didn't tell anyone. We walked for days, expectation closed in the knot of our two hands, and pretended to go about our daily lives.

The first hormone test was fine.

We put off the ultrasound. Then one day we went. There was no heartbeat. The probe pressed against my flesh as it searched in vain. The room remained dark, without a heart.

The doctor turned on the little light over his desk and took up his papers and a pen.

"Maybe it's early. Maybe you got the date wrong."

It couldn't be. We hadn't made love since, so as not to disturb those cells.

I went back home, inert. I threw myself on the bed, pulled the covers up over my head, closed myself in the dark.

I want to sleep. Let me sleep.

I threw my shoes on the floor, tore off my clothes. Fuck you, fuck you to everyone and everything. Another blighted ovum, another dried embryo, another spider without a heart. I looked at the marks on the old wooden floor. Where was our misfortune hiding?

This time they had to scrape it out.

Diego came with me as far as the opaque glass door. He walked beside the stretcher, hand on mine.

I was calmer. I had accepted the injustice. Diego was pale, his voice too loud as he joked with the nurses.

"I'll wait out here, baby. I'm here. I'm not going anywhere. I'll be here."

He caressed my head with a heavy still hand and looked at me with too much intensity. His eyes were a different color, darker, the dilated pupils eating up the rest.

Later he told me he'd smoked a joint. While he waited he went down to the ground floor and slipped into the hospital chapel, where he sat before a plastic Madonna lit by a fluorescent light, just him and a nun. He couldn't remember a single prayer. The nun helped him with a Hail Mary.

He came out with his eyes wide open.

"I don't want to see you suffer again, my love."

Months went by, one after the other, useless as empty boxcars.

I bought new clothes, a pair of boots that fit like gloves and a frock coat with a high belt to pull tight around my too-thin waist. My head seemed smaller. I cut my hair. I wanted to feel my skull. My eyes looked out from that mass of dark and heavy tissues like an animal's, a wound hidden in shiny fur.

Diego's gaze was almost fearful. He said he liked my hair, said I still looked beautiful, that it showed off my features. He found himself with another woman, a little fox with a bony face and long, still, inscrutable eyes.

I didn't want to talk about it.

Diego's work was going well. Now he spent his mornings teaching at a private photography school. He was out the door before me to make his eight-thirty class. His students idolized him and followed him around like acolytes. If the light was right, he brought them to take pictures outside, far from the photo studios he so disliked. Groups of scooters moved around the city together, from parks in the center to the Tiber Delta fishing nets. His students imitated him, dropping onto the ground beside him and capturing images that were upside down and slanted. All the girls had crushes on him. Many of them were pretty, with a cultivated eccentricity. Now and then I'd take my scooter and join him during my lunch break so we could grab a sandwich together. I'd watch him linger with the students, smiling, and then draw near with my fox face.

"That one's cute."

He'd nod without any conviction, without any interest. He didn't look at women. Even when we sat in a café, with his students all around us, rolling themselves a joint, he was more interested in the dogs going by. He liked hunting dogs with their wide ears, delicate muzzles and spotted cloaks.

But I didn't want a dog. I made all the usual excuses: we'd have to walk it all the time, we wouldn't be able to go on vacation without worrying about it, we'd have to keep regular hours rather than come and go whenever we liked.

In reality, I didn't want to give in to the idea that we were beginning to be a bit sad together, that we needed another living being to help fill the silence of the house, the silence of my thoughts, his thoughts, thoughts of a child who hadn't come.

I remember the end of 1989 well. Three things happened: the fall of the Berlin Wall, the death of Samuel Beckett, paper-thin, and, on the same day, the death of Annamaria Alfani, my mother, a death that was hesitant like her life. One morning she started getting bruises. She became pale as a candle and dark spots sprouted all over her stomach and legs.

It wasn't a long illness. I barely managed to do anything for her. All she wanted was *stracchino*. She craved it. So when my lunch hour came I'd leave my office, stop by an expensive deli and race to her side. I'd feed her with a spoon and clean her mouth for her. Then I'd take off my shoes and lie on the bed beside her to watch TV. There was a bean quiz. You were supposed to guess how many there were in a glass jar. One day my mother said three thousand seven hundred twenty-three and got it right. She watched her own end with the same eyes with which she watched the television screen, without real interest, as if her mind were on something else. An example.

She detached herself with serenity, folding her hands. It was one of her favorite positions. She often lay like that, one hand over the other.

My father lost weight, down to the bones. I invited him to supper but he didn't want to come, so I went over to his house and made him fried meatballs like Annamaria's. Armando hardly touched a thing.

Gojko pulls his jacket over his head. It's raining again. He crosses the street to get cigarettes. He lights one beneath the rain, smokes it even though it's wet, and finally throws it away half smoked because it's gone out. He turns toward me. I see his face, his hair glued to his forehead, his jacket over his head like a cloak. He looks like a woman, like his mother.

We've just come out of the art gallery. We're walking to the restaurant with a small group of people. I'm afraid for my heart, the pain that's taken hold there. I wish Gojko would stop turning to look at me, that he'd let me disappear. I stop beside a window full of jewelry and look at a silver filigree pin shaped like a rose.

"Do you like it?"

I hadn't noticed Pietro behind me. Here he is, his breath staining the window. He's pulled up the hood of his sweatshirt. It's blue like his eyes, which tonight are so dark they look black. He points at the rose sitting in the center of the display on its meager velvet cushion.

"Do you like it?"

"Like what, darling?"

"That pin there. The rose."

I nod. "It's very pretty."

I breathe against the glass, against that rose. Diego once asked me the same question, pointing at a silver filigree rose in a window not far from here, in the same Turkish market. He pinned it on my shirt in a bar.

Pietro's watching me. He sees that I'm unsteady, as if I were drunk.

"Are you tired, Mom?"

"No . . . no."

"It's because of the pictures, isn't it?"

I turn toward my son, toward the long bony face like his father's.

"Did you like them?"

He doesn't answer right away. He hangs his head, bites his lip.

"They hurt, Mom."

For the first time in months he seems sincere. There's no little laugh waiting in ambush behind his tense face.

I take his hand. It's cold.

"I'm sorry, Pietro."

He swallows, his throat moving in the dark. "Diego was great."

He studies the little rose on its cushion in the window.

"I'm nothing like him, am I?"

"You're the same."

"Hey, baby!" Diego smiles as he comes into the room.

It's the waiting room of a private clinic, a glacial aquarium. In front of me there's an empty couch of pearl-colored leather, identical to the one I'm sitting on. The windows have iron fixtures, warehouse-style. A huge abstract painting fills an entire wall, red stains, bubbles of light and blood navigating a dark background.

Diego's here, thank goodness. I've been staring toward the door, hands resting on my legs. He's finally here with his mussed hair and the smile that always cheers me up.

"Am I late?"

I shake my head. "No. I just got here."

He sits beside me on the couch and kisses my cheek. He's holding his motorcycle helmet in his hand. He smells like himself and like the city he's just crossed. He kisses me and takes off his motorcycle gloves. I smile an awkward, tense little smile. He rubs my shoulder.

"Am I going to have to jerk off again?" He laughs.

I try to laugh, too.

When the geneticist read the results of Diego's tests, she nodded, satisfied. *Fortunately, the quality of your husband's sperm is excellent. That means we can concentrate on you.*

I start crying, my face immobile and composed and the tears streaming down. Diego doesn't say anything. He's used to these tears. It's a script we play out every time, more or less the same.

"Do you want to leave?"

Diego has said more than once that if it turns into a torture we shouldn't bother. I'm the one who insists, the one who makes the appointments.

"Where were you before you came here?" I ask.

"In the studio."

"Do you have to get back?"

"Don't worry. It'll wait."

Lately all he does is photos for ad campaigns. He aims to satisfy his client's tastes. He doesn't mess with the images anymore, he just does what they ask for, photographs that are crystal clear. It's not creative work, and that's why he likes it, because he can do it without thinking.

The medical procedures have cost a lot. Another year has passed, the worst in my life, the year of laceration, of chastisement, of legs spread wide, of speculums and needles inside.

They injected me with hormones to stimulate ovulation and then they sucked out the ova and analyzed them. They're imperfectly shaped. The nucleic acids aren't in the right order. I form clots where I shouldn't. They injected me with cortisone and anticoagulants and then stimulated my ovulation again.

My ova were better. There were a few decent ones, in the end. They whirled Diego's sperm around in a centrifuge and did the first insemination and the second. The pregnancy began. There was a heartbeat. After fifteen days it was gone. A week later I fell off my scooter and got five stitches under my chin. The geneticist said, *There's something here that doesn't make sense.*

They did a hysteroscopy. The geneticist smiled. "Were you aware that you have a uterine septum?"

"What's that?"

"A membrane that divides the uterine cavity and prevents the fertilized egg from implanting."

We sought out the best doctor we could find. He was in Milan. We took a train, stayed overnight in a hotel. I put on a green cover-up in the private clinic. They removed the septum. Diego helped me as I limped along that shiny corridor, my hand pressed against my lower belly. We took a look through the nursery window at the white garden with its crop of dark little heads. We were outside the aquarium. We hugged. I said, *I want to do it and I will.*

It was time for more ovarian stimulation with Profasi 500 and Pergonal 150. I swelled up. My mood changed. My libido went to Antarctica. I was strict. I didn't let a cigarette cross my path. Now I'm here waiting for another insemination.

We're finally called into the room, the big room with its immense polished glass desk beneath what looks like a painting by Burri, one of his wounds.

The geneticist is kind, with his mustache and flesh like a man from another era. He moves his hands. I look at his wedding ring, the tufts of hair on his fingers.

I step behind the curtain, lift my skirt, spread my legs. He turns on the monitor, inserts the cannula and moves it around. I wait.

He's an honest man, in the end. He touches his head, opens a hand. We're back at the desk. I'm once again wearing my moribund fox face. He looks at us, moving his eyes from Diego to me, and shakes his head. He's sorry, he says, he's very sorry, but there's no point in trying again.

Despite the hormones, I have fewer ova than the last time. His voice is higher than usual, maybe because he feels uncomfortable saying what he has to say. No assisted pregnancy program would take me, not even as a candidate to receive eggs from a donor, because my uterus lacks elasticity. *It's an aged uterus.* The operation to remove the septum created excessive scarring, something that can happen, unfortunately, with soft tissue.

His voice says, "You're incompatible with life. You're ninety-seven percent sterile. That's total sterility according to our parameters."

I nod, my hands clenched in a tight little rose of bones and yellow skin.

Diego stands, rubs his hands on his jeans and sits back down. "And that three percent?"

The doctor grimaces. "It would take a miracle." He smiles. "We're in Italy, of course. A miracle can always happen, they don't cost a thing."

He accompanies us out, something he's never done before, all the way past the reception area to the main door. He's sorry, too, it's as if he were a priest evicting two members of his flock.

"Thank you."

He didn't want a cent this time. He dragged us right past the payment desk.

We go down the stairs. I touch the shiny paint on the banister. It's a beautiful building from the 1940s, white and smooth as a ship.

I can't suffer anymore. I've already suffered. I may even feel relief. I will never be a mother. I will always be a girl and I will grow old that way, dry and alone. My body will not take on another shape. It won't multiply. There won't be a God. There won't be a harvest. There won't be Christmas. I'll have to look to the world in all its aridness and narrow passageways for the meaning of life, to these stores, to this traffic, and that's how I'll grow old. Dead, that's how I feel. Serene, at peace, because my time has passed.

The crossroads of life is here, as I cross this street on the same legs I've always had. There's a sign on my chest, like the kind beggars carry, or a dog tag. STERILE WOMAN.

I open the windows. The apartment feels dark. Maybe pollution coming up off the streets has dirtied the walls. There's an empty room at the end of the apartment. It's where we hang clothes to dry when it rains. It hasn't been used since we did the work on the apartment. It was supposed to be the baby's room.

The corridor is long, too, perfect for playing ball or riding on a tricycle.

I walk with my beret and overcoat like a gendarme's along the same streets as always. I've become more diffident at work, especially with women. They know we've had some problems but not the whole story. Viola tells me she's pregnant beside the coffee dispenser while we wait for the little plastic cups to fill. I give her a hug that's more or less sincere. We get a shock when our stomachs touch. I smile. It must be something synthetic in the fabric of our clothes. She nods and lights a cigarette. She's already had two abortions. This time she wants to keep it. She's already thirty-seven.

"I've reached my expiration date, like yogurt."

Later, when she isn't looking, I look at her stomach. I like her. She's one of those hapless people you can't help but liking. But now I can barely stand to be in the same room as her. She seems unkempt, stupid.

I translate an article about male impotence. In an interview, a man says, "If you're blind you can ask your woman to see for you with her eyes. If you're impotent you can't ask her to make love for you." I cry.

The world is divided in two. I belong to the dark half, along with burnt forests, seas suffocated by algae and the women of Chernobyl.

Diego comes to get me. I put my arm through his, stiff and uncertain. Suddenly it's as if the city were full of pregnant women. Before I never noticed. Now they're like an army. I don't look at them when they pass me. I notice them from far away like a hunting dog and then watch Diego out of the corner of my eye.

"Why don't we adopt a child?"

He's fertile. He can afford to be magnanimous. I'd like to punch him. I smile and wait for the flames to subside.

I'm afraid of other people's children, their genetic profile, the baggage they may bring from their family of origin. You can't trust a tire without air in it. I'm closed within my leaden body. The world can keep its children and I'll keep my incompatibility with life.

"We're not married. We can sponsor a child through distance adoption." Distance.

Chapter 6

I step into a church in the center of the city. It's full of baroque gold, dingy arches, frescoes speckled with reflected candlelight, gloomy allegories. It's almost Lent, time for repentance. I take a seat on a little gold chair beneath a side archway. I'm alone but for a couple of old maids in the dark depths, women whose miserable bodies can't ever have born fruit.

I'm ashamed to believe, to give myself over to anything so medieval. I know about the scientific origins of life, the microorganisms in the primordial sea. I'm familiar with agnostic thought and the reflections of the freer mystics. I've made love, married and divorced, traveled, fed myself on open-mindedness. What am I doing here with these women? It's a Wednesday afternoon. The stores are full of chocolate eggs. Children are looking forward to their Easter surprises while He waits for Calvary.

I feel ill at ease on this chair, out of place, like a thief, like those faithless tourists who come in, their mouths covered with sandwich crumbs, to take a peep at the frescoes. I want to leave right away but instead I stay, and cry.

I had always thought I could master anything, control my every step. All those years I took the pill—what a joke.

I'm closed off from the banquet of life. Maybe I should simply bow my head. Not everyone is meant to have children. My hands clutch my purse, my wallet with all its credit cards, my documents with my particulars: blue eyes, brown hair, female. Dead womb.

Intelligence is one of my traits, but I've been abandoned by everything that served me in the past. I lack the courage and innocence faith demands. God is merely a distant accomplice to the afflictions of man. But the geneticist spoke of a miracle, a last possibility in the hands of the unknown. The truth is that I'm here for that miracle. I've made this grotesque attempt and now I'll leave with my tail between my legs, discouraged by my weak faith, my inability to believe in any reward.

I'm about to get up but something holds me back and makes me bow my head, like a hand pushing down from above, guiding me to humility.

I may not believe in You, but You may be big enough to believe in me.
I've learned to pray.
Give me a chance to read a better sign in this destiny. That's all I ask You.
I touch myself with holy water. The Archangel Gabriel hovers beside me in an Annunciation full of fear. The Madonna is little, miserable, crushed by her vision, by her task.

In the dressing room at the gym I spend a lot of time putting on lotion. I'm anxious when we make love. I'm afraid to return to the light. I concentrate on the search for a motionless pleasure lying deep within myself, compressed into a distant solitude. Everything disturbs me, the slightest noise. Diego collapses beside me. We're two separate bodies.

He looks at my back. He tells me we don't have to make love. It would be fine just to cuddle, to hug.

I look at his naked body, his fertile testicles.

I assail him, demanding a violence he doesn't possess. If we fuck, we'll be saved. We'll be a couple. Otherwise, what are we? What will we be?

My stomach is hard and muscular. He liked it better before, when it was a warm sack full of benign noises and white spider webs. I know that he looks at me wistfully. I don't care. This hardness is my defense. It's best he get used to the fact that mine is not a mother's belly. I'll be a lover all my life. I'm a creature made for sex without consequences.

His eyes and his wistfulness bother me. So do the photos on the wall. Sometimes it feels as if those feet and those puddles are mocking me, mocking my incompleteness. Something hidden in this apartment has made us unlucky.

The former tenants didn't have children, either.

But they loved each other very much, the porter told me. I'll have to hope for the same good fortune. I think of the life that awaits us, old age, our four lonely legs.

Leave, Diego. Leave.

Sometimes I think it would be best if he found someone else, one of his students, someone with full ovaries and a uterus without scars.

It would be easier if he didn't love me.

I wait for him outside the studio. I imagine I catch him making out with another woman in the shadow of a wall, his tongue running over her tongue. The thought makes me shudder, but part of me hopes it will happen so this limbo will end, so I can kick him and spit in his face and tell him I was right.

But here he comes. Alone or in company, he's always the same, with his woolen cap and thin face, his long crooked body. He waves and walks toward his motorcycle, the shoulder strap on his bag splitting his back evenly along the diagonal.

We sit at the table. Here they are, our four elbows, near each other like every night. Our big table could fit at least two little kids but there's no one here to make a mess. We're well-off, sterile, organized. We've become too polite, too considerate of one another. Moments after dinner there's nothing dirty left. I load in our two dinner plates and close the dishwasher. The red light goes on along with that little noise of things cleaning themselves in the dark.

"You'll see. Sooner or later you'll find someone else, and you'll have a baby." I say it to his back from within my thin body wrapped in black cashmere. "I'd understand. You know you mean so much to me."

He grabs me by the neck, forces me to look at him.

"What a terrible thing to say. The only thing I know is that I love you."

All our friends start having children. Their houses smell like wet laundry, semolina, fennel tea. I make up reasons not to go see them. I convince myself that they're boring, that they stink of cooking and domestic stagnation. I buy a new dress. Spending money gives me a little burst of satiation. In the dressing room, my thinness is a virtue. The fabrics adhere to my flat stomach. I try things on, toss them aside, trample them underfoot.

Maybe I'm sexier. Sometimes, when I'm putting on my makeup, I imagine someone punching me in the face, a big boxing glove crushing my nose, my eyes surrounded by black.

We go to the movies, to concerts, to restaurants filled with artists and homosexuals and people concerned primarily about themselves. I leave my Armani coat in the wardrobe and walk to the table on my high heels.

This will pass. One day I'll stop thinking about it. There are plenty of people without children, people who don't want them. The supermarkets are full of products for singles, individual servings, ready-made foods.

But we're not like that. We bring food to the cats in the courtyard. A pigeon builds her nest on our balcony, shedding feathers and cooing incessantly. I know I should chase her away with a broom, throw away her eggs. They hatch and two sodden little black creatures emerge from the smelly shells. Diego toils over a cardboard barrier because he's worried cats will get them or they'll fall over the edge. In the end, the little pigeons fly away to the overhang with the rest of their family and I have to scrape away a carpet of white and black shit.

I call in the workmen. They repaint the apartment, put in a bathtub with a hydro massage, take out the kitchen tiles and paint the walls bright colors. I go up and down the stairs with paint chips and fabric swatches for the curtains and the headboard on the bed. I'm agile as a fly. I feel a new vitality.

"How do you like the new couches?"

Diego nods and tries them. He liked the old one just fine. It was more comfortable with its floppy cushions and dirty armrests. But if it were up to him we'd never change a thing. He's thirty-one now, and his face is still boyish, but he's grown slower, more hesitant, and he's developed a dry cough that comes out in bursts when he's nervous. He still loses things, just like always—his glasses, rolls of film—but now he insists on finding them. He wearies himself looking all over the apartment.

My father helps him in this domestic treasure hunt, bending down to look under the furniture, looking on our shelves with circumspection. He doesn't want to be nosy, he just wants to help us.

He finds the roll of film and hands it back to Diego. A moment later, the car keys are missing.

Dad jokes that Diego's getting old. He can feel how tired we are. The night I told him we can't have children he put a hand over my mouth to stop me from speaking, from suffering. He brought his face close to mine and kissed the hand over my mouth. He kissed my destiny, our bloodline that would go no further. He kissed my wound the way he kissed my skinned knees to heal me when I fell off my bike as a child.

It's all right, darling. It's all right.

I worry about Diego's cough. I take him to get a chest X-ray. There's nothing, not even bronchitis. His voice is hoarse because the coughing has inflamed his vocal cords. His voice is querulous, like an infant's, hard to get used to.

I buy him a thick scarf and prepare the nebulizer for him like one of those overly anxious mothers who make their children ill in order to keep them by their side.

He breathes in the mist from the nebulizer and smiles.

I'm a wreck, he says.

He seems happy to be one. He waits for me to smile, to bless him.

The Christmas tree ends up dying out on the terrace. I take the lump of dry dirt and throw it in the dumpster.

The room at the end of the hall is a gym now. It was the architect's idea. There are big mirrors and a wall bar on the wall and a treadmill in the center. At night I run on the conveyor belt in the dark, the room barely lit by the light coming in off the street. Sweat runs into my mouth. It has a bitter taste of toxins and rage, like something discharged by an ancient, extinct creature. In the mirror I can see the reflection of my body, moving alone. This room was meant for the future. Down on the street someone is laughing. The conveyor belt is going faster than I am; by the time I notice, I've already fallen.

I've got a bandage on my dislocated wrist when I visit Viola in the hospital after her baby is born. I find her sitting on her bed in a mussed dressing gown. Her face looks the same as when we are at work or when we go to a café. The only difference is the slightly slack belly and the IV stuck to her wrist with white tape. She's just sitting there on her bed in the ward. The dark-skinned woman in the next bed has a transistor radio glued to her ear.

Viola lights up when she sees me.

"Hey, look who's here!"

I look around and wonder why she didn't choose someplace better than this. But Viola is so disorganized. When her water broke she called the ambulance and they brought her to the nearest hospital.

"Want a cigarette?"

"Are you allowed to smoke?"

"Who gives a shit?"

Out on the balcony, which is barely the size of a doormat, we cling to a rampart black with smog. Fumes from the kitchen rise up from a grate beneath us.

Viola looks down at all the sick people and visitors in the hospital yard as she puffs on her cigarette.

"Are you happy?"

"Yes," she says, her weak face to the wind.

She and the baby's father, a tattoo-covered imbecile, broke up while she was pregnant. She went on by herself, prosaically. There's no poetry in that belly, no love story, just hasty realism. Yet there's something sweet about her all the same.

I help her clean her neck with some wipes and tidy up the drawer of her bedside table, throwing out an overturned juice and a sticky magazine. Viola nods in thanks. I go downstairs and get her a pack of cigarettes and an ice cream. It seems odd that no one's here with a woman who's just given birth.

"Where's your mother?"

"On a camping trip."

Everything clashes with the sickly sweet maternity I thought I'd be forced to swallow, like a punishment. Viola seems more like someone who's broken a leg falling from her scooter than someone who's just had a baby. There's something cheering about her inertia.

They bring the baby in. Viola passes him to me right away as if he were a folder or a sandwich.

"What do you think?" she asks me.

He's a dark little thing with a squashed nose and an adult expression. He looks like an Afghan. He looks like his father.

"All he needs is a tie . . . he looks like a man already. He'll walk home on his own two feet!"

Viola laughs and says I'm right, thank goodness. The Afghan doesn't cry. He just lies there, calm.

"Let's hope he sleeps."

"Has your milk come in yet?"

Her breasts are still small. She picks up the baby and draws him to her nipple and grumbles that the nurse said to do it because *if the baby doesn't suck, the milk won't come.*

Viola says the nurse can go to hell, and her white suspenders, too.

I help her, even though I don't know how to do anything. I move near her on the pillow, hold the baby's head and tickle him under the chin so he'll open his mouth.

Viola watches me and says I'm better than the nurse. I laugh and blush.

When we hug I smell her exhausted sweaty smell. Before I leave she cries and smiles at the same time. "That must be the hormone levels going down."

I follow the nurse who brings the baby back to the nursery. I stand there and look at all the metal cribs on the other side of the glass, at the plantation of heads, seeds sticking up above the snow.

As I climb into my car I think Viola might not be a good mother. She's too needy herself, too unfortunate. Then again, who knows? I have to accept the fact that children sprout randomly, like weeds, wherever the seeds are blown by the wind.

I don't bother reading the letters from the two children we're sponsoring in Romania. I'm not interested in establishing a relationship with them. Filling in the deposit coupon and sending in the money are enough for me.

Diego is marking up some photos of a skeletal model wearing black makeup and scraps of camouflage material. With her visor and military boots she looks like a soldier creeping through the jungle.

The slaughter in Rwanda is on the news. Dad's the only one paying any attention. Black figures fill a river of red mud. I move closer.

"What are those?" I ask.

"Dead people."

I look at the bodies disemboweled by machetes, heads far from the bodies, brothers who started killing each other from one day to the next. A short-lived shiver goes down my spine as I turn off the television. I'll send that river of black orphans some money, too.

My father is drinking a whiskey. Diego's sleeping. He was feeling down tonight. I could tell from his cranky voice.

Out of nowhere my father says, "Listen, Gemma. Why don't you adopt a baby?"

My voice when I answer him is devoid of emotion. I say we've distance-adopted two children and that's enough.

He nods, but he's troubled.

"You're two good people."

"We're not married, Dad."

He nods, his bowed head weighing on his neck, and says that's something he hadn't thought of. He goes toward the corridor to get his coat. He rings the bell right after he leaves.

"What, Dad? Did you forget something?"

"Why don't you get married?"

"Good night, Dad."

We got married. At town hall, just the two of us and very few relatives. Duccio, Diego's new manager, stood up for Diego with his red suspenders and a pin-striped suit. Viola was at my side with the little Afghan in her arms. It was an anonymous sad Thursday, a day like any other. We did everything in a hurry, with no preparations. I was almost brutal about it. We waited the requisite number of days after declaring our intentions and then, when they let us know the date and time, we went to a room with two bronze suits of armor flanking the entryway alongside a flaccid Italian flag. Also waiting to get married was a couple in their fifties, a second marriage for both. I was wearing a stiff gray suit. At the last minute I'd tied a flowered scarf around my neck to liven it up. I looked like my mother. Diego was wearing the same corduroy jacket he'd been wearing all winter. He'd added a little mustard-colored bow tie, a crooked butterfly on his sports shirt, his only nod to ceremony.

At the exit, Viola pulled a packet of rice out of her purse. It was still vacuum-sealed. We waited ridiculous, irritating moments while she opened it with her teeth and passed it around. Then, without any surprise, those little pebbles thrown from too near struck our tensed faces.

Diego took the wedding picture. He put his camera on self-timer, set it on a column and ran toward me and the wedding guests. I don't remember if I ever saw the print.

Afterward, a few of us went to a restaurant full of German tourists near the Campidoglio. I don't remember much about that day; it was poisoned by my bad mood. Diego raised his glass to the table of Germans and they showered us with whistles and German good wishes. The United States was bombing Iraq. The night before we'd stayed glued to the television to watch B-52s and Wild Weasels release intelligent, laser-guided missiles.

"They say they're targeting strategic objectives, then they bomb a hospital, a bus, and their spokesperson apologizes from behind a bottle of mineral water."

My father was waving his arms.

"Do you know what's written on those missiles? The boys in the Apache Battalion are having a great time. One missile says UP YOUR ASS, SADDAM. The next one says UP YOUR WIFE'S ASS."

He'd had a bit too much to drink. He sat there mulling things over as he slowly chewed his food. For some time now he'd been finding less and less to like in the world. My mother's fixation on banalities helped balance his mood. Now that she was dead, Armando was more of a rebel as he wandered alone through his unchecked thoughts.

There was a brand-new wedding ring on my finger and a disagreeable expression on my face. I wasn't happy. I had gotten married so I could adopt a child. Our names would now travel together through the infinite tunnels of Italian bureaucracy. I was worried that the legal testimony of our love would somehow rob us of something. As I signed the register at Diego's side, I felt no happiness, only the bitter taste of defeat. Our wedding was the definitive confirmation of my deficiency.

I crumbled bread on the table. Every so often Diego rested his head against mine. Dad raised his glass and started clanking his fork against it for attention. He thought it was important to say things aloud on certain occasions. He was mute for a moment, his mouth open, until the pause became too long, almost pathetic. He looked up and down that miserable tableful, just a few friends, modern and jaded. He pressed his eyes shut for a moment to call his bushy eyebrows and his thoughts to order. Then he brought out a few words.

"I wish the bride and groom health, peace, a full plate and everything that comes next."

He looked at Diego and me as if we were a single body. A lump closed his throat. He pretended it was a burp, covering his mouth and excusing himself softly.

"I miss Annamaria," he mumbled.

Viola complained that the meat was tough.

"Order something else," I snapped.

Duccio didn't even wait for dessert. He had to get back to his models.

Diego's bow tie went into the pocket of his corduroy jacket, where I found it some days later.

We didn't make love that night. Diego opened a bottle of champagne he'd left to chill for a toast. We linked arms. Our necks got wet, our clothes. We grew giddy, loquacious. We were afraid of the silence, afraid of finding ourselves naked and defeated.

The telephone woke us. It was Gojko, whistling the wedding march into the receiver. We had asked him to stand up for us but it would have required official documents and trips to the embassy. We were all lazy and reluctant to deal with bureaucracy, so nothing had happened.

"In any case, you're the real wedding witness, the only one," I said.

"I know," he replied. "Unfortunately I'm only the witness." He chuckled. "I wish I were the killer." He asked us about our honeymoon in his usual manner. "Under which rich sky will you be going to fuck?"

Diego smiled, rubbing his head, and looked at me. "We're staying in Rome to work."

"Are you crazy? After you get married you have to go somewhere! You have to take your woman and go."

Who knows what he was imagining—a Bosnian-style wedding full of commotion, the bride covered with embroidery, a field full of men drunk on slivovitz? He certainly couldn't have imagined our composure, the silent house and the two of us sitting in bed, drowsy and boring.

"Take your wife and go to a hotel!"

Diego smiled. "I'll give it a try."

He hung up the phone, looked at me and turned off the light. "Let's go to the Grand Hotel."

I muttered a response worthy of a first-class nag. "Why should we throw away money like that?"

He turned over a couple of times in bed, then got up. In the morning I found him on the couch, bare-chested, one arm falling to the floor and the champagne bottle empty. On the television a fat man with a mustache was selling naïf paintings. I picked up a slipper and the empty bottle. I looked out the kitchen window at passing cars and the market stalls. I stayed glued to the glass, absently allowing the things I saw to blur into a single mass of dirty, slimy colors.

Two days later we submitted our adoption request and began the whole rig-
marole of certificates and bureaucratic offices, official stamps, questionnaires,
birth certificates. I didn't mind the out-of-body pregnancy, the bureaucratic
mildew. It made time pass. The problem had moved from my body to the
shelves of public offices. I went around the city on my scooter, put the kickstand down and ran along the stairs to befriend porters and haughty, thickset
clerks.

My father went to a notary to sign his consent for inheritance purposes.

We were called into police headquarters to speak to a plump, flat-nosed
man with a superior attitude and an expressionless, squashed, albino-white
face, like one of those fish that live beneath the sand. Diego had a criminal
record: he'd been tried and convicted for a minor offense with the Marassi
ultras.

The police officer's lighter is all I remember, a little stub of gold that he
turned over and over in his hands. He spoke softly and rarely met our eyes.
He licked his lips constantly.

Diego was smiling and lighthearted at first as he went over episodes from
another life. He was wearing his woolen cap. The police officer looked up.
"Please uncover your head."

Diego took his hat off, excusing himself.

Diego was swaying, eyes shining, trying his best to remember those years.
When the police officer told him to stop fidgeting, he froze. A flash I'd never
seen before darkened his expression. The questions became more and more
insinuating. He answered them with annoyance. The light changed. The police
officer licked his lips once again. A faded sadism blossomed in his pale face.
Suddenly we felt like two criminals. He knew everything about us, the trips
to Sarajevo and the rest. I stuttered over my words, justifying our recent
marriage. The police officer stared at me with his swampy gaze. At one point
I caught him looking at my chest. I adjusted my shirt. Diego jumped to his
feet. The police officer said he hadn't finished. Diego said, "What do you
want? Do you want to take us into custody?"

From that day on we felt as if someone were spying on us. Every so often a
police car would slow down as it passed beneath our apartment.

The national health psychologist was kind and disinterested. We walked to an office in the hinterlands, a mental health center in what must once have been a lovely little 1920s building, now surrounded by a garden grown wild. Doctors and nurses smoked at the windows and junkies wandered around. We sat next to a hazy woman carrying a wallet in a crumpled department store bag.

The psychologist smiled at us when we entered his office. We waited while he finished his telephone conversation. Then we answered his questions as he filled out the questionnaire. He pronounced a very positive judgment without even really looking at us.

Finally we go in for our first session. The psychologist assigned to our case, a robust woman, lingers in the doorway with a social worker, a dull girl dressed in a vest and tie, like a man. Then, looking at us without seeing us, the psychologist moves toward us and sets our case folder on the table. She has thick hair, little eyes made up with eye shadow and a bunch of noisy necklaces. She must have been beautiful once. I look at her fleshy lips, the white teeth she constantly flashes, her sensuous mouth. She raises her eyes and I know in an instant that she'll hate me. There are women who hate me at first sight. I've learned to recognize them immediately, learned to defend myself.

I try not to think about it, try not to let myself be influenced by my perception of her as I answer her questions. Her voice matches her robust physique. It bounces off the walls with their posters of children and clasping hands. She smiles and tells me to go ahead. But it feels as if she's doing everything she can to discourage me. Her eyes move from me to Diego like marbles. I feel fragile, uncertain. She's weighing our imperfections. It's obvious that Diego is younger than me. My back is bent, I'm hugging my arms to myself as if I had a stomachache. It's clear that I'm the sterile one. I talk about useless things, dodging her questions. I can't tell her the truth: that I want a child with the same eyes and shoulders as the man I love. This woman reads the truth as if I were a book: that I'm here because it's all I have left. It's my last chance. If I'd been able to have a child of my own I wouldn't be sitting here in front of this noisy woman with her necklaces so she can show me up in a lie. I'm not motivated by altruism. I'm afraid Diego will leave me. I want to fasten him to me. I put on a confident air and speak softly. But what I'd really like to do is break down and cry upon this table full of folders and documents of people who have suffered, like us. I had hoped the psychologist would convince me. I thought it would be like speaking with a priest, an expert taking me in hand. Instead, this woman is doing what she's supposed to do, scrutinizing potential parents. She tells me the truth, that it's a long and painful journey, a terrible trial for the psyche and the soul.

"Even the closest, most motivated couples find themselves fielding terrible blows."

I smell something acrid. My armpits are soaked with nervous sweat, dripping sorrow.

At home I can no longer hold myself back. "What a bitch!"

I feel wounded, stripped, as if a hand had reached inside me to scrape away at the most intimate spaces and take away the last clots.

Diego closes himself into the darkroom, far from me. He can stay there. When he moves past me in his sweater, I want to pull it off him and pull out his hair. He didn't defend me. He left me to flounder on my own. While I was speaking the psychologist looked at him and said, like a slap, "Does your wife sound sincere?"

Diego sat there without opening his mouth, without saying a thing. Then he nodded, but moving automatically, as if powered by inertia.

I skip the next interview. I have a problem at work, a ridiculous excuse. In reality I don't want to go. I feel exposed.

We had hoped it would be easier. We had dreamed there was a child already waiting for us. Now we know we'll have to wait a long time and go through hours and hours of investigations. We know we won't get a newborn because they don't give them to couples without experience.

In my pregnancy book it says the first two years are the ones that count. The hammer strikes malleable metal. Later, you're working on material that's already solidified.

An advertising executive Diego knows from work invites us to dinner. He and his wife have adopted a child. Little Ludmina is blond and ethereal, like Tinker Bell in Peter Pan. Their house is modern and telegenic with its dark plates, the kitchen with its island counter in the center. The mother is

English and blond like the adopted daughter, who really does look like their child. Could this be why they chose her? It's a petty thought, but I can't help but think it because I know it's the truth. I've become adept at observing the depths. It's a very pleasant evening, red wine in wine-bar glasses, a timbale of white cabbage with béchamel. They seem to be a harmonious couple. They're very kind to one another. The father puts on his baking glove to open the oven door. The mother feeds the daughter, who's six but still likes to have help, and later takes her off to bed. Ludmina says good night to the guests. Her stuffed animal when she waves it is like an extension of her arm. The mother comes back and lights a cigarette. She pulls out little ramekins of custard cooked in a bain-marie. After a while the little girl comes back. She wants water. She says it in Russian. When she's tired she speaks her own language. The mother puts out her cigarette, gives Ludmina water and takes her to her bedroom. A little while later Ludmina is back again. She's still thirsty. The father takes her back to her room. The little girl keeps coming back. Her face is different now, less ethereal. A fatal air of chagrin descends over this fashionable table without any frontiers—an Italian man, an English woman, a Russian child. Gradually the telegenic charm falls to pieces. The little girl, who was so tired before, has no intention of returning to bed. The parents look at each other as if they'd have an argument if they could. The father's cheeks are red as if he'd like to yell but can't because he has a plug in his mouth. The mother smokes another cigarette. A bit of ash falls on her sweater. She brushes it off and looks at the little hole. They've got guests. Smiling, they apologize. They let the little girl do whatever she wants. She starts throwing pillows and jumping around. She turns on a terrible talking toy. The intimacy and warmth, worthy of a television commercial, are now shown up as lies. The father gets up and speaks softly in the little girl's ear. The mother goes over to her and the little girl kicks her. They serve port, accompanied by this little nuisance. The little girl finally collapses watching old *Tom and Jerry* cartoons. We watch them too, for a while—the volume is so loud we can't help but be drawn in. The mother takes the cassette out of the VCR. She tells me about their trip to Russia and the first time they saw Ludmina in the orphanage, a bunch of poetic nonsense, then bits of truth. The child rejects her because she remembers her biological mother, and when she's angry she says, *You're not my mother*. It's better with the father but she's very aggressive. It's better that way, it's a way of getting out the pain and rage she carries from the orphanage. There were bars on the beds there. It was like a prison. "You can't imagine how they keep the children, it's beyond words." She cries. Then she makes an authentic and terrible pronouncement.

"I love Ludmina, but if I had to go back, I don't know if I'd do it again. We've taken on so much pain that didn't belong to us."

She looks at me from her polite blond naïve face, which has probably aged over the last two years.

You don't adopt a single child, you adopt the pain of the world. It's a litmus test of your incapacity.

The fifth session with the psychologist goes better. I've learned to be sincere. I cry without speaking. The psychologist says it's fine to cry.

The next week I talk. I say I never saw my mother naked, that she put deodorant in my gym shoes and made me eat off plastic plates to save time. I cry about nothing, those plastic plates, that sterility.

After two months I admit openly that I see adoption as a last resort. I say I'm not sure I'm capable of loving anyone. I've come to like speaking the truth. It tastes better. It's more outrageous. I say I'm afraid of losing Diego because he's younger than me, because I'm the sterile one and he has an excellent sperm quality. I talk about the ordeal of needles and blighted ova. I don't cry anymore. I study my hands.

Today Diego is crying. He trembles and coughs his bitter cough.

The psychologist leaves us alone to regain our composure. When she comes back she offers us candy. It's comforting to chew those little spheres of gummy licorice.

Diego's hand is in mine. We're like two little children who met at day care and whose love for each other is much larger than they are.

I look at Diego and say, "I want a child with his eyes, with his neck." I look at the psychologist and ask, "Do you think I'll find that child?"

The psychologist nods, robust and diligent. "Yes. You'll find him."

I hug her. Today she's my mother, my real mother, my adoptive mother.

The next time, Diego talks about his father, the machine room, the sawdust-covered wharf.

At our last session, the psychologist says, *We find something else in these children because we dig deeper. Gemma, you'll find Diego's neck. Diego, you'll find your father.* She tells us we've learned to dig.

I walk close to Diego. We have no destination in mind. We go to our old haunts, the barge that's now a fashionable bar. Nothing's left, not the pleather couch with obscene graffiti where we made love so many times. There's a white parquet floor. We order *bresaola* and cry out of love for each other as we eat the dark dry meat. Our flesh is alive and red. I watch the river outside. It's the same as always, yellow and angry. I'm not sterile anymore. My hands are soft. Diego says, *We have our entire lives ahead of us.*

We go back home. There's a child before us, the nape of his neck so close we can almost touch it.

The psychologist trusts us now. She reassured us. It's not a leap in the dark. There's room for choice, interviews to help you decide. Diego says, *No decisions.* The first child who comes into the room, the first one who looks at us—that's him. You don't choose children like peaches at the market.

We are a father and a mother. We're ready.

Our leave-taking takes place in a pizzeria, the dirtiest pizza of our entire lives, mozzarella and shit. The three of us cry. The psychologist says, "I've never met a couple like the two of you. You're so good, so honest."

Our request is refused. We are unfit for adoption. Diego has a criminal record. That soft hairless cop dug through the past.

Dad brings us loquats, Diego's favorite fruit. He washes them, breaks them in two and says, "Let's go somewhere else. Let's go live in Iceland."

Diego stands at the window. I look at his neck.

I've grown. It's absurd, but I have this feeling that something is coming toward us. It's crazy, tonight of all nights, to feel such confidence.

Today Gojko is in a bad mood. He seems older than his age, walking as if he were already senile, dragging his feet, his arms detached from his body, his big hands open. He looks like one of those abandoned windmills on the banks of the Drina with their stocky bodies of dark bricks and broken falling poles and yet still waiting for the sky and the wind.

"I didn't think it was possible! Who'd have thought my generation would decide to follow evil backwards, dig up the dead of the Second World War and the battles with the Turks just so we could roll around in hatred? It's unbelievable. We had our whole lives before us, U2 concerts, girls who loved us and would have listened to us. What else did we need? Why did we opt for dirty seeds, poisoned wells, decaying carcasses?"

The three of us are sitting like stranded tourists on a bus stop bench beneath an opaque plastic shelter. The metal disk of a sports center armored in black pipes looms behind us like the carcass of a prehistoric beast. The wide naked road before us is slightly muddy thanks to the rain that's just stopped. An old Opel passes, leaving behind a black trail of exhaust. Pietro covers his mouth with his hand.

Gojko smiles and looks at Pietro. "You lead the good life in Rome, huh?"

"Yeah," Pietro mumbles. "It's okay."

There's something menacing about the way Gojko's hoarse voice sticks to his words. Rage seems to be advancing across his face.

"Everything here seems kind of dull and sad."

Pietro shrugs and looks at the road ahead of him, the empty boulevard, the peeling tree with its thin trunk bent over like a fishing rod.

"No. I like the square with the chessboard."

"The square with the chessboard is full of pathetic old refugees. You should have stayed in Piazza Navona, in that bar facing the fountain by Bernini. You're lucky to be Italian."

I put a hand on Gojko's leg. It's meant to be a consolatory gesture but I'm squeezing his flesh. I'm scared Gojko will say something to Pietro. Maybe I've been wrong to trust him. He's been through too much. His calm suddenly appears to be malice in disguise.

"Ask your mother what this city was like before the war."

"It was beautiful," I hasten to say.

I turn toward Gojko. He's disagreeable, unrecognizable.

"This is where she met your father. You know that, don't you?"

Pietro nods, this time with bowed head.

"He was a really likable guy. Your mother, on the other hand, was very snooty, but with her looks she could get away with it."

Pietro scratches at his pants legs with his nails, which he keeps long so he can play the guitar. He's agitated, too.

"Cut it out," I tell him. "That's irritating."

He stops scratching without complaint.

Two kids with cheap acrylic OLIMPIK SARAJEVO sweatshirts are playing soccer in the open space in front of the metal disk. Gojko kicks their ball back to them, then stands and joins their game. He's still agile. The ball stays glued to his foot.

"I want to leave, Mom. I want to go back home."

"*Italijan!*" Gojko hollers. "Hey! Del Piero!"

The boys come toward Pietro. Gojko's told them to. They look alike. They have the same eyes, the same red blotches on their cheeks. They look like brothers.

Pietro smiles and shakes his head. He's never liked soccer. It's not his sport. He mumbles that he doesn't have the right shoes, but then he stands and joins them.

I watch him beside Gojko as they struggle for the ball. Pietro is gentler. Gojko means business. He plays with that slightly pathetic frenzy men his age get when they're playing against boys.

One of the boys from Sarajevo knocks Pietro down and steals the ball. Pietro pulls himself up, shakes the dirt off his jeans, and stays behind, jumping alone. He's got his hood on. He wears it when he wants to defend himself.

One of them moves toward him again with the ball. Pietro manages to get it away from him and kicks it hard against the wall. He yells that he's scored a goal. The boys whistle with their fingers in their mouths and say it was out of bounds. Gojko shrugs. There's something that unites him to these two boys, a sort of cruelty. They play gracelessly, viciously. Pietro limps. His face is tense beneath his hood, his eyes on the ground studying the ball as if it were an enemy. There are four of them. It's every man for himself but it's really as if they were all against Pietro. I watch Pietro alone in a field of enemies. He's long-limbed and graceful in his expensive jeans and shoes. He's handsome, full of light, well mannered. The old-school sensei Giuliano found for his judo lessons taught him old-fashioned courtesy. He's played water polo and tennis. He's used to fair play. He doesn't give up, but he's not capable of hurting another person. I try to see him as these boys must see him. They seem ugly and opaque with their acrylic sweat suits and their blotchy cheeks, their unmoving eyes that overflow with envy. I think they hate him. They're all children of the war, their mothers sick with cancer, their fathers alcoholic and unemployed. They have squat bodies and they play rough, kicking my son's shins.

You can't pity everyone. I don't like these boys. I don't like their sweaty faces. They look as if they were made of some shoddy inferior substance, flesh without light, full of rubble and dust.

My son is safe. He's made it out of this concentration camp. Take your hands off him, you boars, you wrecks.

The snipers used to fire from this hill. They played with their victims, hitting a hand, a foot. Some aimed for the testicles, a breast. They had time to kill, so first they had some fun.

For me it was like shooting at rabbits, one of them said in an interview. He didn't feel at all guilty. He couldn't understand why there was so much interest in his story. He wasn't crazy or sadistic or anything else. He had simply lost the meaning of life.

Pity dies along with your first kill.

He was dead, too. That's why he was smiling.

On the way back I call Giuliano. I put a finger in one ear and clutch my cell phone to the other as I walk because there's traffic now, smelly and noisy.

"Hello, my love."

"Hello, my love."

I ask him to help me find a ticket so we can come back early. He says he'll try. "But weren't you supposed to go to the sea?"

"The weather's crummy. The food's no good. Pietro's complaining."

They're meager excuses, cheap as my heart, as my fears. Giuliano can tell. He leaves me in silence for a while.

"Giuliano?"

"I'm here."

Wait a while longer, he's thinking. I can tell. I can see his face, his eyes as they narrow. I know the expression he has when he's thinking of me.

"Where are you?"

"Walking."

"What's there? What's in front of you?"

I don't understand what he's asking me.

"There's an ugly street full of traffic, a cell phone store, a bakery, a plaque with the names of dead people on it."

"Don't run away."

In front of the hotel I don't look Gojko in the eye. He senses my distance. "Good night."

"Good night."

"Tomorrow?"

"Tomorrow let's sleep in."

I turn and feel his bastard eyes boring into me.

Pietro opens a bottle of water and takes a long drink. Then he sighs. He burps and excuses himself.

We try the television. A German channel gets the best reception. It's a game show we also have in Italy, one of those format shows they export all over the world.

We lie on the bed watching the phosphorescent box full of laughing people. Shiny fake money like pirate's booty falls across the screen.

I never watch this stuff but right now I let it pass through me without defending myself. I think it's good for me. It's relaxing. It gives me back some of my stupidity.

Once I asked Diego what it felt like when he did heroin as a teenager.

The biggest asshole looked like a decent person. The Marassi Stadium looked like the Maracanã. My little Vespa was a Harley-Davidson. The world was easier to bear.

I watch the screen, the images that enter and leave. After a little while my thoughts depart. I am utterly emptied. My mouth lolls drowsily against my face.

Pietro slides down the wall and puts his head on his pillow. I turn off the television. One of Pietro's feet hits mine. He doesn't immediately move it away. What's got into my son tonight? He seems less angry.

"What are you thinking?"

"Nothing, Ma." But he has the wakeful voice of someone who's still present in the world. He doesn't move his foot. He leaves it there next to mine. I look at his hair in the dark, reach out a hand and caress his head. At home he'd have chased me away with an ill-mannered gesture and a grunt. Here in

Sarajevo he accepts my caress, even moves imperceptibly closer and cuddles against me like a baby. I hug him. I hug my son for the first time in a long time. Maybe he's been wounded by this strange day, this city where he was born, by chance, he believes, because his father was a photographer who traveled the world. Now he's breathing more deeply. He may be sleeping.

A few days before my mother died she told me she dreamt of me still inside her womb, such a vivid dream that she was still confused when she woke in the morning. She lay in that bed, near death, and touched her belly with disbelief. She'd been so certain I'd returned to the womb.

"That's ridiculous," I said, wounding her.

And then it happened to me, too. Pietro was little. He had a terrible ear infection. Pus was dripping out one ear and his fever was going up.

That night he slept with us, his minuscule, boiling-hot body by my side. I dozed off for a while. Then I dreamt that I opened my legs and gave birth. There was no pain, no blood. I woke with a scream that trailed off in a long whimper.

Giuliano turned on the light, wide-eyed and frightened. "What's wrong?

Pietro was sleeping. His fever was going down.

"It was just a dream," I reassured him.

"A nightmare?"

"I'll tell you about it tomorrow."

Tonight my son is sleeping next to me, curled against me like a big fetus. Tonight, in this hotel, in the pale light coming in off the street, I fear Sarajevo's soft voice, what it may sing and tell. I listen to Pietro's breathing.

"Maybe someday I'll tell him," I'd whispered to Giuliano that other night, after my dream. "I'll tell Pietro I'm not his mother."

Chapter 7

The Dubrovnik sun floated through every particle of sky over the red roofs of the old city and the white stone of the city walls. We were enchanted as we approached the port. A real vacation at last.

We went to the ferry hold for our car. The loading door opened with a stinking blast of black smoke and diesel fumes. We could see Gojko out on the pier. He was wearing white pants and dark glasses. His skin was already baked by the sun. He stood with one foot resting on one of the big cables that anchored the boat to the pier. As he chatted with a white-uniformed official he helped the flow of traffic out of the ferry by gesturing to the drivers to straighten their wheels.

Diego stuck his head out the window, put two fingers in his mouth and let out one of those whistles he had learned in the Genoa alleyways.

Gojko turned and saw us. A huge smile that showed all his crooked teeth split across his face. We were still in line. He ran to us, scrambling like a cat over the hoods of other cars. He hollered his happiness as he hugged Diego's head to his chest. He kissed him, looked at him and kissed him again. Then he let out another yell.

"*Dobro došli, Diego! Dobro došli!*"

He came to my side of the car. I tried to protect myself from the onslaught. He literally pulled me out of the car, lifting me like a piece of straw.

"Hey, beautiful! *Dobro došli u Hrvatsku!*"

He took Diego's place behind the wheel and drove the car down to the pier. Then he and I walked arm in arm like a brother and sister through the little streets that had been polished by the sea. He insisted on buying me a hat with the red and white Croatian coat of arms. He put it on my head. I looked in a tiny mirror. I loved it; it made my face look much younger.

Diego had stayed behind to lean out over the walls and take pictures of the port from above. Gojko glanced at him over my head.

"Has he been making you suffer?"

He said this with a deep and threatening expression in his eyes, a Balkan man full of ancient honor.

"No. It has nothing to do with him."

"There's plenty of time," he said, and didn't ask more.

He turned and shouted to Diego. "Hey, artist, take a picture of me with your wife!"

I still have the photo. Gojko is wearing his boastful martyr face. I'm in that Croatian hat, my skinny legs sticking out of my shorts. I don't have a face because Pietro dropped some oil on the photo when he was little.

We sat with a bottle of wine and a plate of little black olives beneath a hibiscus trellis at a tavern behind the Stradun. We had a contest to see who could spit the pits the farthest. Diego won. He always won. His thin cheeks were surprisingly powerful.

Gojko asked Diego for one of his shoes. Diego laughed and tossed him one of his flip-flops. Gojko studied it for some time with a disgusted expression on his face before handing it back. Then he bent triumphantly over his own feet and took off one of his loafers so he could show us the name Dior on the inside. We nodded, amazed. Gojko lit a cigarette and smoked it beneath his dark glasses.

"Where did you steal them?"

He said he wouldn't let us provoke him; he preferred to offer us another round of drinks.

The sun had moved. The turquoise-blue sea was motionless below us. We were almost drunk.

Gojko wore his shoe half on with the back squashed down. Maybe it was tight and hard to get back onto his sweaty foot. There were two military tanks down by the port.

"What are they doing here?"

"They belong to the Armija. Every once in a while they send them out to do a patrol." He watched the sea through his American sunglasses. There had been problems in Krajina, people killed at Borovo Selo. One of the fourteen cadavers was returned without eyes, another without a hand. Diego asked about it.

Gojko smiled. "Disputes between neighbors. Nonsense."

He pulled out a gadget he appeared to be very proud of, a half-naked rubber woman with a clip in place of her head. You could put whatever head you wanted on it.

He rummaged through his pockets and pulled out a passport-sized photo that he put into the clip. I recognized it. It was the photo from my press credentials during the Olympics.

He set the sexy doll with my head on the table.

"You were with me all winter long."

Diego punched him.

The island of Korčula was covered with vineyards all the way down to its crooked coastal inlets. We stayed in a little Venetian-style inn with just a few rooms. We never went back for lunch. We walked through the light-colored rocks and bushes of the scrubland on the cliffs to a little beach that quickly became ours. We stayed in the water all day long. I studied the bottom for hours, the little fish that swam near my body in the sea as clear as glass. The rocks on the beach changed color with every hour of the day, attracting the light and seeming to arrange and rearrange themselves continuously in a secret order known only to them. Early in the morning it was like walking on an immense brooding ground of little eggs about to hatch. At sunset the rocks took on the vibrant blue of the sea and looked like the backs of moving insects. At night the white moonlight made the rocks evanescent; they took on the metallic reflection of dying coals.

Gojko had found an inner tube at a mechanic's shop. He idled in the water, his elbows resting on the black rubber, and read a book. Every so often he'd stop reading to sing at the top of his voice. "*Kakvo je vrijeme . . . Vrijeme je lijepo . . . sunce sija . . .*"

There was a huge peeling spot on his forehead. He stuck wet pieces of newspaper on it for protection. When he grew tired of his watery post, he'd walk bare-chested beneath the sun to a distant drink stand. He would return bathed in sweat and bearing cold beers and fish kebabs for us all. Diego photographed salty puddles that looked like faces, funeral masks of ancient warriors. He was thirty-one. He'd improved with time. His face was ascetic and carnal at the same time. He had that dimpled chin, like a child's, and a touch of melancholy in his deep-set eyes. I was thirty-six. My body was still young, but my thinness did not suit my face and the sun accentuated all my little expression lines. I preferred the dim light of our hotel room to the harsh fluorescent light in the bathroom, and sat on the bed to put on my makeup, a sliver of face in the mirror in my compact. At night we dined in the little restaurants near the port—crustaceans, mussels *alla buzara* with garlic and toasted bread, the flavorful goat's-milk cheese of the islands and pitchers of local wine. I noticed girls passing back and forth in front of our table, seasonal waitresses, islanders infected with the tourists' euphoria. They glanced furtively at Diego. With the suntan, his face looked as if it had been sculpted in wood and then burnished. After all, there were three of us. Maybe it looked like I was Gojko's wife. I moved toward Diego and kissed him so as to send those little Croatian adventurers on their way.

I didn't know it that summer, but the war was already there. I didn't think about it. Gojko spent the whole day floating in his black rubber donut, scribbling poetry, selling trinkets. After dinner he'd disappear to go sweat against some random body. And yet, in retrospect, the war was already in his eyes, in his desire for extremes, his wish to snatch whatever he could. Maybe it was for our benefit, so that his two Italian dear hearts would enjoy the sea, the mussels, the wine. One last bottle before the shadows. I now know that Gojko's frenzy was the tarty, happy-go-lucky daughter of a dark foreboding.

"All the Serbs in Zagreb have become Chetniks and all the Croatians in Belgrade are Ustaše." He spit grape seeds into the sea. "Propaganda. Television. First the propaganda, then the history." He laughed as he told us about the leaders whose names we were hearing for the first time, a bunch of imbeciles, men who blow-dried their hair into puffs and plastered their faces with makeup before they appeared on TV. Milošević had taken to carrying around the mortal remains of Prince Lazar like a crazed undertaker and Tudjman wanted to change restaurant menus and road signs. It was impossible to talk seriously about it. Gojko would just laugh and draw a cartoon, Tudjman introducing his wife to a friend with a little bubble up above: SHE'S NOT A SERB, SHE'S NOT A JEW, SHE'S NOT A TURK, TOO BAD SHE'S A WOMAN. He wouldn't even buy the newspapers. "They all talk to themselves. All they have to do is fart for their own assholes to sing their praises." His sense of humor protected us. We felt safe at his side.

He was overly electrified. Sometimes his restlessness bothered me. He was like the sea, up and down with the tides, banging against the rocks, seething and whirling. Then, on certain nights, when the tide sucked the water away and the beach was laid bare, he was like one of the little crabs that scrambled over the cliffs like small children when their blankets fall off.

One night as we made our way back to the inn, I said without thinking, *You're stupid.* I was tired of hearing his booming heavy laughter in the deserted alleys.

Later, in the empty hotel lobby, a last glass of Travarica wine in his hand, he climbed with his Dior loafers into the depressing tile-covered fountain like something out of a Turkish bath and started to yell. "It's true. I'm stupid. Poets are stupid, like flies against a window. They bang against the invisible to snatch a bit of sky."

A German couple with two children who looked like angels checked into the room next to ours. We met them in the hall coming back from the sea in their sandals. The mother walked ahead of me on her swollen legs, which were tanned in splotches and crisscrossed by dark threadlike veins. She was a young woman already gone to seed, without the slightest hint of sensuality. The father had a beer belly and rock-climbing sandals. They smiled at us and I smiled at them and at those two marvelous children.

"When they grow up they'll be as ugly as their parents," I said, laughing, back in our room.

Diego looked at me, struck by my caustic remark. They were quiet neighbors and spoke in low voices when they were in the room. But now we had to put up with those miniature bathing suits hanging off the railing of the balcony next to ours. The wind blew away the little girl's blue-flowered suit. I stood and looked down at it in the silence of the courtyard as a cleaner passed through with a bag of trash.

I hear the sounds through the locked, white-painted door between our room and the room next door. It's late. The children are sleeping. Their mother rinsed their feet and then tucked them into bed. It's always late when we return to our room, and usually it's silent next door. But tonight the Germans want to unite their two graceless bodies. I hear the unmistakable sounds of sex. Something acidic climbs up out of my stomach to corrode my throat.

Tonight's fish *brodet* was too spicy. Nausea rises in my gullet. It's the food, the heavy wine, the awkward ugly bodies rubbing against each other next door. I feel disgust for all the sex in the world—thrusting, thrusting until death, the seeking out of holes. I picture the man's big naked belly and the woman's sex, huge and flabby like her legs and the rest of her body. I hear the squeaking old bedsprings. It's their vacation. They have deutschmarks. This is a good place for Germans to take a summer vacation. Will there be a war? Maybe yes, maybe no. It's June, the month of vacationing mothers and children, and tonight is a night for fucking, for putting the finishing touches on the wreck of a bed. The Germans ate their dinner, walked hand in hand over the polished stones, bought plastic windmills for the children. They were in a good mood when they got back to the hotel. They put the children to bed; the two little cherubs are sleeping with their blond ringlets pasted to their foreheads. They killed a few mosquitoes. Then they slid into bed. They're a seasoned couple. They know how to extract pleasure from each other noiselessly. I hear the minimum, the sounds of the bed and of their breathing, no shouts or obscene words. I want to get out of bed because it's hot, because I have an upset stomach, because Diego's sleeping through it all. Then I hear a sudden cry, like the cry of a seagull when it challenges the water and comes back to the surface with its head wet after having passed for a moment through the sheet of glass that is the sea.

It was one of the children. Now I hear sobs and the voice of the mother as she lovingly lows. That wreck of a woman is fucking no more. She freed herself from the beer belly's tool and got out of bed to bend over her little darling and reassure it with her warm breath like a cow's.

So that's how it is to make love when you have children. You leave the frenzy in a rush, dripping with juices, and bend over your child to console him, to help him through his nightmares. The German is a good mother. Now she's singing a lullaby. She's young, not particularly attractive, worn out like a middle-aged woman. She possesses no beauty but her child loves her all the same. She's like a shield of flesh, a tower of love. Her child thinks she's beautiful, buries its nose in her heavy scent of hair and sweaty skin and recognizes her womb odor and the ivory mud of birth.

It's dawn. I'm out on the balcony. It's no use trying to sleep. The air is still and fresh, an intense cobalt blue. Hatred strikes me, hesitant at first, then ever clearer, hatred for the whining child and for its mother and hatred for myself above all, which provides some consolation.

The next morning, Diego sits in his bathing suit eating a sweet crepe dripping with honey and cheese.

"I don't want to come to the beach," I say.

There's always a crisis in the middle of a vacation, a lull after the enthusiasm of the first few days. Diego smiles and says he's tired, too. He'll stay to keep me company.

"One of the German kids kept me up last night with its crying."

"We can change rooms."

"Yes. Let's."

I see the German woman in the corridor. She blushes when she sees me. Maybe she's worried about what I might have heard. As she moves past me I ask, "What was the matter with the child last night?"

She says the little girl woke up crying because she lost her bathing suit. She'd already cried about it on the beach. She must have remembered it in her sleep.

"It was old, but she liked it so much."

I think about the suit on the ground in the courtyard and the cleaner who picked it up and threw it in the big wastebasket. I wanted to yell down to him not to do it. I knew it had fallen off the Germans' balcony railing. Instead, full of bitterness, I let him do it, almost as if it made me happy to see him throw away the faded scrap of cloth.

In reality all three of us were a little sad, so we pretended to be happy. Immersing ourselves in nature gave us back to ourselves. The days passed and the sea drained my body. The salt wind restored my strength. Snakes reawakened beneath my peeling skin. Diego avoided swimming because the saltwater hurt his eyes. He preferred the cliffs. I trailed after him with my Croatian hat, the two of us barefoot beneath the burning sky as we climbed to the top. I could hear Diego breathing. His feet looked like prehensile webbed claws. Seabirds made their nests in the rocks and squatted over their mineral cradles. They studied the wind and then, all of a sudden, they lifted off and glided low to capture fish. Diego tried to catch the moment—a fish brushing against the surface of the water, the bird as it immersed its beak for the capture, the opening in the sea, the rapacious body as it risked drowning to challenge another element and the culmination, a moment-long struggle in a sliver of sky, the life of the bird, the death of the fish.

Diego takes my hand. It's a clear, brilliant day. There's something unreal about the things around us, like a shining copy of the real. The islands seem to be literally sitting atop the water.

"I'd like to live here. One day, we'll come here and leave everything behind."

It's such a clear day that we can see Italy beyond the design of the islands, a dark line on the horizon.

"We're so close."

Gojko keeps an eye on me. Despite his dark glasses I can feel his gaze as it lingers over me. I sink into long silences. I repeat the same gesture over and over again, gather up the grainy sand and let it slowly slide through the hourglass of my closed fist.

A group of island kids shows up around two, when the day's at its hottest. They come running out of the underbrush and race toward the sea like a bunch of little boars fleeing the maquis. Their bodies are frail, their swimsuits encrusted with salt.

One of them, the littlest, breaks away from the group every now and then. He walks toward us, then stops to crouch to the ground. He stays there, rocking ever so slightly on his folded legs. He looks like an egg.

He must want money like the kids down at the port who dive when the ferries come in from Dubrovnik. How old can he be? Seven, eight at most. His frizzy hair is covered in salt. It stands up in tufts like goat hair. Today it seems like he's come closer than usual. His eyes as he watches us are black and still like big shiny buttons. I doze off. When I wake he's still there. My legs are slightly open. He's looking at the triangle of my bikini bottom, the swelling between the pubic bones. I close my legs, adjust the cloth. Who is this child?

Now he's in the water up to his waist, immobile, studying the water around his body. I can't understand what he's doing. Then, all of a sudden, he sticks his hand in the water. He's trying to catch fish. Diego walks toward the rocks. The boy lifts his gaze from the water.

The other kids are too interested in Diego's camera. There are too many of them, they have too many hands. "Be careful," I tell Diego. "They might steal it from you, or throw a lens in the sand just to spite you." But he lets them touch it. He's not afraid, even though two of them are big, with thickset, aggressive bodies and clearly defined muscles. One of them has a red mark on his face, like a splash of sauce. The other one is the only member of the group to own a pair of flippers. They are black and yellow, identical to the pair a French tourist spent hours looking for on the day before his departure. The kid doesn't take them off his feet, but he doesn't swim. Instead, he walks on the pebbles like a ridiculous penguin.

Diego takes their picture in front of the rocks. They stand in bunches, posing and snickering. The smallest one doesn't even seem to be part of the group. No one pays him any attention. He's in the water still, immobile as a signpost. The rest of them cluster around Diego. I watch him as he crouches on the pebbles, his miserable disciples huddled around him. He's taking apart the lens, he's explaining something—in what language, I have no idea. Now the camera hangs from the neck of the boy with the red birthmark, who's taking pictures. Diego is laughing.

He turns toward me, his tanned face still full of that smile. He puts the camera away in its leather case.

"They wouldn't leave me alone."

"Did you get some good shots?"

"I don't know."

He never knows if his photos will be any good, if there will be anything to save, a single image worth dozens of spent rolls. While he works he doesn't see things clearly. Potential masterpieces turn out to be crap. The image he wants reveals itself from among the mistakes. Beauty crops up randomly, the way it always does in this world.

The next day, at sunset, the child comes back. Diego is taking in the last rays of sun. He likes it best at this time of day when it's red and meek like all things as they come to an end. He's taken off his sunglasses and his face is full of that marvelous light. He slithers silently, snakelike, to open the camera case, take out the camera and glue it to his eye.

The child is crouching down as usual, like an egg, his back to us. I didn't see him arrive. A few minutes ago he wasn't there. He came with this gentle light, out of the bushes like a lost goat. Diego moves toward him on all fours. The child is in the water, trying to catch a fish with his hands. He slides one hand in like a beak, like those hungry birds. Diego shoots. It's a split second. The child caught a fish. For a moment he held it. I see the picture, a seagull kid and a fish flying against the setting sun. Maybe this is the shot, the random beauty.

It lasted a split second. Right afterward the fish is gone and the child is gone and the sun is gone, too, leaving behind an opaque and uniform sky that looks like it could never have contained it.

I see Diego fall to the ground, exhausted, as he holds his Leica. I think there must be an angel who lands every so often because it feels sorry for us, for all the things that flee from our grasp, that won't stay in our eyes.

One day in the future, his eyes full of everything, Gojko will look at this shot and say, "Now I know what art is." His greasy gaze, stupid with intelligence, will cut through me. "It's God when he feels nostalgia for men."

Gojko isn't with us. He's been lying low for days. He only comes down to the sea in the afternoon. He says he has things to take care of in the old city and that the sun gives him a headache. He says he's working on a poem. Maybe he's tired of us. Maybe we're more boring than we used to be. His Dior loafers have turned into beach shoes, his white pants are dark in the front and full of stains. Our vacation is coming to an end.

We're back in touch with the world back home. Diego's talking with Duccio from the phone booth at the inn. He's already got two jobs lined up for next week. I've started packing. Point-blank, Gojko asks me, "Why don't you two have any children?"

The wind carries a noise, notes from a violin. Gojko rises and walks toward them. He comes back later, singing and swaying on his legs. He's had a few glasses of wine with his friends, a group of kids from the Sarajevo Music Academy. They're staying near the beach in what used to be a forest ranger barracks, a big crumbling gray house with a patio made of stones like the dark pebbles on the beach.

When the wind changes, the sounds of the instruments harmonizing among themselves float down to us. They're getting ready for a concert, Gojko tells us.

The child seeks us out, as if he'd got a whiff of our departure. He comes mixed in with the others and their racket. As usual he studies us from afar, from behind the shield of his wildness.

It's windy. Around two, Diego and I walk to the first shack that sells things to eat. We order Pag cheese and pickles. The plastic tent connected to the shack shakes, its sides rattle. The wind is rising. The sea is rising, too. High waves fall on the beach, tight as bales of hay.

We go back to get our things. Our towels have been blown onto the rocks. My Croatian hat blows away, too. We go.

We could just as well not have heard that cry, what with the deafening noise of the wind, like a herd of cattle in flight. The light-colored dirt rose up off the path and swirled around us. A few more meters and we'd have been past the ridge, looking down on the first houses of the village, the wild geranium bushes, the yellow walls of the fish market. A few more steps and we wouldn't have heard the cry, "Ante! Ante!"

We see the excited huddle of boys down below on the dull spit of the beach as they holler that name. In a flash Diego goes tumbling barefoot down the cliffs, eating up the trail we've just taken, the shortcuts with the falling rocks.

Now his heels are moving across the beach pebbles. Without stopping he throws off his backpack and the camera.

"Wait!"

When I get to the beach it's already late. Diego is a little bird head moving through the waves. The kids mill around me dumbstruck like stupid lost goats. I'm dumbstruck as well. The child isn't there. There's no egg rocking back and forth on its heels. I look for him, though I know I won't find him.

I grab the yellow and black flippers, though they're too big for my feet. I jump in the water and try to make my way like Diego past the wall of breaking waves. But it keeps chasing me back. I drink and choke and think as I choke that each of the three of us has taken a turn during this strange vacation at wanting to die.

Soaking and defeated, I look at the sea beyond the barricade of foam. Time passes. Time stands still. Around me the kids are gray in the face like spent candles. For a moment I think I see Diego riding above a wave and then diving through its crest. For a moment I think of those birds that glide over the water and risk their lives to catch a fish.

The musicians have come down from their gray house. The boy with the red birthmark ran to sound the alarm and now there's a knot of people on the beach. Gojko arrives with his zipper down and his shirt wide open. He must have been fucking one of those musicians who smell of salty anchovies and cheap makeup. His hair is mussed, his face gloomy like a tragic actor's.

He looks at the inlet, the rocks that rise up out of the sea where the pebbles of the beach come to an end. He climbs up and disappears behind the rocks.

He reappears a few minutes later, exhausted as a shipwreck victim. Diego's with him, holding the boy tight, one arm dangling. He moves forward with that little trophy of flesh. I run to join them.

Diego smiles at me despite his breathlessness. The current pushed them into the little cove beside the beach and they climbed up from there. Ante is white, stunned by the water. Diego rubs his back. Gojko pours a glass of rakija down his throat. The kids herd around us and study his shivering teeth that beat together like a hammer against a nail. They laugh at his wizened hands, soaked through with water, and his purple lips. It's as if he were a mutant fish caught in a net. Ante spits out some seawater, pulls himself to his feet and runs away into the maquis.

The kids touch their heads and gesture that there's something not quite right with Ante.

We go back to the hotel. It's cold this evening. The wind is gone but it's left behind a brisk air. We huddle in bed without even rinsing the salt from our bodies.

Ante no longer comes to the beach. The other kids tell us his mother punished him, that she whipped him with a piece of rope, the same one she uses to tie the goats to the shed at night. The sea is as calm as glass. The boy with the birthmark slaps at the water with the yellow and black flippers stolen from the French tourist. Diego lies facedown, his eyes toward the maquis, toward the cliffs. Every so often Ante peers out at the sea from the underbrush and studies the beach without daring to go beyond the vegetation. The others yell that they see him, blow raspberries, throw rocks.

Diego gets up and moves away with the camera around his neck. He goes to see whether or not the seagull eggs have hatched and to take the last pictures from up above.

First I let him go, but then I decide to follow. I scratch my legs on the

bushes as I try to catch up. He moves quickly, as if he were following someone. He passes the musicians' house. Their instruments lie beneath the big
mulberry tree that looks as if it were sleeping, worn out from the heat and
from the weight of its branches. I pause. I see Gojko through a window, his
arm resting on the naked back of a woman. Then I see them, Diego and Ante.
The child has let Diego come close. Diego is taking his picture.

I follow them to the place at the top where the maquis thins out on the
edge of a precipice. There's a worn, thin woman sitting in front of a stone
house. Her pale eyes, sunk deep into her bones, are lifeless as a blind man's.
She looks at Diego and bows slightly. I watch them go into the house.

That night we drink a bottle of Lombarda and eat some cheese on the balcony. We're tired of restaurants. I tell Diego the child resembles him. Maybe
it's his legs, the way he takes flight.

The next day I buy two T-shirts and a pair of gym shoes for Ante and bring
them up to his mother. She's nursing an infant on her saggy breast like a sick
cow's. She explains through gestures that the baby is not well. The milk sticks
in her throat. I return with a bag full of food and then I leave all the money I
have under a beer bottle. She smiles a mournful smile, an ungrateful grimace
like a stray dog's, the kind that growls at you after you've given it something
to eat. She doesn't speak Italian but she understands when I speak it. She's a
refugee from Krajina. She's returned here because it's where she was born.
She has this hovel here and her mother, too, the old woman dressed in black
we've met many times on the cliffs, a goat herder with a stern face and an
acrid smell of alcohol rising off her clothes.

Today Ante takes Diego's hand. His mother lets us bring him back to the
beach with us.

"Thank you," the boy said after the woman slapped him to make him
speak.

It was the first time we'd heard his voice. It was like the hoarse whisper
of a seagull.

He's ours now. He'll stay with us for the rest of our time here. Diego
takes him by the hand and puts the camera around his neck. At lunchtime
I buy skewers of grilled calamari and we eat them on the beach. The child is

hungry. He talks a lot now. He's never quiet. His voice darts and soars until he's breathless. The miserable tissue of his face wrinkles with gratitude when he laughs. We don't understand everything he says, but it's clear he's happy. Now he teaches Diego to catch fish with his bare hands. They plant themselves in the water like two signposts. Yes, the child resembles Diego. I've thought it from the start, when I saw that closed little body like an egg rocking on the beach.

Gojko sees us with the child when we bring him back to the stone house. We pass before the mulberry tree and the forest ranger barracks. The musicians are rehearsing. A flute is tuning itself to a violin. Gojko introduces us to his summer girlfriend.

"This is Ana."

Her black hair is cut jaggedly around her round face. She has the white skin of someone who never goes out in the sun.

Gojko looks at the child and shrugs his shoulders. He knows he belongs to that dull-witted woman and wonders why he's always with us.

Then one night I answer his question. We're sitting in the last rays of the sun on the wide steps in front of a church. Diego has just stepped into the travel agency across the square because we've decided to stay a few days longer. The client's press office in Rome has complained about the delay. Duccio yelled at Diego. We stopped calling.

"I'm sterile, Gojko. I can't have children."

He's wounded. He's always got something to say, but now he just looks around with a hurt expression on his face. He tightens his mouth and squashes his nose with his thumb. He pulls out a crumpled bit of paper and reads me a few lines of his poetry.

> *. . . and life laughs at us*
> *like a toothless old whore*
> *while we fuck her with our eyes shut*
> *dreaming of the ass of a lily*

His eyes are stupid and still.

"We're a luckless generation, Gemma."

He shakes me, pulls me tight. I sit there holding his hand and study his thin nails in his puffy fingers.

"We've really become fond of that child." My tears flood his shirt. "Help me. Talk to his mother. Find a local lawyer, anyone. Maybe we can adopt him, take him into our care. We can give his mother some money."

Diego comes back with the changed tickets and a smile. He finds me there with that miserable face. I stand.

"I told him."

The three of us embrace in the middle of the white square.

And so Gojko went to speak to the mother. He climbed up to the house bearing a bottle of kruškovača, sat beneath the plastic awning, breathed in the stink of goat. The mother produced her usual grimace and said she'd think about it.

"What did you tell her?"

We rented a boat that day so we could go to the island of Mljet. We crossed the salt lake to the Benedictine monastery. Ante was with us. Diego carried him on his shoulders. They really looked like father and son. Gojko and I walked a few steps behind.

"I told her the truth, that you can't have children, that you'll take care of the boy, that he'll have a chance to study."

"Did you tell her we can give her money?"

He looked down and scratched his red hair. "Do you want to buy him?"

"I want to do whatever it takes."

He studied my hungry gaze. "Even the poor have a right to keep their children."

"That woman doesn't deserve that child. She doesn't love him. She hits him."

I ran toward Ante and pulled up his T-shirt to show Gojko the scabs that were beginning to fall off.

Gojko shook his head. "It's God's decision."

I said he was a damned Croatian hypocrite and told him to go to hell.

We went back the next day and the next. The woman smiled, accepted our gifts and shrugged.

"*Patre*," she said. It was the father's decision.

Thus began an endless series of phone calls from the booth in our hotel. The husband who'd stayed behind in Krajina was never there, just relatives. Ante came up to the room and rested between us in the bed. I'd started teaching him Italian and giving him showers in our tub.

They set up bumper cars in the dusty square beside the old pier. We spent an evening there until it was just the three of us bumping into each other and laughing. When Diego banged into him, Ante yelled *Belin!* just like a boy from the center of Genoa.

That night Ante cried when we said good night.

The next day we got hold of the father. Ante's mother summoned Gojko to the phone booth. I watched him through the window and saw him deflate entirely. He listened in silence and then spoke again.

When he came out he was exhausted. Ante went into the booth. His father wanted to speak to him.

He didn't say a single word. We saw him nod just once. When he came out his face looked different, broader. His big eyes turned toward us.

"*Moram ići za ocem,*" he said in his seagull voice.

Gojko translated. "I have to go with my father."

In September the child would return to Krajina, where his father was a soldier in the Croatian National Guard. The man refused to give up his son. He'd take the child with him into combat rather than leave him with his wretch of a wife.

Tearless, wordless, Ante bade us goodbye and offered us his little wrinkly hand.

"Is that God's decision?" I asked Gojko.

I gathered our rags together. We stretched out on the bed beside the closed suitcase. Tomorrow a new occupant would inhabit this room and chase away our scent. We went out and walked in the little streets of the center, winding our way down to the port. Gojko was sitting at a table at a restaurant beside the sea where his friends were playing a symphony by Haydn on a little stage.

"Haydn was strongly influenced by Croatian music," he whispered.

And who gives a shit? I thought.

His conquest, Ana, was the only one who didn't play an instrument. She turned the pages for the cello player, an old man with a long beard that curved upward at the end like a tongue. The wind moved the musicians' clothes and hair. The music flowed over the water. For a moment it almost seemed as if it might console us. In any case, we were already drunk. We'd downed the last bottle of Lombarda and the hell with everything. At a certain point I started to feel sick. I don't know exactly what I said. Diego touched my arm and I brushed him away. *Let me get it out of my system.*

There was an interlude. Ana, Gojko's brunette, sat with her face resting on her hand, watching me as if studying a view out a window. I looked at her red nail polish, those dancing red bits, and from the depths of the wine and my nausea, started telling her about my trials. In Rome I'd never spoken with anyone and now I was emptying myself to this stranger. Maybe it was her nail polish, like little fish floating toward me. She lit herself a cigarette.

She said something in patchy Italian. "You can get help from another woman."

She blew smoke rings as she told me about an Austrian woman who had a restaurant in Belgrade. She didn't have a uterus so she paid a woman from Kosovo to bear her child.

I watched Ana's little pointed mouth. It sat, red like her nails, in her wide face without cheekbones. I couldn't decide whether she was a good fairy or a witch. I moved away and threw up behind the cliffs.

Early the next morning found us at the pier in our sunglasses and clean T-shirts. Two tourists on their way back home. We got there early and sat drinking orange soda at the little dockside café. There was no sign of Ante. We were waiting for him, though we didn't have the courage to say so. We were restless. It felt like he might be hiding behind one of the pink walls, spying on us. We stayed on the pier until the last possible moment. Gojko came running, shirtless. We could hear his ruined Dior loafers as they slapped against the pavement. It was a strange leave-taking, and the verses he dedicated to us were strange as well.

Will the white thread of dawn
be enough to separate us from the night?
Will we see each other again?

We boarded the ferry. We leaned against the railing like two birds. Ante appeared as the boat pushed off. We saw him coming along the pier. He stopped because he didn't want to get too close to the sea—he didn't know how to swim. He wasn't much taller than one of the big iron mooring bits. He waved an arm, a single black arm that stayed in my sight.

When we could no longer see him, we went inside, where we were greeted by the boat odors of damp carpet and fuel, saltiness and rust. A television was on but there appeared to be no signal, just a confused screen and a noise.

Diego said he had to go to the bathroom. Later I found him behind a hanging lifeboat, closed in on himself like an egg, rocking back and forth on his heels. I looked at the sea and pictured myself taking Diego by the hand and jumping in over the foam. Who knows if we would have been able to find another life beneath all that water? *Fish*, I thought, *we're nothing but fish, gills that swell and close. Then along comes a seagull from above and it feels like we're flying. Maybe that's what love is.*

A rumble interrupted the silence. Instinctively I ducked and covered my ears with my hands. It was a group of military airplanes flying so low over the sea they made waves. They came very close; for a long moment it felt as if they might hit us. I saw the ashen faces of the sailors who stuck their heads out of the portholes. The planes had taken off from the base in Dubrovnik as other squadrons lifted off simultaneously from Spalato, Fiume, Pola. We learned this later, when the television at the bar started working again. Diego sat in an armchair with one leg resting on the chair in front of him and his sunglasses on. Sandal-clad tourists with fanny packs around their waists and cups of coffee in their hands crowded around the images as they flickered in and out of focus. The sailors were all there. Even the captain stood with his eyes glued to the screen and drained a beer right from the bottle.

"Who in the hell's driving this boat?" I asked Diego.

I managed to wring a smile out of him. He pulled me close.

We spoke in English with a Norwegian reporter who had filmed the tanks of the federal army planted all along the border. Then, naturally, he'd taken advantage of the opportunity to visit the islands. His hair was tied back in a blond ponytail. He blinked his eyes continuously and spoke too fast. He was skeptical, pessimistic. He had interviewed Milošević, who'd said repeatedly, *Wherever there's a Serbian tomb, that is Serbia.*

"Croatia is full of Serbian tombs," the Norwegian mumbled.

The military planes were gone. Diego looked out at the sea beyond the salt-encrusted window. A ray of light went right into his mouth.

Chapter 8

It happened so fast. On television we saw Zagreb and Zadar being bombed and then Dubrovnik, where we'd spent the day. Every so often I thought I recognized something—the wall I'd skirted in my flip-flops as I slurped a nauseating banana ice-cream pop. We sat on our new couch with the feeble quiet of Rome outside and an October that was, as always, generous with light. I bit my nails to the quick and remembered our vacation and the things we'd seen in Dubrovnik: the Pile Gate, the long pedestrian boulevard of the Plaça, Onofrio's Fountain, the clock tower, Orlando's Column.

Diego hadn't taken a single photo of the city, just bits of people in motion and café chairs. We saw those very chairs on the news.

That's how the war began for us, with those overturned chairs in the rubble of a café, the café where we'd been a few months before, where Gojko had pulled out that shapely doll and stuck my photograph in the clip in its neck. Now we telephoned him frequently. He reassured us. He had relatives in Zagreb who'd had to leave their house. "They're on vacation in Austria."

I don't know if it was pride or what, but it had become difficult for Gojko to talk about his country, which was exploding bit by bit like a pan of popcorn.

At work, too, I notice that no one wants to pay much attention to this war. After all, we're putting out a scientific magazine. Viola says, as she chooses a pastry at a café, "The Balkans. No one understands a fucking thing about the Balkans."

She bites her sandwich and says the bread is stale and the tuna's old; she should have gotten the one with spinach. "And no one gives a fuck. Rightly so."

"What do you mean, *rightly so*?"

"Come on. Who gives a shit?"

She's wearing her usual expression, annoyed and good-natured. She shrugs. Then she points to the sandwich press behind the counter and says they're burning my sandwich. She complains on my behalf.

"How's the baby?"

"He's in day care."

The real news is that we see the war on television every night. It's close to us, just a few miles away by sea, but it's far away as it hums on the TV screen.

It's November 18. I know because it's my father's birthday. We made a cake and said goodbye at the door the way he says goodbye lately, as if we might not see each other again. He may be a little depressed. Most mornings he comes by the house early. He rings the bell and says he's coming up with some mangoes. Lately he's mad about mangoes. He cleans them and slices them. The remains of the cake are on the table. Now, as I listen to the news I run my finger over the silvery paper and lick the bits I've gathered. I give Diego a fingerful as well. He presses the remote control.

The voice says, *The city of Vukovar has surrendered to the Serbian militia after a siege lasting eighty-six days.*

There's a clip of a man filmed from behind as he runs clutching a child. The cameraman follows his flight. The child has surrendered. His arms are limp like a rag doll's. Maybe he's been wounded, and the father is running to the hospital. I notice that a bit of the man's ass is hanging out of his pants. He isn't wearing a belt. Maybe he was sleeping and got dressed in a hurry. I look at that detail, his pants falling down and the hand doing its best to hold them up.

The image stays in my mind when we turn off the television and sit staring at the black screen that emanates a last bit of luminescence. The tragedy of this war, to my mind, is encapsulated in that image of a man trying to save his child and keep his ass covered at the same time.

We no longer talk about the child from Korčula. We came back home with our sorrow and then it went away, gently. But Ante is still with us. I believe that when you find a child in the world he stays with you no matter what happens. Some people lose their children and go on finding them every day, in photographs, in the wardrobe. That's how we continued finding Ante—in a painting at the modern art gallery, in a hare that stopped in front of our headlights and watched us for a long time as if it wanted to tell us something. In the nape of Diego's neck, because that's where he remains, like a love that had only just started. When I spy Diego sitting on the toilet for too long, his jeans around his ankles, his head leaning against the tiles as if he were sleeping, I ask him what he's thinking about.

He's thinking about the boy, about the bumper cars.

Winter marches on, dragging cold days. Exhaust fumes come out of cars to poison the air and attach themselves to the clothes hanging on the balconies of the houses that overlook the highway bypass, which I see on my daily route to work. Bundled up against the cold, I race along on my scooter. It's cold at work, too. I have a little personal heater and Post-its from my boss, most of them marked URGENT. I unstick the little bits of yellow paper and roll them up and play with them. How can an article on the magnetic effect of a new synthetic fiber that will revolutionize the way we do our household cleaning be urgent? The magazine has become nothing more than a catalogue of advertisements disguised as scientific information. This was supposed to be a temporary job, a few months and then on to something else, but instead I've been promoted to assignment editor. I get my coffee from the dispenser at the same time every day. As I wait for the liquid to flow into the little brown cup I think that it's unlikely I'll ever leave. I'm good at what I do—and quick. It's because I'm completely uninterested in my work, and that's just fine. Passion hobbles me and makes me awkward. I have a hard time living up to the things I hold most dear. I grow anxious and start scratching, as if my blood had suddenly begun to flow too quickly and burn beneath my skin. A few days ago I found the notes from my research thesis. The days when I thought I'd continue studying for the rest of my life seemed like ancient history. I thought of Andrić and the pathological solitude that made him disagreeable and paranoid. In the last interviews he gave, he seemed irritated with the questions and sick of his work, as if he'd revealed too much of himself and then regretted it. And I thought I'd understood something I'd never grasped before: it's possible, as one grows old, to become suddenly reluctant to give of oneself, unfeeling toward the world, because nothing has ever truly rewarded us.

"Who knows what it's like right now in Sarajevo?"

It's Diego who's speaking as he leans up against a balustrade at the Pincio.

We meet up at seven p.m., give each other a kiss and walk arm in arm to the wine bar where we've become regulars. It takes us in like a greasy belly. We eat a few pieces of toasted bread covered with spreads and drink little glasses of red wine. There's a bench, a window with a view onto the street. People rush along on the sidewalk. We watch them pass as if they were figures made of ash.

We rest our hands in each other's on the table and smile at the boy waiting on us. We don't bother talking about work. Diego doesn't want to. He doesn't bring home his rolls of film anymore. He has an assistant who does everything. And even when he does have time, he doesn't go out anymore with his camera around his neck to look for puddles. He stays in the apartment and falls asleep on the couch. The piano lid has been closed for months.

It's not that we're sad, exactly. We're like logs floating placidly downstream without giving a damn. We've become more indifferent. We hardly see anyone anymore. We come up with excuses. We like to be alone. We love each other more than ever after that strange vacation. It's a different love. I read recently in the newspaper about a couple who jumped off a highway overpass. The owner of one of those vans that sell sandwiches was the last to see them. They were calm, even happy. They ate roast pork sandwiches and drank a beer. There were clouds piling up behind the hills. The van owner said it looked like it would rain in the afternoon. The two of them glanced up at the sky and smiled. That rain would never get them. Diego and I sit in the wine bar in complete harmony, as if we had nothing left to lose, nothing to ask for. As if we were about to stand up and throw ourselves off an overpass.

Maybe this is love at its peak. Elation, like what a mountain climber feels when he's made it to the top and then doesn't know how to go anywhere else because the next place to go is the sky. We look out the window at the rarefied landscape, the world we left behind to begin our climb, the world that now seems so far away. We've managed to reach the peak, and we're alone.

Diego's hand is on the table. His wrist is white.

He's seen the herd of refugees, lines of human beings along the dirt roads, the desperate old man in front of a stable full of dead animals, the woman with a single earring in a lone ear, the forty blind children from Vukovar who don't see the war but feel it with their egg-white eyes. Maybe he'd like to be there, among those people, with his camera and his old hiking boots.

We set our feet to the asphalt, brushing against the walls as we go. The wine has descended to our legs and to our swaying, clasped hands. It's easier now to return to the collection of rooms and possessions that have spent the day on their own and bear the stench of silence.

We turn on the television. We wait for the late-night news, which gives more time to each story. They wait for children to be safe in bed before they show the bluish useless corpses and the men pressing triggers and loading mortars and destroying the work of other men. What kind of thrill can it bring to cause things that it took centuries to build to collapse in moments, to disperse all traces of human goodwill? That's war, the reduction of everything to the same nothing, a public toilet and a convent in the same heap of rubble, a dead man next to a dead cat.

Every so often the reporter falls silent, the cameraman keeps filming and we hear the voice of war. It's a recognizable sound, like the clinking of dishes in the sink, a silence broken here and there, a fabric cut by an agitated tailor. The footsteps of someone running away. Deaf rocks sinking into the mud. A burst of gunshot, not even all that bad, like a necklace breaking. Then the hard report of a mortar. The camera shakes. A splash dirties the lens, then the sound of voices talking, like kids in front of a school. A head sticks up out of a burnt car, small and lively like a chick that's just broken through its shell.

In the meantime we move about the apartment, do our things. I put on face cream. Diego opens the windows and looks out at the street, the orderly nighttime traffic, the opalescent trails of red and white lights.

It's easier to get through at night. We dial the area code and then the number and wait through the emptiness, through the leap that goes from nation to nation across kilometers of earth and sea, but our call doesn't go through. When the call is dropped it's as if an elastic has broken and bounced back on us. We try again and again until finally we hear a faint, distant ringing sound at the other end. We envision it as a fuse running through the cables as they cut across forests and plains full of poplars and fields of sunflowers and then glide alongside rivers that hurtle over the rocks of mountains named Zelengora, Visočica, Bjelašnica. Finally, the fuse crosses the city of Sarajevo and reaches the pinkish building where the gray, government-issue telephone sits in its place on the sideboard with inlaid mirror glass, beneath the portrait of Tito.

When Gojko answers, his voice sounds so close it's as if he were in the phone booth on the street below our bathroom window. He yells to his mother to turn down the TV. It's Diego who speaks with him, holding the receiver. I stand beside him, my head glued to his. Diego wants to know how they are, if there's anything they need. Gojko says he wouldn't mind a case of Brunello di Montalcino.

"I'm not kidding. Do you need something? I'll send it. I'll bring it."

"Don't worry."

"How's your mother? How's Sebina? Maybe it would be best at least for her to leave."

"The war hasn't reached us."

"Will it?"

Gojko says it won't. No one will touch Sarajevo.

I grab a piece of Parmesan and a pear and bring them with me on a plate to Diego. That's how we eat now, wherever we are when one of us gets hungry, a mouthful for me, a mouthful for him. I put the food in his mouth.

There's too much stuff in this apartment. We should throw most of it away and keep only the couch or maybe just the piano and then sit leaning against the wall like we used to do a few years ago, when we were young.

Diego's naked. He's taking pictures of the television. At night he shoots the blue of the television screen, the war we see in the box. That's how he takes pictures of the dead of Vukovar, their waxen mouths lacerated by their last breaths.

The apartment is bright around him, our knickknacks and light-colored curtains and car keys, a normalcy drenched in butter and unhappiness. Diego shoots, crouched on the ground. He's using his wide-angle lens. He shoots diagonally and captures the things in the margins. Afterward he'll print long oblique blue photographs like cinemascope images of the television floating in that varnished nocturnal space, black stuff all around and only the blue light, the blue that illuminates death.

"Come on. Come to bed." His ass is skinny, like a dog's.

We make love. His body is a cloak of skin and bones.

He sweats, collapses beside me, coughs a dark short cough.

He smiles at me, his childlike face creasing into bunches of wrinkles.

He goes back to watch television. A car commercial. Then a girl who's been hung. She's wearing a red sweater. Her legs dangle open. She's thickset like the cows in her stable.

It happens at the hairstylist's, in that hot bubble of hair dryers and the good smells of shampoos and dye. I like going there, like resting my head on the sink coming up out of the wood floor. The girl rubs away the city grime and the dirt of my thoughts and for a moment it seems like maybe everything will go down that drain behind my back. I lift my head. They wrap my wet hair in a little black towel and I walk toward the mirrors in this big salon that's like a New York loft in the center of Rome. Here there are no down-market ads for conditioner and hairstyles, just big grayish paintings, fleeting sea scenes that speak to a better future when normal people will have perished and only the stylists will be left.

I wait for Vanni, the man in charge of this refuge for hair damaged by smog and other little afflictions. It's lunchtime. There's a bit of a crowd, rich hens under the helmets, lawyers and accountants and monumental whores waiting for some politician. Parliament is just around the corner. A boy dressed in black presents me with a pile of magazines. "Would you like something to read?"

I have a book with me, but I don't feel like concentrating. I feel like floating in this limbo, this glamorous aquarium. I leaf through ads for clothes and lipstick, an article on hymen reconstruction, bra ads, a story about a trip through London flea markets, letters from women who have been disappointed by men. I stop. There's a photograph of a woman with a baby in her arms. The headline says, in red, "The Stork Comes from Afar."

I read the interview with this Frenchwoman who became sterile after being treated for cancer. Her sister donated an egg that was fertilized in vitro and then implanted in the uterus of a third woman, a Hungarian girl—the *stork* in the headline. The technical name for this is *surrogate motherhood*.

Vanni joins me and plants a hello kiss on my cheek. He's chewing gum. He's gay, stocky but athletic. He walks barefoot over the carpet of hair like a yacht owner on his boat. He raises strands of my hair and looks at himself in the mirror as he looks at me. He holds his breath and starts cutting. He touches my hair like an artist with his medium. He rubs my head with his expert hand and the cut materializes.

"Do you like it?"

"I like it."

He glances at the magazine, grabs an ashtray and stands beside me smoking and chewing gum. We talk about the article. He says, "Even the Madonna, when you think about it, loaned her uterus to God."

It's raining. I watch a drop that's bigger than the rest as it slides down the window. A long, watery laceration cuts the night in two. The sound of my breathing is like the rhythm of the earth; that drop is a prehistoric tear that divides our world from theirs.

This morning Dad brought mandarin oranges. Before he comes to our house he wanders through the market below, taking in the scent of things. *It's the good part of the city*, he says, *the last place where human beings still mingle. Everywhere else is solitude.* He has a dog now, a sort of Italian pointer with ragged hair, a good excuse to go out for a walk. Dad sets the brown paper bag on the table and the fresh smell wafts through the house. *Vitamins*, he says.

The three of us sit in the kitchen. We peel mandarins. Diego eats the peels, too. He likes them.

Our suitcases lie open on the floor. Diego made a perilous climb up the ladder and pulled his backpack out of the storage cabinet because he'd rather take it than some other bag. He tossed it down to the floor. When he picked it up he sniffed it and recognized the smell of voyages and nights spent in airports, of dreams and wounds.

It's my old skin, he said.

Dad's dog prowls around it and sniffs it, too.

"Your dog's not going to pee on our luggage, is he, Dad?"

"Come here, Bread. Sit."

"What kind of name is Bread?"

"I was eating a sandwich on the side of the road. I tossed him a piece of bread. That was it. He wouldn't leave my side." Dad pats the dog, who moves closer to him and stretches his neck out in a single smooth motion. The mandarins are finished. Dad looks at our suitcases. He hasn't taken his eyes off them since he got here. "What will the weather be like there? Rainy?"

As he speaks he's taking the full garbage bag from our garbage can.

"Come on, Dad, you don't have to bring out our garbage!"

"I don't mind."

"Come on!"

He's stronger than me, more stubborn. He holds the garbage bag with rage. "For Christ's sake! Let me do something!"

He insists on taking us to the airport the next morning. It would be quicker and easier to go by taxi. Instead we've got this man, my father, who wakes at dawn and waits for us in his car, too early, like an overzealous chauffeur. Over the intercom he says, "I'm here. Take your time."

He likes the dawn. He's so happy it's as if he were off on a fishing trip. He's shaved and even put on a tie, like a real chauffeur. He smells of aftershave and of the coffee he got at the café.

I sit behind the familiar gray nape of his neck just like when he used to bring me to school. It bothered me that I wasn't good at math. *Copy someone else. Sit near someone who will let you copy.* I'd blush at this advice, which seemed beneath my dignity. *You don't understand, Dad!* But the point was, he understood everything. *Learn what you enjoy learning, Gemma. Leave the rest to the others. Don't worry about it so much.*

He concentrates as he drives, paying attention to everything, and it's as if he wanted to send us a message to be careful. There's never a moment's hesitation. He knows exactly where to go, which ramp to take in order to leave us in front of the right entrance. It's as if he'd done a test run. He opens the trunk and runs inside to get a luggage cart. He doesn't draw out our farewell. He doesn't want to be a burden. This morning he wants to be a professional, the kind who brings his passengers to their destination and then heads off to other engagements. He doesn't have anything else to do but he pretends he does. He climbs back into the car and nods, his jaw tense in the mirror. He says just one word: *Call.*

Maybe he'll stop in Fiumicino to take a walk on the beach while he waits for lunchtime. He likes fried hake. I imagine him devouring a plateful. He'd get some wine, too, a chilled bottle, and drink it, bringing the color to his cheeks. He'd indulge all by himself. I know him. All his life he's tried to set a good example for me, though I've always been a bit obtuse. I'll only really understand what a privilege it is to have a father like him when he's gone, like flies and wind, like everything, always.

There are flies on the bread basket, one of those plastic baskets you get in restaurants at the beach. My father eats and drinks and enjoys the salt and the blue sea view. From where he's sitting he can see the planes take off and circle around before they find their route.

We're on one of those planes. He lifts his chin to accompany us with his eyes. Just a few minutes ago we were near him and normal-sized with our bodies and our smells, and now we're destinies up in the sky. My father watches the distance between nothing and everything, between that fart of white smoke in the middle of the clouds and his love down here, clutched in his aging heart.

"What are you thinking?" Diego asks as the wing of the plane follows the traces of the sun reflected in the window.

"Oh, nothing."

Daddy's on the wing.

There's something you're not telling me, isn't there, Gemma, honey?

What, Dad?

Don't tell me. It doesn't matter.

Chapter 9

We're in business class, with big seats, real-glass goblets and cloth napkins. I didn't want to fly coach, not on these run-down planes, didn't want to deal with cramped seats and harried flight attendants. I wanted to be able to stretch my legs. This isn't a pleasure trip. It's treatment. When you're sick, if you can afford it, you choose a private clinic, a room to yourself, a nurse who behaves like a hotel maid, curtains to keep the world at bay. I thought the plane would be empty. Who wants to fly over a war? But the plane's full of men bound for clubs full of opalescent lights and butter-white girls who have just started to dirty themselves. It's the beginning of the fire sale; it's a huge draw to be among the first to grab at purity. These men will return to Rome with jars of caviar and an icon or two. There are Russians, too, headed home, like the two men sitting next to us with their hard black briefcases, which they did not put in the overhead compartment but prefer to hold beneath their seats where they can be supervised by their feet in their shiny black shoes, Italian shoes for two businessmen from the former Soviet Union. What were they trying to sell? Pieces of their crumbling country—oil pipelines, buildings, mines, nuclear warheads? For a moment I imagine that their briefcases contain pens that can kill and vials of cyanide, like the spies who came in from the cold in American movies. But the Cold War has melted along with all the rest. At most they're probably carrying a few pieces of Parmesan.

The curtain that separates us from economy class is closed now. The Russians have drunk glass after glass of champagne with no change to their facial expressions or tones of voice.

The attendant who is looking after us has a plump face and a short nose. Her cap is perched precariously upon her teased hair. It looks like a little boat riding the waves. There's something charming about the way she pours our drinks and gracefully extends her chubby arm without spilling a drop.

More, please.

I've been looking forward to this for a long time but now it's no longer clear to me why. I moved mountains to get on this plane, and now I'm thinking that if someone—a madman, a hijacker—opened the door, I'd jump out, too, into the powdery white of the clouds and the cold of this altitude.

It was a sudden decision. I bought the tickets and made sure our passports were still valid. Let's go see, try to figure it out. It can't hurt.

I did it out of love. That's what the woman said in the article I read at the hairstylist's. *I helped a woman like myself. I wasn't an incubator. I was the stork.* I sip my champagne. *More, please.* In the sogginess of drink and altitude, I flagellate myself a bit. If it's something a woman does out of love, then why are we going to an impoverished, disintegrating country? The Italians across the aisle talk in loud voices. What makes me any different from those whoremongers? I'm looking for a woman, too, for a womb, and I have to make this trip to find one because it's illegal back home.

"Listen." Diego puts one of his earphones over my ear. It's R.E.M. Together we listen to a bit of "Losing My Religion."

That's me in the corner . . . that's me in the spotlight.

"Don't worry."

Then he falls asleep. I look at his hand. What is a hand? Who decided what form it should take?

A woman stands up and gets a bag from the overhead compartment. Thanks to a bit of turbulence she almost falls on me. "Excuse me."

She has a pleasant face. Her husband is sleeping, too. A skull with a few gray hairs, his mouth open against the pillow they gave out at the start of the flight.

They're sitting in the row behind us. After a while she touches my shoulder. "Are you scared of flying, too?"

"No, I'm afraid of the land."

"Pardon?"

What the hell am I saying? I don't know. It must be the champagne. I correct myself. "I'm scared of landing."

She's a talker. "I'm not scared of landing because you can already see the houses."

She moves to an empty seat in the row next to ours. She's neither old nor young. She has a nice smile. She opens her bag and pulls something out, first some lip balm, *Have you noticed how your lips dry out when you're flying?* Next comes a box, which she opens to reveal a pair of little red sneakers with a pink border. She pulls them out.

"Do you like them?"

I nod.

"My husband got them in New York. He has to go there a lot for work." She rubs the shoes affectionately, raises them to her nose, smells them. "Look. There's a surprise!" She smiles.

I wonder if maybe there's something wrong with her. Maybe she's a pill popper.

"They light up. See?"

She sticks her hands in the shoes, bends over and moves her hands to simulate footsteps on the floor. It's true. Little lights flicker through the transparent rubber sole.

"They don't have them yet in Italy."

"Are they for your daughter?"

She smells the shoes for a while before answering. "She isn't a daughter yet."

It's the opening she's been waiting for. She's one of those people who look around when they're traveling for a funnel to pour their voice into. Now she's found me. Her husband is sleeping. He must sink his head into the pillow like that out of self-defense. I'm treated to the entire story. For two summers in a row, she and her husband have hosted a little girl from Chernobyl, an orphan, one of those children who come to get rid of the radiation. She and her husband have donated a refrigerator and a projector to the orphanage and befriended the woman who runs it. Now they're going to visit the girl, Annuška. The shoes are a present for her. The woman and her husband are too old to adopt Annuška, but they hope they can take her as a foster child.

"Our lawyer has spoken with a Ukrainian lawyer." She gestures—thumb sliding back and forth beneath index and middle finger—that it's a matter of money. "With money you can do anything in Ukraine."

Annuška is seven years old and at their age they can only adopt a child who's nine or older. She brandishes two fingers like little knives and her voice becomes a plaintive whisper. "Two years. What can two years matter?"

She moves the shoes again and shakes her head with a nervous gesture, as if she were brushing off a recurrent thought. It's a gesture I recognize. There's a code known to every woman who's desired motherhood in vain.

"Two years. I even tried to falsify my documents. I'm not ashamed to say so. They force you to break the law."

I ask for more champagne and wonder in the meantime if I've met the woman I will become, wonder whether life is what it seems or a series of luminous signs, like these fucking shoes and the little light over the exit.

The woman goes on and on. "When Annuška first came she'd never seen an armoire. She was so scared she hid under the bed. We took it apart and had her fold her clothes and put them on a chair because that's what she was used to. This summer she wanted the armoire. We got it out of the cellar and put it back together again. My husband was sweating like a pig. I thought he was going to collapse. It was the most beautiful day of our lives. Annuška was laughing. She wasn't scared anymore. She kept getting into the armoire and knocking on the door for us to open it and set her free."

The woman bends over and once again moves those shoes over the carpet so that the little soles light up. For a moment it feels like I know Annuška. I can see her running in her American shoes. She won't get lost at night. I remember the day I went with Diego when he took pictures of the children who'd just arrived from Chernobyl at that summer camp. They seemed phosphorescent.

"What about you?" the woman asks.

I touch the armrest, the black hole left by a cigarette.

"Do you have children?"

I stick my finger in that old hole.

"Not yet."

She smiles, sighs. "You're still young. You have time."

Diego's opened his eyes. He checks the time and stretches.

"Your husband looks like a kid."

Diego smiles.

I hear the woman say, "And where are you headed?"

He answers over the nape of my neck.

"We're on vacation." He thinks a moment, then smiles. "To the Black Sea."

We meet Oksana, our interpreter, at the Kiev airport. She's tall and thin. She's waiting stiffly in the crowd of people in the arrivals hall, a sign with our neatly printed surname clutched in her hand. She has a serious expression and the solemn posture of a soldier. She relaxes when we approach her. We shake hands. She smiles a faint smile and nods, almost bows. Her hair is tied back in a ponytail. She's wearing a light blue coat with short sleeves above her bare wrists. A cloth bag hangs from her shoulder. She asks about our trip. She speaks Italian well, with a slightly humorous accent. We follow her ponytail amid a shifting anaconda of shabby-looking people who don't seem to be about to board a plane; they look as if they were here to take advantage of the heat coming out of the radiators. I ask Oksana about the abandoned packages beside the exit.

"Mail."

"Aren't they going to deliver it?"

"Sooner or later."

A mustached man leans out of an old Fiat van, puts it into reverse, opens the door and takes our bags. We sit among all those empty seats. Oksana opens the glass window that separates us from the driver and says something in a low voice. Then she takes a seat facing us.

"Do you have dollars?"

"Yes."

"Dollars are okay."

"What about lire?"

She smiles. She doesn't want to offend us. "Dollars are better."

She watches us, awaiting further questions. She has the rigid grace of a classical dancer.

"How far do we have to go?"

"A little more than a hundred kilometers."

All I ask her is when we can see the doctor.

"Today."

I look at Diego. "Let's leave our stuff at the hotel and go right away."

"Okay."

He's also looking at Oksana, her serious face as she leans toward us, her high clear brow. Vans, tractors, buses brush past us on a road that cuts across albino fields and then endless plains of still-green ears of something.

"Is that wheat?"

"Yes. Chechnya is our oil, Ukraine our wheat." She smiles. "That's what Stalin used to say."

Diego asks about Gorbachev and the aftermath. She shakes her head.

"A mess. A real mess."

Diego says it's normal for a transition like that to take a long time. "It could take twenty years."

Oksana nods. Her head bobs on the pedestal of her neck. "Twenty years. Like me."

"You're only twenty years old?"

She nods. I'd have said thirty, maybe because she's so thin, so serious.

For a while now we've been looking out at dilapidated factories rather than fields. The city seems to have no center, only outskirts. Oksana gets out before us and accompanies us into the hotel, where she talks to the concierge.

The walls in the room are papered in shiny sky-blue satin that's stiff as plastic. It's all the same, the curtains, the upholstery on the head of the bed. We drop off our luggage, wash our hands and race out the door.

The clinic, a massive and spare construction in perfect Soviet style, was a few blocks from the hotel. We took the escalator to the second floor, where we spent some time in a waiting room with white linoleum on the floor. There were a few certificates on the walls as well as two big laminated posters like something from a medical school classroom. They showed the male and female reproductive systems with the pink sacks of the scrotum and the ovaries, the seminal tubes, the fallopian tubes and an infinity of red and blue filaments, the veins and arteries. I looked at the immense cross-section of a penis, soft as an abandoned proboscis, and the orange vagina that looked like the inside of a mussel. Sadness rose from my stomach to the nape of my neck. I glanced at Diego. He was smiling to himself with a stupid expression.

A woman with a white lab jacket stretched tight over her stocky figure called our name. The doctor's desk with its green glass top was too large for the otherwise modest room. Behind him there were two flounced curtains and various framed honors.

He stood, shook hands with us and gestured for us to sit. "Please," he said, in Italian.

Oksana sat beside me and translated as Dr. Tymošenko apologized for not speaking Italian. He knew only a few words but was planning on learning more because he had begun to see lots of Italian clients. "Our country is a pioneer . . . in this field."

Oksana translated without hesitation, her face inscrutable. I had the impression she knew by heart the doctor's little speech, which continued on in this vein. On the walls to either side of us hung images of smiling children in the arms of smiling mothers. They must have organized the whole thing into a set series of stages, like a visit to a spa where you'd have cold treatments, then warm stones and then oil. First the depressing waiting area with those listless reproductive organs, then this reassuring room with its happy mothers and embroidered curtains like something out of an alpine hut. I was tense, waiting for some hidden trick.

Dr. Tymošenko's white lab jacket was clean but grayish. He had Mongol cheekbones and salt-and-pepper hair slicked back with gel. He told us we could smoke if we liked.

"We don't smoke."

He lit a cigarette and waited.

I did the talking. I told our story. Occasionally, Oksana put a hand on my arm to signal that I should pause for her to translate. I watched her and tried to understand whether or not she was good at her job. I gestured brusquely to Diego to give me our medical files, the enormous pile of sonograms, tests, money thrown to the four winds. I showed the doctor the picture of my uterus and the rest.

"Deformed uterus," I said.

I waited while Oksana translated the words. The doctor opened the file, looked at a sonogram, nodded. He twisted his mouth. One of the windows overlooked a playing field with an old basketball hoop that no longer had a net. I looked at that empty metal eye and cried.

The doctor waited calmly. He must have been accustomed to this, too. My sobs were hard as rocks.

I stood and went to the window. Diego joined me, and we hugged behind those two people we did not know. I looked at the playing field and the line of identical flat-topped houses visible in the distance. They looked like abandoned seaside cabanas.

I sat back down. I was calm. The mud had moved on like a kidney stone, which hurts terribly when it's passing but then, when it's really over, simply leaves you a little tired. An enormous woman came in with a steaming samovar. We drank tea. We discovered that the doctor spoke French, and so for a while we talked without Oksana's help. Then he went back to Russian. He opened a drawer and pulled out some sheets of paper.

Now I was clear-minded and alert.

He drew three circles, A, B and C. Above the circles he made a triangle with an X. He pointed with his pencil to the X.

"This is your husband." He looked at Diego and smiled.

Mother A was the donor whose egg would be fertilized with X's seminal fluid and inserted into the womb of surrogate mother B. He made a new pencil line to connect one circle to the next until finally he got to me, circle C.

Too many circles, I thought. *Too many mothers.*

"I'd rather there be just one woman."

He said there was no problem; it was also possible to do everything with a single woman. But it was more expensive.

"The surrogate mother of a child who does not belong to her genetically has no rights. The natural mother, on the other hand . . ."

I knew it was riskier, but I wanted to see the face of the woman, smile at her, establish a relationship.

Oksana translated but my eyes were on the doctor, his big hands, his mouth as he spoke, his small deep blue eyes. I was wondering if I could trust him, if he bore some sign of goodness.

We followed him on a brief tour of the clinic. We stepped into a room with a bed, an iron cupboard, a shelf full of ampoules and medicines, one bucket full of cotton wool, another full of specula. I saw an old plastic container with a handle. Maybe that was where they put the ova, the seminal liquid. It looked like an old-fashioned beach cooler.

The doctor sat on the bed and with nonchalance began talking about money. He wanted to be paid in foreign currency, either dollars or deutschmarks. There would be no other fees, nothing for the surrogate mother's upkeep during the pregnancy, nothing for the local lawyer. They would take care of everything.

"And if the mother changes her mind?"

Oksana translated. "They don't change their minds. These women offer to do this because they want to."

For a long moment I had the impression that there was not one ounce of truth either in the man's gaze or in any of the words he had pronounced.

We walked back to the hotel. It was raining. Oksana insisted on covering our heads with her umbrella as she followed us. We told her she could go ahead, that we'd be fine on our own. Instead, we got lost. All the street signs were in Cyrillic and no one spoke a word of any language we knew. Many of the stores were closed, with faded PRADUKTI signs and half-empty windows. We ducked into a bakery. There were a few loaves of bread on a wooden shelf, like rocks on a tomb. The few people on the streets turned to look at us.

Diego took pictures of the puddle reflection of an old woman sitting beneath a cement kiosk. She sat motionless without ever changing her expression as this boy knelt and took pictures of the dirty water at the end of the road. Then Diego stood, his knees all wet, and rummaged in his pockets for a ten-dollar bill. The old woman had a yellowish face that seemed to be made of some spongelike substance, dry and unhealthy. She threw herself to the ground to thank Diego. He tried to hold her back, to rein in her exaggerated reaction. He kissed her head through her headscarf.

We resumed our walk.

We found the hotel. It rose up out of the cement in the gloomy light of that rainy afternoon.

I took a shower beneath an onion-shaped showerhead that sent weak jets spurting to fall far from my body against the plastic shower curtain. The beds were small and separate. We moved them together. The noise of metal against the floor scraped inside our ears. The bedcovers were fitted tight around the beds like straitjackets. Diego didn't complain about the shower. He stood by the window taking pictures of the view, a long gray wall with a ring of barbed wire on top, like the wall around a barracks.

We went downstairs to eat. A singer in a red-sequined dress like a mermaid's outfit, her eyes swimming in green eye shadow, was singing for the diners, mostly single men and a few couples. Our waiter, with his swollen belly, big feet and black-and-white uniform, really looked like a penguin. We sat at a little table. They brought us a big menu with translations in French and English. We read through it and called the waiter over. It was farcical.

Every time we pointed to a dish, the penguin would shake his head and shrug his shoulders. *Nyet.*

They had borscht, so we ordered it. Then the man came back to our table and pulled a little container out from under his jacket, as if he wished not to be seen by the maître d'. It was caviar. The price was ten dollars, cash, to be paid to him. We bought it. The cash slid out of sight. Another payment brought a bottle of special vodka.

Now the maître d' smiled our way with a little bow whenever he passed our table on his way to other diners, women with teased hair dressed in miniskirts and pointy-toed boots, men in shiny jackets. They brought the caviar with blini and sour cream, and it was delicious. Diego had a little black egg on his nose. I smiled, leaned toward him and cleaned it off with a finger. He looked down my silk shirt like a boyfriend and for a while we felt like a couple on vacation. After we'd finished eating we stayed on our padded benches. Diego raised his glass of vodka to the singer and she sang us a song. *Volare, oh oh oh oh.* We laughed and applauded.

Back in the room we made love. The beds made an infernal racket. It was entirely sexual, a release. We didn't mind. At least we were alive.

"Even if nothing happens, who cares?" I sighed. "We took a trip. We made love."

Diego, at the window, points his lens at the dark.

"What are you taking pictures of?"

"A light."

It must be the big spotlight on the barracks across the way.

The next morning we went down to the breakfast room. We found two big containers of boiling water, some eggs and some sweets, along with a lingering, stale kitchen smell of meat left soaking in its broth. Oksana joined us there, the same elastic holding back her hair, the same pallor. We put a cup of tea into her pink hands. She said the doctor was trying to find the right person for us and that we'd hear from him in the afternoon.

We took a walk. Diego photographed an old wooden church and a statue of the Cossacks next to an eternal blue methane gas flame. Even in the center of the city there was a strange silence and an overwhelming impression of absolute misery.

Oksana came back in the afternoon. A taxi, a prune-colored Škoda without bumpers, took us to the clinic. The doctor had found a woman who might work out.

"Who is she?" I asked.

Oksana was sitting next to the driver. She turned toward us and said that the woman was trustworthy. "She's done it before."

I thought about the woman who was waiting for me somewhere, a woman who gave away her children for money. *A professional*, I forced myself to think. *What could be better than a professional?* I looked at Diego's hand on the seat. It was closed into a fist. It was immobile and anything but serene, the skin taut as if he were clutching a nail.

Before we left, Diego and I had discussed the moral boundaries of our journey. Diego said, *The only law is the law dictated by our conscience. The important thing is to stay true to ourselves. Otherwise we'll come back home and that will be the end of it.*

I had dragged him into this adventure after a night of tears and desperation. Now, I was irritated by his serious face and his thoughtful gaze.

The woman sat facing away from us as we walked into the room. She did not move when the doctor came to greet us. I glanced at her without really seeing her. We sat down and only after a while, as the doctor spoke, did I study her carefully. I pulled her out of the context and secretly swallowed her up. I saw a hand, an ear, a short, masculine haircut. She was a simple woman, dressed humbly but with dignity. She had a long, thin face and a well-proportioned nose. She was clutching a bag with a stiff, fake leather handle. I took in her bony ankles and her comfortable oxford shoes like a church lady's. She nodded as the doctor spoke. Oksana translated.

I smelled grass and ashes. I asked if she was from the city. It was the first question that came to mind.

She smiled in my direction and then faced Oksana as she answered. She lived in the country, about twenty kilometers away. We exchanged a few pleasantries. The fat lady came in with the samovar and served tea. The woman bent her face toward the cup as she drank, clearly worried about making noise and taking care not to dirty the saucer.

Then she stood and made a little bow. Oksana translated that she had to go because she didn't want to miss her bus back home. She held out her hand. It was so cold and meek that it seemed almost incorporeal.

"Thank you," I said.

Diego stood. He hadn't said a single word. She extended her hand to him, as well, and he bowed as if he owed her something.

The woman patted Diego's hand, a kind, brusque, comforting gesture like a mother to a son.

She left without a trace, carrying away her smell of ashes and her plastic purse.

"She's perfect," the doctor said. "She's a dependable woman and very reserved."

It was a brief and informal meeting. That was the procedure. We hadn't really talked about anything.

"There will be time for that," said the doctor. "You need to go back to the hotel and think about it overnight."

"How old is she?" I asked.

"Thirty-two."

"Does she have children of her own?"

"She has three."

"Does she have a husband?"

The doctor burst out laughing. "Of course she does!"

"How can we know for sure . . ." I couldn't bring myself to say it.

The doctor understood anyway. It was as if he were responding to a questionnaire he'd answered many times before.

Oksana's voice explained that after the insemination the woman would stay for a few days in the clinic, where the doctor would do tests to make sure that the fertilization had worked. Once it was certain, she would be sent home.

He smiled. "Your interests are our interests." He touched his head, the gel that imprisoned his hair, and said, in a sharper tone, "Our women are humble and generous. They see themselves as neutral creatures. They would never give away the children of their own husbands, rest assured."

We had less appetite for our caviar than the night before. We were distracted by an infinity of thoughts. Every so often a word would spill out of one of our mouths onto the table. The singer had the same red dress, the same velvety powder around her eyes, the same husky voice. I kept thinking about the meeting, about the woman. She was clean and unassuming, with a light down on her face and disorderly eyebrows. She clearly didn't use tweezers. She had shoes and hair like a nun's. The doctor was right. She was perfect. A few glasses of vodka slid down to make a nest deep inside our bodies.

"So? What are you thinking?"

"She seems like a decent person."

"So, she's the one . . ."

"Do you want to dance?"

We danced among the backs of clumsy men and women with robust buttocks and sickly sweet perfume. We danced, clutching each other, lost.

The doctor came to get us right after lunch. We climbed into a blue sedan with leather seats that smelled like whatever detergent had been used to clean them shortly before. The streets were almost too quiet, deserted even in residential areas, where we saw light-colored houses with Alpine roofs overlooking the endless plain. The radio was tuned to a news program punctuated by brief musical interludes. We gleaned that they were talking about the war and asked Oksana to translate for us. She turned to face us.

"They've signed a cease-fire agreement in Croatia."

The doctor laughed. "That's what they like best, to sign agreements they don't respect."

We drove by an area that was fenced in with spikes and barbed wire and stretched for hundreds of meters across the countryside. Inside we could see a semicircle of enormous warehouses. Diego asked what it was.

Oksana said, "They're . . ."

The doctor turned and said, in his clumsy French, "They're abandoned mines."

He turned onto a dirt road. The car moved slowly. We reached a country house in a little rural village. The earth around it was muddy from a recent rain. I saw a bed frame and a child's bike leaning up against a shed.

A stocky, dark-complexioned man wearing a red and brown argyle sweater came to greet us. He probably wasn't past forty, though he looked older. The woman was waiting for us inside. She greeted us and gestured for us to sit. She set on the table a tray with glasses and a bottle full of reddish liquid, cherry juice, and touched her chest to explain that she'd made it. We heard crying. She went out and came back with a small child in her arms. He must have been a year old at most. She gave him a spoon to play with and sat down. The husband was talking, moving his hands like knives on the table as if he were cutting something. He and the doctor were speaking in Russian and more than once I heard the word *dollars*. Oksana translated for Diego. "The first installment at the beginning of gestation, the second when she reaches the fifth month, the third upon delivery."

She had studied Italian by correspondence, and the terms she used were harsh and bureaucratic. She couldn't be aware of how much they hurt. Diego swallowed.

"Okay. That's fine."

The child was pale like his mother, and his eyes were the same dull brown as hers. He was wearing a felt outfit of a nondescript color. Now the mother was looking at me.

"I want to know if she is happy to do this, if she's doing it out of love. This is important for us."

Her husband responded in Russian in his nicotine-rusted voice.

Oksana translated. They were very happy. The woman was glad to help us.

He stood and gave us a tour of the house, a few tidy rooms all with the same wine-colored ceramic tiles, curtains at the windows, lace lampshades and a few heavy pieces of light-colored wooden furniture. The man opened the doors wide and we stuck our noses in. Everything was bleak, with the same smell, but clean.

I asked if I could spend some time alone with the woman. She was shy and elusive. Her overly invasive husband had kept a constant eye on us.

She brought me with her when she went to fetch wood. Outdoors it was much more disorderly. There were tools piled everywhere and heaps of construction materials. Oksana walked behind us. I asked the woman her name. We talked about the countryside and the still-bitter weather. She said she had studied for a while to become an engineer but then had to quit. She looked mostly at the ground but raised her eyes every so often to look at Oksana, who had to translate. The constant intermediary made me feel uncomfortable. It made the conversation less intimate.

"Listen, Tereza. I only want to know if this is your choice or if it's your husband who . . ."

She shook her head and repeated that she was happy to do it, that she would have done it without payment but that she needed the money so that her children could study. She said she liked being pregnant, that the hormones of life put her in a good mood.

"What will you tell your children afterwards?"

She laughed and I saw that she had two chipped teeth, right in front.

"They won't notice. I'm very thin, and I always dress this way." She gestured to the baggy dress that danced around her frame.

I asked the question I had to ask.

"And won't it be hard for you to give away the child?"

She was wearing a pair of rubber galoshes for the mud. It seemed like she didn't want to answer. I turned to Oksana. "Did she understand what I said?"

I had inadvertently spoken in an authoritarian tone, the voice we use when we speak to children and old people, to dependent creatures.

"No," Oksana said. "It's natural for her. She knows the child isn't hers."

Finally Tereza looked at me. "*Ja eto dom.*" I am the house.

She was bent over. The outline of her soft belly, ruined by pregnancies, was visible beneath her clothes. She stuck a hand into the straw in the henhouse and pulled out two eggs that were still warm. She insisted I take them. They were good to drink raw. I shook my head, then stuck them in my coat pocket anyway. My hand stayed there on those warm eggs.

After a while she said, "You mustn't think I'm a bad woman."

Her husband came out to look for us and made a strange whistling sound as if he were calling hens. Tereza hastened toward the house. I walked behind her and observed her buttocks and hips the way someone might study an animal. She wasn't poorly built. She had long muscles and thin ankles. She had no physical defect, no anomaly. She was neutral, that's what she was. She wasn't happy and she wasn't sad, she wasn't beautiful but she wasn't ugly; she didn't evince a great warmth but she wasn't disagreeable. I'd been looking

at her face until three seconds before and already I couldn't remember anything about her. She was a good candidate—perfect, in fact—because she
wasn't anyone. She was Mrs. Nobody, a circle from the doctor's chart.

· I walked around for a while by myself in the area in front of the house. I
sniffed the air, glanced here and there, checked out the territory, the square
meters in which Tereza would live with our child in her womb. Like a cautious mother, I bent to move a rusty metal spike.

I went back inside. Diego was taking pictures of the child, who was now holding on to the edge of a ramshackle playpen. He looked at the lens of the camera
without any interest. He was colorless and inert like his mother. He didn't have
a single childlike burst of spirit. He stood there, imprisoned like a fossil enclosed
in resin. There was something eternal about his misery, useless flesh reproduc-
ing itself over the centuries, blooming and disappearing without a trace.

"Let's go."

It bothered me that Diego was taking pictures of that child. Sometimes
it even bothered me to see him taking pictures. He wrapped himself around
the camera as if it were a heart, something pulsating that had come out of his
chest, something he held tight in order to live a few more minutes.

"Let's go."

His attitude bothered me, his hollow missionary face. There was too much
defeat in his way of loving. One day all of this would end. One day he would
photograph our child for hours and hours and all the others, all the Antes in
the world, would slide away.

Diego was silent for the entire trip back, dozing against the window.

"What comes next?"

Oksana translated. Tomorrow Tereza would report to the clinic for blood
tests. The doctor would check her follicular activity. She was about to ovu-
late. It was a question of hours. Ovarian stimulation would not be necessary
because the woman was extremely fertile.

The doctor turned. "Unless you want twins or triplets . . ."

I laughed, splitting my sides. It had been ages since I'd laughed like that.
Now I liked this direct, rough man, a true Cossack dedicated to the cause of
human fertility.

Diego did not laugh. I took his hand.

I wasn't going to let him influence me with his bad mood and his scruples. Now I was worried about the woman, about *moi malenchii dom*, my little house. I would leave extra money for her, of course, and I would send her vitamins and minerals like magnesium and iron. The fertilization now seemed like a simple detail. Something would happen, and quickly. It would take a handful of minutes in the clinic with the embroidered curtains.

The doctor was chatty and relaxed during the drive back. He answered all my questions, assuaged all my fears. The woman would be monitored through constant checkups, and they would send all the sonograms and test results to us in Italy. We could come and visit at any time. He suggested that I, at least, should plan to stay in Ukraine for the last months of the pregnancy.

"That way you won't have to explain things, and if you want you can simply say you gave birth abroad. It's important that you participate, put your hands on the surrogate mother's belly and feel the movements of the fetus. This will help you. You're about to go through a very emotional time. You'll have to be very careful with your health. Often it's the legal mother who gets ill. You'll feel weak, and when it's time for the birth you'll feel real contractions."

It felt like I was a step away from life.

Diego looked out the window as he listened. Every so often he took a picture, a tractor moving across a field, a man on a bicycle. He hadn't taken a single photo for months and now here he was taking pictures of this nothing, these ugly fields, this dusty sky.

We passed by the long fence with spikes and barbed wire that surrounded the mine, with all those posters that said who knew what. Diego raised his camera and took a picture through the window. I asked what they mined in that bunker. Oksana didn't turn; she shrugged very slightly.

That night the singer was dressed entirely in white, like a big cloud. The maître d' brought us caviar. He'd had his tip. Then the vodka descended, and we began to speak.

"Her teeth are broken. That woman has broken teeth."

I tried to smile. "So?"

"You really didn't notice anything, my love?"

"What was I supposed to notice?"

He brought a hand to his cheekbone. "There was something, a mark, a bruise."

I had in fact seen that darkened eye when she turned toward me to say, *I am the house.*

"It must have been the baby. He must have stuck something in her eye. Or maybe she got scratched in the fields."

Diego nodded. "Maybe."

Later on I couldn't sleep. There was an unpleasant smell in the room. My coat was drying on the radiator. Those damned eggs ended up breaking in my pocket because I forgot about them. I threw the shells in the toilet, turned the pockets inside out and cleaned them as best I could. Now the stink of drying egg wafted out from the radiator.

"Her husband beats her. That's what you think."

He wasn't sleeping, either. "I don't like that man, and the child is sad, too."

The next day we went out early. Oksana came to get us at the hotel. We invited her to have breakfast with us. She pressed her white face to the cup of warm tea, then pressed the cup against her cheek. She had come on foot and she was cold and more tired than she'd been the previous days. When Diego went up to the room to load his camera, I asked her point-blank, "Do the men here beat the women?"

She was in less of a mood to smile that morning. She said that early in the morning, on the streets, the women examined each other and took count.

"There's no work anymore. The men drink until they fall down."

Her voice was veiled. She kept rubbing her red nose and her colorless lips that seemed incapable of regaining their natural color.

"My brother worked on a ship. He lost his job. Now when I open the door he takes two steps into the house and falls. That's how low it's brought him."

I took her hand. "Oksana . . ."

All her youthful pride seemed far away now. It had crumbled in an instant.

"Kasimir, my eighty-year-old neighbor, threw himself from a window. He didn't have anything left to eat."

She cried for a moment without changing expression. Then she laughed.

"My cousin Epifan works in a factory. They pay him with rolls of toilet paper, mountains of toilet paper. It's the only thing that abounds in our house."

I wanted to help her but not to wound her. I reached for my purse. She looked daggers at me, raised her hand. "*Nyet!*"

I lied and said I was looking for my lip balm.

That afternoon we went back to the clinic. Tereza was there. They'd done some tests and she was putting her clothes back on. Without asking permission, I stuck my head in the door. She was bent over the little bed. For a moment I saw her back. Her shoulder blades were like the wings of a plucked chicken. There was a mark on her back, too, a bluish bruise that spilled downward from her neck. I smiled at her. Her husband was in a corner of the room. He came toward us. I turned and studied Tereza's eye carefully. It was darker and puffier than the day before. The doctor said the follicular activity had begun. Her husband rubbed his hands against the cloth of his pants. It seemed like the most horrible noise on earth.

"*Nyet*," I said.

I saw the doctor freeze where he was standing, then hunch over.

"This person is not right for us. Please excuse us."

There's a huge barrel of frying oil in the middle of the street. It's Saturday, market day. A girl with wet braids devours a dark pastry. An old lady stands beneath a dripping tin canopy selling mismatched drinking glasses and brass candleholders. The cold came overnight. There's stiff white grass at the edges of the road. The freezing wind hurts our faces and blows sleet around. There's another old lady selling heavy socks and yet another offering clumps of beetroot and a rubber toy rabbit. They stand there almost motionless, like the icicles coming down from the roofs. Diego doesn't take any pictures this morning. He buys everything and throws it into his backpack. He pulls handfuls of nearly worthless karbovanets out of his pockets and sends those old women home to sit in front of a warm stove.

More caviar. It's Sunday. Tonight the singer has decided to move through the crowd with her microphone. She weaves her way among the tables. She comes toward us. Maybe she's noticed I've been crying. She briefly caresses my hair and stays beside us for a moment. Close up, she looks older.

Diego wants to leave as soon as possible but I insist on staying. "It's just one more day." I watch the women on the street, a gas station attendant, a worker painting a wall. I inspect them with my eyes, hover over their bodies. I'm seeking the thing I lack.

"This isn't okay," Diego says.

"Leave me alone," I reply.

Oksana follows us with her light blue coat and her white neck like a statue's. I ask her, "Would you do it?"

Oksana doesn't answer. She pretends not to have understood.

Diego twists my wrist until it hurts.

The doctor won't let us go. He's set up another appointment. Diego has a strange expression on his face. He looks ugly this morning. There's something crooked about his features. Last night he slept as far as possible from me on the bed with its tight sheets like a straitjacket.

The new woman is there, on the same chair, in the other's place. She's younger, more voluptuous. She stands and smiles. Her teeth are intact inside her fleshy mouth. She's taller than Diego. Where the other was odorless, this one smells like she's just come out of a cheap perfume factory. A sweet stink invades the air. She's wearing a white shirt with a cameo on her chest and a dark skirt like a schoolgirl's. She must have dressed like that especially for this interview. Now she's trying to gauge our reaction. Like her voice, her lively eyes dart every which way. I check her skin. It looks okay. She has bleached hair, darker at the roots. Her face is strange, like a clown without makeup. Then I realize that she doesn't have any eyebrows, not a single hair, just a bony puffiness. She looks like an unfinished painting.

I seek Diego's eyes. He's looking outside at the playing fields and the basketball hoop without a net.

We're walking outside. I ask Diego what he thinks.

"Do you really want to know?"

"Of course I do."

He continues to touch every cement column we encounter as if he were counting them. He doesn't turn toward me. "I think she's a prostitute." He stops for a moment, rocks back and forth and smiles. "I think we're disgusting, my love."

Oksana finally tells us the truth about the abandoned mine while we're riding in the van that takes us to the airport. It's a uranium mine. Until very recently, the little city beside it was not shown on any maps. It didn't exist.

"A friend of mine lost her little boy, but my grandmother is almost ninety and she's lived there all her life. She has a garden; she says the uranium is good for the cabbage."

The abandoned packages are still in the airport, in the same place as before, only more battered.

I hold Oksana's face tight between my hands and bury my chin in her blue coat before I say goodbye. Diego gives her all the dollars he has left. This time she accepts the money and puts it in her cloth bag.

We had a layover of a couple of hours in Belgrade. We ordered tea at a café and sat at the counter to drink it. A man next to us was eating a sausage, red and long and dripping with grease. Diego pushed his tea aside and asked for a sausage and a beer.

I watched him devour it without saying a word. He wasn't eating it. He was tearing into it. I said, *Let's go take a walk*. He said, *You go*. I was moving my legs and making his stool shake, too. I fluttered through the ashes, like in the aftermath of a fire.

"Sit still."

I kept moving my legs.

"Please."

He had grease on his chin. He looked at me with a dark gaze pulled up from who knows where, pulsating and distant despite our nearness. "We may have to leave each other." He stood.

"Where are you going?"

"To take a piss."

I couldn't find him anywhere near the bathrooms. I wandered around among the people waiting for flights and ducked into sad shops full of bottles on shelves and cartons of cigarettes. Then I stopped looking. I thought backward. I asked myself where, in which rotten moment, we'd begun to lose each other. I went to the bathroom again and rinsed my face and then I went to the gate. An attendant was already taking the boarding passes.

I sat until the last minute in a row of chairs clamped to each other. Someone put a hand on my shoulder. I turned to find the woman I had met on the flight from Rome smiling down at me. A Russian scarf tied like a headband divided her thick bangs from the rest of her hair.

The girl she'd hoped to take as a foster child had been adopted by another family.

"French."

"I'm sorry."

"They took the younger brother, too. He's three. This way they'll be together. It's a good thing for the children. We would never have been able to take them both. The French couple is young."

I hugged her. I could feel her body trembling, her breasts packed into her stiff bra.

Diego comes running out of the desert of dispersing people. He sits next to me.

"I thought you wanted to leave me."

"I came back."

"Our flight left."

"Whose shoes are those?"

"That woman we met on the way. She gave them to me."

"Why?"

"I don't know. Look, they light up."

I put my hands inside the little shoes and crawl between benches and pipes, pressing down to make the soles light up. Diego follows the little lights with his eyes. His hair is messy, his beard scruffy, his eyes tired but still alive. He takes his Leica and shoots a picture. I smile, my hands stuck in the shoes.

"So it's true," he says.

"What?"

"That life speaks through light, just like photography."

He helps me stand up and leans on me. "I know who we can take these shoes to."

I feel the impact inside, like a broom that passes and scratches as it cleans.

"There's a flight to Sarajevo. That's what I came to tell you."

The airport is practically deserted, populated only by airport employees and a few local travelers. The baggage claim belt isn't moving, and when they do turn it on it bears just a few isolated suitcases, stuff that goes around and around but no one picks up. An Australian cameraman is filming a taxi driver in front of the door of his car. He has one of those sunken faces you often encounter in Sarajevo, the bones surfacing out of the nicotine-tinged skin. Gojko is there interpreting. He sees us and flushes, impatient. He gestures to us to wait and shrugs his shoulders to let us know that he was drawn into this by chance. He can't like what he's translating.

. . . They said they will leave us a bit of ground, enough for our tombs. This is what they said in our Parliament.

"Fucking nihilist," he says, and with a gesture sends the taxi driver and the fool of an Australian off to hell. He kisses us and embraces us in his usual manner, throttling our chests with those long, motionless arms that all of a sudden become strong as a vise.

"Beautiful woman, skinny photographer."

None of us had imagined we'd see each other again so soon. It's a March morning. Nine months have gone by since the vacation in Croatia—time enough for a pregnancy, time enough for a war.

He holds us tight and presses his forehead against ours. He asks us if it took a lot of courage to come.

"It was harder to stay away."

He says we're his friends and hugs us again. His little honey-colored eyes fill with tears. "Once in a while, the poet takes a piss." He even makes a gesture as if he were pissing and laughs.

Diego takes a deep breath, spreads his arms, takes another breath. The air is still cold even though it's already spring.

Gojko is wearing a Gore-Tex jacket. *It's German*, he says. He made a trade with a journalist from Reuters Deutschland. He takes it off right there in the airport drop-off lane. He's wearing a cotton T-shirt underneath. He wants us to hold his jacket and feel how light it is. He puts it back on as we head toward the car.

He says he doesn't feel the cold anymore, that the jacket's solved a lot of problems. He can stay out all night even when the temperature is ten below zero. He talks about Gore-Tex, the literary magazine that publishes his poems, the radio station where he works now and then. He wants to take us there because the people there are quick thinkers, like blades on a helicopter. I look at the streets, the linden trees, the lead-colored buildings. I breathe in. Why didn't we come before? This city is like a pocket for us. Coming here is like slipping our hands into the dark to feel a warmth that comes from deep inside.

We head into the city. Gojko's voice is warm mud. He tells us that there are a lot of journalists in the city now, thanks to the International Conference on Bosnia-Herzegovina sponsored by the European Community. He's working as a guide again, like he did during the Olympics.

Diego asks him about the impending war.

Gojko throws his cigarette butt out the window. "The whole world is watching us. Nothing will happen here."

He takes us to the kafana near the Markale Market with upholstered walls and Bosnian blues coming out over the loudspeakers. Gojko smokes another cigarette. We look at his face. It's a bit puffier than it was in the summer. He lowers his mouth to kiss my hand where it rests on the table. He grabs the camera from the red vinyl bench and shakes his head because Diego is still using that glorious Leica from his first days as a photographer.

The first picture Diego takes is in that café. Gojko and I are on the bench, hugging. Gojko holds his fingers in a V for victory in front of our smiling faces.

"So, do you two still love each other a lot?" Gojko whispers to me.

Diego answers, "Yes."

"Too bad."

We go out and walk through the cold. People are immersed in their own routines. The stores of the Baščaršija are all open, with their piles of spices, copper utensils and white tunics with gold trim.

What did the faces of the Jews look like as they beheld without recognition the evil headed their way? They must not have been much different from the faces I see here, this old man engraving leather, this girl wearing a veil and jeans as she steps out of the madrassa, her books held tight with an elastic strap.

We sat on the bleachers in the big gym, one of the ones they'd built for the Olympics. Sebina was standing next to a pile of blue rubber mats. We watched her for a while before she noticed us. She hadn't changed much, just grown a few hand widths taller. Her bare legs were stocky and white as candles. Muscles rose out of her skin like little sausages. She was barefoot. Before every exercise, like a seasoned athlete, she'd take off the little wool shawl she used as a muscle warmer and then put it back on immediately afterward. The gym was dimly lit. There were a couple of fluorescent panels down below but their light barely reached the bleachers.

She saw us. She raised her eyes and rested them on us. Did she recognize me? We spoke on the phone. I'd watched her grow in photographs. Every Christmas I sent her a toy and some money, and she sent little holiday cards, angels cut from paper. She stayed in place with the others, disciplined. But everything she did from that moment on was for me, for my eyes as they watched her on the parallel bars, the balance beams, the horse, where she gripped the handles and pulled herself up, body straight, head turned toward us. In her letters she'd told me about this passion, but it was something else to see her in action. She missed a landing and fell, but then she crossed the room with a series of cartwheels like a little flame and landed in a perfect split.

We met in the long linoleum corridor lit by the distant lights of the dressing rooms. I called her. She was looking for me. She turned toward me and ran. She had the same squashed face from when she was born, the prominent upper lip. I picked her up, I think Diego and I picked her up together, both of us greedy for that smell, that pale sweaty skin.

"Darling. Sweetheart."

"Gemma! Diego!"

"Sebina."

What is joy? It's this lonely corridor, rancid with good smells, this little body embracing us.

She was tiny, so much smaller close up.

"You're so heavy," I said.

"To su mišići." It's the muscles.

Now Gojko lived on his own, but he went almost every night to fetch Sebina. He'd wait for her near the showers. Sometimes he'd help her dry her hair, other times he'd simply plop her hat on her head and off they'd go. When he felt like it, he'd take her out for pancakes with honey and apples in one of those places with high stools where you eat looking at the wall and smell of frying oil when you leave. They'd talk between mouthfuls without really looking at each other. Like any big brother, like the father who wasn't there, he'd ask her about her day and about school. Sebina always spoke too quickly, and Gojko had a hard time following her. She liked only two things about school: the window in one of the corridors that overlooked the parks along the Miljacka where couples went to make out, and the experiments they did in the chemistry lab. She wanted to be a champion gymnast. She was almost too small, though.

"I'm the shortest one."

Her brother wiped her mouth with his hand. "Short people are more firmly rooted to the ground."

If she was sad, he'd read her one of his poems.

The girl sat on the ground
before a pyre of corollas
like winter flames.
Help me, I'm tired.
We peeled roses until sunset
swathed in a sickly sweet perfume
that befuddled, like a drug.
Who will drink all this grappa,
I asked her.
You will, if you return.
I wasn't sure I could find my way.
She waved at me from the window,
her melted plaster face
her hands dripping with the blood of petals.

Sebina liked her brother's poems, but she asked too many questions.

He said, "Poems cannot be explained. If they reach the right place, you feel it. They itch you on the inside."

"Where's the right place?"

"Look for it."

Sebina twisted her mouth and looked at him skeptically from out of her funny face. She prodded her stomach, her legs.

"Is a foot okay?"

"It's a bit low."

"I feel your poem itching me there."

Gojko put her on his shoulders and climbed the stairs of his old house, where he left her with Mirna.

We went into a restaurant for pita bread stuffed with everything—meat, potatoes, squash. Sebina started yawning, her eyes lost and watering, like any sleepy child. She didn't complain. She folded her arms on the table, rested her head on them and fell asleep. We stayed talking. Diego crumbled up one of Gojko's cigarettes, then opened his little tin and made a joint. Gojko watched and mocked him.

"Since when have you been doing drugs?"

"This isn't drugs. It's hash."

Gojko glued himself to the joint, bathing it with his mouth.

"Well, then. Let's smoke."

"Your sister . . ." I said.

"She's sleeping," Gojko said.

The two of them smoked while I rubbed the nape of Sebina's neck. At one point I bent down and buried my nose in that well of flesh and found that old smell of milk and forest. It had remained over the years. It struck me as the odor of the future, there ahead of us just like long ago. I looked at our bodies in the mirror that ringed the wall and it felt like time hadn't taken anything away. Diego was weeping, motionless, seemingly oblivious to the tears that rolled down his face as calm as sweat. I touched his shoulder.

"I'm fine," he said. "I'm in heaven."

We walked back in the dark through the friendly streets. Sebina was sleeping on her brother's neck, her abandoned arms capturing the rays of the streetlights.

It was freezing cold. I touched Sebina's hands. They were frozen. We hurried toward the hotel, a little red door like the entrance to a house. We asked for the key and went up to the room. Gojko didn't want to leave us, and we didn't want him to go. He had managed to find a room that was bigger than most, with wood floors and a big wool rug. He'd even tried the bed. "I took a nap," he said, and in fact we could see a bit of a depression in the middle of the bed and wrinkles on the bedspread.

"Do you two still make love?"

We'd just come from that desolate trip and the cold had done nothing to dispel our limpness.

"Tonight we're dead tired."

"That's when it's best, when your body is empty. That's when you fly."

Later on Gojko switched on the television. Karadžić was talking, his hair blown dry into a puff, his face made up like a doll's. It was a long, glossy interview. He spoke of his work as a psychiatrist and as a poet. As he spoke, some of his verses rolled across the screen in superimposition. Gojko snickered as he read.

"Psychopathic Montenegrin!" He scratched his head, his arm, as if he'd been attacked by a terrible itch. "How on earth can anyone believe a lunatic like that?"

Diego was lying across the bed. "It's the lunatics we need to worry about."

Diego closes his eyes. His arm flops onto the bed beside Sebina, who's still sleeping right where we set her down.

"Aren't you going to get undressed?" But he's already asleep.

Gojko lights a cigarette. I tell him to go open the window and smoke there.

I look at the clock. It's almost three.

"What were you doing in Belgrade?"

We sit on the edge of the bed. I look down as I talk. I tell him about our trip to Ukraine, the women there. Gojko listens with a serious expression and then he starts laughing.

"Are you crazy? You wanted a baby from a whore?"

Diego's body is stretched out next to him like a big child's.

"He didn't even take off his bib."

It's true, Diego's still got the napkin from the restaurant in the collar of his sweater. Gojko stands and takes it off and then uses it to blow his nose. He pretends to cry and bangs his head against the wall.

"Why? Why don't you need a man? Why is life so unfair?"

He hugs me from behind and tickles me. I push him away halfheartedly.

"I've been unhappy for so many months, I don't know who I am anymore."

I move toward Diego and tug at his boots, those old Camperos that are so hard to get off. Gojko watches this weary, maternal gesture.

"You're afraid of losing him, aren't you?"

"I'm thirty-seven."

"He'd never leave you."

I drop the boots on the ground and slide off Diego's socks. I stand for a moment looking at those long feet, white on top and red at the sides.

"I want to have a child with feet like this."

Gojko pulls a face. "What's so great about his feet?"

"They're his."

"I see."

The still-open window vibrates in the metal window frame. Gojko closes it. It's deepest night. We can see the cathedral spires with their little crosses that look like they're made of glass.

That night the four of us slept in the same bed. Gojko was too tired to carry his sister on his shoulders. I had no intention of really sleeping. I settled on the far edge of the bed and lay there stiff and precarious like the blade of an ice skate. I waited for dawn and finally fell into a brief light sleep, protected at last by the light of day. When I opened my eyes again, I found Sebina's little face bent over my own. The first to wake, she had already combed her hair and washed her face.

"Wait."

I got up and gave her the shoes from my suitcase.

"They light up when you walk."

She got hiccups. Her body reacted to the excitement by literally fragmenting her breath. I helped her put the shoes on. There was room for at least a year's growth. She stared at her feet and shook from those little spasms that would not stop.

"Try them!" The shoes lit up.

She didn't seem so much happy as desperate. I understood her desperation. It was the same thing I felt when I reached the peak and understood that I had everything, like a sudden intimation of the rapture of nothing. I thought she might faint. I yelled to scare the hiccups away and then couldn't believe I'd produced such a savage howl.

Sebina started and stared at me, her mouth hanging open.

I didn't know why, but we were motionless in the face of something. We were rebelling.

"Walk. What are you waiting for?"

She smiled. The hiccups were gone. She started walking around the room while looking at her heels, those plastic bubbles that lit up from within. She came back and gave me a kiss on the mouth. I felt the softness of her lips against mine.

Gojko had rolled off the bed onto the rug and continued sleeping. Now his sister was walking on his stomach to wake him up. She put her shoes in front of his face. Gojko opened an eye, studied those luminous soles and turned toward me like a snake.

"Fuck, where did you find them? I want to import them!"

Sebina began to holler in a high shrill voice, remonstrating her brother. She wanted to be the only one in Sarajevo with shoes like that!

Diego was awake now, too. He smiled as he watched her luminous steps. "That way we'll always find you, even in the dark."

Gojko had moved into an old dilapidated building near the old synagogue. It didn't have an elevator. There were a few elderly tenants left, but no families. Rather, the building was inhabited by young people: university students, aspiring artists, budding intellectuals. They were part of Sarajevo's new generation. They went to concerts and frequented literary cafés and art-house cinemas. They met up at the Čeka and gathered at night beneath old statues of Tito to yell along with U2, *I wanna run . . . I wanna tear down the walls that hold me inside.* Gojko lived on the top floor in a shared apartment, a sort of mini-commune, one of those chaotic places where kids live for a while before settling into real life. At thirty-five, Gojko was the oldest housemate, but the place was a good fit for him. *If friends down below see the lights on in the windows, they come on up.*

He opened the door and a dense cloud of smoke and spices assailed us. A boy stood playing the saxophone near a window. He was bent over the keys, his cheeks puffed out, his eyes closed. His figure reflected in the thin glass that had been blown and cut by hand the old-fashioned way; it seemed to move like water.

Because of the advancing war we had expected to find a depressed world of aimless people. Instead, we found music and chitchat and a pair of girls stirring soup in the kitchen.

We went back almost every night to that apartment suspended high above the seraglio of the old city, and maybe there we found what we'd been missing, the human warmth of smiling young faces, and time—yes, time, the old Bosnian habit of taking a pause from life to talk, to be. We found time that expanded along with our breath, the needs of our bodies and our spirits. We saw Mladjo again, the painter, who was now portraying bodies of all ages on canvas smeared with pure colors and showing these modern shrouds in a warehouse in Grbavica. We saw Zoran, too, the lawyer with the acne-covered face, and Dragana, who was now acting in a theater along with Bojan, her boyfriend.

One night I saw Ana again. She hadn't lost her smile, either. She was leaning against a door with an empty glass in her hand and a black sweater stretched tight over her prosperous chest. I watched her neck darken with the shadows of whoever walked by. I remembered her half dressed on the island of Korčula, lolling on her belly beneath the mulberry tree. As we spoke, I realized she was rocking on her heels, slowly leaning forward and then slowly moving back as if she were standing on a threshold, unable to decide whether or not she should proceed. I looked around and felt a chill penetrate my body. All these kids who were talking, who seemed alive, all of them were standing on the same threshold.

"How do you manage not to be scared?" I asked her.

"We're together. It's important to stick together."

I watched the young saxophone player bent over his instrument as if it were the body of his beloved, as if he were making love for the last time.

Chapter 10

Pietro turns over in bed and covers his face with his pillow to block out the light.

"Get up. It's late."

"Is it raining?" he asks from beneath the pillow.

"No."

He's up in a flash. "Really?" He moves toward the window and stays there awhile, stuck to the glass, his eyes on the uncertain sun in the muggy sky.

This morning Gojko is taking him to the water park, the one advertised all along Marshal Tito Boulevard. He opens the wardrobe and empties his bag onto the bed, then locks himself in the bathroom. I can hear the water running pointlessly.

"Turn it off. People are dying of thirst."

It's something I say all the time, to Giuliano, too. I can't stand it when he leaves the water running while he's shaving. Some things have become a part of me, my shadow. Like that woman, dead on the pavement next to the beer factory where people lined up to get water, her legs folded as if she were sleeping, her head resting on the plum-colored stain of her blood beside the tank she hadn't managed to fill.

Pietro comes out of the bathroom in his quick-drying surfer trunks. Danka, the girl from the hotel café, will be going with them. Pietro invited her last night.

"What do you think, Ma? Should I ask her?"

He'd been thinking about it for a while but hadn't dared mention it.

"Of course!"

He takes a few steps, then turns around. "Never mind."

"Why not?"

"What do I say?"

"You'll think of something."

He stands up once again and sidles over to the counter where Danka is filling glasses with ice. For the first time, I see him approach a woman. As I watch him I think he's charming, despite the shyness and long arms. To ease the tension he's drumming with his hands on his jeans. He sits, raises those indigo eyes, smiles.

He comes back to sit beside me.

"What did she say?"

He grabs a bag of Bosnian potato chips off the display rack and starts munching on them. "It looks like she'll come."

Danka, mounted on a pair of platform sandals and wearing tight jeans, looks thin and very tall this morning. She has a silver ring in her belly button. Pietro notices it right away, shining in that pale strip of belly. It must be enticing but intimidating. He looks away, starts horsing around. He shows her the towel he's bringing, one from the hotel. Danka laughs and says it's not allowed. Pietro hides it under his T-shirt and pats his terry-cloth belly. They laugh again.

Gojko shows up in last night's jacket and shirt, a pair of flip-flops on his feet. We get a coffee, Italian espresso, in the café across the street from the hotel. The man standing next to us is reading a book. His whitish hair is as long as his beard. He looks like Karadžić when he was captured, disguised as a holy man, the same long white robe, like an Indian guru, the same lamb's gaze. How many of those people must there still be, killers going around unimpeded like Karadžić, who went to soccer matches and was practicing medicine? I ask Gojko how he felt when Karadžić was arrested.

He puts out his cigarette, pushing the butt against the ashtray until he burns his finger. He says Karadžić wasn't arrested. He was sold. Karadžić's arrest left him cold.

Gojko's flip-flops have synthetic grass in them that massages his feet. He takes one off so I can see it better and stands there with one bare foot on the sidewalk. Then he almost falls into me when he puts it back on. He's glad it's not raining, glad summer's finally here. I ask him how high the slides in the water park are, whether they're safe.

They jump in the car, slamming the doors.

"When will you be back?"

"When it closes."

I go up to the room and fill my little backpack. I want my arms to be free so I can walk.

The old men are already at it playing chess in the square. The birds are there, too. A new battle is beginning. The giant chessmen are back in their starting places. I look at the two facing armies, one black, one white.

As I pass the circular building of the covered market, I speed up, eyes on the ground. Then I stop in front of a bank that wasn't here before. A car bearing the words HEINRICH BOLL FOUNDATION in little blue letters is parked in front. I shake my head and laugh. I've got a book by Boll in my backpack.

The music school is across the way, a corner building flanked by a steep street. It looks exactly the same as before. Only the paint has changed, a pale sky-gray. Nobody pays any attention to me. I go up one flight. There's a smell of closed spaces and bodies crammed into little rooms, the smell of every school and place where people grow, where they sweat. I move along the corridor over a rope-colored carpet held in place with brass borders. The old floor sways beneath me. Perhaps they simply covered it over after the war. Arpeggios and chords rain down upon me as I climb, a violin rehearsing, an upright bass. I let myself be sucked into this place of perseverance, of solitude, of hands, breaths, craziness, an old eccentric teacher, a young autistic talent. The doors are padded and covered with leather. FLAUTA. GITARA. KLAVIR. VIOLA. I push one open and see two young faces and a teacher bent over a keyboard, ethereal as a flickering flame, and beyond them a coffee dispenser.

I ask the piano custodian if I may go on with my tour. He comes with me. He has an elderly face and a short smock like an altar boy's cassock. He walks with a limp. We climb higher. The landing is crammed with kids. Perhaps they're waiting for an audition. A crouching boy moves his hands over the keys of a clarinet held far from his mouth, not emitting a sound. The custodian explains that in the common areas of the school, playing instruments and talking aloud are forbidden.

The sound of the black, double-soled shoe he wears on the foot of his shorter leg accompanies me as I climb. He stops, opens a window and shoos away some pigeons brooding in the space between the glass and the iron bars. We're almost at the top.

The wall still says TISINA. Silence. Underneath, there's a gaping chasm, created by an explosion. The custodian says it's been left this way as a reminder of the time silence was violated. He lights a cigarette and touches his rigid, skeletal leg, nodding to himself as he remembers. I ask him if I can stay here for a few minutes. He leaves me alone, dragging that rigid leg along behind him.

I sit on the ground in front of the gaping wall. On the other side, a corpulent woman with a strange hairdo of rolled braids is teaching solfeggio to a group of kids. She waves a pencil in emphasis, like an orchestra conductor.

I look at the writing on the wall, absurd and solemn at the same time. SILENCE! I imagine the impact, the shell that violated the silence of these walls accustomed to absorbing notes. I watch my life through this dismembered wall, this abyss no one has ever filled.

The referendum for Bosnian independence had just taken place. The streets were plastered with nationalist posters. Mothers of soldiers in the federal army took to the streets wrapped in banners demanding their sons be sent back home. There was alarming news. Some even said that as far back as the preparations for the Winter Olympics, while the ski slopes were being leveled, there were those who were thinking ahead to the trenches for the coming war.

Gojko dismissed it all as stupid alarmism.

"Propaganda finds its converts in the countryside. It's easy to convince a peasant that his neighbor is a Turk who wants to steal his land and slit his throat. But here we're not Turks, we're not Chetniks, we're not Ustashas. Here we're just Sarajevans."

But Diego knew the language of stadium mobs. Karadžić had been the psychologist for Sarajevo Soccer, Arkan the head of the Red Star Belgrade ultras.

"Wars begin in peacetime on the edge of the cities, while you sit around in your cultural centers discussing poetry."

Interminable arguments accompanied us homeward each evening.

Diego and I left our hotel and took a rented room in the apartment of an elderly couple. Jovan, the husband, was a biologist, a white-haired and silent old man who suffered from the cold and wore flannel shirts buttoned to the neck. Velida, his wife, had been his assistant all her life. She was thin, with lively green eyes, and always wore gray, like a nun. We did little favors for each other. I passed her the foreign newspapers Diego bought once a week. They couldn't afford them on their pension. When she cooked something good, Velida would leave a plate of it for us in front of our door. A little balcony separated our room from the rest of the apartment, so we could come and go without disturbing them. We had our own key and a bathroom, as well as a burner where we could make coffee.

That night, Diego was out taking pictures in the direction of Grbavica. I was alone and upset. It was very late. Gojko knocked on the door, stepped into the room and threw himself on the bed. He'd spent the entire day in Parliament translating for an American, arguments between politicians that went on until late. The members of the Bosnian Serb Party had abandoned the proceedings. He was exhausted and depressed.

"*Šteta.*"

I turned. "What's a pity?"

He shrugged. "*Ništa.*" Nothing. "Are you really leaving?"

I nodded.

He closed his eyes. I let him sleep for a while but his snoring was too loud. When I went to wake him, I could smell the stink of alcohol. He must have tanked up with the American. He looked at me with a strange expression in his eyes, like a lost child, a child who's had a nightmare and can't tell his mother from an ogre.

He takes me by the neck, strokes my cheek.

"My love."

"You're drunk. Go home."

He pulls his wallet out of his jacket, rustles through bits of paper and reads me a poem.

My sister is sleeping, what a pity.
Her hands are growing
far from me

as the day dies.
Tomorrow I'll take her skating
she'll stop on Vase Miskina Street
in front of the window display of computers
they've just turned on.
My sister believes in the future,
what a pity.

I smile and nod.

"You think it's awful."

I shrug. He can think what he wants. He's impossible, still young but aging badly.

"Does Sebina want a computer?"

Gojko turns.

"I came to invite you to a concert."

It's the end-of-year recital at the music school. He wants to introduce me to a girl.

"I told her about you."

I'm putting the blow dryer in my suitcase. I freeze. "What did you tell her?"

He takes a step toward me and puts a hand on my stomach, low. He holds it there, not moving. I can feel its warmth, a friendly fire that penetrates. I'm sweating. He doesn't move, just stays there, that shameless hand just above my groin. I breathe, and don't brush him aside, and maybe all of a sudden it feels like I want him, because there's something of his that I share, something defeated, a solitude I no longer share with Diego. I breathe and feel the breath descend into my belly, below his hot steady hand that's pressing on me.

Diego comes in, his face like a cat at night.

"What's going on?"

Gojko doesn't move, like a corpse. I give him a light kick.

"I'm drunk," he says, and leaves.

I watch him from the window as he moves away along the dark street. Diego watches my head, my hand holding the little embroidered curtain.

"Did he make a pass?"

"No. He invited us to a concert."

That's how we end up going to the music school. It's a rainy afternoon. Water flows in torrents through the streets. While we wait for the concert to begin, I rest my wet feet, one at a time, on the cast-iron heater. Around us, country women in galoshes stand next to women in summer sandals and long evening dresses with damp hems. A robust woman with a whistle hanging from her neck is setting up chairs. This little cultural event clearly means a lot to these people. Their chitchat is cautious, polite, and even the miserable quirkiness of the gowns has its grace. I think of Rome, the mixed crowds that flock to so-called *events*, women in rags worth thousands, nightclub intellectuals, politicians, people with no purity, the *spirit of our time* the ad men were always talking about.

Not everyone gets a seat, but no one complains. No one even leans against the wall. It's warm in the room, I fan myself with the program. A continuous stream of musicians comes and goes on the little wooden platform. They are all young, the boys wearing bow ties, the girls dressed in black, their dresses altered for the occasion. They thank the crowd, rise behind their instruments and bow their heads. The second group comes in, then the third. I can't take it anymore. Gojko touches my knee and points to the brass section.

She's the tallest in the group. Her face is too white, her lipstick too dark, her hair rust-red. She's waiting her turn. She stands clutching her instrument, a trumpet, as if she were holding her heart. She's wearing a velour dress that skims her thin hips and her breasts, which stand out despite the dark dress. I devour every detail in a flash, like an ordinary woman curious about a more beautiful creature. I search for a flaw. She raises her chin. I'm a bit too far away to make out her features. I need a little pair of binoculars like the ones ladies use at the opera. I can see the blotch of her face, traces of expression. She starts to play, surrounded by violins. She empties her cheeks, tightens her lips and bends over the trumpet, then raises it along with the music, which has become an onslaught. I don't know if she's any good, I don't know enough about music. I don't care. She plays with her eyes shut and moves around a bit too much. She shakes her head, that red hair hacked into imprecise tufts. She looks like a bird with too many wings.

They're playing Shostakovich's concerto for piano, trumpet and strings. The music changes, becomes darker, more insistent. The wail of the violins is overwhelming, the trumpet enters in bursts, the girl is trembling, her cheeks filling and collapsing, emptying slowly. Now her fingers on the valves are like soldiers on the battlefield, facing off, retreating. The blond boy at the piano looks crazed as well. He's running back and forth, dragging his body behind his hands, crashing down here and there like a dying moth. The trumpet is the cry of an owl in the night. The girl's chest rises, then falls, wounded. Her red hair is a trail of blood. Nobody dares move. All are entranced. Outside, the rain is still pouring down. You can't see anything through the windows. We're locked in a watery prison, and the music, too, is a prisoner of the water that won't stop coming down. It's hot. I fan myself. The woman beside me is crying, solitary tears that leave tracks down her immobile face. They are like veterans of a great sorrow yet to come, a pain the music anticipates.

I put my hand on Diego's. He takes it automatically, as if he were holding a used glove. These last few nights we've tried to make love, starting but not getting very far. We laughed about it. It's something that happens to failed lovers, finished lovers. Once upon a time I was his love. Now he goes out with his camera, that's how he makes love, with whatever he comes across in the world, like a priest. Then he returns to his housekeeper.

The girl plays, quivers around the trumpet, dies inside it. Then she comes to, like an aging actress who dies onstage every night. Now she's sputtering out a kind of march.

I look at Diego. His eyes are closed. The concert is over.

The woman beside me is the first to stand, red in the face and clapping. The trumpet player joins the others. She's as tall as the boys. She crosses her legs and takes an exaggerated bow. The groups that played earlier come back in. They all squeeze together on the platform. Now it's a concert of shrieks. The conductor throws his baton in the air and then everyone is throwing something, a bow, a score, like brand-new graduates with their black hats. Diego's opened his eyes but doesn't stand. He claps softly.

"I fell asleep," he says.

"That's Gojko's friend."

Diego thinks I mean the plump violinist with the braid in a crest on top of her head. I say, *No, the one with the red hair hugging the blond piano player.* Diego looks at her—her hair, her black lips.

"What is she, some kind of punk?"

Gojko stands and lets out a whistle that would bring down a forest.

"Great, huh? They dump out your innards, dance on them and then put them back in your gut where they belong."

Then for a moment I think they're all crazy, as happy as if the war had already come and already finished, as if this were a festival of reconciliation.

We stand there against the wall, Diego and I, hemmed in by the flesh of women who resemble little embroidered lampshades and by a Bosnian cowboy wearing a crusty jacket with a rain of fringe. We're in the room next to the concert hall. The woman with the whistle has set up a table with trays of sweets and homemade sarma. Now, along with the smell of rain and of damp clothes letting off warm steam from bodies, there's the smell of Sarajevan food as well, spices, animal fat, tangy cheese.

The girl comes toward us. Close up she seems much younger, like a child all made up. Her sweaty hair looks like dripping rust. She's changed her clothes. Now she's wearing torn jeans under her velour dress. There's a safety pin in her ear. She carries her instrument case over one shoulder and a canvas bag full of stuff. Her hands are full of pastries.

"This is my friend Aska."

She looks at Gojko, smiles and swallows, then extends a greasy hand our way.

"I'm Aska, Gojko's friend."

She speaks *enough* Italian, she says, because she spent a year at the conservatory in Udine. She's hungry. She can't eat before she plays because *otherwise I'd throw up on the others' heads*, so now she's starving. Her accent is without inflection. She separates her words and closes them, every one a caesura. Her voice is like one of those little monotone voices that come out of the machines in parking garages, *Welcome, insert ticket, please wait.*

"Aska, like Andrić's sheep," I say in a whisper.

"Yes. It's a name I gave myself." She laughs.

I look at her soaring forehead, her long deep green eyes like leaves, stained with black makeup that's run into the whites.

She kneels and puts the pastries on her trumpet case. Then she's taking off her high-heeled shoes and putting on a pair of bright purple combat boots.

We compliment her. "People were crying."

She stands up and thanks us without emphasis. "People have no sense of irony."

An elderly man with a yarmulke comes by, an instructor who speaks to her, swathing her face in his trembling hands. She listens to him, serious, then steals a cigarette from the packet of Drinas sticking out of his pocket. The old man smiles and lights the cigarette for her. Now Aska is the one talking, looking at him intently, smoking in his face. When she speaks her own language, her voice is different, more melodic. She races over the words just as, minutes earlier, she raced over the notes.

She says she's in a hurry. Now that she's eaten and had a smoke, she has to get to a gig. Her motorcycle is parked out in front of the school, an old wreck that looks like something from the army. She wraps a black scarf around her head. Maybe she's Muslim, maybe she's cold. She crumples up her dress, ties a knot in the back like a tail and climbs on, legs wide in her jeans, her purple combat boots, her trumpet case over her shoulder.

Diego wants to take her picture but doesn't have his flash. Maybe the cone of light from the streetlight will be enough. He tries.

"It was a pleasure to meet you," she says to us. She starts her motorcycle and plunges into the night on that old carcass of a bike.

Later, Diego asks me to tell him Andrić's fable of Aska the sheep.

"She's a rebel sheep who only wants to dance and doesn't listen to her mother's scoldings. One day as she's dancing she gets separated from the herd. When she opens her eyes again the wolf is right there. He's hungry but he can wait. He likes watching that stupid little sheep as she dances. She can feel his black eyes on her snow-white fur. She knows her life is about to end, knows she should have listened to her mother. She's terrified, but she keeps dancing because it's the only thing she can do. As she dances, she moves backwards. The wolf is still there. All he'd need to do is reach out a paw, but the little lamb dances so well that he wants to enjoy it a while longer. He's sure to come across another little lamb, but he'll never see a lamb who dances like this."

"How does it end? Does the wolf eat her, or does she escape?"

His eyes are acting up again. I prepare an herbal infusion and wring the gauze over his eyelids.

He takes my hand from the darkness of his covered eyes. "What's wrong?" he asks.

"Gojko says that Aska would be willing to help us."

I studied old Jovan's still face as he reclined in his worn green velvet armchair. There was a clean little embroidered cloth on the back. Velida changed it almost every day. He could hear very little and he watched TV without even trying to make out the words. The television set was ancient, black-and-white, with a little antenna that didn't pick up the signal very well. The absence of colors and the pale grainy veil cloaking the screen brought to mind stock images, old film clips from the Second World War. The Serbian army had crossed the natural border of the Drina and was advancing through Bosnia. I remembered the long night of the first man on the moon, that distant signal. I was a little girl. I sat beside my father, who was watching the television as if it were the last piece of something he would never see again. Suddenly he felt himself a part of a single generation of men that went from the wings of Icarus to Leonardo's flying machines to the Wright Brothers' first Flyer, a generation that was now leaving the earth's gravity for good to take a seat on that diaphanous, distant eye. The deep-sea diver on the screen, white, unsteady as a small child on the moon's lead-colored crust, he was my father himself.

My father believed in the future, like Sebina. He believed that common men would take to moving through the skies, full sail ahead. Mournful tanks were advancing across the screen, and the only signal that came in was a disturbed image on that ancient television.

Velida stood to free the two blackbirds from their white cage in the kitchen. They never left, just flew through the rooms, at the very most crossing the street to perch on the balcony of the building across the way and then coming back when Velida called them, tame as hens. She turned off the television with an irritated gesture, almost a challenge, rummaged through the vinyl albums on the shelf and slipped some jazz onto the turntable of their old gramophone. Then she made coffee, with maniacal care, without spilling the tiniest bit.

I breathe in the calm of those rooms, smell the perfume of objects accumu-
lated over the course of many years. Art books, scientific volumes, crock-
ery on the kitchen shelves, photographs of Velida and Jovan when they were
young, the clock on the wall. It's as if nothing is ever to move from this house,
a little domestic labyrinth where blackbirds fly and come to a stop on the
couch next to the cat, who doesn't even look at them. "It's odd for a cat not to
pounce on a bird," I say to Velida.

She lifts the ladle. "I taught them to respect each other."

We're in the kitchen. I'm helping her make sarma. We mix the rice with
the meat, lay out the grape leaves, fill them and roll them. Velida's gestures
bring to mind eternity, stuffed grape leaves endlessly boiling and satisfying
palates. It's relaxing here in this kitchen with this ancient biologist, who ban-
ishes the black of the world by turning off the television and dicing an onion.

"Why didn't you and Jovan have children?"

Her eyes are red from the onion, but she's smiling.

"We didn't want them. Jovan was too caught up with his research and I
was too caught up with him. And so it went."

"And you've never missed having a child?"

She could lie. She's accustomed to reserve, to solitude. But she doesn't.
"Always," she says. "Always." She piles up the stuffed grape leaves in a pan,
crumbles red pepper. She's smiling again.

Earlier, in front of the television, I asked her what she plans to do if the war
reaches them, engulfs them. She shrugged and went to let the blackbirds out.
Now she answers. She pours a bit of vinegar into the pan and says they will
never leave their home. She says she's had cancer twice but God must not want
her. He's left her there to cook. "People are only afraid when they have children."

A pleasant smell is coming out of the pan. I tell her God is right to leave
her in that kitchen. She asks why I don't have children.

I tell her the truth in a moment, easily. She looks at me with her biologist's
eyes and shakes her head. She tells me that my name, in the process of gem-
mation, indicates the first draft of a new individual.

I told Gojko I wanted to meet Aska on my own. We met in a bar I'd never
been to before, a turban made of copper and glass in the middle of a park, a

funny, Austro-Hungarian reworking of Ottoman design. Inside, the elegant decadence of a turn-of-the-century Viennese café mingled with the smell of pickled cucumbers and bosanska kafa. Aska was half hidden by a curtain of mirrors. Her black trumpet case sat next to her. She was deep in conversation with Gojko.

I moved toward the table and held out a hand. "Hello."

She stood and hugged me warmly. She was wearing a black sweater full of slashes and the jeans from the day before. The safety pin was still there in her ear, but she wasn't wearing makeup. In close proximity to her hair, to the skin on her neck, I breathed in her smell, rosewood and cedar.

She ordered for me. Austrian *bavaroises* and local pastries made with honey.

While she eats, I study her face. We're sitting very close. In the day's inclement light, I look for hidden damage, a little flaw, but she's beautiful, her face is a perfect oval, austere, and there's a natural swelling under her eyes and in her skin, which is transparent, like water. It's a sensual tiredness that ruffles her beauty. She is observing me as well, the crumbs on my mouth, the ring on my finger. We talk a little.

"How old are you?"

"Twenty-two."

I had hoped she was a bit older. I look around. A middle-aged woman is talking and smoking and clutching her pack of cigarettes in her free hand as if it were her own breath. At the end of the room there's a door, the bathroom maybe. Suddenly I think I should leave now, get up, say I need to use the bathroom and instead leave this sheep with those puffs beneath her eyes like swollen petals.

And now I think she resembles me the way I was a few years ago, the expression on her face haughty and foolish at the same time.

Gojko shoots me a malicious glance, like a panderer, a procurer.

It's hot in the café, and Aska's taken off her sweater. Underneath, she's wearing a T-shirt with a gray print on it of a young face. It's not clear whether it's a man or a woman.

She asks me if I want the last *bavaroise*.

"It's yours," I say.

I'm full. I was never actually hungry. Aska eats the *bavaroise* and licks her fingers.

She has strange eyes, with a shadow of sadness like little boats forgotten on a river. Her expression as she looks at me is serious, and even when she laughs she doesn't strike me as someone who would make fun of people. Gojko treats her like a younger sister, with the same gruffness he sometimes uses with Sebina. He asks her who the girl on her T-shirt is.

Aska tells him, *You're old, you don't know anything.* The girl is a man, a legend named Kurt Cobain.

That's how I discover she's a fan of Nirvana, that she listens to them at night, in the dark. She says they carry her away.

"And where do they carry you?" Gojko mocks.

"Somewhere you could never go."

He lights a cigarette, throws the pack on the table. He sneers, grumbles that Nirvana is a bunch of *lukavi*, slick operators. "Fucking millionaire nihilists." He gets up, says he has to take a piss. He does it on purpose to leave me alone with Aska.

At the bottom of her T-shirt there's a sentence in English, something Cobain said. NO ONE WILL EVER KNOW MY PLANS.

I want to leave the café.

"What are your plans?" I ask her point-blank.

She tells me she just wants to leave. She's from Sokolac, thirty miles from Sarajevo. She supports herself by playing gigs now and then in clubs and by giving trumpet lessons. In fact, she doesn't have much time now because she has to go teach the son of a Baščaršija jeweler. She puffs out her cheeks to show me that the boy is fat. He can't even spread his fingers over the valves. She says it's all the rage among well-off Sarajevans to give their children music lessons. She says that she's young and doesn't want to get old doing this. She smiles. One of the three guys in Nirvana is Croatian. If he could do it, so can she. She wants to go to London or to Amsterdam and start a band. That's why she needs the money.

"What did Gojko tell you?"

"That you need a *roda*. A stork."

"That's right."

There's some cream left on the plate along with a few grains of sugar frosting. Aska scrapes up these remnants with a spoon.

"I'm ready," she says.

She looks around, plants a fist under her chin and draws near me with her green eyes. I can smell her breath.

She's brazen and businesslike. She wants to be paid in deutschmarks, in cash. Her head disappears and reappears as she puts her sweater back on.

"Are you only doing it for the money?"

She lifts her trumpet case, smiles and says she likes to tell the truth, that I can trust her because she isn't afraid of the truth. "What do you want me to say?" She touches her earlobe, one of those kitsch earrings. "That I'm doing it for love?"

She tells me music is her entire life. She spent her childhood in the country cleaning rabbit hutches, husking corn and playing the ears like flutes, like keyboards. For many years, Sarajevo was like San Francisco for her, but now it cuts into her like a tight bra. She says she'll never marry, never have a family.

I ask her if she's Muslim.

She grimaces. She never goes inside a mosque, though now and then she reads the Koran.

"What does the Koran say about renting out your womb?"

"The Koran says to help others." She doesn't mind the idea of lending her womb to a mutilated woman. That's the word she uses, *mutilated.* "Each of us has to give something back." She stands up, puts on a long plastic coat to cut the wind while she's on her motorcycle. She shrugs. She asks me to let her know soon. She has to arrange her future.

Diego doesn't say anything. I look at his hollow neck, his head hanging on his shoulders. He's exhausted. His pants are muddy. He climbed up to the Jewish cemetery and photographed the city from above. There was fog down below and it looked like the minarets and the tops of the building were sticking up out of a cup of whey. I tell him about Aska. All he says is, *I don't know.* He puts his rolls of film in order, numbers them and puts them all away in their black capsules.

We found a doctor on the outskirts of the city on the state highway to Hadžići. Gojko picked us up in his car. Aska sat in front with her hacked-at red hair and black-painted nails and big dark glasses like Kurt Cobain's. I looked like her mother, with my knee-length skirt, my eyeglasses and chignon.

The doctor was thickset and had a somewhat obtuse expression, like certain farmers. He didn't ask many questions. He kept sucking in air through the space between his two front teeth. All I remember is that mouth curling up like a rabbit's, that irritating noise.

Aska put her hand on Diego's and said he was her boyfriend and that they wanted a child but that she couldn't have sexual intercourse. "I have muscle spasms that make it impossible."

Gojko lowered his head almost to the floor. The bastard was laughing. And again I felt the thrill of our youth together, when we were crazy and free. The doctor wasn't interested in our eccentricities. He prescribed a series of tests for Aska, requested a down payment of one hundred deutschmarks and told us to come back the next week.

Aska left the room wagging her behind and winked at me before she put her superstar sunglasses back on.

We wait for her outside the music school in a hidden café because she doesn't want her friends to see her. She moves her mouth like a beak, *Quack quack, they talk too much.* She doesn't want to explain anything to anyone. She never seems very happy to see us. She laughs, accuses us of being like overly anxious parents. I wring my hands in the café and little bones crack. I'm the anxious one. Diego's calm, too calm. He acts like a guest.

"We need to know you better."

Aska snorts. *That's stupid, because people never really know each other, not even husbands and wives know each other. Everyone has a secret life.*

"Do you two know each other?"

Diego smiles. Their eyes meet and it seems like they're close to each other in a flash.

The sheep has traveling eyes, always a little tired, that pull themselves up like wet wings, blink and like wet wings descend. But when they touch you they leave a trace, the sorrow of beauty. I look at her lips. They're chapped from all her trumpet-playing. She never stops licking them. I look at her breasts, her arms, the bits of her body I can see below her costume of modern calamity: punk absurdity, Sarajevo-style. I don't care that she decks herself out that way. She's not my daughter and she's right, we'll never be friends. She whitewashes her face, paints her lips dark and fierce.

She'll go to London, where she won't make anything of her life. She'll waste it on the streets, in the din of clubs. I don't care about her destiny, I care about her immediate future. I care about her flesh. She's joking with Diego. I let them go on about music. She's beautiful, despite the paint, bursting with health. I smile like an amiable mother. "So, you want to leave Sarajevo."

She's chewing. Every time we see her she stuffs herself, orders sandwiches, sweets, says every time that she hasn't eaten since morning. She says you can't play for too long if you really play, because the music eats you alive.

She detests Madonna and Michael Jackson.

Now she's talking about Janis Joplin. All of a sudden her face changes, becomes sad. She stops eating and looks straight ahead. "Every so often God picks someone and says, *You, come with me.* You can't say no to God. He plants himself in your body and tears your soul apart. Janis took drugs to put up with God."

I ask her if she takes drugs, if she's ever taken drugs.

She looks at me with hate in her eyes. She says no. Then she stands up and says the session is over.

We're crossing Goat Bridge.

She's telling me about her mother, who died just a month earlier. It was because she didn't follow her path, Aska says. People get sick when they don't follow their paths. "Last night I fell asleep to 'Smells Like Teen Spirit.'" She laughs, says it's almost impossible to sleep to that song, but she fell into a sleep as heavy as lead. She dreamt she was walking, naked and pregnant, along Marshal Tito Boulevard. She was very tired, her belly was heavy and she couldn't understand why she kept walking instead of sitting down. Then she saw the tanks coming toward her. She knew they were going to crush her, but she kept going forward as if it were the only thing she could do, like the unknown rebel in Tiananmen Square. She was sure she would stop them.

She looks down at the gentle waters of the Miljacka. "Sarajevo has too many bridges." She spreads her arms in the wind and stands there like an angel with open wings and red hair, her pathetic Sarajevan grunge outfit, big dark glasses and a safety pin in her ear. She tells me to open my chest, to breathe. We stand there like two foolish angels, me in my suit, her with her bracelets, infinite metal circles that sound like a bell on a sheep's neck.

"Why can't you have children?"

I tell her my story.

"It's not just your womb. It's life itself that's denied you every day, time and time again."

She hugs me without excessive emotion. The safety pin brushes against my mouth. It's as if my future were hanging from that pin.

Diego takes our picture from behind. He says he likes to see us together, that Aska reminds him of a girl in Genoa who worked in a warehouse full of old navy military uniforms, stiff cloth that smelled of damp.

"Did you like her?"

"She was a lesbian."

Aska asks me if Diego and I love each other.

"Yes, very much."

She nods, looks at the water below, bends down to pick up a pebble and throws it in.

Diego frames us, hugging on that bridge. Then Aska wants to put her eye to the viewfinder and take our picture.

Diego is talkative, like he is with his female students. "You can take pictures of reality, or you can search."

"Search for what?"

"Something going by, something unseen, something that will appear later."

He tells her that this is why he loves to photograph water, because it moves and inadvertently something is included, a passage, a reverberation.

Aska presses the shutter release button, gives the camera back to Diego, smiles. "Who knows, maybe I took a picture of something unseen."

I smile, and it's my stupid smile again, because once more I can sense the child there, floating toward us on this sidewalk. I turn to observe them. They're walking close together on the sidewalk without looking at each other. For a moment I think there's a resemblance. They're the same height and they have the same way of walking, hips wobbling, leaning forward and stiff, as if they were trying to avoid some danger by going defiantly toward it.

In the meantime, we've given her the first five thousand deutschmarks. She counted them at the table in the café.

"Wouldn't it be easier to put them in a bank account?"

She doesn't trust the banks. Yugoslavia is losing bits and pieces and she's scared someone in Belgrade will end up with her money.

We take a taxi back to the doctor's. She's clutching the card with the test results. "Everything's fine," she says. "I don't have AIDS."

I brush against her leg, the holey tights showing bubbles of snow-white flesh.

"I'm nervous, Aska."

"Why?"

Who can guarantee she won't want to keep the baby? That she won't say, once she feels it move, that she can't give it up?

She reassures me. She takes off her glasses so I can see her eyes, without makeup this morning. She's given me her word.

"But how can you know now?"

She says she knows. She doesn't want children. She wouldn't know what to do with one. "All I care about is my music."

"What will you tell your friends?"

She thinks for a moment. "I'll go away for the last part. That's what I'll do."

"Where?"

"There's a place I like on the coast."

"I'll come, too."

She nods beneath her dark glasses.

I already feel better. The car moves along and I imagine a little white house, off-season, full of damp smells. I take Aska's hand because I'm imagining the two of us walking along a beach, hand in hand, she with her belly and me putting one of my shawls over her shoulders, making her tea, taking care of her. It will be nice, just the two of us, the wintry sea and a window with droplets on the outside, steam on the inside.

We've stopped in front of the little clinic.

"I'll play music all the time for your baby. That way, maybe he'll be a great musician."

She saddens all of a sudden. I tug one of those locks of strong red hair.

"No Nirvana. I'm begging you."

"What do you want me to play for him?"

"Mozart."

"Forget it."

"Chet Baker."

"Okay."

The doctor wasn't there. The door was bolted shut. Aska climbed the stairs, rang other doorbells. The only person left was a woman in a wheelchair.

She came back to us, tired arms at her sides. "They've all gone away."

"Where?"

"I don't know. There's no one left."

We heard voices and after a while saw two men in camouflage uniforms on one of the balconies. They stood there like two office workers taking a break, smoking, looking at us. It seemed like they were laughing at us. For the first time, I was afraid. We waited awhile under the gate, stunned, like chickens closed out of the henhouse after sunset.

The taxi was gone. We headed back on foot. Aska walked on the other side of the street, looking like someone on her way back from a ramble in the countryside. She hummed, tried to grab the bud-covered fronds of a prune tree. We were on the edge of the road. Very few cars passed, leaving behind the stink of their old mufflers. Diego gave me his hand, weightless and distracted. One of his lenses was scratched. It had fallen on the stairs at the clinic. That was his sorrow for the day. He was sick of these pilgrimages. It was out of inertia, or love, that he let me drag him along, but it was like following a wife afflicted with a solitary obsession.

I stopped to look at the sky, the retreating sun driven away by the night. There wasn't a single star. We walked back through the dark, fumbling along until we reached the lights of the city. Aska lived in one of the outlying neighborhoods. We walked her to her house. She invited us to come up, though she didn't have much to offer us.

"That doesn't matter."

We climbed the stairs.

Now we really were orphans, and she was our mother. It wasn't a real house, it was more like a dormitory, with little apartments one next to another like dressing rooms.

"These houses were lodgings for the Olympic athletes."

Inside there was a table made of light wood, glued to the floor, and a corner bench covered with the same brown carpeting as on the floor. There was a line of glasses on the wall behind a metal grate. It was like the inside of a camper. I took a few steps to go to the bathroom and glanced into the bedroom, which was also little and dark. On the wall was a poster of Janis Joplin with her old bag-lady face and frizzy hair, slits for her eyes and one for her mouth, the wind of delirium. Beneath the image, the words ON STAGE I MAKE LOVE TO 20,000 PEOPLE. THEN AT NIGHT I GO HOME ALONE.

We stayed and talked for a while. Aska took some glasses from the metal grate, put milk and a spoonful of cocoa powder in each one and stirred. She put her finger to her cheek and turned it back and forth, the gesture meaning that this drink was good, that it would make us feel better. She said she always cheered herself up by eating sweets, like a small child. But she didn't seem at all sad. She'd taken off her purple boots and was walking barefoot. Her feet were white, with long thin toes. I took off one of my shoes and put my foot next to hers. We laughed, because mine was much smaller and wider. I told her she could have been a basketball player. She shook her red head and told us again that all she wanted to do was play her trumpet. She was born with the trumpet inside.

"It's a strange instrument for a woman."

"It's mine."

"Why?"

"It takes all your breath, your soul."

She glued her lips to the mouthpiece and started playing "Diane," eyes closed, swaying zombielike, Chet Baker–style.

Diego watched her with his mouth slightly open, the way you watch someone you care about who might make a mistake. The evening heated up like that, with the chocolate milk and the music. Diego rolled a joint. Now he was drumming on the table with his fingers. I was hugging my knees to my chest, my head back against the wall.

I felt good. I'd taken a puff, too, and now I felt a few little tepid shivers inside, blades of straw moving gently.

And so it had gone. We would leave our little Sarajevan friend behind and this evening was worth five thousand marks. By now I was used to defeat, holes in the water. Always the same, always the same little pond. It was a sweet, vibrant night. A farewell whose taste I already knew. Aska stopped playing, shook her trumpet. Some saliva fell out. She made another round of milk and cocoa powder. She pulled her safety pin out of her ear and started fiddling with it.

"Why do you dress like that?"

"I started to spite my father."

She tells us about her father, the prayer leader at the mosque in her village. They fought for years, but since her mother's death they've made up.

"My mother's dead, too." I'm sad. Diego is wearing the sweater she gave him. I think back to that day, her shy eyes, uncertain about everything, like always. It seems I resemble her more than I ever realized.

Diego takes my hand and kisses me. "What are you thinking about, love?"

"Nothing. My mother." Yes, I'm thinking about her, an insignificant woman to whom life gave so little.

Aska asks, "Was she sterile, too?"

I laugh, like I've never laughed before, revealing all my teeth, all my unhappiness. "I was born."

Aska thinks it's funny. "Oh, yeah. How stupid."

It's the joint taking effect. *But maybe she's right*, I think. *Maybe I was never born. Maybe I'm the shadow of my desires.*

And once again that fable comes to mind, the sheep dancing so as not to die.

We hear the sounds of gunshots up in the hills and stick our heads out a little double window. Aska has to hold the frame up with one hand because the hook is broken. The air is cold. We can't tell for sure where the shots are coming from.

Aska doesn't seem worried. "It's been happening almost every night for a while. It's just a bunch of stupid kids having fun."

She and I go back to the kitchen to heat some water. She's busy trying to keep the gas burner alight when she says it. "If you want, we can do it naturally." She's just had her *menstruacija* and in about ten days she'll be ready for mating. That's the word she uses, *mating*. I laugh. She's playing with that safety pin. She says for her the mating would be no problem. I think of rabbits in the country and their rapid couplings. My face is burning. I'm dumbfounded with joy, an unsheathed excitement.

"It could be a problem for me." But before I finish speaking I know it isn't true. It isn't a problem. I look at her rust-colored hair and already I've leapt over the depths of ambiguity. All night something has been floating in my stomach. And before, too, when I was looking in that room, at that bed, I thought, *It's nothing. Another joint and I'll sit on the bench while they lie down under the poster of Janis Joplin and we'll all go back home alone, Aska, all of us, into the depths of our little bodies, born not to last.*

She's still talking. She says she's not interested in sex, she finds it useless, like anything else that's too goopy and wet. I can watch if I want. "Like in a clinic." She laughs.

I thank her. *"Hvala."*

"You're welcome," she responds, not catching my irony. She says it another time. *"Za mene parenje nije problem."* For me, mating is no problem.

I let that sentence slide into my chest, went back to sit on the bench and waited for the effect to sink down deep, down into my belly.

Diego was watching us. He could sense something, the new wine of an intimacy.

"What are you two doing?"

"Ništa." Nothing.

I told him to roll another joint. I wanted to laugh and laugh, for everything to melt into long languid laughter. We were done with clinics, needles, withdrawals of seminal fluid. We were done with everything that had made me suffer. Goodbye to ejaculations into glass, hello to coitus in the flesh, Aska's white warm flesh that now seemed like my own. It would be like the three of us making love together, being warm together, like a little while ago, when the three of us huddled together at the window, the two of us and our sheep.

It was just the flesh we needed. She was young and Diego liked her. Anyone would have liked a morsel like that, a Sarajevan dimwit as beautiful as the sun, made just a bit ugly by fashion, by stupidity toward herself.

We looked into each other's eyes for a little while longer. She wasn't embarrassed. She didn't lower her eyes, she held them there, abandoned in

my own, guileless. She was simply not as happy as before. Now she was leaning against the window and I was learning something about her. She was
slightly disconnected from the world, as if there had always been a little void
to cross, to violate, between her and everything around her. There were no
bridges for her, there was a flowing river, and she was looking for something
to grab on to in the water, a rock sticking up, something. Now she'd found it,
that rock, and little did it matter that it was her own body.

I thought she had waited for me, that she had come my way to help me,
that she'd been born for that purpose, that it was her destiny. She'd floated
between us by chance, like a child when a couple makes love, and this was
a night of love, with those distant gunshots almost keeping us company,
admonishing us, teaching us that life has its risks, its harshness, and that one
might as well get straight to the point and risk everything once and for all,
go all the way. I looked through the windowpanes at the profiles of the hills
outlined by the glimmer of moonlight. What were we, sheep or wolves?

"Aska wants to go ahead anyway."

Diego burst out laughing. He was flushed.

"What, you mean I'm supposed to . . ."

His eyes met mine and fluttered away, like a moth against a light. His shirt
was open, his curls pressed against his forehead, his lips chapped from the
cold. Red blotches of embarrassment assaulted the skin on his face like a violent allergy. We stumbled along through the night, dazed, that strange game
thrusting us forward. By the time we found the way back to our room, to our
bed, my mood was already more confused, my throat thick. Diego took off his
pants and got in bed without taking off anything else. He lay there under the
covers in his shirt and bare legs. We stank of chocolate milk.

"How does Andrić's fable end?"

"It's a happy ending. The sheep keeps dancing. The wolf waits so long to
eat her, he doesn't notice that they're too close to the village, and the peasants
surround him and kill him. The mother gives the dancing sheep a good scolding and the sheep swears she won't stray so far ever again, and since she is so
good, they send her to dancing school."

I clutched his thin legs. We kissed for a long time. Months had passed
since we'd last made love. Now we were suddenly excited.

Dawn was already upon us, a nearby glimmer like a pond in the night, and far away the darkness of the mountains.

The next day I went to look for Gojko at the radio station. I stood in the recording studio and waited for him to finish his show. It was late morning, but in there it felt like night. Gojko sat beneath a wan yellow light with his headphones on. His voice, hoarse from cigarettes, rustled through the microphone, sensual and soft. He was reading a poem. When he saw me he blew me a kiss and dedicated Mak Dizdar's verses to me:

Kako svom izvoru
Da se vratim?
(How will I return
to my source?)

We sat in the entry, by the door, and had a coffee from the little machine.

"What do you want me to say?"

"The truth. What do you think?"

Now and then someone came in, bringing air into the room.

I was there for advice. The coffee in the paper cup was too hot. I spilled some on my shirt.

"Those two want to fuck, that's what I think."

I shake my head, puff out my cheeks. I'd like to say something. I wait to recover from the blow. We look out the windows at the inner courtyard, the branches dotted with little dusty flowers.

"Diego is completely crazy about you, out of his mind." He gets up, goes to the bathroom and comes back with a handkerchief dripping water. "But he's a man. And a man's pickle doesn't follow the same path as his heart. It takes the low road. Through the sheep pens." He laughs and says the sheep is a clever storyteller. He doesn't like her, but he's certain she'd never keep the kid. "She's young, she wants to have fun. May I?" He rubs the wet handkerchief over the coffee stain. "Take what you need. Stop suffering. Get this damned kid, so we can send him off to war." He laughs again, but he's sober.

I look at him. He's handsome this morning. His blue shirt suits him. So do his glasses. He may be the best person I know, the most sincere, the most alone.

"I'm afraid."

"Of a sheep?"

Gojko looks at the skin showing beneath the wet silk of my shirt. "What a yearning," he whispers.

"Why were they shooting on the hills last night?"

"The assholes want to make sure we know they're there."

We walk for a while, arm in arm, beneath the white pollen dust coming off the trees.

"Is something going to happen?"

"No. They'll leave."

He looks at me, looks again at the pink skin beneath my wet shirt. "Water can't be divided."

"After I give you what you want I'll disappear."

"Maybe we'll come see you in London, or Berlin. When you're a rock star. We'll come to cheer for you."

"Maybe."

"You'll pretend not to know us."

"No. You won't really come."

We saw each other just a few more times, quick, formal encounters. Aska was always in a hurry to get away, agitated, clutching her trumpet case like a shield.

In fact, something had changed.

Diego's eyes were nervous, his lashes like insects in flight.

They rarely looked at each other, and it was precisely there, in that avoidance, that the knots were being tied. I noticed but didn't say anything.

All I had to do now was wait. They were the ones pulling the sled. I wasn't risking a thing. Diego was mine like every drop of my blood. And I wanted our child to be born out of pleasure rather than sadness. I was sick of crooked ghosts, sad women, opaque children. I liked the banquet of her youth.

Aska had become more severe, more inward.

Now it seemed to me that all her nonchalance was false, like the way she dressed and hacked at her hair. She reminded me of the dolls I ruined as a child with markers and scissors.

Diego spoke very little when the three of us met. Every so often, when I said something, he'd nod. The rest of the time he seemed almost inert.

"I don't know if I can go through with it," he'd said.

He clung to me like a child, as if he were afraid of losing me. We had agreed: just once. If nothing happened, we'd leave.

He kept asking me, "Are you sure?"

I wanted his child. That was the only thing I knew. I closed my eyes and thought of the baby. I acted calm, spoke only of practicalities. I had become like one of the doctors. I had learned from my torturers. I used the same quiet tone, the same bureaucratic jargon. The cycle was regular. In a week the sheep would be fertile.

There were riots and a death. The father of a groom was killed in front of the Orthodox church.

Aska was beside herself.

"They were waving the flag with Chetnik eagles in the heart of the Baščaršija!"

I took Diego's hand, placed it on Aska's on the riverside wall and put mine on top.

"Everything will be okay," I said.

It was a sort of ritual. I stood there feeling the warmth emanating from that tangle of hands, the little nerve endings, the microscopic adjustments, all the tension flowing through that embrace. I thought of the marks on the undersides of our hands, in the dark, those palms one atop the other. And once again I asked if destiny would help us.

Aska tried to withdraw her hand, but I held it down. Then Diego tried to free himself and Aska and I pushed downward with all the weight of our hands. "Where do you think you're going?"

Diego was restless. They had that carnal appointment, and they could no longer look each other in the eyes. They would look later.

We went into the zoo, walked between the cages and the enclosures. It was windy. A light-colored dust rose up off the ground to dirty the air. The bears were agitated, holed up in a kind of empty tub covered here and there with moss. Aska had insisted we come. It had been years since the last time she visited the zoo. It reminded her of her childhood. She bought a pack of peanuts and fed them to the chimps. She wandered around the cages making funny noises. A peacock answered her. I went off to get a bottle of water.

When I came back, Diego was taking her picture. Nothing was happening. She had stepped into an empty cage, where she was hanging from the bars like a depressed monkey, her red head lolling onto a shoulder. I felt something, the weight of intimacy.

Diego had lowered his Leica and was looking at her with his naked eyes. Aska was walking ahead, her fingers running across the bars.

In the middle of the night I call my father. His voice is alert, as if he'd been expecting my call.

"Dad."

"Dear heart."

He doesn't say anything. I hear his breathing, the rustling of his lungs, of his life through this gray, government-issue receiver. It's been ages since I last called.

"Do you need anything?"

"No."

"What's that noise?"

"It's raining."

"When are you two coming back?" He tells me about his dog. "I don't cook anymore. Every night we go out to the Mexican restaurant." The dog likes meat, my father likes tequila, they're perfect companions. He makes me laugh. Joking with him is a way of beating this rain, which is getting me down.

"What's that noise?" he asks again.

Now I'm the one breathing into the receiver. Thunder, I tell him. But it was gunfire, deaf, insolent.

"Be careful."

I tell him he's far away and there's no way he can understand. "People here are mixed together like water, one drop within the next."

He says the news in Italy isn't very comforting.

"They'll bring bad luck," I grumble, and laugh because I've started to sound like Gojko.

I hang up. Diego's sleeping, one of his long feet hanging out of the bed.

It was Aska who put the date on the calendar, three days, the best ones, the most fertile, the ones right in the middle of her cycle. And instead of a circle she'd drawn a heart. We'd decided to go for the second day, the one in the middle of the heart. We'd piled our six hands on top of each other to celebrate with a propitiatory rite.

Now I thought of that heart. The calendar was right there, hanging in our room. I looked at it every night and counted down the hours.

A few days beforehand, we chose the place for their meeting, an inn like a mountain hut, an isolated house at the end of the city, one of the last structures on Mount Trebević. Upstairs there were a few rooms, a single corridor and a couple of bathrooms at the end. We went into one of the spotless rooms, clean-smelling like a clinic. A little barred window looked out onto the woods. *Are there thieves?* Anela, the owner, had laughed. *No, squirrels.* They snuck into the rooms to gather crumbs. The bed was covered with a white, hand-embroidered cloth. I lay down. I felt audacious and unconventional, like Gojko, like the third inhabitant of a single heart. Aska and Diego leaned against the wall, two shy little squirrels.

Chapter 11

The woman who ran the inn at the foot of Mount Trebević kept right on setting the tables for breakfast every morning. There was nothing to eat, not even stale bread for the chickens, nothing but chipped cups and glass that had fallen from the window frames. But she held on to her routine. It was a way of not giving in to the men who'd occupied the heights. She persisted, like an animal that carries on living for as long as it manages to stay standing. She rose early each morning, fetched water from the well, made coffee. Every day, waiting for peace, Anela set the tables for her guests. She studied the dawn and the old iron rooster on the door, mauled and damaged by drunken soldiers who'd used it for target practice. Who on earth would have come to the inn in those times? There were no tourists, no couples in flight, no traveling salesmen from Dubrovnik or Mostar. All the same, every single one of the infinite days of the siege, Anela set her wooden tables. The devils had come in and taken everything they could get their hands on. There wasn't a thing left in the place, not even a plum. She'd picked up the cups, glued them back together and set them out every morning on the bare table. They sat there, motionless, like tired doves awaiting peace. This was her pride, her resistance.

I'm wearing my backpack and my rounded sunglasses that make me look like I have two black eggs stuck in my eye sockets. It feels hotter. I'm sweating in my shirt. I can feel the cloth sticking to my back. I climb toward Bistrik. There are traces of shelling on the smog-blackened stones at the base of the walls. Little Ottoman houses with dark wood bay windows. I stop. It seems like the old inn is about to slide onto me. I recognize the structure. With its narrow base and the walls that seem to grow wider and lean crookedly forward the higher up they go, it looks like a mistake made by a distracted architect. It makes me think of the ancient headstones in the Muslim cemetery.

The woman is out back on the cement patch where the yellow plastic cases for empty beer bottles and the gas tanks are. She's giving corn to a pair of dwarf chickens who hover around her feet. I greet her. She doesn't recognize me, but I wouldn't have recognized her, either, if I had seen her somewhere other than here. I know it's her because she's here, because I was looking for her. My first thought is that she's alive. She's an old woman, dressed in black, with red cheeks and a toothless smile. Anela's never left here.

We talk for a while with my limited Bosnian. I tell her I came to this inn before the siege. She turns and points to the woods. The line of fire was there, a hundred meters away. She would go out in the morning to get the eggs, bend over among the wooden cages and then, with feathers sticking off her here and there, fry them for her guests. I look at her red hands, her weathered peasant face. When I speak to her she wears the same expression now as before, pretending not to understand and thinking in the meantime. So she's alive. She's come back to life, too, a marginal figure, a broken shell I had banished from my memory, along with everything else that was lost. Now, though, I'd like to hug her. I drag her into the world by an arm and put her back where she belongs.

Anela doesn't remember me but she looks at me and her eyes are swampy, barely holding back the tears.

After the war she sold the inn. She didn't have enough money to fix up the rooms that had been damaged by the shelling. She makes herself understood with a few words of German and Italian. She kept a room on the ground floor for herself. The rest belongs to a print shop. The breakfast room is full of printing presses. She puts her hands over her ears; the noise makes it hard for her to sleep. She says she got used to the shelling, but now she's older and it's irritating to shake all day long along with the walls of her room.

"*Srepljenje,*" she says. Patience.

They let her stay. The owner is a rich man who made his money through the tunnel they dug beneath the airport, through the black market—eggs that cost one mark when they went in on the Butmir side and ten when they came out at Dobrinja. But he's not a bad man. He's let her stay on as a sort of guardian and he gives her a small monthly salary.

I ask her if I can look at the rooms on the second floor. She tells me there's nothing now but storage space.

"I came here with my husband . . ."

She looks at me. For a moment I think she might have recognized me.

"He was a photographer."

She nods and says there were lots of photographers. She puts her hands on her hips to show how she used to pose.

She disappears through the metal door of the print shop and comes back with a ring of keys. She tells me I'll have to be quick and not to touch anything. She can't come with me because she can't manage the stairs anymore. She sends me off with the same brusque gesture she'd used to drive away her chickens.

It was Anela who gave us the keys that night. We paid in advance. She nodded like a mother. She took Diego's passport and returned it without writing anything down. She turned toward the grate that held the keys to the inn's few rooms.

Hand against the wall. Hand. One of my hands against this old wall. I touch the wall as I climb the stairs. I'm more than fifty years old and there's no point in being here. This is the hallway. I recognize it immediately. I take a deep breath and move forward. All the rooms are on the same side. Up here nothing has really changed. It's all just darker and dirtier. The smell of war is still here, coming out of the wall and the cracks in the doors. This city must be full of places like this, buildings that have ostensibly been restored and are being used again but that contain abandoned passageways as sinister as unburied corpses. Here and there on the walls are grainy splotches where the plaster has been touched up, where wounds have been closed, suture points along the walls like on a sick body. There's a torpid, asphyxiating heat and an unpleasant smell of sewage. I push open a door. The bathrooms are still there. The old plaster is puckered, the toilets seatless with blackened bowls—the source of the unpleasant smell. I count the doors and confront the room. It's the one closest to the woods, to the birds, mushrooms and squirrels, the one that was too close to the line of fire. Once inside, I close the door and wait for my heart to calm down. Dusty boxes, reams of paper. Light filters in through the window gratings. I let my backpack slide off. I'll just stay a few minutes and then leave. The important thing is to remember that it's a place like any other, a timeworn room invaded by a fine luminous dust. The sink, small and lonely like a baptismal font in a forgotten church, still grips the wall. Around it lie bunches of I don't know what, folders, a papery mixture of old wedding invitations and piles of flyers black with humidity, wilted by the heat. And then I see that iron foot, the base of a bed. That bed. It's drowning in heavy packages wrapped in brown paper and closed with twine and munici-pal stamps, like old mail that's never been posted.

I trip and manage not to fall. There's Diego sitting before me on the bed. The mattress is unmade and there are burnt patches here and there. Shirt-less, his long hair held back in an elastic band he stole from me, he's play-ing the guitar. His feet are bloody, the feet of a boy who's walked over glass. He doesn't look at me. He's singing . . . *Spring is here again* . . . *Tender age in bloom.* . . . Aska trembles next to him on the burnt mattress. The windows are broken. Gusts of frigid air come in. I'd like to toss them a jacket, a blanket, anything. Cover them. I smile. They're not cold, I think, because they're dead. For years now they've been prisoners of this old bed, of this room.

That night Diego and I joked and walked arm in arm. We climbed up the little streets. Behind us the polished iron mouths of the Travelers' Fountain said goodbye. We were lighthearted and yet full of terror when we arrived at the inn. We stopped to kiss, sucking in each other's flavor. The gunshots stopped, like a distant game played by children who grew tired and went to bed.

I give him my final instructions and kiss him deep into his throat.

"We're crazy," he says.

We're young again. This nighttime walk is so similar to the snowy walk we took the first time we met. We're stray cats. Life carries us back in time. We're daring. To hell with propriety. To hell with second thoughts. Here's the big red door of the inn, the lonely crooked poplar like an elderly man, the iron rooster and the sign that says GOSTIONICA. Inn. We knock. Anela complains that it's late as she opens the door. She was about to go to bed. She has to be up at five. She lets us in and smiles. It's a night like any other, before the broken cups, before the white craziness. She gives us the keys to our room and to the main entry and tells us not to make noise.

We go back to wait for Aska on the road. We sit on the steps of a nearby house. A sliver moon hangs like a white mustache in the black sky. The branches of the poplar vibrate in the absolute silence. Diego breathes on me and presses me up against the wall. There's no sign of the sheep.

"What should we do?"

"Let's wait a little while longer."

It's not cold on this mild April night. If we were to walk away now, none of what is to come would happen. But life is like water, disappearing beneath the earth to resurface where it can, where it must.

I caressed Diego's hair, the soft, freshly washed curls. He rested his head on my legs. Time passed. The waiting went from vibrant-seeming to less certain. We looked around. A pearly fog was advancing through the dark.

The Nirvana fan had taken us for a ride. Her courage was an affectation like the rips in her clothes and her studded belt like a futuristic warrior's. She'd stolen some money from us, that was all. The album cover for *Nevermind* came to my mind. She kept it beside her bed like a relic and every night before falling asleep looked at that image of a newborn with open arms pursuing a dollar bill.

All of a sudden a blast bursts through the night, followed by an agitated silence. We look up at Mount Trebević, at the evergreen forests that cover it, immobile in the dark. Down here the fog is like almond milk or white powder. It eats up the meters as it moves along.

"Let's get out of here."

Yes, let's leave this night and this city that's started to be painful. We're already thinking about a consolation trip to the heavenly islands along the coast, deserted now because the tourists are too scared to come.

But here's Aska after all. We hear her scooter as she turns it off and then see her figure come forward through the fog. There she is, waiting in front of the big red door, her trumpet in its black case slung over her shoulder.

When I see her I know I've already seen this nighttime scene, with its foggy border that eats away at the contours of her body, like in images of saints. She's our Madonna, complete with messy red curls, holey tights and combat boots.

We whistle and wave our greeting. She says *ciao-ciao* in Italian. She loves to say *ciao-ciao*. She pronounces it in a strange, guttural way that makes it sound like the call that comes out of the gullet of a wild turkey.

"I'm late."

"We were about to leave."

"There were a lot of people in the streets."

It's true. People are taking their time going home.

She doesn't approach but waits for Diego to come to her. All I see is her hand against her leg, a gesture that's slow and perhaps a bit sad, as if she were caressing a body beyond her own, a dog's back, a child's head.

I could have gone in behind them and waited below. I could have fallen asleep on the little couch beside the breakfast room. But all of a sudden I was embarrassed. I felt ridiculous.

Diego and I pulled ourselves upright and alert after all that mushiness and said a hasty goodbye. No, I didn't want to hang around like a watchdog. I couldn't have stood the pain, the pornography. We hugged and Diego turned. I saw his eyes fill with fear and excitement.

Aska didn't come near me; I didn't want to go near her, either. We stayed in our places, one here, one there, on either side of the road. The fog was rising, erasing things as it came.

Listlessly, I made my way back. The cardigan I was wearing drooped with damp, and my hands dug deep into the pockets. I regretted my decision after just a few steps. The night was full of ghosts. I heard the panting of Diego and Aska in that little fresh-smelling room. I felt shabby and lost, a bitter unhappiness I recognized from my childhood, when a petty disagreement could leave me feeling mortally wounded and isolated from my friends. That ill-tempered child had returned. I clutched her to me along with the limp cardigan. She was the truest, most deeply buried and wretched part of me, the bud—the *gemma*—of my inabilities.

I thought again of my mother . . . *Gemma, Gemma.*

They must have put the metal gratings on the windows to keep the squirrels out. I can't tear myself away. Maybe a squirrel is watching them in my place. I see Diego's lips rest on those eyes, on that mouth devoid now of its lipstick.

They walked up the stairs hand in hand, embarrassed. They talked for a while, crossed their legs on the bed and played their instruments, softly, because the other guests were sleeping. Then Diego rolled a joint. He wanted to dull his senses. In the dim light that filters in from the outside they look into each other's liquid eyes, laugh, move toward each other. He caresses one of her hands lying still on the bed, one finger at a time. Then he moves toward her with his now-heavy head and rests his forehead against hers. Their lips touch. Soft skin opens ever so slowly. Now they can smell each other's skin, necks, ears. They can each smell the scent of the other's history, childhood and all the rest—small pains, dust, death that is so near. He pulls her velour concert dress over her head. She lifts her arms to help him. He buries his head in the hollow of one of her armpits. Her breasts move toward his bony torso, the little nipples of the boy from Genoa. They aren't afraid. They hear each other's hearts now, the heartbeats wandering in that red buried universe. The joint has taken effect. Everything is deep and near. Entering each other means entering life, a man and a woman, a passing child who observes the sepulcher of love. The dark has become phosphorescent. Aska's pupils dilate into Diego's. A distant planet draws near. She falls onto him. Again and again they fall onto each other, planets that pass over each other, swallow each other. The sheep moans, lost in the woods, and dances for him, for the clawless little wolf who's licking the nape of her neck and bleeding.

I cross the Latin Bridge and sit next to the Travelers' Fountain. I feel a hand on my shoulder. It's Gojko.

"What are you doing here?"

"I came down to bring out the trash."

He throws the bag in the dumpster and watches me.

"I was waiting for you. I couldn't bear to leave you alone."

I cry on his shoulder and thank the night for this big sweet body.

"Are those two fucking?"

"Yes."

We talk about whatever. I ask him what he's been up to. He was at the radio station, then at Parliament. He pulls out a piece of paper. He wants to read me a poem. I tell him no, I'm not in the mood. I'm tired of poems. He doesn't get angry. He burns it with his lighter, then lights a cigarette. I take one, too.

We watch the piece of black paper crumple in its moribund nocturnal dance.

"Too bad. It was nice." He takes leave of his poem. "Farewell, lost words. Burned by a cruel heart."

Dawn is slipping between our steps. The colors of the parked cars and the ivy gripping the wall beside us begin to show themselves. Gojko breathes on me. I'm crying again, my mouth trembling. All of a sudden I think that this

is the last burst of life and that we won't see each other again, that something
will happen to us. He moves closer, his eyes serious and calm. He doesn't
want to laugh or mock life, not right now. He breathes on my face.

"Do I stink?"

"No. You smell good."

He comes closer. We kiss each other like we've never kissed. I can feel his
teeth, his rough tongue like a cat's. I feel his weight, a motionless consternation, falling onto me. I feel the liquor of his heart and of all the poems he's
written that no one will read.

"Let's go to my house."

He lowers his head and raises it again. His little eyes dilate. It's the right
night.

"Let's go make love just once before we die."

It was a moment, a moment that passed, a moment that burned itself up
like the blackened piece of paper in the night.

We were a sham, a pathetic couple, stupid satellites around those two
young planets. I gave him a light blow on the cheek.

"We're not going to die, Gojko."

Off to bed. Like two foolish siblings.

The bed is there, right before my eyes; that is, what remains of it—an iron
frame, its feet rusted by the rain. It's too wide to go through the door, so no
one bothered to get rid of it, and now it's covered with junk from the print
shop. Season after season this bed has waited for me. It survived the war. It
floated through my dreams with its incessant squeaking, like a swing in an
abandoned garden that squeaks and goes through its old routine with every
gust of wind.

I move closer to the bed, push aside a couple of heavy packages. They fall
to the ground like bricks, stirring up the dust. I'm thin, I don't need much
space, just a narrow strip of this iron frame. I lie down and pull up my knees,
my feet still in their shoes.

Pietro's back. He drags himself hunching around the room with heavy steps
and the smell of chlorine. He complains; his back is on fire, Gojko fell on him

and weighed a ton. Danka scratched him. Her nails are too long and she's too much of a fraidy cat.

His footsteps make the floor shake. I shake, too, like old glass in a window frame.

I'm curled up on the bed, my eyes open in the semidarkness.

"Be quiet," I say. "Quiet."

Pietro throws open the shutters. "Why's it so dark in here?"

The light assaults me.

"What did you do, Ma?"

"Nothing. I walked."

He looks at my feet. "You haven't even taken off your shoes."

"Leave me alone for a while."

"You've been alone all day. What's the matter with you?"

I tell him I don't feel good, that I need to rest for a while. He says, *Come off it.*

I clean my eyes hastily with my hand. I don't want him to notice that I've been crying, but he sees me with his lynx eyes, so different from my own.

He keeps complaining but now he's broadened his subject matter. He grumbles that his friends go on really cool trips in August. They go to America to see the waterfalls, or to Dubai to see the world's highest tennis court, where Federer played. And here we are in this disgusting city.

I don't answer. Let him say what he wants.

I want to huddle in the dark. I want Diego and his arms gently hugging me, as if I were made of glass. Instead I get this ugly rasping voice.

He turns around and around on himself in the few meters of the room, hectoring me with every step. He yells that I'm just sitting on the bed, useless, and his back is sunburned.

He's used to seeing me come running, tail wagging, whenever he needs something. He's taken off his T-shirt. He moves around the room like a monkey in a cage.

"It hurts. It's on fire."

"Take a shower."

"Don't you have any lotion?"

"Look in the bathroom."

I hear him dump my bag out and throw everything around. He comes back with a little tube.

"Is this it?"

I nod. He tosses it onto the bed.

"Will you put it on me?"

"Do it yourself, Pietro."

He turns around, irritated. "Why?"

"Because I don't feel good. I told you."

He climbs up on the windowsill and pushes the keys on his mobile phone.

"Hi, Dad."

Leave me alone, Pietro. I cooked for you, I folded your clothes, I spent hours bent over your homework. You have your whole life before you. All I have are these old legs, these bones as empty as bamboo. Today I'm as pathetic as this city. I'm a sick cat rubbing up against the wall.

I hear him mutter that everything's disgusting and I'm out of it.

"Here, you can speak to her."

I don't want to talk to Giuliano. I want to be quiet and still.

He throws the mobile phone on the bed. "Here. It's Dad."

What little I have to say comes in a voice from beyond the grave. "I'll call you back," I say.

Maybe I have a fever.

Pietro climbs down from the windowsill.

"Why didn't you talk to him?"

"I'll call him later."

He pounds my back, my legs.

"What are you doing?"

"You're all dusty. Where have you been?"

I gather my skirt around my legs like a sick cat with her tail.

It's true. I'm dirty and sweaty.

"Leave me alone."

He picks his phone back up and stalks around the bed.

"Because you . . . because you . . ."

That's how he starts, without really knowing where to begin, just like usual, only today his anger is immense, a wave that blocks his vision.

"Who do you think you are?"

I should get angry, but I don't have the strength. My body is in pieces. I watch him from a distance. He's ugly now, graceless.

"Who do you think you are? You've always been ashamed of Dad."

He kicks the chair. Some clothes fall off.

"Dad has a belly, Dad wears a uniform."

"Pietro, what are you talking about?"

"And you never went to the carabinieri banquets, because you don't have anything to say to the wives of the other officers. You didn't even go to the memorial for Salvo d'Acquisto! I went and you didn't! You were busy!"

"What are you talking about? What does that have to do with anything?"

Now I look at him and I'm scared. I should get up from this bed, put lotion on his back, take care of him, spread something cool on this rage.

"You're selfish! You didn't come back here for me! You came here for that fucking Diego!"

He yells again but I've stopped listening. I look at his blue eyes, reddened now and muddied with rage. I throw his shirt at him. "Get out of my sight."

He stalks around again and I worry for a moment that he's going to jump on me, bite me. He's like a puma, a young puma, mouth poised to bite. He points his paw at me.

"Stop acting like you're so great, Mom. You're nobody."

He goes off, taking his sunburned back with him.

He'll go to the Internet café, that cave full of blue screens, and sit chatting with his friends, that army of hominids he disowned me for in the turning point of this last year. He'll come back with his eyes popping out of his head and look at me as if I were a distant relative.

It's true. I'm nobody.

I go into the bathroom to rinse my face. In the meantime I'm still crying.

I climb up on the windowsill to call Giuliano.

"I'm sorry. I'm so sorry."

"Whatever for?"

"That I didn't come to the memorial for Salvo d'Acquisto."

He laughs, but he's touched as well, because it's really stupid, and stupid things always touch us. But otherwise we're strong. He served with the peace-keeping troops in Lebanon. I was in Bosnia.

I tell him about Pietro's anger. He says, "Pietro's jealous. It's normal."

He sighs, and now his voice is shiny like the flame on his uniform cap.

"You're surrounded by jealous men."

I go out to find Pietro. I stick my head into the Internet café. It's full of kids bent over screens, cigarettes in their mouths. I don't see Pietro. I walk to Titova Street and empty myself of everything as I go. I'm always so scared I won't see him again. How many times have I waited at the kitchen window to hear the noise of his scooter and catch sight of his battered helmet, no longer myself but like I am now: a figure on a dark sheet of paper, waiting for the scissors to cut me out? Giuliano is calmer than me. *You're too anxious*, he says. *You'll worry your life away.* He's right. All mothers share these fears, but mine is another sort of affliction, darker, more desolate.

Then I find him sitting next to the Travelers' Fountain among lingering pigeons and nighttime passersby.

It's the same fountain, the Sebilj, where Diego and I stopped like travelers exhausted by a voyage that had just begun. Diego took some water with his hands. *There's a legend that if you drink a sip of this water you'll return to Sarajevo at least once in your life.*

"Pietro."

I don't touch him. I follow his lead.

He walks alongside me, head low. He's got a package in his hand. I glimpse the red paper as he sticks it in his pocket.

"What's that?"

He doesn't answer, just studies his feet like a gold prospector. I sniff. For a moment I worry about what might be in that red paper. A lot of his friends smoke joints starting first thing in the morning. He doesn't smell like smoke, at least he doesn't seem to.

I sit on the bed and unscrew the lotion cap. He comes near, T-shirt pulled over his head, back hunched. His burnt skin drinks in the coolness. My hands move over his young wings as they rub in the lotion. He doesn't say he's sorry, like he used to when he was younger, but he's breathing more calmly now, like a lamb that's regained its peace.

The peace groups called for an antiwar demonstration. It was like a river. Sarajevo was full of people, especially young people. Many came from elsewhere.

The parking lot beside the station was full of buses. From the first light of day the demonstrators wandered around the city, chanting slogans and eating sandwiches like soccer fans at an away game. I was awakened by the cries that came up and bounced around our room. I put my head out the window and saw the procession passing below. Later I went to see Velida. We ate quinces and drank coffee, lulled by the tumult of the human wave below. It let off an energy that was contagious.

We went out on the balcony and spent most of the day there, watching the demonstrators down below like two old ladies. Every so often she recognized someone from the university and waved. This tranquil swarm of students and miners in their work uniforms and women and fathers carrying their children on their shoulders could have been a peace demonstration anywhere in the world. A long white banner bearing the words MI SMO ZA MIR, We Are for Peace, floated over the bodies.

I hadn't seen such a crowd since the opening ceremonies of the Olympic Games at the Koševo Stadium. I thought of the torchbearer as he lit the brazier, the baton twirlers and that stupid wolf Vucko, the mascot of the 1984 Sarajevo Olympics. It all seemed so far away. Now there was another wolf, one who fired warning shots at the stars by night as if he wanted to extinguish them all.

Later, when the procession had moved on toward Parliament, I went with Velida to do some shopping. The grocery store felt oddly deserted. Many of the shelves were empty. A woman dragged a cart full of canned goods. Velida shook her head and walked with the superior gait of a proud little bird.

"What's with people, grabbing at everything like that? They've gone mad."

I asked her if she also wanted to stock up. Maybe there was a problem, a suppliers' protest, something we hadn't heard about.

Velida bought less than usual. There was an entire wheel of cheese she could have bought, but instead she asked for a small wedge, enough for that night's dinner.

"We've never stocked up and we never will. If they think they can bring us this low, they're wrong."

It was dusk. People walked quickly, staying close to the walls. Everyone seemed to be in a hurry to get back home. Isolated groups of demonstrators ran below our window as if they were being followed. The 1977 student demonstrations back home came to mind, the slogans, the brawls and sudden fights.

Night fell suddenly. The sun slid behind the mountains and a sliver moon appeared among the thick and distant clouds. It was still possible to see but only barely. Cries rent the dark. I put on my shoes and zipped up my jacket. Diego wasn't back yet. I wanted to go find him. I couldn't stand it anymore. I was tired of casting my gloomy shadow over his absence.

I reached the boulevard. The lanterns were not lit. After just a few meters a policeman stopped me. I tried to say something but he wouldn't listen. With wide eyes he explored the night. Then he raised an arm and yelled, "*Natrag! Natrag!*" Go back, go back. As if that were really possible.

I asked Velida if I could keep her cat with me for the night. I didn't want to sleep without something living beside me. I put on one of Diego's sweaters and stretched out on the bed. At dawn I heard shots. They were different from the others, closer, more agitated. I learned in that instant to distinguish between warning shots, fired into the sky, and shots to kill that end up buried in flesh. The cat was standing, neck stretched out, ears vibrating like little radar antennae. He'd been the first to perceive that evil hissing sound. He took refuge beneath the bed and began meowing a deep and graceless lament that sounded like the cries of a human.

We didn't look out the window anymore. Velida and Jovan had already lived through one war, while I hadn't, but instinct told me what to do. We drew the blinds and closed the shutters.

We spent the entire day in front of the television looking at the people who had rushed to Parliament. The radio played the same song over and over again, "Sarajevo My Love."

Gojko turned up that evening. His hair was standing up like a cat's and one of the lenses on his glasses was broken. He'd spent the last two days in Parliament with a huge crowd in an unreal climate of enthusiasm—the European Community had formally recognized Bosnia-Herzegovina—and of agitation because of the threat of war. President Izetbegović had been derided, while the men of the special police forces had received ovations.

He told me about what had happened. Someone had fired shots from the windows on the top floor of the Holiday Inn, where the hawks of the

Serbian Democratic Party had their rooms. The people gathered in front of the Parliament building threw themselves to the ground and tried to hide beneath each other like a terrified flock of animals. Many of them started running for the other side of the Miljacka, but shots were being fired there, as well, perhaps from the Jewish cemetery—that's what he'd heard people saying in the streets. The Serbian militia had occupied the Grbavica neighborhood.

Then the television brought the news that a girl was dead. She'd been killed as she tried to flee across the Vrbanja Bridge. I thought of Aska, wondered if her waxen face had born some sort of sign.

Now the Jutel announcer said that actually two young women were dead, students who'd been part of the peace demonstration, young lilies.

Gojko lit a cigarette and didn't even bother inhaling. He buried his face in his hands and began sobbing uncontrollably. I watched his cigarette as it burned down between his closed fingers and then fell to the floor and died. It was terribly clumsy, the sobbing of a beast. Hands glued to his face, he held up the rubble of the tragic future that had finally reached him.

When I look back I know that for me the war began with those sobs.

He regained control of himself. The river passed, leaving him with the gray face of a drowning victim. He smiled and worried about me, just like always.

"Let's go find the photographer."

Gojko drove with his headlights off, those broken glasses on his nose. Barricades had sprouted up overnight to divide the city. We managed to cross the Miljacka but it was impossible to reach the last houses at the base of Mount Trebević. Hooded men guarded the dark. Terror paralyzed my legs and moved up my back like a long nail. A burst of gunshot struck us, a hail of cartridges that stuck in the side of the car. We turned back.

I don't remember exactly how it went, don't remember the exact moment. Maybe no one does. Sebina, yes. She said she was watching *The Simpsons*, that happy family of pranksters. When the program was interrupted, she ran for her mother, who was at the kitchen table correcting her students' homework.

"Mama, what's happening?"

Mirna took off her glasses and looked at her daughter on the threshold.

"Don't worry."

Rumbling sounds came down from the mountains, the sounds of life vacating the city to make room for madness. They didn't know yet. They hugged. Mirna had work to finish. She touched the pile of papers. They were already floating away, along with the little lives who had written them, along with the table, the two of them.

It didn't last long. Soon *The Simpsons* started chattering again with their funny cartoon voices.

No, I don't remember the precise moment normality was suspended for good, when even the dogs fled to hide.

There was washing hanging from the lines. It was spring, the season for cleaning and windows opened wide. Every so often a crow screeched on the streets and no one paid it any attention. It was a peaceful city. No one thought in any particular way about the ethnicity of his neighbor or of his wife. They felt fondness or hatred for one another because they felt a connection, or because of a smell, just like anywhere else in the world.

The streets were full of people. More than one pair of arms bore a sign saying WIR SIND WALTER, We Are Walter. The entire city was drawn into a single heroic heart. They looked up as if they were watching an air show. They kept their eyes on the mountains. Who was hiding up there?

They'd started targeting houses. The first mortar shots fell far from us. We heard the blasts. They sounded like a recording, like something coming out of the plastic speaker holes on the radio.

Velida said, "Who could want to kill us?"

Then a shell fell so close it shook me. It felt like it went into my stomach. They were firing on the Baščaršija. For a moment we sat looking at each other as still as the dead. Velida's little face stiffened into a dull-witted fixedness as if she were already dead.

The cups shook and the books shook. The little blackbirds hid under a bunch of cotton wool.

Velida yelled, "Jovan! Jovan!"

"I'm here."

The old biologist hadn't moved from his armchair. He was sucking on one of his cigarettes, his fingers yellowed like his hair. Things fell off the shelves. The windows were still intact, at least for the moment, though they were shaking like my teeth. At a certain point I held my chin in my hand to stop that metallic noise. I gathered up a few things and closed myself in our room, where I clutched a pillow. I couldn't stop my teeth from shaking, and I had the same terrible pain in my stomach as when I'd miscarried, a hand that grabs hold and takes everything away.

It was three days before Diego came back. He came into the room like an animal silently crossing the night. We stood still in a long embrace, immobile like sandbags, all our strength drained away. He felt so heavy. He'd run. Sweat from his neck drenched my cheek.

"My love."

He held his hands over his ears and moved his head ever so slightly back and forth. A mortar shot had momentarily deafened him and now there was a lacerating whisper in there, a noise like suction. He didn't look at anything, just sat on the bed. He took off his boots and kicked them away with his last strength. He collapsed next to me. I let him sleep. I curled myself around his back to breathe in his smell, his usual smell but stronger, like when he had the flu and stayed in bed with fever and that man-dog smell remained on his sheets and the collar of his pajamas. I stayed there in the half dark, my eyes shut. He'd come back. His breathing was troubled, as if it were too much, as if it clogged his nose.

At dawn I found him awake on the bed, arranging rolls of film.

"What about Aska?"

"What about her?"

He hardly seemed to remember her. He spoke as if from a distant planet. He brought his hands to his ears once again and shook his head like a piggy bank. He looked at me.

"Nothing happened." It was almost as if he were apologizing. "I'm sorry," he said, with a gloomy smile. "Forces beyond our control."

They'd been imprisoned in that inn along with a few other guests. They'd spent the hours like the rest of us in Sarajevo, glued to the television in the breakfast room, where not a single cup had remained intact because the mortars were just a few hundred meters away.

He shook his head because of that noise stuck inside him. He still couldn't believe it.

"It's crazy. Everything's crazy."

I hugged him and we quickly made up for those horrible hours we'd spent far apart.

"They say it won't last, that it will be over soon."

Later I made the sign of the cross. Nothing had happened. The mating had not taken place and now I felt as if I'd been freed. Red projectiles fell through the night. I would forever be free of that desire like an ingrown toenail. I'd feared everything during those terrible days. I'd imagined the two of them dead and buried in the rubble of that bed I'd pushed for them to occupy.

I pressed his hand to my chest so he could feel my heartbeat. Diego opened his fist and pressed his hand against my heart. We'd taken an absurd risk and now I was asking his forgiveness.

It was a lesson, the hardest of my life.

I looked at him. There were scratches on his face and white powder in his hair.

"Did you take any pictures?"

"No."

He went into the bathroom, filled the tub and covered himself with water, even his head. I went in after him. His eyes were open. We looked at each other across the water, inhabitants of two different elements.

"Do you still love me?"

He pulled his head out of the water. "Always and forever."

We wanted to leave right away, but instead the days went by. Gojko had been to the airport. People were storming the planes on the tarmac at Butmir. The last flights out of the city were full, like cattle cars, with people in the aisles and in the toilets.

We stayed in the house in front of the television. President Izetbegović tried to calm the population. The war in Croatia would not reach Bosnia. He invited people to go out into the streets.

But the city was surrounded. On every hill there were cannons, mortars, Kalashnikovs, machine guns, precision rifles.

The Armija, the glorious Yugoslavian army that should have protected the city, had cleared out the barracks. For months they'd carried away all the weapons, piece by piece, and placed them on the surrounding mountains. For defense, they had said. Now it was too late to ask why the weapons of Sarajevo were pointed at Sarajevo.

Gojko continued to hope.

"It won't last. It'll be over in a few days. We have the eyes of the whole world upon us."

He accompanied crowds of journalists around the city to film the passive, unarmed civilians and the holes made by the shells.

"The important thing is to let the world know what's going on."

The kafanas were still full of opinionated kids with their beers and cigarettes, talking over one another. Free voices, strong and incisive and certain they would be heard, certain they would carry beyond those mountains to the tables of Europe.

The kids believed the world still had ears. Jovan did not. He was a Serbian Jew from Sarajevo. He took his shoes off whenever he entered the house, as the Muslims did, out of respect for his wife. He no longer read the newspapers, no longer listened to the newscasts. He spent hours watching his feet encased in their woolen slippers.

It was May, the month of primroses and dandelions and little swallows on the banks of the Miljacka.

Everyone subscribed to the illusion that it was just an attack, the result of agitation that would soon come to an end, the way the earth settles after an earthquake.

In the meantime, the UN officials transferred their headquarters to Stojcevac from the rest home in Sarajevo.

In the meantime, the post office and the Marshal Tito Barracks were burnt.

In the meantime, people discovered that snipers were posted throughout the city. The daily vivisection had begun. The sophisticated viewfinders followed people, homing in on the color of their eyes, the sweat beneath their noses.

Who were the snipers up in the hills? *Chetniks. Animals.* Had they come from elsewhere, or did the city itself hatch them? Kids who made their slithering way up the mountains to join the demon, to kill their university classmates and childhood playmates.

Her back upright, Velida covered her eyes with her hands. "It's not true. It can't be true."

We stayed on to keep those two old people company. At night we played cards on a little table covered with green felt. Velida served blueberry brandy and little sweets made with honey. We heard the deaf sound of the mortar rounds as they dropped through the night. Shells were raining down on Dobrinja, Vojničko Polje, Mojmilo. I thought of Aska and the cement camper-like building where she lived in Mojmilo, where once upon a time the Olympic athletes had lodged.

For me the mating would be no problem.

It felt like centuries had gone by.

I wondered if her slightly wandering gaze and her eyelids that fluttered like wings had been clues to her destiny. Every day I went through the list of the dead in *Oslobodjenje* with the fear that I would find her name.

One day Diego came back with his first dead body on a roll of film. A woman on the ground, apples rolling out of a bag.

He lifted the strap from around his neck and pulled the camera away from his chest as if it burnt. He flung it onto the bed. He was full of rage. It almost seemed as if his anger was directed at that mechanical eye because it had forced him to look . . . at that body, fixed in that pose in the image he had captured and forever unburied. His hands seemed to be trembling as he removed the roll of film and deposited it in the dark of a tin can.

"I feel like an undertaker."

Our kafana was no longer there, pulverized when a shell hit it full-on. All that remained was a spectral hole and a futuristic tangle of metal. Fortunately, none of our friends had been there when it happened early one morning. The only victim was a poor Albanian handyman who slept in the back.

The glass fell out of our windows, too. We did what everyone else did and covered the frames with sheets of dark plastic, opaque curtains through which the light barely filtered. At night dark fell early. There was no longer any electricity. Velida and Jovan preferred the inner area of the house. At night they sat there in front of a candle, waiting for the flame to burn down into the wax. They had no intention of leaving the city, nor would they go down into the basement as many now did. "We'll see what summer brings," Velida said. "In the summer we won't need heating. It will be like camping."

She and Jovan had camped many times near the waterfalls of the Bosnian national parks, where they'd spent hours bent over pools of water studying microorganisms.

We grew accustomed to the alarm sirens and the hiss of the shells. I thought I'd never sleep again. I spent the nights awake, my eyes wide open, my hand in Diego's. I pictured our house in Rome, the living room, the kitchen, the photos hanging in a long line on the wall. I pictured the quiet street below, barely populated at night apart from someone now and then walking a dog. My father had the keys. He went to water the flowers hanging from the windowsills. He'd sit in the silence, make himself coffee, rinse the cup. It had been a week since our last conversation. The last time he had been unable to speak, as if silenced by sorrow.

I'd said very little. I'd managed to send a few of Diego's rolls of film with a friend of Gojko's who was headed back to Zagreb. I begged Dad to make sure the photos were published in Diego's name, not the agency's.

Later we learned to sink into sleep as a way of escaping for a few hours from that concentration camp. We'd wake early in the morning to take advantage of the light. Diego would go out and I'd hug him tight. Nowadays everyone hugged like that when they met again and when they said goodbye, as if they would never see each other again.

Sebina's gymnastics coach was dead and so was the pharmacist. The bodies stayed there for some time because it was too dangerous to go near them. The snipers were waiting with their viewfinders. Only at night did people drag the bodies away, and then at night they buried them in the old Muslim cemetery—silent funerals, mourners as light as moths risking death to bury the dead.

We learned everything that May. We learned to recognize the harsh voice of the Kalashnikov, the hiss of the shells after the mortars exploded. If you heard it whistle across the sky over your head after the shot, it meant you were safe. If you didn't hear anything, it had already completed its arc and was about to fall near you. We learned that the mountains were usually silent the day after a riot of explosions. We learned that at a certain point the snipers took a lunch break and that toward sunset their aim worsened because they were drunk on rakija.

We learned how to move, to run like rabbits through the open spaces, the cracks between buildings, the intersections visible from the hills.

I wanted nothing but to leave, but Diego couldn't pull himself away. He'd walk kilometer after kilometer with the camera around his neck and his backpack on his back. When he returned he'd bring back something to eat or candles for the night.

I almost always stayed in the house. Every so often I'd go with Velida to the market. There was hardly anything to buy anymore, just a few vegetables from the gardens of Sarajevo, and the prices were ten times higher than before. The bread factory was still working, but the lines were very long.

We learned that the truces were not really truces. They lasted a few hours and then the staccato music of the shots started up again. The streets changed faces every day, crumbling and miserably recomposing themselves. Objects had been set up to block the snipers' view, blocks of cement, the carcasses of trolleys, sheets of dark plastic stretched from one building to another. The city had begun to organize, with volunteers and weapons gathered here and there. Regular troops from the Bosnian Territorial Defense Force were fighting in the trenches. Groups of criminals took advantage of the situation by sacking the houses of Serbian Sarajevans, professors and members of the middle class. It was the commerce of war, of expropriations and the black market. Incredible characters approached you to change money or sell you anything you could imagine. The white tanks of the UN forces stationed inertly here and there, like chickens in the sun.

And yet at night, life continued, surviving in cellars and clubs to the sound of bitter jokes. There was still beer, the legendary Sarajevsko Pivo, but it tasted different, bitter and strange as the jokes. People hoped everything would be over before summer.

We found a new kafana. You went down a little stairway into a basement grotto full of smoke. At least down there we were safe. Music from Radio Zid covered the alarm sirens and the eruptions in the sky. We had to break the curfew to get there. The girls wore fashionable clothes and makeup. Ana and

Dragana danced with their arms around each other. Mladjo the painter had taken to cutting human figures out of pieces of plywood and armoire doors. He'd color them and leave them in the middle of the road to mock the snipers. Everyone wanted to have fun. It was important not to concede a thing to the animals in the mountains.

Every so often Gojko would bring a journalist a touch braver than the others for a glimpse of Sarajevo behind the scenes. Gojko would help him lighten his load of deutschmarks by getting him to offer drinks to everyone. We'd sit studying our dirty glasses. One night Gojko stood and read a poem dedicated to a dead friend:

You didn't leave anything
in your old house,
only the wrinkled bed
and a burning cigarette.
You didn't leave anything
in your old life,
only Igor, your dog,
his full bladder
awaiting your return.

At night we stay close to the walls. Other human shadows silently move away, like seaweed. We navigate a dark aquarium. There is no light, just spent candles. It's total darkness. The moon is a lantern held by a ghost. The red light of a tracer bullet lights us up for a few seconds before it drops like a falling star. We're alone. Diego smells like a dog. Water's scarce. We wash ourselves in a shared basin full of water.

Mirna has her glasses on and she's planning lessons for her students. School is closed, but she and some colleagues are thinking about organizing small classes out of their homes. Those who can continue to go to work by foot or—the more fortunate—by bicycle. The trams aren't running and there's no gas for cars.

Sebina laughs and says it's better without cars. Their building was black with smog.

Mirna wears heels when she goes out. I smile. They're not the most practical shoes. She's serious about it. She has no intention of changing her life, of jumping around all day long like a rabbit. Her overcoat is just as it should be, as well. She tightens the belt with a decided gesture. She hasn't been this thin since she was a girl. Her pallor is visible beneath her makeup. She, too, has no intention of leaving Sarajevo.

"The people who wanted to go are gone already. We're staying."

I tell her that we'll be leaving as soon as we find a place on one of the convoys headed for Zagreb or Belgrade. I say I'd like to take Sebina with us to Italy.

"It's so much easier for foreigners," I say.

My goddaughter looks at me, swollen with Bosnian hatred. She looks like her bison of a brother. She hollers that she has no intention of coming with me. She wants to stay with her mother.

"It's just a vacation," I try to say.

But my goddaughter is the cleverest child in Sarajevo! She calms down and sits, legs crossed, on her pink movie-star armchair. Then she says, with poise worthy of a head of state, that vacations are for times of peace. It's wartime for them. In any case, they are better off than others, because Gojko works with the foreign press. They've moved Sebina's aquarium into the kitchen, which overlooks the inner quadrilateral of courtyards. Gojko's managed to procure a little electric generator.

Night has fallen. The aquarium is illuminated, a phosphorescent blue bubble in that black flood. We sit around it as if it were a fireplace. Our voices float like the fish with their barely visible blue noses. Sebina's chin is buried in her knees; her thin mouth is curved in a smile. Gojko teases her, persecuting her with his black humor. He tells her to be careful because with all these hungry people someone might decide to catch her fish and eat them.

When I stop by she always comes to greet me on her roller skates, which she wears buckled onto the light-up shoes I gave her. She pretends she's one of those girls she's seen on TV wearing skates and a miniskirt to serve American fast food. She bends over and sets an empty plate and a glass in front of me. She takes my order on a little pad of paper.

"What would you like, ma'am?"

"*Uštipci, kolači,* and strawberry cake."

She sets a book before me, then an oven mitt, then an upside-down cup. I stuff myself, chewing air. She laughs. Then she says, "A nice strawberry cake wouldn't be so bad."

We don't have any eggs or butter but we try to make a cake with plum jelly, oil and dark flour. The result, cooked in a pan over a camp burner, is hard and full of holes like a pockmarked face. But we enjoy it and press down on the plate with our fingertips to gather the crumbs. Then comes the blast that reverberates for a long time in our ears. It comes from behind, unexpected, and thunders through us. The bomb must have fallen very close by. Everything shakes. Moments later we realize we're alive by sheer chance, the sheer chance people in Sarajevo now call "miracle." If we'd stayed where we were a few minutes ago, before we decided to make the cake . . .

The fragment, a piece of twisted metal, pointy like a spade and longer than an arm, tore through the plastic in the window and drove itself into the wall. The wall around it is full of deep cracks revealing lower layers, like a sculpture by a conceptual artist. The wall is like earth that's been torn open by drought, the steaming metal fragment like a big evil spade. Tito's photo is still in place, though it's fallen over on its side. I imagine Diego will take a picture of this image. It calls out for a witness.

My heart goes back and forth like a little pendulum as it counts the seconds. There's no collapse. We wait, our breath stuck in our throats, for the house to settle from the blow. The aquarium is still intact. Sebina is watching it, watching the multicolored scales that flutter through the roiled-up water. We watch life as it endures, the fish trembling like the lilies on the new Bosnian flag. It's just a moment before the crack moves invisibly across the glass. A buried tremor was imprisoned in the water and only now is it exploding. The aquarium splits in two and falls in a thousand pieces to the ground. The fish spill out into the dust and leap into the air with dirty backs. Sebina hollers. I yell for her not to go near. The ceiling could fall in. But she dives into the dust and so I crawl over to her and we move about in that rickety mess trying to save those little worthless creatures. But they are worth something. They're worth more than everything now. They're a symbol, like the lilies. I pour water from the tank they use to fetch water into a pan and we throw the fish in there. Later Sebina's eyes are swampy with pent-up tears as we watch the fish swim around in the filthy dusty water. They're all alive except for one, a little floating thing like a cigarette butt.

"The little one died," Sebina whispers. "My Bijeli."

I console her. It's a miracle the rest of them survived.

Later Gojko will bring a new aquarium, and God only knows what it took to find it. But Sebina pestered him for days on end, because she can't leave her fish in the pan. Gojko regrets having given them to her. You can't find fish food, not even on the black market. *Because living things die.* It's become increasingly necessary to go down to the cellar and stay for hours, and Sebina doesn't want to leave her fish.

"It makes my heart hurt," she says.

"Everything you love makes you suffer. It's a rule."

She thinks for a moment. "Is that why you don't want children?"

I could cry. I pinch her and smile. "You're enough for me."

"I'm not your daughter."

"You are a little bit."

She studies me from her mischievous face. "Yes, maybe a little bit." She makes a gesture with her hand, a bit of love closed between two little fingers.

That morning people walked calmly through the streets, the women wearing scarves, the men ties. The idea was to give the middle finger to the men up in the hills, to the club of the Chetnik three-fingered salute. It was a message for them. *Shove your precision rifles up your asses.* That's what the scarves and the orderly footsteps were meant to say. They were a testimony to the fact that life went on. They'd hit the maternity clinic. The *Oslobodjenje* building had become a target for idle snipers with nothing better to do. The city would seem to have emptied and then it would fill with life again, like a pasture. Graffiti had appeared on the wall below our house: WE DIDN'T DIE LAST NIGHT.

My throat tightened every morning when I saw it.

There had been a lot of turmoil the day before. The Zetra Stadium in the Olympic village had burned. The metal cover so dear to everyone's hearts had turned to liquid. Firefighters and volunteers toiled for hours. People now knew they could expect quiet from the mountains after the worst bombings.

A cease-fire had been ordered, without retractions. Sanctions had been enacted against Belgrade. There was no way to avoid standing in line for water, for bread, for medicine. People risked their hides standing in a row like pigeons, but that day was a hopeful day, women chatting on the sidewalk, children playing around their legs. It was sunny. It happened in Vase Miskina Street, where one of the biggest roses now lies. The little door is still there. The place no longer sells bread, but it's there.

The names are written, small and orderly, beside the Muslim star and moon and a verse from the Koran.

They were men, women, children at play, and they had no idea their names would be carved into the wall and photographed into infinity by tourists. It was the breadline. There was a lovely smell. It was the kind of hopeful day when rabbits peer out of their dens. It was the end of May. Swallows pecked up the crumbs that fell out of the bread bags when people broke their bread open as they walked. There were a few lucky people, the ones who'd been first in line and who had left right away with a fresh loaf or one of those unleavened breads with no salt. But some of the early birds stayed on to chat with an acquaintance. Three shells fell, two on the street, one on the market across the way, and everyone who was there splattered. The square became a theater set, with red rags everywhere. Images of that disgusting red and the blood-soaked bread would travel around the world.

"Who'd have thought there was so much brain in a child's head?" an old man said, gripping his cane. "It wouldn't stop coming out."

A woman sat on a little wall. She wasn't crying. She clutched two dead children like cut flowers, one on either side. Another woman tried to grab her own leg, sliding along after it on her elbows. One man was funnier than the rest. He was folded over on himself like a glove someone finds on the road and sets on a fence in case the person who lost it comes back to look for it. Sad mismatched gloves, covered with mud. The man lay there like a lost glove over a metal barrier that divided the road into lanes, but he no longer had a stomach, just a big, slightly ragged circular hole. Behind him you could see people fleeing and people on stretchers. He lay there like a special effect.

That day Gojko was like a crazed man. He ran immediately to the scene and hollered to the journalists to turn on their cameras.

"Now they'll take note of us."

He picked up a loaf of bread and broke it in half. It was full of red blood like sauce. He offered it to the journalists.

"Here, take some and eat, all of you. This is our blood."

Then he dashed off, desperate as Judas on his way to hang himself.

Later there was silence. It had been a hopeful day. Those young men had come with their camouflage uniforms and their sky-blue helmets. People mistook them for guardian angels and thought it was over at last. Instead, the hospital was full of flesh to be sewn up. Even the mountains were silent. Televisions the world over broadcast that one truculent sequence. The animals in the hills closed themselves into their dens and toasted their fame with rakija.

We left two days later. The electricity was running again. All Sarajevo's washing machines started running in the night. I took it as a good sign. Our bus to Zagreb even had air-conditioning. It was usually used to take pilgrims to Medjugorje. From Zagreb we had no trouble catching a plane. There were so many things I wanted to say to Diego. What I said was, "How does a plate of spaghetti sound to you?"

Diego smiled.

His eyes were red. The first thing I planned to do was take him to see a doctor. Now I thought God would never rinse our eyes of what they had seen.

Chapter 12

I look at the sky out the window, the clean sky of peacetime people, tourist aircraft, birds that migrate and return. The brief flight ends and we descend beneath the white wing of a fortunate sky and a light sea breeze.

Dad's waiting for us. He's lost weight. He's wearing clip-on sunglasses and the sort of cotton shirts convicts wear on furlough. He hugs us with a wide, hopeful smile, as if we'd returned from a vacation. He lowers his head immediately and takes my suitcase. He'd like to take Diego's as well.

It's as if he were an enterprising tour guide working hard for his tip and we're two disheveled and dusty tourists just back from a safari.

How'd the hunting go? Have you brought back some kind of trophy, a tusk, a tail?

Yes, we've brought back a dirty tail that slides behind us and threatens to trip us up. A wounded tail. It will take time, a few days, and then it will fall off, a bit of flesh that will stink and then die, and then we'll be ourselves again, the way we were before, enjoying life's comforts and aperitifs in the sun.

Dad puts our bags in the trunk. Diego lets his backpack slide off his shoulders and it's as if he's abandoned a piece of himself on the ground, the body of a child.

He sits in the back and stretches out on the seat. Dad keeps his eyes on the road. There's a lifeless smile glued to his mouth. He doesn't ask anything, just waits for me to talk.

This morning, Dad's an intrepid driver. He moves quickly, like an ambulance driver. He's got two wounded people with him.

I look at the road signs, the smooth wide asphalt lanes that lead to Rome, the calm flow of traffic, the cars that have passed inspection, their exhaust pipes in order. This normality seems like a miracle, a special effect. In my mind's eye I see the uncertain carcasses of burnt vehicles. I turn toward Diego.

"How are your eyes?"

They're closed, two swollen pink bubbles crisscrossed by little veins. They look like the stomachs of newborn birds. Dad springs to life. He'll call the eye hospital. He has a friend there, the head of a department.

"A photographer's eyes are so important. They're the aim and the view-finder."

Diego puts a hand on Dad's shoulder and smiles.

The architecture changes as we move along. We pass elegant Umbertine buildings, Fascist buildings with geometric balconies like the decks of ships, buildings from the 1970s and then the Baroque buildings of the center, which drink in the pink rays of Roman sunsets.

There's the white spider of the Vatican and all around us the shadow of churches, the gold of art galleries, the stink of cloth warehouses, the hoarse voice of the ghetto and the weighty voice of the political potentate, herds of tourists and the nobleman reduced to rags who sits beside the flavored-ice kiosk with the pigeons as they peer into the yellow muscle of the Tiber.

For years I've wanted to leave here and for years I've stayed. Today I thank God for this Western world I live in and for its dirty peace.

People are going about their business, coming out of stores and offices, crossing the street, stepping into cafés for sandwiches, running to the gym.

I want everything, to hug each street, to take long slow walks with a straight back. We're out of the concentration camp.

Home. The smell of closed spaces and the last thought we left between these walls. The file folder with my medical records and sonograms is still on the table. The night before our departure I left it there after going through it on all fours on the carpet. I set a foot inside the door and walk in. There's the noise of the clock hanging in the kitchen, the dark open mouth of the fridge with empty holes for the eggs. The smell of the carpet. Diego's photos, feet waiting for the subway.

I push the shutters outward over the dirty windowsills. A ray of sunlight slithers like a snake over the photographs. Diego's on the couch. He took a few steps and stopped there, in that white pit. He says all those feet on the wall are stupid. We have to take them down.

I don't answer, but now I know he'll never again like the photos he took before. He looks at them and says it doesn't seem like he took them.

I open everything wide and let in the light. With long strides I reclaim the meters of my wood floor. We're safe in the belly of our apartment. Dad's not with us. He didn't want to come up. He helped us put our bags in the elevator and turned on his heels. "Sleep," he said. "Close the shutters and catch up on your sleep."

Fortunately, there's plenty to do. Rub the sponge over the kitchen table, put clean sheets on the bed. Diego helps me. He takes care of washing the floor. He wrings out the floor rag as if he were wringing someone's neck. We settle into cleaning the house by chance. It's a sort of outlet, a way of taking care of ourselves. We could just call the cleaning lady and go out. But this morning it's a privilege to move freely around, to cross in front of the wide-open windows. There's nothing better than cleaning house, a physical response to futility. We fill a huge garbage bag. Diego throws away mountains of contact sheets and bad shots. I throw out all the medical tests and sonograms. I'm done. Covered in sweat and Roman dust, we hug in the middle of the living room. We turn in unison toward the window as if we were turning toward a photographer. Or a sniper. Who knows, maybe the notary in the building across the way has inserted a precision rifle through the air-conditioning vent.

Later we go down to wander about the market stalls laden with seasonable vegetables—red tomatoes, boxes of cherries, *puntarelle* in bowls of water. We do the shopping, snatching at life. Diego's wearing sandals that look like something one of the apostles might have worn. He fished them out of the storage room. People say hello and ask where we've been.

"Abroad," we say. Abroad.

We pack our fridge with things to eat and make a multicolored salad. We stuff ourselves with vitamins. We eat fresh bread and open a good bottle of white wine. I put my feet up on the table. Diego rubs them. His eyes are shut and there's a joint in his mouth.

We don't talk. We know everything. There's no need to speak. Our bodies need time. We've been somewhere else and now we're back.

It's nighttime. I look at him next to the glass that separates us from the world, from the voices that rise up off the street, people on their way back from dinner at a restaurant. He walks his fingers over the miracle of intact glass within its wooden frame. We saw all those windows covered with plastic sheets like bandages over the eyes of a wounded man. I ask myself when we'll be able to get past the glass and look out again.

We picked up where we left off. It was as if we'd saddled ourselves with the body of a lover we no longer loved but toward whom we felt a sad affection, an oppressive sense of duty. In the morning we showered and then we embarked on days that no longer seemed to belong to us. Diego did his best. He went out every day just like old times. He had his motorcycle again and his white shirts and he seemed himself. I stayed near the door, my back against the wall, breathing. The silence of the house made me restless. Without realizing it I walked the way I did in Sarajevo, close to the load-bearing walls, as if I feared a sudden collapse.

I'm in the office. The director complained about my long absence.

"Gemma, you're an assignment editor."

I shrugged. "I still don't have a regular contract."

I look at the gray computers, my colleagues' faces. Viola brings me a cappuccino and a pastry from the café. She won't leave me alone. She sets her ass on my desk and talks and talks. I think that she's not clever enough to survive in Sarajevo, what with her laziness and low self-esteem. Her good nature would not be enough to get her across the street. A sniper would have latched on to her steps and had his fun. She's the classic prey. To be honest, I've always taken advantage of her myself, joking with her but never really confiding anything. I look at my colleagues, aged kids like me, people who raced to get through university and then wound up here, little sharks who've grown old in this pond meant for toads. I imagine myself putting a bullet through their foreheads and seeing them crumple at their miserable workstations. How many of my colleagues would I get rid of today, along with their little quirks and their querulous voices?

I call Diego. "How's it going?"

"And you?"

We're closed inside a conspiracy of silence. We don't talk. We both try to do the same thing: steer clear of it, take our distance from those days by putting other days in between us and them, these other days that drag on and on.

I write an article about manure. In India they use it as fuel. In Norway a man used it to build himself a house. A shitty house, I think, and laugh to myself. One thought consoles me, and I cradle it as if it were a doll: I'm glad I don't have children. Last night I saw a dead child on TV. His mother was washing his body for burial. I was cutting bread in the kitchen. I dropped the knife and made the sign of the cross. *Farewell, useless life.* I turned off the television and went back to cutting the bread. *He's not your child, Gemma,* I said to myself. *You don't have children. You're lucky.*

We go to dinner at a friend's. We're back to normality, clothes at the dry cleaner's. It's Duccio's birthday. The terrace is open again after the winter. Below us flows the Tiber, adorned with the lights of summer events, book launches, bullshit. There's Castel Sant'Angelo with its angel stretching into the night. I'm wearing heels and my shoulders are bare. Diego's wearing his loose-weave linen jacket. His hair is unbound and he's grown sideburns. We're fed up with being sad. It was a pleasure to leave the house, hand in hand, fresh from our showers and lotions. We're beautiful tonight, like a couple of actors. A glass of champagne right away, then another, seized from the silver tray borne by a faceless waiter who's nothing more than a white outstretched arm. Divine goblets, cool and opaque. Two each, to start feeling good.

There are people from Diego's work, worldly folks tainted by culture. A bit of everything, just like in the bowls of crudités for the dip, a tuft of green and a carrot, a strip of pepper and a radish.

"Hi. How are you?"

"Fine, and you?"

We nibble on lobster canapés and breadsticks wrapped in prosciutto.

We find ourselves in a corner of the balcony, a hand on a shoulder, dusty-eyed. We watch the slow rumination of the party. Then Duccio comes over with a guy and mentions Sarajevo, says we were there. He leaves us with this waxen-faced carp with glasses and a cigar. He's really not so bad. He wants to know. He wants to talk with us. He's a journalist, the type that sits in the newsroom and leaves what's actually happening on the ground to his younger colleagues.

We don't feel like saying anything. We mutter a few yeses and nos. In any case, the carp keeps the conversation going. He already knows everything anyway from the news wires. In a few minutes we're surrounded by too many people. They've dragged us over to a big wicker sofa. Sarajevo and the war there are fashionable, the sorrow of the year, an opportunity to shake one's head, to criticize America and Europe. Everyone wants fresh news from the city that's been transformed into a field of rabbits to be hunted. I force myself to remember, to restore human dignity to the rabbits. But how can you recount the smell of those modest houses, better than our own, and the women's courage in putting on makeup when they go out? How do you recount that lifeless hand, nothing but a rake of human flesh lying motionless upon the dust?

The armchair journalist is now singing the tune of ethnic hatred and barbaric races. A trendy man and a lady intellectual argue. The man says Europe is afraid of Islam, while the woman says that no, Europe is afraid of Germany, with its banks and its factories, like in the Second World War.

It's always easy to look good when you're talking about international politics. It's not as if anyone ever says anything of any use to the world, or reveals anything true about him- or herself. The dead child being washed by the Muslim mother is nothing but a fart. These people out here on the terrace are playing Risk.

"What's on your mind?"

"Gojko."

He would have thrown glasses and trays of canapés to the floor. Or maybe he would have held forth and blathered nonsense, peddling his ass for a good tip. *What the hell? The truth is too obvious, too stupid, and everyone wants to feel intelligent.*

This war, so near and so violent, provokes a morbid curiosity. The woman next to me is all right. She scratches an already tanned leg and looks at me with a face that's sincerely pained. She filled out a form and donated money to Caritas in Sarajevo. I try to say something about the civilized, enlightened people I know, something about their infinite dignity. She nods, but she doesn't seem all that interested. The East has its stereotypes, its bad smell.

Diego says nothing. He's been silent all along. There's a red stain on his linen jacket. We'll send it to the cleaner's.

There's a girl, someone's daughter, with bushy hair and little breasts like lupini beans. She adores Diego's work, adores the puddles. She, too, has questions about Sarajevo, the city in vogue. Diego puts an arm around her and steers her to the railing overlooking the riverbank, the skyline of the holy city, the white spider. He sticks out his arm and starts shooting, ratatat-tat, ratatat-tat, ratatat-tat.

At first the girl doesn't understand. She laughs. Then she moves away.

The photographer's been drinking. He aims at passing scooters and fashionable people stationed at the kiosk that sells colored beverages. He yells, "Enjoy Sarajevo . . ."

Everyone turns toward him. I feign laughter and cross to his side.

"Let's go home, my love. It's late."

Duccio is at the door in his red suspenders and black T-shirt.

"What the fuck's eating you?"

Diego snaps Duccio's suspenders. Duccio absorbs the elastic blow, the photographer's last blast.

One night Diego yells. I'm cooking eggs. I run into the living room. Gojko's on television. It's him, alive. His hair's grown. In Italian he says, "This war isn't a humanitarian issue. We need to defend ourselves. Send Kalashnikovs, not cans of macaroni!"

The journalist wants his microphone back. Gojko holds on. Now he's yelling in his own language. He's angry at Mitterrand, who went to Sarajevo to take a walk, and at the UN blue helmets, who just stand there like broken traffic lights.

"Is he drunk?"

"Completely."

Tonight our friend seems devanged. His crazed eyes linger for a bit longer on the screen.

The eggs burn. We eat cheese for supper.

We wait for the war to finish. In the meantime, a shell has fallen on the department store, another in Titova Street, another in Rade Končar Square. Diego gets angry at the television and hollers at the correspondent, who's wearing a bulletproof vest and a summer shawl. He says, *Get the fuck out of the way! Let me see what's behind you.* He moves from channel to channel in search of news programs. They show the same footage on every channel, repeated on every broadcast. But Diego can't tear himself away from the screen. He watches those images as if he were hoping to catch something he missed earlier, like in the puddles, like in his photographs.

We watch to see if we can recognize our friends in the frightened figures that cross the screen for a few seconds in the news clips from Sarajevo. We don't look at the dead. We take a step back.

I watch for Sebina's gap-toothed smile. What's happened to my goddaughter? I write her almost every day but never get an answer. I wonder if the building with blue gratings is still standing. I study the TV screen. Why don't they show that street in Novo Sarajevo? *Where are you going with that camera?*

It seems like they're always showing the same streets, the same buildings. The cameraman takes a few steps outside before ducking back into the Holiday Inn to take refuge on the couches there with the rest of the international press.

We try to call Gojko almost every night. The phone fills with unknown, incomprehensible voices, radio frequencies or who knows what. It sounds like stomach noises, indigestion.

Supper burns again tonight. There's a story about the Sarajevo zoo. The panther and the baboons died in their cages. The zookeeper couldn't get to them with food and drink. I look at those hairy bodies, motionless in the dust, and tears stream down my face. Maybe I'm crying over the animals because I no longer have tears for the humans. I cry because I remember that day at the zoo with Aska. She bought a packet of peanuts and put her hand through the bars to feed the animals. Then she went into the empty cage and sat rocking her head.

We eat cheese for supper again. Playing with the rinds, Diego makes a letter *A*. I see it later, when I'm clearing the table.

Diego does his job. He gets up, gets dressed, puts up the kickstand on his motorcycle and leaves. He goes frequently to Milan now, where he works all day and catches the last flight at night.

"How'd it go?"

"Fine."

When he comes home I try to ask him questions but it's all he can do to keep his temper.

"Nothing happens, you know."

"Who was there?"

"The same people as usual. Who the fuck do you think?"

He comes near, rests his head against mine, rubs against me with his smell. He apologizes. His eyes are driving him crazy. It's because of the lights and the black cloths, magnets for dust. He rinses his eyes with cold water in the kitchen. His hair's wet when he lifts his head. The water drips onto his shirt, which dries almost immediately. Hot wind rises up off the street. How on earth are Gojko and the others managing without water?

We eat at our usual places in the kitchen, sitting across from each other at the little table that comes out of the wall beneath the window. We like it. It's like eating on a train. You can look outside at the street and at passersby. Diego chews and looks out at the night. Then he takes my hand and slowly spreads my fingers on the table.

"Do you want to know what I did today?"

He touches my veins, slides a finger into the spaces between one finger and the next, a gesture as tired as his voice. He's mumbling tonight.

"I spent the whole day photographing a can of tuna."

First it was open, then closed. He spent hours finding the right light to emphasize the streaks in the tuna and to make the oil shine.

We laugh. He tells me the tuna had its own makeup artist who kept moistening it with oil and changing it the minute it got the least bit wilted beneath the lights. She'd take it into the dressing room like a tired model. He says they used a mountain of tuna, which in any case they wouldn't have sold because the tuna they usually put in cans, obviously, is of a lower quality. It's not the best white meat, it's the pickings.

"So it's a trick."

"Like everything." He pauses. "The world is going to hell," he says, "and so are we."

His laugh reveals all his crooked teeth.

He's hardly eaten a thing.

There are cherries, in cozy loverlike pairs. He swallows a few without even spitting out the pits.

He says, again, "I spent the whole day photographing a can of tuna."

He gets up from the table with a pair of cherries dangling from each ear. He takes three steps and throws up on the carpet. He apologizes for not having made it to the bathroom.

"Are you sick?"

"I'm fine."

On Sundays he closes himself in the darkroom. He spends the day there with his basins and his fluids, his eye on the enlarger, running negatives over the illuminated panel. He likes to shut himself in that prison, the only space that's really his in our house.

He hasn't sold a single photograph from Sarajevo. He's produced a few prints that he's kept for himself in a gray pile.

The Somali cleaning woman comes to clean our house. Sometimes she brings her daughter. I don't mind anymore. In fact, I like to see her sitting in a corner in the kitchen. I'm calm when they're there and calm when they leave. I don't feel anything.

The mother empties Diego's wastebasket full of torn-up prints. A piece falls out. It's black-and-white, so the locks aren't red, but it's obvious whose curls these are, whose half of an eye. When I notice it's too late. The woman has already carried out the garbage. I'm left with that fragment. I look at it and throw it away.

It's August. Almost everyone but the hostages—the elderly, the destitute, the handicapped and the terminally ill who can't be moved from their hospital beds—has left the city behind. The TV broadcasts footage shot from above of highways choked with lines of cars. The café is closed. The restaurant is closed. The smell of steaks and fried artichokes no longer wafts in through the window.

We've found a little place that doesn't sell alcohol. We drink milk with almond syrup beside poor patrons from the neighborhood, big women in slippers and partially buttoned housedresses that show their thighs, old men in their undershirts. It's some kind of employees' club. They let us in because it's summer. In the winter they set up an old-fashioned dance floor. There's a trellis and a bocce court where old men play beneath a white concentration camp lightbulb and one of those insect-killing contraptions with blue fluorescent lights hanging from the wall. It's for the mosquitoes but every night it kills a ton of moths whose carbonized bodies fall to the metal base that someone will empty later. We sip our drinks and listen to that terrible noise, the zapping sound and the frying wings. It's the soundtrack of our summer.

There was a time when I wouldn't have lasted a minute in a place like this. Now it doesn't matter. I let the moths drop and die. With his milk mustache, Diego reminds me of a child. He lights up a joint. An old man notices the strange smell and turns. Diego raises the joint.

"Drugs," he says.

The old man nods, throws his bocce ball and scores.

It's the kind of place where people mind their own business. It's a neighborhood of desperate clandestine people, happy borderline cases. It took a while of riding around on the motorcycle, clutched tight on these summer nights, before we found it. It's no accident it's here. In every city there's at least one place that evokes war.

Diego says, "I want to go back."

He says it while the contraption's frying. Don't those stupid nocturnal creatures see what's about to happen? Why do they line up to touch that light, to die? What the fuck do I care? I'm drunk on milk and almond syrup. My legs are slightly open on the plastic chair. The fleshy bits are sweaty. Diego's gray. He hasn't spent a single day in the sun. He's wearing the ancient white T-shirt from when he used to go running. His eyes remind me of a woebegone bird.

"Did you put in your eye drops?"

"I want to go blind." He laughs.

Anyway, I've known for a while. He's never really come home. This isn't peace. And Aska's been here with us on these evenings of pretend truce.

"You want to go back to her, don't you?"

He doesn't answer, just smiles, his lips curling ever so slightly. I can't even get angry. How do you get angry with a sad child?

On the way up the stairs to our apartment I kick him. I let him go first and then I fling myself at his youthful T-shirt and yell that I saw the bit of photograph and the *A* he made with the cheese rinds.

He turns and protects himself with his elbows.

In the apartment I don't even bother turning on the light. I go straight to the darkroom and dump out bottles of fluid and toss all the lenses and the exposure meter on the ground.

Diego doesn't move. He watches me from the couch, calm as a gecko.

Later he says, "Shit. It's just an estimate, but I think you've trashed five or six million lire worth of stuff."

I'm on my hands and knees picking up pieces. I apologize. I'm really sorry, because I'm the tightfisted one. He doesn't give a damn.

"Someone needed to get mad," he says. He doesn't mind discovering that I can still be jealous.

He calls to me with a voice from old times. "Come here."

He plants a long kiss on my lips. Then he licks his lips and says I'm the flavor of his life.

I look at myself in the bathroom mirror while I rub the makeup off my eyes. I don't like myself. All I ever see is my void. How can I be jealous of a poor girl who's dying along with her city? Of that punk sheep dancing with the wolf on her trail?

Later we watch TV. We laugh at a funny summertime program, amateur videos of cats licking parrots, brides whose skirts fall off, children who trip a hundred times.

We make a move. We leave behind the deserted summertime city and, for a change of scene, go to the seaside to spend some time with Dad.

We take the motorcycle. I press against Diego as we ride through the muggy wind of the highway and over the softened asphalt. The apartment smells like it always has, a hostage of time, the smell of my grandmother, the things she cooked, her sweat after the long walk back from the beach. The smell of her sighs and reprimands. Who were they for? Me? The fish?

First thing in the morning Dad takes his dog out for a walk along the waterline as lifeguards rake the beach and open the umbrellas at the bathing establishments.

The sea is disgusting, flat and syrupy.

Diego takes a glum swim.

"You can't see a thing," he says.

We leave before the paddleballs arrive along with the radios and the coconut-scented lotion.

That lacerated coast is across the sea. The islands, where until last year people went on day trips in their yachts and on cruise ships. On clear days we can see the rocks no one looks at anymore. The sun seekers have abandoned them; it's as if they belonged to another sea.

Here people swim and eat popsicles, buy bikinis and sheer tunics and bargain with vendors burdened like camels for the best price beneath the hot summer sun.

Here in this shallow water I've never liked I remember how I used to be. I remember the time I was stung by a weever fish and its shock paralyzed my leg. A boy came running with ammonia. It was the first time I really looked at a man.

Dad says he's decided he doesn't mind this horrid place. He didn't get along with his mother, either, with her anxiety and her murmured reproaches. Thinking back, though, thinking of all the trouble she went to, taking the bus all the way from Rome to change the sheets for her summer renters and argue about damage to a wall or the tub, it's easier to see her side of things. We talk about it one evening. Diego listens. At a certain point Dad apologizes for having left me here all those summers.

"Children shouldn't be left to grow sad. Not even a dog, of course not a child."

"You had work to do, Dad. You couldn't do otherwise."

He thinks. "There's always an otherwise."

Ever since my mother died he's been angrier with himself. Diego looks at him. He's always missed having a father. I sense that tonight he's come here to find him.

It's a pleasant evening. We eat in the kitchen and leave the door onto the narrow little balcony open. The balcony's too small to hold a table. This is a humble apartment with thin walls. You can hear the voices and televisions of other vacationers. You can't see the sea, just a forest of antennae. Dad serves us mussels in sauce and mixed fried fish.

It's the first good meal in ages. We use our bread to mop up the sauce from the mussels and open another bottle of beer. Dad smokes and talks about my childhood, when I was an unpleasant child, too introverted for anyone else to like me. All we had was each other.

Diego takes advantage of the opportunity to hear stories about me. And Dad stands up and imitates me, his arms folded like mine always were. I was always a little haughty. It makes me sad to remember myself.

"Mother Superior, that's what her grandmother used to call her." He laughs.

I punch him on the arm.

Diego watches us. It's a sweet evening.

We don't know it yet, but it's the last one we'll spend together. Maybe someone up above knows it. There's a strange light around us, God illuminating our farewells.

It's the last supper for the young apostle. His wet hair is tied back in a ponytail. He's got a joint in his mouth. Dad asks if he can try it.

"Dad, what are you doing?"

He shrugs. "What's the big deal?"

Dad went to bed, laughing, and we went out for ice cream. One of the bathing establishments stayed open at night, the round cement dance floor full of people, sun-baked girls with huge white earrings and bangs hanging over their eyes like schnauzers and boys with slicked-back hair and bright-colored, skintight T-shirts, local tourists who'd come from inland to enjoy the coast.

Then Diego asked me to make love. He closed his eyes, begging like a blind newborn puppy nuzzling for milk in the dark. There on the beach, like two teenagers, with the hammer beat of the dance music and voices coming from the club.

"Let's go home."

He dragged me onto the sand among the lounge chairs, where he grabbed on to me like an oar in an oarlock and set to struggling in the still night as if he had to bring me to safety through a storm.

The next morning I woke up alone. We'd gone back to the seaside apartment to sleep. The rumpled bed was full of sand. I figured Diego must have gone to the café that had good pastries and a rack full of newspapers. He was always starving when he woke. Breakfast was the one meal he needed. For a moment I pictured him sitting at one of those plastic tables, sated, enjoying the pleasant sun.

I went out to do some shopping. When I came back I noticed the open garage door. Dad was tidying up the shelves. He was cleaning a rusty wrench with a rag dipped in turpentine.

I dropped the bag full of tomatoes and half a watermelon and leaned against the cool wall.

"Where's Diego?"

Dad looked up from the wrench and took a couple of steps toward me. "I'm sorry."

He speaks slowly, the way he used to talk to his students. I listen in the unreal atmosphere of this garage that resembles a hangar. He tells me that the reason Diego wanted to come here was so he could leave, because it's so close to Ancona, the port for Adriatic ferries. He tried to dissuade him . . . He shakes his head.

So instead he went to a military supply store and bought him a bulletproof vest.

"It's a really good one," he says. "With inserts. The kind they use in Northern Ireland."

His eyes are shining as if he were crazed. I look at him and wonder if he's gone mad.

I picture this poor old man trying on the bulletproof vest, imagine him testing it by pressing it and punching it. And then he deposited it on the bony shoulders of the son he never had, the boy he loves and has allowed to leave like a son going off to war.

Dad raps on his head with his knuckles. Stubborn.

Now he's wearing a useless expression, desperate and guilty, almost as if he were asking for my help.

There's my little-girl bicycle with its white basket. We used to pedal together among the pine trees, me in front, Dad behind. I hate my whole life, my childhood and this fruitless adulthood.

"Here."

It's a folded sheet torn from a pad of grid paper. Not even an envelope, as if there were no longer any need for prudence.

One line.

My love, I'm going. Diego.

Back in Rome, I dreamt of his voyage almost every night. The motorcycle climbing dirt roads patrolled by militiamen. I saw the boy's face, the tired eyes peering through the dark of that land with no more light.

I lived in front of the television, so I saw the pyre of the National Library. The journalist said, *Ashes are raining down all over the city.* All the books held there for centuries had been reduced to a thick swarm of black wings. The ashen rain of an August day was burying the memory of men, burying the symbol of that open city where cultures had mixed like water. Now the Miljacka was a long, soot-black mourning band that ran along the riverbed. I thought that nothing would be left. I remembered the thin girl with glasses who took the books down from the shelves and carried them along the corridors in piles of no more than three or four at most. She walked carefully, respectfully, as cautious as if she were carrying a small child, before setting them down in front of the students along with a photocopied list of rules and an invitation to turn the pages slowly.

She must be there now, on all fours, bloodied with soot like the other young volunteers who were digging in the hope of saving something, a page, some piece of themselves in that martyrdom. For a moment I thought I saw Diego but it wasn't him, it was someone else.

Then he called.

"It's me." His voice sounded metallic but incredibly near.

"Where? Where are you?"

He was at the Holiday Inn. He was using a Canadian TV journalist's satellite phone. It was hard to hear; he was in the lobby and someone next to him was hollering in English. Someone was laughing a bit farther away but still audible.

"How are you? Talk louder!"

"Fine. I'm fine."

He seemed extraordinarily calm.

I asked him about his trip. There was a pause, as if he'd forgotten. He said he'd gone through Medjugorje, where he'd attended a mass, the only man among a bunch of weeping peasant women. In the Serbian enclaves kids greeted him with their hands raised in the three-fingered salute. Everyone stopped him: Serbs, Croats, Muslim Green Berets. But his press pass and a few hundred deutschmarks were enough to get him through. On the last leg, over Mount Igman, the most dangerous part of the trip, he'd stayed near three UN tanks escorting trucks full of humanitarian aid.

There were so many things I wanted to say. For more than six days I'd been shut up in the house waiting for this moment, the telephone always beside me. Now I was completely unprepared.

I said something really stupid. "Didn't they shoot at you?"

He paused. I heard him cough. "No. Not yet."

I asked about Gojko and Sebina, Velida and Jovan, Ana and the others. They were all alive.

"And Aska? Have you seen her?"

I stood holding the receiver, listening to the dial tone without making up my mind to hang up, as if he could come back from afar.

He'd traveled all those kilometers of burnt villages, mines and blown-up bridges to return to the city from which everyone was trying to escape. He had traveled in the opposite direction of the convoys full of refugees and orphans fleeing the siege. Now he was there, in that casket.

I called my father. "He's there."

I heard him weep and clear his clogged throat.

"Did he tell you where he's staying?"

"I don't know anything, Dad."

This was my war front, this peaceful city, this clean empty house without Diego. His jeans weren't lying around anymore. Neither were his cigarette butts, nor the rolls of film that ended up under the couch. The mess was his, and maybe the life of the place was his, too. Alone, I didn't make a mess. I didn't exist. I was neutral, odorless. I cleared my plate the minute I finished eating. The bed was always made. I stood in front of the piano. It reminded me of a big white funeral urn. It held the ashes of our best days. I waited for peace to come, the UN resolutions. I heard the Pope imploring all parties to lay down their arms. Meanwhile the men responsible for the horror were drinking mineral water in Geneva.

He was there, on the front he'd chosen, the one with the exploded window glass.

In the middle lay the no-man's-land that was my abandoned body, scorched earth between two trenches.

Lost and incredulous, I wandered through my days.

Almost every day I went to the Foreign Ministry for news. I waited for hours
to speak with an official. "I have to join my husband."

I wanted permission to fly on one of the military planes going to Bosnia.

"It's very risky. You should wait."

"I can't wait."

I am determined to cross no-man's-land to reach the other front. Then Gojko
calls. I hear his hoarse, cigarette-muddied voice. It's dawn, a September
morning. Diego's fine. He's staying with him in the shared house. It's difficult,
almost impossible, to make phone calls. Gojko doesn't have much time. He's
calling on a satellite phone from the television bunker, a favor from a friend.

"How are you all? How are things going?"

"We're hanging in there."

According to the news the city is completely destroyed. Almost all the
buildings have fallen. Gojko answers, "No, we're still standing."

I ask about Sebina. He says she can't go to gymnastics anymore.

"Send her to Italy."

"It's practically impossible to get out now."

It's the beginning of September. On television they say that an Italian military plane, a G22 on a peace mission, has been shot down on the slopes of
Mount Zec just outside Sarajevo. It was carrying a load of winter blankets. A
missile split one of its wings in two. Young military wives wait in shock before
their televisions. The heroes have been reduced to bits of flesh on those inac-
cessible peaks, more than two thousand meters high, but nonetheless their
wives hope and hug their children tight, while the children wonder who all
these people are, the journalists who knock on their door each day, the door
no one ever usually knocks on, the door their father went out of in his uniform, alone, as usual.

At night my thoughts go to those widows and their big half-empty beds
purchased on installment. They're probably doing what I'm doing, lying still
in the dark and drying their tears so as not to dirty the pillowcases.

I think about the children, the arms that will never again wave goodbye
to their fathers.

When the caskets are brought back to the military base in Pisa, they're draped in the red, white and green flag of death. The airlift is suspended. The martyred city is isolated from the rest of the world, at the mercy of its persecutors.

The official's voice on the phone is rushed. He doesn't have time for me. "The humanitarian flights have been suspended, ma'am."

"But I have to go."

"It's hell over there."

"My husband's in that hell."

"I'm sorry."

My resistance is made up of little acts. You have to move slowly so as not to disrupt the balance. Don't move a thing. Maybe, that way, evil will forget about us, move beyond us. I wake in the middle of the night. I'm sitting on the bed and I'm running. I dreamt the phone was ringing. It was the official. *Ma'am, I'm sorry, but your husband was an imbecile. Some people get what they ask for. May I offer you a coffee?*

In the office, as well, my eyes are on the telephone. *Now*, I say. Now they'll call from the Foreign Ministry to give me the news. I pick up the receiver and check to make sure the phone's working. Then I console myself. Viola comes over with her useless smile. If anything had happened I'd know it already. The city is full of journalists and volunteers, people who go there and back without dying. The thing is, I know him, his way of seeking out the fringes, the lesser bodies of water. It's the decentered center that attracts him. I'm afraid he's moving around without any cover.

On television they show images of the Bosnian concentration camps. They've discovered at least five. The worst one is next to the old iron mines. Toothless and mutilated human skeletons, things we haven't seen in a long time.

Then Diego calls, and this time he seems to have more time to talk. I hear an explosion and ask what it is. He says it's the music of the day. "Wait."

I hear other noises, disjointed fragments. I call his name. "Diego! Diego!"

He comes back. "Did you hear? Random machine gun fire. Mortars. Grenades. They've fired at an ambulance."

"They even shoot at ambulances?"

He laughs. I wonder if he's gone mad or if he's just drunk.

Then comes another week of silence. I go to the hairdresser's. I take my seat in this temple of well-being, even let them polish my toenails. The women around me have elegant bags and obligations in this city that has resumed its normal routine after the long summer pause. I have nothing but my abandoned body. And this head, to which I've tried to give the external semblance of order. I'm a hostage in this no-man's-land. When I step out, soaked in perfumes that don't belong to me, I look like a doll. It's raining and I don't bother opening my umbrella. I'm glad for the rain to ravage me.

Chapter 13

Batteries, vitamins, camping lights. What else? Everything. They needed everything. Antibiotics, tablets for disinfecting the water. Cigarettes, powdered milk, canned meat. I'd walk into stores and pull out a crumpled sheet of paper. Gojko had dictated the list to me, and now I was following his orders. My fear had passed, and I was driven not by courage but by a sense of purpose, insignificant as it may have been.

I'd already prepared a package and sent it through Caritas, but it never arrived. The best packages were ripped apart and plundered. Now the package would come with me, an enormous wheeled suitcase made of stretchy but resistant fabric.

The saleswoman in the luggage shop looked nonplussed at the thin, strange woman who sat on the black suitcase to see if the fabric would hold.

"What do you need it for?"

"A cadaver."

She laughed at the humor as dark as the suitcase. I paid and dragged the suitcase toward home.

There's a dried-up woman, a sterile woman, ravaged by silence. She's dragging a big empty suitcase along the sidewalk. Soon the suitcase will swell with all manner of things. Filling that suitcase will be her reason for living in the days to come.

The layers, packed and repacked at night. First the hardest, bulkiest things, then the little objects, the most delicate things, glass bottles of medicine. The suitcase sits and watches me. I'm no longer alone.

Everything I put in there is a hope for life.

Don't forget sanitary pads. Women can't get them anymore.

In the pharmacy I stop and skim the pink and purple bundles. Extra-slim pads, absorbent but super flat, the most expensive kind, the ones that don't show under even the tightest pants. They take up the least space. I arrange the packages in the suitcase, a huge layer of pads. These thin pads should do the trick. How much flow can such hungry women have?

Dad brings things, too. He really seems to see the suitcase as a coffin.

"I'm going to bring him back," I tell him.

He doesn't say a word. He obeys my pain, my fury.

The suitcase takes up time, fills entire days. We fight because of it. *I told you, I can't carry bulky things! It won't hold another fucking thing, can't you see?* And I throw the blankets he's brought in his face.

It's as if it were supposed to grow by night, fill up like a big belly, like a shipping container, as if it were supposed to save, feed and dress all of Sarajevo. My eyes glitter when I look at it. I get up at night to check the expiration date on the antibiotics and the energy bars. There's nothing that isn't useful or necessary. I look at the suitcase the way a mother looks at her daughter's trousseau.

How much life is contained by that war?

How much death is contained by this peace?

Life has come back to me from my feet upward, from my sex, my belly.

I go into a UPIM department store to buy a mountain of markers and drawing pads.

"Are you a teacher, ma'am?"

I say, "I'm going to Sarajevo."

The woman, heavyset and worn out by the routine of her job as a cashier, changes expression and becomes an enormous palpitating mother. Her face flushes in splotches, a sign of her humanity. The stock clerk, who's got a pierced ear and a junkie's teeth, helps, too, and so does the manager in his striped tie. They drag things up out of the basement, unsold stationery and clothing.

"Please, ma'am. Take it. Bring it with you."

The stock clerk is the angriest. He swallows.

"They use the knives we use to take the pits out of olives to take people's eyes out of their sockets."

He used to go to Yugoslavia on vacation. He even dated a girl from Split. Paradise, he says.

The girls at the gym kick their legs. It's the newest thing, a plastic step. They step up onto it and back down, sweating.

I'm at the back. I look at the little asses in their thong leotards. I step back down off the plastic step. I'm in shape from running on the treadmill. You have to be in shape to go back to Sarajevo. You have to have what it takes to sidestep death, so that it will take someone older than you, someone who's not in such good shape.

In the dressing rooms the girls rub lotion on their sculpted bodies and prance around chitchatting about men and diets as they put on makeup and pull up their stockings.

My eyes are heavy. The warmth of the showers and blow dryers makes me sleepy. Goodbye, girls, goodbye. Goodbye, little twits.

Dad has become better than me at finding things for the suitcase. He wanders around the market stalls at Porta Portese buying little sets of wrenches, spools of copper wire, transistors, even a night viewing device. The suitcase will burst. I look at it. It's the last night. Finally, I can go. I've finally got a place on a humanitarian flight.

Viola calls me. They've discovered a lump in her breast. She cries about her breast and cries because I'm leaving. "You're my best friend."

I've never been much of a friend to this accident-prone girl. She's created the whole thing on her own. But tonight I think it's actually worked. There are people who penetrate you like cancer, though you're not sure when it happened.

"Are you scared?" I ask.

"Who gives a shit about the lump?" I can't tell if she's laughing or crying. "What about you? Are you scared?"

I'm afraid of everything, the trucks on the highway, the crowd at a concert. I'm afraid of lightning. Of course I'm afraid of a war.

Dad comes over with a crate of just-ripening peaches. I refuse to take them, but then we make a last layer before the woolen things.

Armando sits on the suitcase and presses down with his rear end. I pull the zipper closed around him. Now the suitcase is an enormous closed body.

I drag it around the house and make sure I can lift it. I have to be independent. No one will be there to help me get my humanitarian baggage off a luggage carousel.

I keep it beside me during the flight, which seems to go by in a flash, probably because all my fear has come back and now, if only I could, I'd be on my way to New York. The inside of the plane is bare metal. There are a few naked seats attached to the wall. The rest is empty space occupied by boxes and by piles of military cloth. We fly over the sea and then over land.

Something acrid rises in my throat, as if my stomach were fermenting. My arms and head are rigid. My feet press into the vibrating metal. The deafening noise of the engines burns the sky. Now I know. I feel it. It could happen here. We're inside. We've become a target for the men in the woods. Once again I see the TV images of scraps of planes downed by missiles, pieces of cockpits and wings that went crashing down through pine branches in forests as thick as mud. My mouth is completely dry, my tongue inert gray flesh like moldy bread.

There are only three other civilians on the plane, two doctors and Vanda, a volunteer for an independent radio station. They're on peace missions to this land without peace. Vanda is robust and masculine and disheveled-looking in the way Slavic men sometimes are. She's the most relaxed one in the group. She's already been to Sarajevo twice since the beginning of the war. She's like a big expert mouse that has figured out how to navigate confinement. She's dressed like a war correspondent from the movies. The pockets covering her vest look like hiding places for hand grenades. She cracks her gum over and over again, little explosions that make me jump.

The smell of Dad's peaches wafts out of my suitcase. Vanda smiles and cracks her gum. She probably thinks I'm a nut. She asks me if I'm flying back out tonight. She says the intellectuals usually stay for a few hours, just enough time to say they've been there, enough time to catch a whiff of the smell of burnt ants.

"Burnt ants?"

"That's what dead people smell like."

Maybe she thinks I'm one of those pen-and-ink profiteers. "I'm coming to stay with my husband. He's a photographer. He's been in Sarajevo for weeks."

She asks his name and says she knows him. She saw him at the end of August. "He's nice. Crazy."

"Crazy? Why?"

"He was swimming in the Miljacka while they were firing from above."

I shake my head, but she's sure. "He's got curly hair, right, and a beard?"

"No, he doesn't have a beard."

"Then it must have been another Diego."

Another Diego, I think, another Diego, and the plane goes down while I'm thinking this. It makes a spiral landing because it's wartime, a very abrupt descent. For a moment I get a narrow glimpse of the mountains. Then I feel the landing gear as it touches down.

There are three customs desks at the airport and three sets of barricades. Soldiers from warring armies get coffee from the same dispenser, the only one left. I watch the surreal scene, enemies bending to retrieve little cups from the same metal hole. The airport is controlled by the blue helmets who protect the landing strips and guarantee the distribution of humanitarian aid. In fact they're hand in glove with the Serbian troops. There's no tension. They all look very tired. Egyptian soldiers, their blue helmets floating on their thin dark faces, drowse on the remains of the seats. We wait a long time for an armor-plated jeep from UNPROFOR, the UN's "protection forces," to bring us into the city. Maybe they're bargaining a bit of truce, because I hear one of the blue helmets talking with a guy wearing a camouflage uniform and a black beret with an eagle.

"Can they go now? Okay?"

". . . Slobodan? Free?"

The Serb nods. Why on earth, I wonder, is a UN official asking a soldier from the aggressor forces for permission to pass? But there's no time for astonishment. This airport has already become a joke, a gangrenous foot at the bottom of the suffering body of the city. If this is the door to the world, there's no hope for the mice.

Heads bowed and without looking around, we climb into the jeep. We pass the first checkpoint, mountains of sandbags and piles of metal, railway ties uprooted and set atop each other. Faces in ski masks, Kalashnikovs clutched tight. The driver yells.

"Keep your head down!"

The jeep is making its way along sniper alley. It skids to avoid rubble in the street. I see the *Oslobodjenje* building through the only crack of light.

There's nothing left, just the elevator structure, like a popsicle stick after the popsicle's melted.

We sped down the ramp that led to the underground entrance of the Holiday Inn, a dark belly protected by sheets of UNPROFOR plastic and full to bursting with journalists and television crews, and then we were in the immense lobby. Seedy figures sidled up to ask me if I wanted to buy a bulletproof vest, if I needed a car, if I wanted to change money, if I wanted to buy information. A guy with fresh stitches on his naked leg clutched a bomb fragment under his arm as he went around in search of someone who would buy his story. I waited in that casbah. There were no vacancies, not among the rooms on the safe side. The only free rooms faced Grbavica. I worried that I'd fall asleep, that someone would take my suitcase. I dragged it to the room that served as a restaurant, where I sat at a long common table full of journalists talking and laughing in loud voices and ate a hot, flavorless meal that seemed delicious.

"Here you need to laugh!" A German cameraman was winking at me.

We went together to the couches in the lobby. He bought me a beer and started explaining the best way to move about the besieged city. He seemed pretty excited. They'd spent the day filming the trenches along the Žuč. He put a hand on my leg and asked me if I wanted to sleep in his room. He smiled, an idiotic expression on his red face. He seemed to take it as a given that I would want to share his bed. After all, it was wartime. I heard an explosion. A few minutes later there was another one, closer by. I recognized the hiss of mortar shells.

I looked up at the long spiral gallery ringed by the rooms. I thought of the time Diego and I looked at ourselves in the reflection of the empty, glittering lobby.

I couldn't remember ever having seen a prostitute in Sarajevo. Now I saw girls in miniskirts sitting on barstools in the company of foreign journalists. A man sitting near me set a pistol on his table as if it were a pack of cigarettes while another guy with a black leather jacket counted a wad of deutschmarks. They were talking about betting and about a place in Marijin Dvor where dogfights were held.

If there's a feeling I remember from those hours, from that prelude, it's a greasy sensation, things flickering before me and then floating away like oil on water.

A hand settles so hard upon my shoulder that it's almost a blow. Gojko kneels at my side and hugs me tight without looking at me.

"Beautiful woman."

We leave through the back. Now he's dragging my suitcase.

"And Diego?"

"He's waiting for you."

He still has his Golf, though now it's covered with dents and riddled with holes. The mismatched doors came from other cars. There's no glass in the windows.

"This is one of the latest Sarajevo city models," he says with a laugh. It seems a miracle that he can still laugh.

It's dawn. We race along in his futuristic car toward a future that may be just like this, the jumbled remains of what came before. The sky is ice, a gloomy blue just beginning to light up from within. I look out at a landscape of fallen and impaled objects. Buildings black as chimneys, tangles of metal, skeletons of cars and trams, the harsh social-realist façades that now look like burnt cardboard. We're trying to get to the Baščaršija. Gojko travels through rubble and along fortuitous passageways, streets I've never seen before. At unprotected intersections he presses the accelerator to the floor and pushes my head down, a possessive gesture. He wants to save my life, but he may be enjoying it a bit, too, playing it up. He yells, letting out an animal groan. All things considered, he's still himself, a Bosnian blowhard in this divided city.

He pulls into the courtyard at top speed. The arches have collapsed. The grass is tall and yellowish. The outside wall of the building has been eaten away by gunshot, but inside it's intact, just darker and dirtier. The stone slabs on the stairs shake as I run. Diego.

He's standing there in the middle of a little garden of candles he's kept burning for me. I hug him and feel something, a hardness I've never felt before. His bones feel like steel. I look at his face. He's thin. His lips are dark. A long beard I've never seen before covers his face to the eyes. I have trouble touching him, recognizing him. His face is like the buildings outside.

I smile and tell him he's a little bit smelly. But he took a shower, he says. With a watering can, Sarajevo-style.

He reminds me of a captive animal, one of the dead baboons at the zoo.

I take his hand and we isolate ourselves in a corner. The house is dark, the windows shielded. There are long cracks in the walls.

"How do you manage to live here?"

He's gripping my hand, his face buried inside it. He's smelling me, rubbing against me, grasping everything he's missed about me.

He stares at me, but his eyes are strange swamps. All of a sudden I think he's not here, that it's not me he's looking for but something that no longer exists.

"My love."

We touch each other like two people who've been brought back to life.

He gives me a bunch of paper flowers.

The old woman who looks like a witch and sells flowers in the Markale Market doesn't have real flowers to sell anymore, so she's created these little ones from pieces of paper that she curls up and colors. They're beautiful and sad. As I look at them I think that Diego resembles them, that he shares their longing for color, for good smells, for life.

He's hungry. I open my suitcase, my treasure chest. He bites into a peach. The juice drips down his chin.

Then the others materialize, Ana, Mladjo, along with faces I've never seen before, people whose houses have been destroyed, refugees from occupied neighborhoods. I pull my bits and pieces out of the suitcase. They hug me tight, as if we'd always known each other. *Hvala, Gemma, hvala.* And people will arrive throughout the day because of the suitcase full of things to distribute. Today the apartment is like the Benevolencija. We celebrate by opening the tins of meat and pickled vegetables and cutting into the Parmesan. Gojko opens a bottle of rakija from his little personal reserve.

I pull back the plastic from one of the windows and peer out. The city, a prisoner of the dark, is like an exhausted mine reduced to nothing but empty holes and abandoned alleyways. The dark soothes as it erases. All I can see is the light-colored stump of a truncated minaret.

Where are all the sounds, the tolling of the church bells, the lament of the muezzin? Where are the smells, the dusty odor of dreggy coffee, the violent aroma of spices and ćevapčići? Where is all the smog from the cars? Where is life?

There was no longer any privacy. In that house, just like everywhere else in Sarajevo, everyone slept together on mattresses piled in the hallway, far from the windows and the parts of the house most vulnerable to blasts from mortars and cannons.

I was the only one who started at every explosion. The others were apparently used to the noise, or else they'd gone deaf. I saw their eyes in rows by the dark light of homemade candles, pieces of rope floating in bowls of water with a layer of oil on top. They were all smoking the cigarettes I'd brought, the gift everyone seemed to appreciate the most, because it's hard not to eat, but not smoking is horrible. They'd taken to smoking anything they could, tea leaves and chamomile and straw from woven chair seats. Ana had hidden a few packets of sanitary pads in her Turkish canvas bag and now she held it to her belly as if it were a pillow. I looked at those strange eyes like the eyes of animals peering out from the dark and at the mouths that drew in on the tubes of tobacco and made them glow.

They were the same eyes as Diego's, haunted, frozen, mute. They all seemed to be looking into the same pit of water, a murky mirror reflecting nothing.

"How are you?"

"Oh, fine."

But my words reached him as if from a distance, like an echo. He raised a hand and passed his fingers over my mouth as if to gauge its thickness. He buried his fingertips in my lips as if they were some warm but unattainable substance.

He leaned against the wall and played guitar in the dark.

Then we lay down on one of those mattresses. Diego settled in with a single gesture, closing in on himself like a fetus, and already he was breathing the changed breath of sleep. It felt like he'd wedged himself into that sleep just to separate himself from me. Maybe he'd simply had too much to drink, like the others. I was the only person awake in that darkness full of the breathing of so many people. I got up to move a jar full of cigarette butts. A few plastic containers for fetching water sat in a corner alongside a heap of everyone's shoes. The windows were covered with those plastic sheets that fluttered and let in the cold. Soon it would be winter. Why were we there, lying on the ground with these people? That's what I wondered as I looked at Diego's back.

At dawn I was awakened by the dull sound of what seemed to be a mortar explosion. It rained upon me through the torpor of the sleep that had taken so long to come. I found it difficult to move. No one else was there. Everyone had disappeared except for Gojko, who was fiddling around with a transistor.

"Where's Diego?"

"He didn't want to wake you."

We ate some of the cookies I'd brought.

"Do you know if he sees Aska?"

He didn't answer me and he didn't look at me.

"Is she gone? Is she alive?"

"She's still in Sarajevo."

"Tell me where they meet."

"I don't know. I don't know what Diego does. I hardly ever see him."

He was devouring the cookies. His beard was full of crumbs.

"I've never trusted you."

"Oh, well."

Now, by daylight, I noticed that Gojko's gaze was dirtier than before, stained by months of war. His youth had disappeared. He dragged around a burden of disillusion and acrimony. There was something ruined about his sense of humor, as well. It smelled of burnt ants like everything else. I thought that I, too, would grow old all of a sudden.

Diego came back after a few hours. He'd gone almost two kilometers away to fetch water. His arms were stiff from bearing the weight of the water tanks.

"So you can take a bath."

We shut ourselves in the bathroom. I looked at the grayed ceramic of the tub, full of yellow lines, and at the faucet that no longer let out a single drop.

We put the water in a basin. I undressed, and for the first time I found it difficult to be naked in front of him. It was as if there were no longer any intimacy. Diego avoided looking at me. He busied himself with the water, running it over his hands as if he were looking for something, a distant glimmer, a passageway.

"Look at me," I said.

He raised his eyes slowly, with difficulty. I was naked. A dead plant with no bark, white wood cut off from its roots.

"What's wrong?"

"You're beautiful."

"What's wrong?"

He reached out an arm and touched my stomach, my belly button, and I felt repulsed by his hand.

He touched me the same way he'd looked at me, with the same distance, as if I were a mannequin.

I burrowed into myself like an egg.

He undressed and settled next to me in that tub without water. He dipped a sponge in the basin and washed my back. I turned to look at him. I looked at the yellowish bones beneath his fine, dry skin, the inert sex surrounded by pubic hair like a dark nest. He looked like an old man.

"Why are you here?" I asked him.

"I'm where I have to be."

The next morning I wake at dawn like the others. Diego is crouching over the suitcase, filling his backpack.

"Who are you bringing that stuff to?"

To some families he knows, he says, old people who can't get around, widows with children.

I dress after he leaves and follow him as far as the Cumurija Bridge.

I see the city by day. There's not a single building intact. The domes of the mosques look like old metal covers of cooking pans lost in the rubble. The shutters of the Baščaršija are closed. In the stores all the shelves have been uprooted. A bird falls on me, a tired bird who probably no longer even has a branch to rest upon.

Rolls of film. Rolls of film lined up next to each other on the table in this miserable room that has become our prison. Rolls of film like cartridges, like cartridge cases. Like black eggs. I make up a game to help pass the time. I pile the rolls of film into acrobatic constructions. Then I lie on the bed and wait. After every blast there's a tremor that moves across the floor and walls and climbs up the table. The canisters of film fall to the floor and roll around.

Who knows if anyone will ever see all the images imprinted upon the celluloid closed inside these dented little cases? They're the perfect pastime for time that never passes. By three in the afternoon we're already shut up in the house. There's no point risking your life after the black market closes and all the water containers have been filled.

It already seems as if I'd never left.

We're back in our old rented room. When she first saw me, Velida touched me as if I were a miracle, glass still intact in its frame. The months have eaten away at her. She's like one of her blackbirds now. Her head is in perpetual motion, a desolate commentary. I bring her the provisions I'd set aside. When Jovan saw the flashlight I'd brought, he shut his mouth tight to hold back his sobs. It's the thing he's missed the most, a swath of light to illuminate the too-dark nights.

The old biologist no longer leaves the house. He spends the entire day in a sheltered corner beside the birdcage. The blackbirds are still alive. The cat with the broken tail is dead. It left the house one day, took a few steps and never came back.

Jovan and Velida look forward every day to peace, though they no longer believe in it. They look at the white armored vehicles of the UN stationed below their windows, doing nothing, useless as pedal carts chained together in an empty park.

I ask Velida for a broom and a rag to clean the floor in our room. Her head shakes the entire time.

"Are you sure you want to stay here with us?"

"Yes."

"You'd be safer in the hotel for foreigners."

There's no getting rid of this thick gray layer of dust as hard as cement.

Velida touches her chest and says that this dust, made up of things that have fallen, has penetrated them and rests like glue on their lungs.

"It's the dust of the buildings where we lived, our library in the old Vijećnica, the university where we taught, the houses where we were born."

In the kitchen there are green layers of leaves on every shelf. Velida says that nettles make an excellent pita filling.

"Everyone in Sarajevo eats nettles now," she says with a smile. Maybe, with such a healthy macrobiotic diet, they'll survive the bombs.

The knowledge she gained as a biologist is coming in handy during this famine. She offers me an herbal tea made from fir tree buds.

"It's delicious."

She asks me why I've returned.

"I want to be with Diego, and he wants to be here."

Her eyes grow cloudy with emotion.

She, too, has followed Jovan all her life. They still kiss each other on the lips, even now that young people and children are dying all around, even though the fact that the two of them are still alive makes her ashamed of their love.

Plastic sheets have replaced the brocade curtains that used to hang over the windows and the pictures on the walls hang crookedly with no glass left in their frames. Velida and Jovan's beautiful apartment has shrunk. They carried their beds into the kitchen, the only room with heat. Velida traded her fur coat and her engagement ring with its ruby stone for an old stove on the black market. They dug a hole in the wall for the vent. Nowadays every apartment has a hole to let smoke out through resuscitated chimney flues and makeshift pipes. The city is a huge encampment.

I'm scared to go out. I stay in the kitchen with Velida, where I watch her thin, curved back.

"How will you manage in the winter?"

They've already started burning their furniture. Jovan chops things up himself. He cuts the legs off the little table in the living room and smashes the drawers from the bedside tables and the sideboard. Velida cuts the rugs into strips and makes blocks of cloth that burn slowly, like coal.

There are no longer any trees in the parks. In just a short amount of time the city has stripped itself of its greenery. From everywhere comes the noise of saws and of branches being dragged like big brooms through the rubble.

Jovan complains. They cut the linden tree below the apartment. It provided some protection from the snipers. He still has a painting he once made of it, the trunk and the big branch re-created with dots of watercolor.

"Trees are life."

He's angry at the profiteers who cut down trees to get rich on the black market.

It's October and not all that cold yet. Other years it's snowed as early as August, but this year, God willing, the snow will take its time.

And so life dies. The trees fall one by one. People need wood for the coming winter, and in the meantime they make space for the dead, who are buried everywhere now, in the parks, in the Koševo soccer field, because the cemeteries are overflowing. Everywhere you find those mounds, dark piles of displaced earth.

The animals up in the mountains continue to attack the rubble. A shell fell on a group of children who were playing soccer behind our house in a peaceful area that had already been utterly destroyed. The Chetniks declared that the shell landed there by accident. They said that it was fired by the Bosnian Green Berets, not by them. The dead children didn't declare a thing. But the soccer ball came right into Velida's house. It unglued itself from its covering and made its way in. She didn't find out about the children until that evening. Now she looks at that ball, which she put in the cat's empty basket, and asks me, "Who am I supposed to give it back to?"

Night never ends now. Diego comes home with rolls of film. He empties his camera and throws them in a corner. He doesn't tell me anymore what he takes pictures of.

At night, darkness engulfs the apocalypse. There isn't a trace of life. The sirens blare their alarm, a forgotten voice that no longer serves any purpose. Night after night, Sarajevo dies when the dark descends like a lid over the city. The survivors, like stubborn ants driven by affection and a desire to share their city's fate, find themselves buried alive in its coffin.

At night all that remains is the wind that comes down from the mountains to wander like a restless spirit around the city.

Diego says this is just a taste of what's to come. One day the whole world will be like this, burnt on the inside, mortally wounded, nothing but rusted debris, gassy chimneys, black tongues of spent fuel. We're seeing the end of the world, just like in the comics, like in the sickest and most apocalyptic movies. He smiles. At night hope vanishes and Diego becomes funereal. I look through the dark at his grin, his shiny eyes. He drinks too much, liters and liters of that awful beer. When he gets up to take a piss he bangs into things. When he's sleeping I touch him to make sure he's alive. I'm scared of this dark, a real abyss. It's as if we were buried below the earth in the depths of an underground lake.

From somewhere comes the sound of a spade digging in the earth. At night Sarajevo buries its dead, slides them silently into the ground. Snipers like nothing better than gatherings in open spaces, so Sarajevo must wait for the dark. The living remain silent, their tears nailed to their chests like the boards of the coffins made from old tables and armoire doors.

The only voices audible in the night are the hoarse barkings of the roaming packs of skeletal dogs, family pets made wild by the war, abandoned by their owners, who left or died or are too hungry to spare any food.

Then dawn comes. Sometimes it's not the mortars that wake you but the birds who come back and sing, and then you think that maybe someday this will really end.

So the survivors can leave the city to have a picnic or gather mushrooms on one of the mountains, Jahorina, Mount Trebević.

So the number one tram can once again go to the waterfalls and fields of Ilidža.

It's incredible to see so many people materialize at dawn. You wonder where they hid, whether they're real living people or people who've been raised from the dead. No one stays home. It's time to go out for food, water, black market bargains and ration cards for bread and humanitarian cans. People do their rounds: Caritas, the Protestant organizations and the Jewish Benevolencija, which is the most generous of them all and helps everyone. They help Sarajevo's Muslims, who years ago helped Jews hide from the Nazis. That's how the first few hours of the day pass. Death is certain if you stay inside.

Every time she goes out Velida says, "I'm going." She pauses, then says, "I'm going to meet my shell."

Every so often someone falls. A woman waiting in line for water. A rabbit.

You mustn't stop to look, mustn't allow your eyes time to see, to feel affection. This is the thing you have to learn, how not to give the dead time to reveal themselves, to become real. You have to move forward without distinguishing between a body and a sandbag, leave it all behind, indistinct, distance yourself from what's real, look only at your own path without giving the dead a name, an overcoat, a hair color. Leave them, learn to move past them at a distance, pretend you didn't see them. Pretend they aren't there.

Because if you stop, if you let yourself slide back, then inevitably you'll slow down.

But children are curious. They stretch their necks to look as their mothers pull them along. Children move toward death like squirrels toward picnic leftovers.

Yet this city where people continue to die emanates a hidden force like sap rising up from the heart of the forest.

Gojko came to get me so I could hug Sebina once again. She reminded me of a turtle with her dry, triangular face and her mouth like a curled piece of straw. I hugged her. We stood on the threshold of that incredibly tidy apartment. I felt her head against my stomach.

"Why are you still here, Bijeli Biber?"

She doesn't want to leave on a convoy full of lonely children.

Some of her friends have left. They send letters and all of them seem sadder than her. She says her room is still there and that, all things considered, it's not so bad. Gojko comes almost every day and they have the things they need, although she's getting really sick of rice and macaroni.

"And then there's this awful smell!" She laughs.

You find the smell of canned mackerel from the humanitarian aid packages in every house and in every burp that comes out of the mouths of people as lucky as they are.

She tells me that she's used now to the alarms and the cellar. Her mouth is covered with the chocolate I brought her.

She doesn't go to practice anymore. The gym has been converted into a dormitory for refugees. Now her voice grows muddy after all her enthusiasm. But she doesn't cry, she simply frowns again and shrugs. She does a handstand, leaning against the wall, then walks on her hands, her hair touching the floor. Her skirt falls down like a limp lily. I look at her spotted legs, the knobs of her knees, the little veins visible beneath her skin, her flowered underpants. She descends into a backbend, her back curving like a contortionist's.

"Don't hurt yourself . . ."

She spreads her legs in a perfect split. It's a little show just for me. I clap. Her smile remains, along with the solitary noise of my hands one against the other.

I ask about the bag hanging off the doorknob. She says it holds their documents, the papers for the house, their birth certificates and blood types and Mirna's driving license along with their money and their jewels and her father's watch, everything ready in case a shell hits the building and they have to run.

She coughs, then uses her asthma inhaler. She laughs and says it tastes bad. "Like a stinkbug."

"Since when have you had asthma?"

Since she started staying home alone. Her throat closes on her. She's anxious about Mirna and scared she won't come back. She paces up and down in her shoes that light up the dark hallway.

"They still work!"

"Of course. They recharge themselves."

News of the dead reaches her, but from a distance, because Mirna protects her by keeping her in the house. But Sebina knows that it's possible to die while you're out walking. She warns me to be careful. "Because they don't know you're Italian. They'll think you're from Sarajevo and they'll shoot at you."

I go out with Diego. I wear the bulletproof vest he never wears. We walk silently through the rubble along with the others. They don't run. They're composed, their eyes just a bit wider than the eyes of the inhabitants of a peacetime city. With their dirty hair and slept-in clothes, the men are more disheveled, but you see some, in jacket and tie, who look like professors or managers. Where are they going? Schools and offices are closed. They cross the dust in their loafers. Their black briefcases must be full of documents or readings to hand out in class. They walk carefully through this metaphysical landscape, almost in slow motion. There's something unnatural about the calm of this minefield. The people make a strange impression, like silhouettes in a theater set. They're stiff with fear. The part of them that runs is their eyes, which move warily, like real eyes looking out of a cardboard cutout. There are signs at the intersections now: PAZI SNIPER! Beware of snipers.

Everyone is thin. There's not a single overweight person left. I'll have to tell the girls back at the gym. Cellulite? Come to Sarajevo, where there's nothing to eat and you walk all day long. The months of the siege can be counted in the sad strips of white growth on the heads of women who can no longer dye their hair. But young women manage somehow to hold on to their elegance as they walk along with their haggard faces perfectly made up.

It's a sign of resistance, a thumbing of the nose at the animals up above, that everyone goes out, obstinately calm, in high heels and lipstick through the passageways opened up by the war, on the obligatory journeys between sandbag trenches and heaps of iron beams.

We reach the beer factory. Diego photographs the long water lines, the uncovered pipe punctuated by little mouths where people fill their containers.

Wheels. There are things people never used to count because there were so many of them, like anywhere else in the world. But now . . . wheels. Everyone talks about wheels. Everyone asks you whether or not you have an old one.

Točak . . . Točak.

With wheels you can drag along the things you manage to scavenge— water containers, pieces of wood, pieces of machinery.

Diego takes a picture of an old man dragging a baby carriage that holds the roots of a tree, a big dirty wooden baby that will be useful when winter comes.

Your day is what you catch, in the lowlands, in the mud of the rubble as the snipers try to catch you.

"Did you know that mothers are their favorite targets?"

No, I didn't.

"The snipers like to see the desperate, wide-open mouths of crying children."

Diego takes pictures of the children who have never stopped playing. They hide inside unstable buildings, below the cement slabs of collapsing ceilings. He kneels down to talk to them. He rummages through his pockets and gives them what he finds there. Frequently he lets them attack him, lets them put their hands on his face, in his hair. He carries them on his shoulders and doesn't even get angry when they touch his camera lenses.

He takes my picture, as well, with the crater of the library in the background.

He says, "Stand there."

I wonder if he still loves me or if I'm just a ghost from the life he lived

before. He moves his head constantly, looking all around. Who is he looking for?

The Beg's mosque is among the ruined buildings. At sunset Diego takes
pictures of the faithful who kneel on their rugs to pray before heaps of rubble.
In Titova Street people stop to read and lower their heads before a typewritten list of the dead that someone hangs each night.

We step into a kafana, a rugged room with tables grouped together far
from the street. There's nothing on the counter but a few pieces of dark cake,
but they serve strong Nescafé frappé with a bit of foam; it almost seems like
Italian espresso. The air is full of Drina smoke and the shouts of drunken
men in homemade military uniforms, militiamen from a ragtag army, combat heroes and former scoundrels promoted to the rank of local commander.
A motionless woman sits with one elbow on the table, her face resting awk-
wardly in the palm of one hand. The gesture drags her features downward,
dilates her nostrils, shows her dark teeth, closes one of her eyes. She doesn't
seem to notice any of what's happening around her. Maybe she's come here to
recover from something frightening.

Maybe she's been disfigured by sorrow.

Bewildered women. Old men still as statues. We drink our Nescafé. For
the umpteenth time I ask Diego what point there is in staying. "Why are we
here?"

Why this absurdity, this punishment?

He doesn't answer. He licks up the last drop of his coffee. His tongue is
white, dirty like mine. "I didn't ask you to come."

And in our room, later on, when we have nothing to eat because we didn't
think about it earlier, and our stomachs are green and sour, Diego's voice
comes to me through the dark. "Go back to Italy, my love."

It's raining. The sky is melting, disintegrating. There was thunder and lightning all night long, nature's blasts mingling with those of human malice. I lie
awake a long time listening to the contest in the sky. It's as if God had become
angry and unleashed his fury into the sky, wetting the mouths of the cannons, the mortars and the antiaircraft guns aimed at the ground, the gashes
of the trenches. There can't be anything much but mud up in the mountains.
Maybe the trees up in the woods won't be able to hold back this flood and the

earth will slide down into the valley like sludge, dragging along orchards and the houses of the *sanjakbeg*s.

The rain targets the plastic sheets on the windows and from now on there's this horrible noise. It's cold. The season is changing quickly. These walls, cracked to the ceiling, no longer protect us. There's a smell of dirty clothes and of damp. Diego is curled up beneath the covers, his head under the sheets, his feet naked and yellow. There's no more gas left in the camping stove. It went out with one last blue puff, a flame that lasted a very short time, just like a spent soul. I go down to the communal kitchen to look for some coffee. Velida is in line, her legs wet to the knees, an enameled pitcher in her hand. She jumps with a start and drops the pitcher.

"It was just thunder," I tell her.

I bend and pick up the pitcher, which is chipped now in two places so that its iron soul shows through.

"One more broken thing." She smiles.

She smells strange, too. The smell of the citizens of Sarajevo. It's not just because water's scarce, because today there's rainwater to wash with. It's the fatigue and the panic oozing from people's bodies, a before-death smell like the one terrified animals let off in self-defense. These are upended bodies, the upset stomachs of people who eat grass and don't sleep and leave their homes with the certainty of death.

It rains on the little line in the courtyard. Women in slippers, trembling soups.

"Look what bad shape we're in."

This morning Velida can cry because it's raining so hard no one will see her tears. A woman shoves us in the line and Velida steps aside to let her pass. Then she gives the woman her milk ration as well. Who knows where the provisioner managed to find real milk. It's been months since anyone's had a glimpse of it. I get angry and tell Velida she's too thin to be so generous. But she doesn't want to turn into an animal. She refuses to take part in this struggle between desperate people.

"She has children," she says. "All I have is Death."

She raises her head. Her wet hair sticks to her scalp like clumps of drenched wool.

"I can see him. I managed to keep him at bay until recently, but now he's here. I've let Death in. He sits in the kitchen with me. He watches me and keeps me company. He asks me to dance."

I go back upstairs with some coffee. Diego is ready to go out. He's wearing a lightweight red raincoat with a rip in the back.

"Where are you going?"

He can't stand being closed up in here. He doesn't mind the rain. In fact, he likes it.

He fixes the raincoat with two pieces of white medical tape from the shoe box that contains our medicine kit.

He goes off with that white cross on his back. I tell him he looks like a perfect target. He shrugs and smiles. Until quite recently I would have thrown myself upon him to keep him from leaving, but I don't have the energy anymore. He's become a fatalist like the Sarajevans. Destiny is like your heart, he says. It's inside you from the start, so there's no sense in taking another route.

Imbecile.

I follow him without bothering to put on the bulletproof vest because it's too heavy, because today I, too, am letting down my guard. I'm tired, and tiredness makes one reckless.

And just maybe, with all this rain, the rifles might be wet and the snipers' vision might be blurred. Maybe it's easier to get past them in the rain.

I follow him through the dripping trenches and deserted entryways, between slabs of walls uprooted by shells and perched in a new, ghostly balance. The inner structure of the walls is bared—the weft, the powder. It's an obscene, internal gaze, intimacy exposed to public view in the public sorrow.

But no one looks anymore. You have to move on.

Eyes pass cadavers without stopping, without turning. War itself resides in these footsteps that press on and in these tired eyes that will not be sidetracked.

It's raining. I walk behind my husband. Every so often I lose him. Then I find him again. I'm hungry.

Diego's got that white cross on his red plastic back. He steps into the covered market. Solitary people move about aimlessly. They seem crazy, walking as they do, heads hanging low like animals behind an electric fence, like patients in a mental hospital. Every so often one of them trembles as if he or she had crossed the boundary into something that doesn't kill but gives a shock and wears away at the nervous system. There's nothing to buy, only miserable objects to swap: a copper coffeepot, a bottle of grappa, a jar of plum preserves, a Bic lighter.

Diego bends over, picks something up and pulls out some money.

All around there's nothing but water, pouring down violently as if tossed by the bucketful.

Diego photographs the people walking around mutely in that watery frame, moribund fish floating to the top.

I'm completely drenched. The ground is covered with mud. I see a bald head that must have blown off a mannequin when it exploded out of a store. Its red lips are shiny with rain, its pretend eyes wide open. I stop to look at the absurd head. It seems so lonely I'm tempted to bend over and pick it up and carry it along with me, set it on the table in a café and talk with it. Diego is crossing the Cumurija Bridge. I'd like to turn back but it seems like there's no going back. I run behind him, behind that white cross.

He skims the Papagajka building, ugly and gaudy, a parrot knocked to the ground by shells. He moves along without looking back and goes into a building that's lower than the others, a former school with a line of rooms as black as caves, classrooms with neither door frames nor doors because they've been burned in the stoves along with the wood of the desks. There's a smell of excrement. Diego seems to know the route by heart. An old map of Yugoslavia hangs on a wall along with a bullet-riddled photo of Tito. A man is busy chopping a surviving wooden board into bits. He doesn't even look at me. I follow in my husband's footsteps. I hear sounds, the voices of people who may be laughing or may be crying. Every so often I see a curtain or a carpet that's been nailed up over a doorway to protect some miserable intimacy, mattresses heaped on the floor and makeshift stoves. This must be a shelter for refugees. I smell wood and paint burning together. Diego's reached his destination. He raises the edge of a plastic sheet and joins a group of people crouched around a weak, smoky fire on the damp tiled floor.

I stay behind and look through the plastic at those poor backs. When I notice, I swallow hard. My breath is like powdered glass. It scratches my throat. Her head is covered so I can't see her hair. She looks like any one of those worn-out Muslim peasant women who've fled their burnt villages. Diego opens his backpack and sits beside her. She leans against his shoulder. She's been waiting for him. They drink the brandy he's brought, passing the bottle back and forth and then sharing it with the others.

Then Aska stands. She's still wearing her warrior combat boots but she's dressed Muslim-style in Turkish trousers. She and Diego go out onto the street. The rain blows back her veil so that the red of her hair is visible beyond the white crescent of her forehead.

I'm filled with a strange euphoria, a violent joy that splits my head. I move forward in the unreal silence of this rain that devours every other sound. They aren't really walking together. He's following her at a slight distance. They look like two lovers who've argued.

I follow them along the obligatory trenches between screens of sheet metal and cement blocks. Now they're out in the open, in one of those unprotected passageways with a sign that says BEWARE OF SNIPERS.

I stop. I feel the fear in my legs, in my gut. The oppressive green of the mountains is visible through the open space. The pine forests look like warriors advancing through the rain. Someone zigzags across and I hear the gunshot. Thankfully, the man makes it safely to the other side. He's bent over, breathing hard. I stink of fear and sweat inside my wet clothes.

I can't believe it. Aska is moving forward. I stare in horror as she crosses. She doesn't run but walks calmly as if this weren't a cursed intersection in Sarajevo but in Rome or Copenhagen.

Diego has stopped as if he didn't want to follow her anymore. Then, all of a sudden, he moves out from under cover and runs like a paramedic with that white cross on his back. He tugs at her, pulls her by the arm, yells at her to run, to get away from there. He shields her with his body.

The gunshot never arrives. Maybe the sniper has finished his shift, or maybe he's also transfixed by the indolent dance of this red-haired sheep.

Now Diego and Aska are safe behind the carcass of a tram. She lights a cigarette. They stay there for I don't know how long, like drenched animals. She smokes another cigarette. He smokes, too. They don't seem to say anything to each other. They crouch in silence, their knees at nose level. Then all of a sudden they embrace, as if they'd made up, as if a few moments earlier she'd risked her life on purpose, as if she'd gone so slowly simply to punish him. He's pulled off her veil. He's caressing her hair. He rests his forehead in her hair and stays there breathing through that wet mantle.

It's as if I could smell that hug, the warm smell of a doghouse, of a shelter.

It's a gesture I recognize from the early days, when he'd left his city and hadn't yet completely adapted to life in Rome. Defeated by an inner fatigue, he'd rest his forehead against my shoulder. He'd stay there, planted in my bones with the gaze of a child who doesn't want anyone to see that he's given up fighting because he needs to be loved.

Aska seems the stronger of the two. She consoles him stiffly, clumsily, almost annoyed by his surrender.

She stands. She's taller and thinner than I remember. She looks like a black candle. Out of that thinness, her stomach blossoms, a round protuber-ance like a swelling. It could just be that her body is worn out by the war, the poor food, the nettles and the flour pastes and the indigestible water stained with disinfectant pills, that her stomach is infected with worms. But I know it's not any of those things. That stomach enters me like a shell. I move back-ward, disemboweled, like the man in Vase Miskina Street, the glove hanging from a barrier.

I leave them behind and wander around that burnt amusement park. I pick up the mannequin's head and carry it under my arm.

I manage to get back home and slip into bed without even bothering to shut the door. It bangs on its hinges, beating out the time as I wait. Bursts of wind come in, along with rain that gets everything wet. Diego comes back, shakes his wet hair and takes off his raincoat and his jeans. He stands there with his white paws and his gaunt face.

"Now you know why I can't leave."

I'm glad for what comes next, the fever and all the rest, the hallucinations, circles in the water, in the mud, in the sky full of red bullets. I see a long line of tombs and all the people I know inside them, everyone in his or her own niche. We talk, smile, pull the lids of our tombs closed and then open them. They slide easily, like the covers of boxes of matches. Velida comes in with one of her herbal teas. Diego hasn't put his pants back on. He stands there with his bare legs. The candlewick fries in the oil. He doesn't come near. He rocks his head.

"Why didn't you tell me?"

He wanted to take care of it on his own. He didn't want me to risk my life. He's not agitated, he doesn't cry. He's nothing. He's as still as this war.

We've been gathering rainwater. There's a cemetery of water basins in our room. Is it contaminated? Who cares? I want to take a bath. The fever is burning up inside. I immerse myself in freezing water that smells like a pond.

He knew I was following him, he says. He let me follow.

"We couldn't go on like that."

He's calm for the first time in months.

They made love that night and all the nights and the days they were together. It wasn't just mating. It was hours of love, of absolute sweetness.

Only now when he's talking about her do his eyes come alive, when he tells me how difficult it was to pull away from her body, from the nape of her neck.

It's easy to grab on to life when it's raining shells outside.

And where's our life?

Far away. Far away. There's no use lying to ourselves. We walked like the dead through Croatia and Ukraine. We stopped over at the airport in Belgrade and then came back to die in Sarajevo, the city where we were born.

From the table, the mannequin head watches us with its wide, makeup-covered eyes.

We looked for a body to rent, a piece of wood floating in the river that was taking us to our ruin, a piece of wood to bring us to the other side. But he's not like me. He can't take advantage of people. He's a stupid boy who falls in love.

He didn't know she was pregnant. She never contacted him. He only found out when he came back to Sarajevo.

He looks at the severed head. Maybe it reminds him of Aska. That's how she lives, too, detached from her body.

She regretted it immediately. She's angry, depressed. Her family was killed in her village, Sokolac. And now she feels guilty. She believes God's punished her.

Diego caresses that head, its wide-open eyes shiny with unshed tears.

"Do you love her?"
"How could I not?"
"And me?"
"You're you."

Who am I? I'm the one in the picture on the press pass. I have to go, have to drag myself to UN Headquarters and get myself a spot on one of those planes that don't even turn off their engines, just unload boxes of medicines onto the Butmir tarmac and then leave again. But I stay. How could I leave? The rolls of film fall to the floor and no one picks them up. There are photographers stationed all over the place, beside the most dangerous crossings, waiting for walking death, a woman who's struck down as she runs to reach her family. They're snipers with film, waiting for the prizewinning shot.

Chilling stories make their way down from the hills. Strange volunteers join the Chetniks on the weekends, people who come from abroad to get their kicks, select marksmen tired of simulations and paper silhouettes.

Sarajevo is a huge open firing range, a hunting reserve.

Chapter 14

After the rain, the snails come out. They push their slimy boneless bodies out of their shells as they move along. After the rain, the inhabitants of Sarajevo go foraging in the treeless fields amid tangles of iron and fresh mounds of earth. They bend over furtively, excitedly, to pick up the shiny little creatures. It's been months since they last ate meat. Then it rained, and today the women smile and unpack their treasure in their empty kitchens. The children smile at the sight of the snails climbing up and falling off the table. Like the others, Velida came home with a bag full of snails that she'd gathered secretly, in an isolated park, because she was ashamed for others to see her hunger.

We dip our bread in the pan. A slightly cloying odor fills the kitchen. Snails cooked in Turkish spices, Bosnian vinegar and broth from the humanitarian packages. A delicacy.

Later Velida will blame this too-good food for having restored a happiness they hadn't felt for a long time, a misleading and harmful happiness.

Jovan's eyes were shiny, and there was a bit of color in his cheeks after months of rough gray skin.

After he finished eating, he lit a cigarette from a package Diego had given him. Drinas that they wrap now in pages taken from books because there's no more paper. Naturally, they started with books in Cyrillic. Jovan was sorry to see his culture going up in smoke, but how could he refrain from having a cigarette after a real luxury like a plate of snails?

Jovan went out when it was silent again, when Velida resumed chopping nettles and the good smell of the snails had disappeared forever.

He hadn't been out for months. He dressed to the nines in his wool vest, a wide tie and his old yarmulke on his head. He picked up the bag he'd used as a professor and said he felt good and that he was going out for a walk.

Unreal words in that ghost city, in those houses without lights, without glass, the best furniture sold and the worst pieces chopped to bits for burning.

"Where are you going, Jovan?"

"I'm going to the university."

Velida didn't have the courage to stop him. She'd always respected her husband's wishes, and it hardly seemed the time to treat him as if he were under house arrest. She simply tried to tell him that the university had been shelled like all the other important buildings. Jovan nodded.

"I'm going to go see if there's anything to be done."

"It's dangerous."

He smiled and came out with an old Yiddish proverb. *If a man is fated to drown, he may die in a teaspoon of water.*

It was too late when Velida came to knock at my door, when it was already dark and past curfew and Jovan had been gone for hours. She wasn't crying, but her head trembled more than usual.

She was worried but still courageous. She had done the right thing.

Today, on a mid-November day, after a meal of snails and two glasses of homemade brandy made with rice from the humanitarian aid packages, the elderly Jovan—a Serbian Jew from Sarajevo, a biologist whose field of expertise was freshwater species and who had spent his entire life studying the evolution of oligochaetes and of unicellular flagellate algae—went out to take a look at the wreckage of his city, at the destruction of his species, the peaceful species comprised of the Muslims, Serbs, Croatians and Jews of Sarajevo.

The dark ate away at Velida's memory-lined face. She had no regrets. If Jovan had felt the need to go, it was right that he had gone.

"We never acted with violence toward one another. We're a peaceful couple."

Velida nodded when the news came. It was a taxi driver who told her, one of the heroes who crossed the most terrible intersections with their doors open in order to gather up the wounded. He was tall, with a beautiful face ravaged by the fatigue of war. He spread his arms, closed them on his chest like a Muslim and bowed his head.

Jovan was struck down on the Bridge of Unity and Brotherhood as he walked calmly toward the Grbavica snipers. This was what people did when they were too proud or too tired. They decided to die on their feet, to walk toward their own snipers as if toward an angel.

Velida cried deep in her throat, little sips of a boundless sorrow interspersed with brief moments of breathlessness. That's how she buried fifty years of life with Jovan. I squeezed her hand. That's all. She was a strong, dig-nified widow, like a warrior's wife. There was nothing but that sound, like the gobble of a turkey, coming from the empty kitchen. A few days earlier they'd argued, one of the few times in all their years together. Jovan had insisted Velida sell his microscope, his books and all his laboratory equipment, but she refused to even entertain the idea. She had sold her gold and the few bits of household silver, had burned her shoes and her books to keep the stove going, but she didn't want to sell Jovan's things.

"I couldn't take his life away from him."

So he took it himself. All that remained were his battered armchair and the worn cardigan that had kept him warm during all those nights in the laboratory.

I think he simply wanted to free Velida of the burden of looking after him. Without him she might be able to leave, sell the microscope, save herself. He knew in any case that he was too weak to make it through the winter. His cough seemed to come up out of a crater. He didn't want to wait for the end sitting down, in the dark of the plastic UNPROFOR sheets. He waited for the rain and the snails. The meal restored some of his strength. With that ephem-eral strength he went out to say farewell to what remained of the city where he was born and had lived.

There's an unmistakable smell in the morgue at the Koševo Hospital, acrid and sweet. We pass the body of a girl with jeans and no arms, then a burnt man with black skin pulling away from his bared teeth and the bones of his skull. They gave us masks soaked in disinfectant to block out the smell. Velida doesn't bother putting hers on. It's as if all her senses were numb.

Jovan is intact. There's no doubt it's him, with the same expression as a few hours ago when we ate the snails. Death hasn't sullied him. The doctor who accompanies us explains that he was hit in the neck and that the bullet came out beside an ear. He shows us the little blueberry-colored hole. Velida nods. There's nothing ugly about it. His clothes are in order, too. The doctor moves away and we're alone with all those dead bodies. I think, *It's flesh that will no longer suffer.* I think that after this abyss there's nothing left. That I should stop suffering now, because that's what happens in here—you simply stop suffering. You lower your head. Velida bends and kisses Jovan on the lips and for a long while stays glued to her husband's face, her eyes closed. When she straightens again there are no tears, but her lips look as dark and dead as Jovan's.

Then I notice the child, the blue child. There's an empty stretcher beside Jovan's and then this child's body with a slightly bluish pallor, like saints in church. He looks perfectly composed. There's no blood on his face. He's got the kind of rough-textured, short-cropped hair that's always tidy. It sits on his head like a fur hat, and it's so alive it almost seems I can smell his slightly sweaty head beneath it, the smell of a child who's been playing. He's a blue lizard, a little saint. He must have died very recently. I step closer to take a better look. There's no one with him. Velida's talking to Jovan, bidding him farewell, remembering their best moments. This gives me time to walk around this place that's more absurd than any reality, this back room of war, where bodies lie heaped together like broken toys. The child is wearing a striped sweater. I look at his slightly opened hand, abandoned as if in sleep. Innocence reclining humbly before death. I look at his fingernails, where it seems his soul has stopped. I should move on because it's clear that I'll never save myself from this sight, that once this child has entered me he'll leave me only when I die. He'll be the last thing I see and the first thing I look forward to joining up with afterward in the pale blue flight of souls. I'll look for his fingernails. I don't wonder where his mother is, why she isn't here to cry over her child's dead body. She could be dead, too. Because I've become his mother, I touch his hand. I know I shouldn't do it. But it seems I can. No one's here to cry over his body, to reclaim it. He hasn't been dead for long. I wouldn't be surprised if he jumped up, planted his eyes on me and scurried off quickly like a mouse frightened at finding himself here.

I've found the prescription for the powerful men of the world, the ones who sit around peace tables clad in jackets and ties. Put the blue child on the table and make them stay. Make them stay and watch death do its methodical work, watch as it eats away at the child from within. Hand out sandwiches, cigarettes and mineral water and then leave them there while the child empties, while he decomposes to the bone. Leave them there for days, for all the days it takes. This is what I'd do.

And now I know that I've become a mother here before this dead child. My pelvic bones have opened. A birth has taken place in this morgue.

I'm shivering, the urge to rebel is so strong.

I hold the boy's hand. I look at his entire body, his elbow, the bruises among the fine hair on his calves.

What can there be after a dead child?

Nothing, I believe, but the deaf echo of our selves.

The child is here with his child's hair, a fur cap that still smells of life. The skin of his eyelids is liquid. Beneath them, his eyes are visible, like grape seeds. His eyes aren't entirely closed. There's a glimmer between his lashes, a road, like a dark walkway in the fresh snow. Veiled eyes withdrawing like the eyes of a saint or a martyr. I take his hand. I'm ready to set out with him. *Why were you born?* I ask him.

Velida comes to my side.

"We can go now."

Then she notices the child and raises a hand to her mouth. "Whose child is this?" she whispers.

"I don't know."

She looks around as if seeking something, someone, the reason for all of this. She, too, is childless. We're two useless women, two bicycles without chains.

"He's the child of war," I say without knowing what I'm saying, what I'm thinking, what I've become.

We're alone among the dead. There's a blue child I'll never be able to forget. I shouldn't have been here today. I shouldn't have been the one to console him, to hold his hand. It happened by chance.

We head for the exit. The disinfectant-soaked mask protects me from the smell. I mustn't look back. We cross the dark skeleton of the city.

At night I think about the snails and their slimy little bodies and about the group of children I saw from the window. They laughed as they gathered the manna that came after the rain. I think of Jovan's red vest and of his chest full of flowing phlegm. I hear the sound of his chest as if from the inside, like in the car hold of a ferry. I think of the somnambulant eyes of the blue child, that narrow and sticky street between his lids. The snail moves across that street as slowly as Jovan, an old man wrapped in a shiny overcoat like the mantle of a snail, accompanying the child across the line of life.

Later Diego also goes to the morgue to bid Jovan farewell.

"I put a cigarette in his pocket," he says. "He can smoke it on his trip."

I look at his back, his ponytail. He squashed a snail when he came in. It was on the threshold. He felt the shell crumble beneath his foot. He was sorry he killed it. He says everything makes him sorry now, because every life is woven into another. It's like a labyrinth.

"Did you see the child?"

"What child?"

"The blue child. Next to Jovan."

He says there was no child when he went. No child.

"The body after Jovan's. Next to the empty stretcher."

He shrugs and turns to face me.

"Why? What was it about this child?"

I'd like to tell him everything but I can't tell him anything.

"He was dead," I say.

I walk in the mud of my tears, drowning in the slits of those eyes that weren't entirely closed and that by now have already been buried underground, covered with glue like a squashed snail. I'll never cry like this again, not even when I'm left all alone. That day I'll be as strong as a Bosnian widow, as strong as Velida.

She said, when we were standing before the child, "Husbands can die. Children, no."

And her sorrow retreated, like the snails in the pot.

Maybe that's what I'll remember.

But tonight I cry over everything, including what's to come, what I saw in the black street of those half-closed eyes.

Then I calm down, but I'm no longer myself. I'm the detritus on the beach after a hurricane, a silent field of destruction, from which some random object emerges, an upside-down street sign.

"Do you know who that child looked like? Do you remember Ante?"

Diego starts as if he'd been stung by a weever fish lurking beneath the sand.

"Ante . . ."

Yes, Ante. The kid in the torn pants, who always kept to himself, perched on the rocks like a bird, the kid who pretended to know how to swim and almost drowned rather than ask for help.

For a few days I'm numb. I remain closed within the blue fire of that vision, nothing but cold matter around me. The thought of that child underground gives me no peace. It hardens like a fossil in rock, a shell. It's the last step of this stairway that climbs into emptiness. I can't touch this ground anymore, with its grazing snails and dead bodies. It seems like all the world's children have died along with the blue child. It's cold. The cold seizes my bones. The children play a sliding game. I don't even look at them. They're like ghosts, creatures lined up for death.

I stretch out a foot to pull the door of the armoire toward me and look at myself in the only piece of mirror that's still intact. My dark brown roots are growing in. The highlights, yellow as a hen's feathers, cling to the ends. I think of my hairdresser, his face, his jargon . . . *light tones, nuances, revitalizing treatment.* I'm on the other side of the world. I'm no longer myself, but I don't care. I spend my time lying on the bed and pushing the tips of my toes against this armoire door and this fragment of mirror that reflects me in pieces. It's as if everything that happened before this war were part of an isolated prehistory. During the long prewar period, before the blue child, I had pictured myself at the sheep's side, my hand or my ear to her belly. Together we'd have been two mothers.

"What's Aska going to do with the baby?" I ask Diego.

"I don't know. She doesn't talk about it."

"I'm afraid."

His gaze lingers on me.

"It's pretty late to be afraid."

And winter began. The war had settled in. The Markale flower vendor said, "This year we're lucky. It hasn't started snowing yet."

She stood there, teeth chattering, before her little tree of paper flowers. Her handmade woolen hat seemed to grow bigger and bigger on her ever-shrinking face, but she never stopped smiling.

There are things I'll take back with me, things that will save me, like the smile of the flower vendor in Titova Street.

One day I asked her name. Maybe she thought it was a devious question, a journalist's question. From her surname I could have determined her ethnicity.

"*Cvječarka sarajevska,*" she said.

What kind of name is that? I asked Gojko. He laughed at the clever old witch. *It's not a name,* he said. *Cvječarka* means "flower vendor."

Cvječarka from Sarajevo. Nothing more, nothing less. Neither Serb nor Muslim nor Croatian. Sarajevo flower vendor. That's it.

Diego takes her picture. He buys bunches of flowers and brings them to me. He surely brings some to the sheep as well.

I'm not jealous. I'm not anything anymore. What surrounds me carries everything away.

Diego tells me about her while we walk, while the color drips off the flowers. He tells me that Aska is very weak, that her family is dead and the child in her womb weighs on her like a rock. But it's the only living thing she has left.

"So maybe she'll want to keep it."

He'll ask her when the time comes.

"In that case . . ."

He shakes his head. It's a remote possibility. No woman would keep her child under this flood of war.

"And you'll stay with her and the child, right?"

My head is spinning. I wonder what I'm doing here.

The bear is dead now, too. He held out longer than all the rest of the animals in the zoo, for months and months, and then he died. His furry body knelt and then lay down. His mouth slowly opened and stayed that way.

I take Velida to the train station, where passengers board the buses to Croatia. Gojko helped me find a place for her. It wasn't difficult. It cost three thousand marks, almost all I had left, but she doesn't know this and I mustn't ever tell her if I want to remain her friend. I told her that she was on the list of civilians to be evacuated because she was an elderly widow. But it's not true. No one leaves without paying. Her only luggage is a little dark brown vinyl suitcase held together with a couple of pieces of string. I pick it up. It hardly weighs a thing. I don't like this half-empty suitcase. It bears no promise of life.

"What do I need?" she asks. "I'm wearing my coat. What else do I need for my new life?"

But she's got the blackbirds. She keeps them beside her feet in a cage that's too small, covered with a rag. She's scared they won't let her take it on the bus. It's her only worry. Beneath her short grizzled hair a smile warms her chapped face. But this morning she's not as pale as usual. It's freezing cold, and there's no place to sit. We stand before the remains of what was once the train station, the departure point for Ploče, for trips to the sea. There are other people sitting on their bundles, women clutching children. If they manage to make it past the military checkpoints, they'll go on to swell the herds of refugees and people in transit with temporary residence permits in their blue passports embossed with the golden lilies of the newborn and already defunct Bosnia. They'll be processed through refugee centers and take menial jobs and be viewed with suspicion by the citizens of the nations where they're granted permission to live. Never again will they be themselves. This is the new life.

The buses finally arrive at sundown, when no one any longer believes they'll come. There's loud applause and laughter from cavity-filled mouths. Velida climbs aboard and puts the cage on her knees. She nods goodbye through the glass and closes her eyes to let me know everything is okay. "I'll write."

In the end I told her about Aska. She already knew. She'd seen her with Diego.

"Where?"

"At the old Turkish baths."

They were walking hand in hand. She was struck by how young and lost they looked. They were like sleepwalkers.

She squeezed my hand and pulled me to her for a last embrace. "Don't be like me," she said. "Don't bow down to Death. You've got to fight, Gemma. Seize life."

Mothers are crying all around us. One of the two buses is entirely full of children. Their lone escort, a burly man with a peach-colored tie, is busy collecting passports.

One day, in my Roman living room, where I sit reading about how hundreds of the children who were evacuated from Sarajevo disappeared into thin air, the man's tie and that bus full of children will come to mind. The missing children may have been adopted illegally or maybe something much worse, something so bad you want to say, *What the fuck are you waiting for, God? Shut it all down. Take away the sun. Hurl down from the sky an asteroid as black as the hearts of the tie-wearing poachers. Make everything dark. Forever. Wipe out the good, too, because evil dwells in its pockets. Do it this instant. Now. Because right now someone's about to catch a child. Save the last one. Shut it all down, God, and show no mercy. We don't deserve a witness.*

Overnight, frigid air comes down to the valley from the gorges between the mountains and paralyzes what remains of life. The temperature plummets below zero. Stiff blankets weigh on people's bodies like cold metal capes. Cold seeps from all sides into the wounded buildings. Ice covers the plastic sheets on the windows. You get ice burns if you touch them. In the foggy dawn the death counts now include people who've succumbed to exposure, mummies veiled in ice like cookies covered with frosting. Winter gardens endure, the plants huddled stiffly beneath taped-together plastic bags.

The snipers of Grbavica, Trebević and Poljine do shorter shifts because of the cold. They can't distinguish the flesh of their hands from the metal of their rifles.

Snow falls, devouring the sky. The city is closed in the silence of its footsteps. The mouths of the waterspouts ice over. Children slake their thirst with snow that eats away at their soft tissues.

Overnight the snow covers the rubble and clings to the black buildings. At first it seems to clean everything up, but afterward, when it's already been shoveled by hand into dirty walls, with broken minarets sticking out here and there, the city looks even bleaker and more desolate. Life stiffens with the cold. Skeletal figures, their backs hunched, drag along sleds and crooked baby carriages full of scraps.

The first shelling of the day leaves blood on the snow.

I hardly ever see Gojko. He's holed up in the bunker at the radio station, where he puts people in touch with their relatives captive in the occupied neighborhoods. Refugees call from radio stations in Croatia and Slovenia to get news of family members who've stayed behind and are living through the siege. Gojko still finds the strength to smile. *They're like voices from beyond the grave,* he says. He's become adept at capturing distant sounds, connections interrupted countless times, voices that emerge through a forest of other voices, sobs and noises like the rumblings of the earth.

"One day I'll speak with the dead," he says. "When this is all over, I'll be a medium."

Once in a while we manage to meet for a soapy-tasting beer in one of the underground clubs that have reopened as life has started to reorganize itself beneath the shadow of war. Kids want to get drunk and fall in love and laugh.

That's how I meet up again with Ana and Mladjo. Zoran, it turns out, was captured by one of the paramilitary groups. He died digging trenches on Žuć hill. They laugh, because Zoran was an intellectual, allergic to manual labor like a cat to water, and it's funny to imagine him wielding a spade in mud up to his knees.

"And besides," Ana says, "tears drown the dead. Laughter keeps them alive."

She's wearing a pair of Levi's 501 jeans and a black T-shirt, and she's become even more beautiful, though her teeth are darker.

"What are you still doing here?" she asks.

Mladjo takes me to see his latest project. We walk to an Austro-Hungarian building that formerly housed an elementary school. The interior has been completely destroyed, but the façade is still intact. He sprayed polyurethane foam on the wall that stands alone like a canvas hanging in a void. Then he sculpted a class on it, an immense gathering of strange children. I see a lot of faces I know: Ana, Gojko, Zoran with his pitted face. Mladjo included everyone he knows from Sarajevo, all his friends, the living and the dead.

What do I remember of that last month? Sebina in a red Santa Claus hat that an Irish cameraman gave to Gojko. She and her mother were on their way to a party at a cousin's house. Mirna wore lipstick and a tidy hairstyle and carried a tray of sweets. When we went past the Zemaljski Muzej, she glanced at the old Bogumil stećci, riddled with holes. Sebina didn't seem to notice the desecration. She was busy jumping between the sandbags in the trenches. She was happy because her teacher had managed to organize a little class in his apartment, which meant she wouldn't miss the school year.

It's hard to say in which part of our bodies love originates before it drips into our bellies. The war was dripping through the very crevices where love had once passed and taken root in my gut. That night, the light of tracer bullets was the only thing to cross the dark. I thought about that growing belly, swollen and white like the Bogumil sarcophagi I'd seen that morning, their floral symbolism disfigured by gunshot. *It's the symbol they want to kill, the symbol*, Gojko said. I knew now that Aska's belly was Sarajevo.

Diego puts his tongue between his teeth and produces a whistling sound like the noise of the shells. He's stopped bothering to send his rolls of film back with journalists bound for Italy. The wind and cold have cut little slits in the green plastic window covering. Like the snipers with their gun barrels, Diego sticks his camera through the holes. He takes up his position and chooses a target, a passerby. But he often shoots without even loading his camera. If I tell him so, he shrugs.

"It's all the same," he says. "It doesn't make a fucking difference."

We no longer talk about afterward. We let the hours pass, encysted in the present. We're like all the other prisoners in this valley. There's no guarantee we'll make it to tomorrow. This precariousness doesn't bother me. It's like walking on waves. If only he were here with me. Instead, we hide from one another, and this siege is ours, a rigid curtain that protects us from ourselves. At night it's forbidden to move about the city with flashlights but often Diego gets up from bed and goes out. His beard has grown so long it covers his neck. His eyes hurt. He's agitated and says he can't sleep. He wanders in a daze among the bones of this devoured city as if he were penetrating the body of death itself.

I touch his thin chest. He shoves aside the proffered bulletproof vest. It's too heavy. His back has become rigid and adult. There's no more time for silliness, for amorous duets.

What I miss more than anything else is the mindless abandon of afterward, when Diego would push my hair away from the nape of my neck and spend hours kissing me in that hollow between the neck bones where hair starts growing and where, he said, he could still smell the odor of my birth.

I no longer look ahead to resurrection day and to the plane that will carry us away. Maybe we'll simply never go back. Maybe we'll die together in this city where we met, where we made love for the first time in Gojko's mother's bed beside an empty cradle. I should have heeded that sign. It was our destiny.

We never talk about Aska. She moves about in the background. Her neighborhood, on the outskirts, is in worse shape than others, but she doesn't want to leave it, and it's easy enough to forget about her except that Diego hollers her name at night, howls like a wounded dog and sits up in bed. That's why he can't sleep—he's scared she'll be hit, that she'll die along with their child. There. I've said it. *Their* child. And I'd like to have Jovan's courage, to go toward that sniper with arms spread wide like an angel's. But this isn't my city. It's not my tomb. I bury myself in the cold blanket. We're like fish buried in a frozen lake, fish blinded by the depths. We brush past each other without meeting.

Diego says it's not about Aska. He would have stayed anyway. He can't leave these people alone. Now that he knows this pain, it's impossible for him to live anywhere else, at least for the time being. He tried to tear himself away but he couldn't.

Life is here, among this ice-covered rubble, and he's never felt it more intensely. Life is Khalia, a little girl who pulls her tiny, rabbitlike brothers and sisters along on a sled, and Izet, the old man who goes every day to the Baščaršija to lean against the dented metal shutter of his shop. Life is the flower vendor selling her bunches of illusion.

Diego never stops saying, *Leave. Go home.* But I can't leave without him, without his love, which he now scatters like birdseed through the streets of Sarajevo.

"You don't need me. You'll be just fine on your own."

He spends his days standing in line to fill water containers for elderly and disabled people who've been left on their own. He builds stoves, drags wood and shovels snow. He shuttles back and forth between the humanitarian aid distribution centers and the houses of the families he's adopted. By now they've come to count on him. His face is greasy with the handprints of the children he carries in his arms up dark, smelly stairways. Almost all the able-bodied men are fighting, digging trenches. Diego risks his life so the mothers don't have to. He hardly ever takes photographs anymore. He says he's not interested, that Sarajevo is full of photographers and reporters, useless people, profiteers. The world's newspapers have had their fill of mangled dead and dirty children in sweat suits. They need more space for advertisements, panettone and diamonds that are forever.

He got it into his head that he'd die in that war, that he'd make up for the peacekeepers who weren't doing a thing. And yet I sensed behind his sacrifice a disappointment in me, in us. I sensed the arrogance of a wounded boy.

Who did he think he was, this thin, hunched boy in the raincoat with a white tape cross on the back and the red ribbon holding back his hair?

He was everyone's father. Everyone greeted him by name.

"*Zdravo,* Diego!"

"*Zdravlje,* Diego!"

He'd learned the language. There were chilblains on his hands from the cold and from the containers of water he was always dragging around.

"You've got stigmata," I said mockingly.

I'd fallen in love with a boy from Genoa with the hoarse accent of the alleyways and a few bad teeth from when he'd used drugs. He was a reckless son who got into fights at the soccer stadium and then acted the lamb with me.

Now he was an old man with the long beard of a hermit.

I pick up some snow and throw it at him, at the goodness in his eyes.

Bastard. My love.

One day a boy in a checked jacket falls to the ground right beside me, and I piss my pants in the snow. Fortunately, he's not dead. He'd bent over to pick up the cigarette he'd been smoking; the shell fragment grazed his shoulder. His hands were so cold his cigarette slipped from his grasp. That's what saved him.

Fate was kind. There's blood and this boy who doesn't understand what's happened. He feels no pain and complains only because his cigarette got wet and went out. Then he notices the blood dripping on the snow and looks at me wide-eyed because he thinks it's my blood, thinks I'm the one who's been hit. He thinks I'm about to fall dead to the ground and looks at me as if I were a ghost. He looks for the wound. He thinks it may be in my neck and that I'm about to start spitting blood. His eyes are frightening, opaque and foreign as they watch me die. Is this the last time the world will look upon me? I feel the warm urine in the cold. It runs down my leg, the one that's trembling. This is what it's like to die without noticing.

Later the boy will say he really didn't feel anything, just a mild blow as if someone had shouldered past him. Then he looked around him, saw the blood, saw me and really thought for a moment that I was the one who was wounded. Only later did his wound begin to burn.

Today, in the water line, I learned that shell fragments don't hurt. They penetrate the body without causing pain. The shock works like an anesthetic.

I no longer go out. I hide waiting in the corridor, far from the windows. Life has been reduced to mere survival.

"Did you find anything?"

"I'd love a carrot. Do you remember what a carrot tastes like?"

We could drag ourselves off to the Holiday Inn with the foreign press. We'd hear the murmur of languages we know, see people coming and going, eat warm food served by waiters. But Diego detests that false atmosphere.

I clutch at him without dignity or pride.

"I was a monster. A monster. I want to see Aska, beg her forgiveness."

Diego looks at me as if I were a fountain, an inanimate object spouting water.

"What can I do? Tell me."

"Call your father. Ask him to send all the money he can get his hands on."

One night he brought back a can of pašteta, a sort of Bosnian pâté that in peacetime turned my stomach. That night, it seemed like the best food on earth. I looked at him, hoping to ask for some sort of clemency or sweetness. I stretched out my hand. He kissed me just to get rid of me, as if he were licking a postage stamp.

We stayed that way for a while. I bent my head to ask for a kiss in that hollow he'd liked so much.

He didn't even notice. He was looking at some pictures he'd had developed in a little hole behind Titova Street where an old man was still developing film and printing photos on old, opaque paper that he cut with a knife.

"Let me see."

People posing, cropped at the shoulder level, images without depth like police identification photos.

"What is this stuff?"

"Someone asked me to do it."

He only works for Sarajevans now, photographs to send to relatives and put on graves.

"Careful."

"Why?"

"Your hands are dirty."

It's true, my hands are greasy with pašteta. But tonight I can't take it anymore, and all of a sudden, before he can do anything, I scrunch up the pictures, all those miserable posing people, and I feel alive, because anger is all I have left.

I follow him like a sick and dirty shadow.

He plays a pickup game of soccer in the snow with a group of kids in the devastated courtyard. He laughs, jumps, dribbles the ball. Then he stays there, bent over on his legs, exhausted. His breath is white in the cold.

The class picture made out of polyurethane foam is still hanging from Mladjo's spectral wall. Mladjo, on the other hand, is dead. He was pushing his father's wheelchair. The sniper picked him off in order to watch the paraplegic alone in the middle of the road, unable to move, unable to do anything for his son.

I follow Diego to the Markale Market. He steps into the crumbling structure. Today it's full of hanging clothes dripping with snow, stuff from humanitarian packages that's landed on the black market. He rummages through bunches of rubber boots and used galoshes. I'm at the end of my rope. Everything disgusts me—the smell of damp used things and broken sewers and communal soups boiling in aluminum pans, this mix of mud and snow. I'm afraid of the stray dogs that tear the dead to pieces. I'm afraid of the hollow faces of the living, their legs in their pants as stiff as crutches, their shocked eyes that rustle over the ground as they search like dogs for whatever they can find. There's nothing in this city anymore. It's scorched earth. The malnourished bodies can barely stand. They sway along in search of something, anything, that might serve life. Bojan the mime and his girlfriend Dragana do a special skit beneath the portico in the pedestrian street. They pretend to eat an enormous imaginary banquet with such skill it makes your mouth water. They take the people who stop to watch them by the hand and invite them to join in the feast. They serve all their fellow diners soups, mutton legs, pita. They lick their fingers and swallow. People laugh and cry, but in the end everyone's belly feels fuller.

Diego comes out of the market with a dark furry coat on a hanger, an overcoat made from inside-out skin swollen with fur. He carries it over his shoulder. It looks like the carcass of an animal. He drags it along with him through the snow.

The next time I see Aska she's wearing the coat. It makes her look gigantic. The buttons stretch over her enormous belly. She's in front of the Ferhadija Mosque, where she washes herself in the frozen fountain. Diego helps her, holding her up. She rubs her face and neck. Then she takes off her shoes and sticks her feet in the icy water.

She walks barefoot through the snow and stops on what remains of the *sofe*, the section reserved for women. She bends and kneels. She stays in that position, leaning forward and straining because her stomach makes it impossible for her to reach the ground in total submission to her God.

I go to her side and kneel next to her. Her eyes are motionless fish behind a slab of ice.

"I'll give you the baby," she says.

A dark smile crosses her face, which is nothing like the face I remember.

"As long as a sniper doesn't get there first."

Chapter 15

Pietro is standing in front of the mirror after one of his interminable showers. He raises his bare arms and studies himself at length before coming to ask me if I notice a difference between one muscle and the other. He wants to know if he's already developed the arm of a tennis player.

"Touch here."

I don't see any difference. I touch two long thin rolls of flesh and then the bone just underneath.

"I've got to join a gym. I have to lift weights."

Now he's sitting on the bed, a towel around his waist. He's getting the sheets wet but it doesn't matter because we're leaving.

I look at his bent naked back, the grains of his backbone, the shoulder blades that stick out of his skin like folded wings.

"I'm ugly," he says.

He says it all the time. He thinks he's full of flaws. His shoulders are too narrow, his eyes too big, his lashes too thick, *like a girl's*. There's a little brown mole with hairs growing out of it on his thigh near his groin. He thinks it's disgusting and because of it refuses to wear anything but knee-length swim trunks at the beach.

"You're so handsome. What are you talking about?"

He hasn't had a girlfriend yet. I'm the only woman who ever compliments him, and of course he doesn't believe me.

The light down over his upper lip makes it look dirty. His teeth, nose and ears are too big because his face hasn't grown yet. His features resemble something by Picasso, distorted horse eyes in a bean face.

He'll be gorgeous. You can tell from his smile, from the graceful way he interacts with small children, the way he greets people he barely knows with kisses on each cheek as if they were dear friends.

His passport says he was born in Sarajevo. To him, this city is a no-man's-land where I ended up by mistake because I was following a father he's never met.

He's only asked once how he was born. He was in third grade. It was for a homework assignment. We used a glue stick to attach a picture of him as a newborn to a piece of cardboard. "What should I write, Mom?" He had to tell the story of his birth, and of course he asked me. I stood up, opened the fridge and took out a steak. I talked to him over my shoulder, inventing our story as I turned that cold piece of meat over and over.

At the end of the school year I saw his essay on a bulletin board next to his classmates' essays. I stood there with a plastic cup of orange soda in the middle of that henhouse of mothers I'd never managed to fit in with very well. I was scared of getting too familiar with other mothers. None of them were like me. I stood there alone before my son's words. The birth he described was trite and sickly sweet, and it was precisely the triteness of it that moved me. We were like everyone else, a *loving* mother and a chubby newborn baby. Our absurd story was lost among all those orthodox birth stories with their pink and blue ribbons. He'd done a much better job of making things up than I had. He stood next to me, a calm expression in his eyes, the pallor of city life on his face, his father's spindly frame. The perfect accomplice. "Do you like it, Mom?"

A tear fell in my orange soda, a stupid tear like my life. I didn't even manage an answer. I just nodded like a pecking hen. I pecked at that long, tepid lie, spread thick with pencil in my child's uncertain handwriting. His innocence was my cover. He was the one who baptized me his mother, who said, *It's you. Here's the certificate.*

What should I have told him?

Every time I went to see a friend who'd just given birth, ensconced in a nest of white pillows and flowers, every time I saw the splendor and smelled the indescribable smell of just-born flesh, of new baby—even the smell of detergent was enough, or of nipple-disinfectant pads for before nursing— every time I smiled and said, *What a lovely baby,* I felt a little lonelier, a little uglier. I'd deposit my little welcome gift and leave the padded den in a darker mood than when I arrived. Then I'd wander around for a while like a stray, no longer myself.

I didn't give birth. You never recover from what you lack. You adapt. You tell yourself other truths. You learn to live with yourself, with nostalgia for life, like old people do.

I didn't take part in the primal event, the regeneration of myself. I was barred from the banquet that normal women indulge in again and again in sated indifference toward women like me.

Birth changes one's bones, shifts them around. My grandmother said every birth was a nail pounded into a woman's body, and that before they die women see the images of all the births they've lived through, when their bodies burst open. They see the nails, the traces of their journey. What will I remember when I die?

Pietro wrote that I put him on my stomach and that he fell asleep there. I should have felt shame, but instead I felt peace. Everything else was nails to throw away.

Gojko came to get me. I heard him knocking at the door. I wasn't sleeping. I was lying with my eyes closed on the bed I'd dragged next to the wall at the end of the room. Fear made it impossible for me to pull myself away from that cold wall. Day was just dawning. In normal circumstances I wouldn't have noticed, but by now I was aware of the slightest variation in the dark.

Gojko didn't say anything. He was holding a lighter so he could see in the dark. He let it go out, maybe to save the fluid.

"What is it?"

I no longer see his face. I'm imagining it in the reflection of the previous moment, of the little flame that's just gone out. He moves a hand to his face and leaves it there. He cups his cheek with it like a shell made of flesh as if he wants to protect himself. It's an unusual, feminine gesture I've never seen him make before.

"What's wrong?"

He shakes his head and mutters.

Fool. Why doesn't he say something? I'm ready. I've been ready since I visited that morgue, since the first snowfall. Jovan has already taught me everything. The body empties itself out like a leaking sandbag. You hear the sand rustle as it falls. Calm is one of Sarajevo's virtues, a calm you don't realize you possess, unexpected as the calm of the dead.

I grab my flashlight and shine it on him. He retreats from its light, shakes his head, moves his hand away from his face and spits on the ground.

"Ahhh . . ."

I smell brandy. Gojko curses and complains that one of his *zub* hurts, a tooth, one of the big ones in the back. He says he keeps the brandy in his mouth to cradle his molar. I look at him. One of his cheeks is swollen as if he'd been stung by an insect, and his eyes are listless and half closed.

Then he tells me that the baby is about to be born and that Diego asked him to come for me.

I go back to my room with the flashlight and drag my suitcase out from under my bed. I take out my backpack, which contains the money Dad sent me through Vanda, the volunteer I'd met on the military plane. We met up in a kafana. She'd shaved her head like a Marine. We split a package of sanitary napkins between us like sisters.

This chilly dawn may be the prelude to a luminous day. We race along the ruined little lanes of Bjelave.

I first climbed into this car a thousand years ago during the Winter Olympics. Gojko was full of that stupid happiness. He reeked of naïveté and presumption. He sang, *Everybody's got a hungry heart*, in English with a Croatian accent and wore faded jeans like Bruce Springsteen's. He was an intrusive boy, *born in Sarajevo*. He wanted to impress me and I thought he was pathetic. *I'll never see him again*, I thought.

Here we are, buried in this labyrinth of skeletons and boulevards. All of a sudden I think that this crazy, violent moment isn't the worst thing. The worst is yet to come, when the cannons leave, and the television crews, too, and the only thing left is the gray flank of this city spilling out a silent pain like mold or pus.

"Are you still writing?"

"No."

He doesn't seem sad or even lost. Now he knows the topography of this new, mined city, divided into zones, where you move like a ball in a pinball machine and only the best manage not to end up down the hole. Gojko's good at pinball. He doesn't bother looking at the destruction anymore. He's used to it. He just looks for a free passage, an opportunity.

"What are you thinking?"

He tells me he has a toothache and that all he's thinking about is his aching molar.

The light in the hospital is dim as the light in a cemetery. Little flashes every so often, then long dark areas and plummeting stairs. I feel the tile floor beneath my feet. It seems to be set directly on mud. An electric cord and then a dangling panel brush against my head. Almost all the wards have been shelled. The beds are parked in the hallways. The bodies look like sandbags in the dark. I try not to look at feet sticking out from under covers and blood-filled IV lines. I move behind Gojko through this tunnel. Figures move toward us, brush against us. Someone yells. Although day is starting to dawn, it feels as if I were advancing through a dirty twilight. A uniformed soldier limps along with the help of a woman in a blue shirt. An old man whose leg finishes at the knee in a bloody bandage sits on a stretcher, smoking a cigarette. Gojko takes my hand and helps me up broken stairs with holes you can see through to the bottom floor. There's a truce in the labor ward. No one is complaining. A woman bends over her swollen stomach like an exhausted traveler over a suitcase.

Diego is sitting on the last step of one of the railless stairways.

This is not any old dawn. It feels like we're buried in a flooded mine, as if we were moving slowly through water. Gojko goes off to find someone to pull his tooth, hollering that he'll do it himself if no one else will, all he needs is a pair of pliers. Diego sees me and stands. I collapse against his smell. I haven't seen him for three days. He hasn't come back to our room to sleep.

"How are you?"

"Fine."

A few words and then the cold vapor of our breaths in this maternity ward that feels like a storage room for old scrap metal. There's no heating. It's like being outside. One day I'll have to tell Pietro about this smell of cold and exhaustion, about the way his father's neck trembled as if he were a goose about to be caught.

"Tell me something."

"What?"

"Anything."

I love you is maybe what he wants to hear. We're sitting on the step. He's got his head burrowed in my legs.

"I brought the money," I tell him. "It's in here." I touch my backpack. I'm wearing it in front, beneath my parka, rather than on my shoulders, because I was scared I'd be robbed at a checkpoint. Only now do I realize that this backpack is like a pregnant belly. Diego smiles an ancient, disconsolate smile. This bellyful of money contains everything, our fortune and our sorrow.

Is this what I should tell Pietro? *Your mommy was pregnant with fifty thousand marks in small bills. They weighed upon her womb, beneath her breasts.* Tell him, *Look how generous the photographer and I were. Grandpa sold his house at the seaside to help us.* It was an enormous amount of money. There were people who bought babies for a pittance in Sarajevo.

I cradle the belly full of money to myself and hold it tight. We hug with its weight between us. It keeps us at a slight distance.

Aska is pacing back and forth in front of the doors to the bathroom stalls. Every so often she stops and leans against the wall between two sinks. I go to her, a few steps across the flooded mine.

The smell of disinfectant isn't enough to mask the strong odor of clogged toilets. Our breaths are white smoke. We're in an Arctic lake, buried beneath the ice crust, the three of us together again after so much time.

I'll have to tell Pietro about this, as well, tell him about this other smell, of prisons and abandoned places, tell him about this encounter.

Aska the trumpet player, Andrić's undisciplined sheep, the rebel who danced before the wolf. When she looks at me there's no change in her expression. It's as if she doesn't remember me.

And yet we were friends, way back when, before the siege ate up the city. We danced one night, our arms around each other in front of a poster of Janis Joplin. Though she was younger and poorer than I was, she held me up, radiant with her wild future as a musician, and I said, *I'm much poorer than you are.* Her hair is not as shiny as before. It falls on her neck in a ponytail. The gray light crossing her face reveals no emotion. I look down.

The sheepskin coat Diego bought at Markale Market hangs open over her dressing gown. Her stomach is gigantic as it protrudes from her thinness. She holds her hands behind her, on her kidneys, and leans her head against the wall. Diego's next to her but in a certain sense it's as if he weren't there, as if he'd left us alone. Aska's belly is big and still.

"Can I touch it?"

The voice rises up out of the depths and I hardly recognize it as my own. She moves her arms away from her body to make space for me and I reach out a hand.

And I'll have to tell Pietro about this, too. One day before I die I'll have to tell him about this hand that moves away from me toward him.

My hand wavers tentatively, then lands delicately on Aska's belly like a lunar module.

I'm no one. I'm just an invader, an iron bird on a planet that doesn't belong to me.

But then, naturally, I know what to do. It's like taking off your clothes, stripping down to go into the water. It's freezing cold, but it's as if my hand were glued to the belly with warm snow. I'm here, and I'd never leave. I breathe.

This is the only water now, amniotic, submerged.

"Did you bring the money?"

I nod with my whole body and point to the backpack hanging off my front beneath my parka. That belly full of money, the most pitiful thing of all, the thing that really makes me miserable.

"*Dobra*," she says. Good.

Then I feel a blow against the hand resting on her stomach. It's like a head butting against me, the head of a fish below the ice.

I scream. I feel that body from the inside and scream.

What was it? A foot? An elbow? A fist?

But I don't see anything else, just a blue mud sky and a wave of nausea that moves down from my head. I know I'm fainting, because I haven't had a thing to eat, because that blow went straight to the empty place between my pelvic bones, the parts that on a skeleton are flat and white.

I'm a broken sandbag. I feel the grains descend and move roughly through my body, all the way down to my feet. My head is empty.

I open my eyes into Gojko's dirty hair. He pushes his bottle under my nose.

"Breathe, beautiful woman. Smell this marvel."

It's brandy from Montenegro, the legendary 13 July brand, a real rarity. They must be a little drunk already. Diego's hands are warm despite the cold and Gojko is euphoric because the tooth's out. He opens his mouth to show me the black hole, baring his bloodied teeth as he laughs.

I see Aska through my liquid trance. She's resting her head against the wall. Then she collapses to all fours between the sinks.

"Do you need something?"

"A cigarette."

I ask Gojko for one of his Drinas. I kneel down and put it, already lit, into her mouth.

She trembles as she draws in and her face contorts in pain.

Now I feel a strong pain in my back. I remember it well, this forked pain that drips down my back and insinuates itself into the deep soft parts like two blades piercing my kidneys and pushing toward my groin.

It's Aska's pain sticking to me. I wasn't ready for this. I move away and go back to sit on the step.

Diego moves to Aska's side and massages her back a little. Then he sidles toward me, head lowered.

Now she's ugly, incapacitated with exhaustion like a rabid dog. Her cigarette falls to the filthy floor. I'll have to tell Pietro about how his mother's head banged against the base of a sink and about the cigarette I'd like to throw away but can't because she's hollering in her own language for me to give it back to her.

I put the butt back in her mouth. She puffs out smoke in spurts. Maybe it helps the pain. She yells again like before, as if she had a rag in her mouth, a stopper.

Women know how to hide themselves, bury themselves like the earth at night, but when it's time to give birth they bare their souls and their courage as the nail is driven in. Fate pounds the nail and a new skeleton passes through your own like a river through a river.

I've remained back in the dark of the earth, eclipsed. I haven't had to reveal myself.

Aska is forced to come out in the open. How many times, looking at the hills, have I thought of her stomach pointing at me like a cannon?

"You have to breathe," Gojko says.

"Who told you?"

"My mother."

We all breathe, swallowing the air into our bellies and exhaling it in bursts, like broken stoves. Aska spits out a few breaths along with us, then groans and pushes us away. Gojko tells her that giving birth is like getting a tooth pulled and that in a while she'll feel as good as he does. He opens his mouth wide and shows her the hole. Aska wants another cigarette. Gojko looks at me. "Get ready, baby. This kid's going to stink of Sarajevo, like an ashtray." He laughs, and if it weren't such a tragedy, it would be a farce. We're like four crazies in a madhouse crawling on all fours around the labor pains of the sheep.

She pulls herself up and rolls like a big insect along the wall toward the only window in that cesspit. It's covered with military plastic that's been torn down the middle, maybe to let some air through, to let out the bad smells. Aska stands in that hole and looks at the sky lit up by the glare of a tracer bullet. She looks at Sarajevo, the burnt houses, the soccer field that now serves as a cemetery.

I'll have to tell Pietro about her gaze as she stands there smoking and contemplating the dead city frozen in cold and mud.

These are his last moments inside her.

Her living belly exposes itself for the last time to the Sarajevan roulette.

Why does she do it? The snipers are staked out not so far from here in the skeletons of the houses to the west. With that lit cigarette, she's a beacon.

Her belly is the dome of a mosque, the Ferhadija Mosque where I saw her prostrate herself.

But I let her do it. She can decide for us all.

There's a rock that's hardened in the depths of my body over the years. Now my blighted ova, one on top of the other, are mounds of fresh earth like all the corpses dated 1992.

It's Diego who takes her by the arm and pulls her away from the window. They stand side by side and breathe, with their shoulders against the wall. She gasps, her neck twisted toward the broken ceiling. He looks at her. Perhaps he looked at her with that same tenderness, the same longing, when they made love.

Should I tell this to Pietro?

Once again, with the intimacy of this gaze, they take everything away from me. Her final gesture is to take Diego's hand, pull it to herself and bite it as if it were a rag between her teeth, as if it were a love about to leave.

"*Dosta . . . dosta*," she moans. "Enough, enough. Get it out of me."

Finally someone comes. A woman in a nurse's uniform and short wool socks takes her away.

Everything takes place behind a white plastic curtain just a couple of meters away. As she went toward the stretcher, Aska looked at me. This look remains with me like a weight pushing down on my shoulders, the sluggish gaze of the refugees, of people who separate themselves from themselves.

It's over very quickly. All we can see behind that white plastic curtain are shadows of limbs and agitated gestures. One of Aska's feet dances in the air. I'll have to tell Pietro about that foot, about the shadows that hold our misery and our fears.

Then we see the midwife's back and elbows. It looks like she's digging. She speaks in loud bursts. Aska whimpers.

Our eyes are glued to the black shadows on the white curtain.

Bursts of gestures, hands digging in a body like the hands that have begun digging an escape route toward the free territories beneath the Butmir Airport.

And now the whole war is here, on this curtain, and it's as if there were a thousand hands, like the thousands of marchers on April 6, all those people yelling for peace. It looks like a long retreat through the snow, columns of exhausted soldiers limping across this curtain.

The midwife digs, pulls, drags, knots.

We stand motionless against the wall like statues beneath the Eternal Flame.

Should I tell Pietro what I was thinking about as he came into the world?

The snipers, their tragic lives. That interview I saw. The boy has blue eyes and he smiles. He says it's just like shooting at rabbits. And I see the blue child. He's playing with a sled, pulling it up the hill by a rope. It's hard work every time. On the way down it goes by in a flash, but climbing up . . . But it's worth it. It's a beautiful sunlit day. The snow is a fresh white covering over the black. The sniper drinks rakija, smokes a cigarette and throws the still-glowing butt onto the ground. Then he takes up his spade, his gun. One day his mother brought him into the world and baptized him. The sniper wears a cross around his neck and believes in the divine trinity of Greater Serbia, or at least that's what he seems to recall, because although only a few months have passed, everything's changed and he's no longer sure why he climbed up into the mountains with the others to fire upon his city, upon his neighborhood. He raises his rifle, puts his still eye to the viewfinder and looks for a target. He likes looking. It gives him a thrill that descends from his chest to his gut and then his testicles. He chooses the very slope, the very snow-covered path where he used to play as a child. Like all men he misses his childhood. Not that he's sorry. When he walked through the mud to cross the river and march up into the mountains, he knew he wouldn't go back. There are other children now on the slope between two gutted buildings. The building on the left is the elementary school he went to. For a moment he thinks of the teacher who spread pašteta on a slice of bread and gave him a piece. He smiled and said, *Hvala*. He liked that teacher. He tries but can't remember if she was a Serb or a Muslim. Now the school is a skeleton like the frame of an unfinished building that someone set on fire. The children are playing. He saw them arrive. He didn't expect them. He never knows what will come along, what will capture his attention, which target, which *cilj*. He likes the word *cilj* because it's a clean word from his everyday work life. *Man, woman, child*—words like these dirty his mission. Children are small targets, *maleni ciljevi*, and he tends not to fire on small targets. They move around too much. But today it's so easy it's an invitation. The *maleni ciljevi* look like rabbits scattered about on the snow. Their mothers let them come out because they couldn't keep their children in all day in the damp of the shelters, and maybe they wanted some freedom to do laundry and prepare soup from bits of grass. The sniper looks for a target. The children are still spots on the snow, little figures with blurry outlines. He turns the small lever that regulates the viewfinder on his precision rifle and sees a mix of snow, bits of sweaters, bits of faces. Too close; the image is fuzzy. He adjusts the focus, moves closer, zooms in, pulls them out of the unknown, the snow. Now the *maleni ciljevi* are children. He walks a bit with his viewfinder, takes a few steps with them, follows their game. He used to play that game himself, sliding down inside a plastic box with his brother beside him. Once he hit a big rock sticking out of the snow. He wonders if it's still there. He looks for it and finds it. He likes finding signs of his past life even though he'll never go back. He feels no emotion. It's like recognizing a territory. This is important for a hunter. His gaze comes to rest on a child. He doesn't know why he picks that child and not another. Maybe because he isn't wearing a hat. The child's forehead is bare, and when he turns the sniper can see the depression in the back of his neck.

Is this what I should tell Pietro? That as he was coming into the world I was thinking about the nape of the blue child's neck, the line where hair starts growing, where life begins? I could see it, in front of me, as if through a sniper's viewfinder.

My heart beats inside the sniper's. I'm the one who chooses the child. I choose him because his neck is uncovered and his hair is short, compact, a fur-covered head. His hair smells. The sniper can smell that smell. He had hair like that as a child, thick, hardened with sweat, noiseless. The child is taking the last steps of his life over the snow. He laughs. His cheeks are red. He breathes out the white smoke of cold and drags his sled up the hill.

The viewfinder on the rifle moves with the child's steps, climbs with him up the snow. The sniper doesn't know why this job fell to him, doesn't know quite how it happened. It was circumstances. There are bags of earth piled around him in the snow. He could change his aim and fire at one of those bags. It wouldn't make any difference to him. The fact is that for every target he strikes, he gets a nice prize in deutschmarks, and he needs that prize because a soldier's take-home pay is low and he wants to buy a car, a BMW with a convertible roof. He thinks about that car, the black seats, the cigarette lighter in the dashboard, thinks about the wind that will make his hair come alive. The rabbit is a child. He moves along, his hair like a furry cap, and below it the nape of his neck. The sniper's body is glued to the rifle. Together they are a single piece. It's the moment of the act, the penis hardening mechanically. The bullet's desire is all that counts. The sniper lets the bullet guide him. He bends his finger, then releases. It's a dangerous moment, the bullet's silent journey through the white air. Like a sperm slowly moving beneath the lens of a microscope. It could encounter something, an obstacle that would change its path. This is the best moment, not quite pure pleasure because it's also painful, like an ejaculation delayed for too long. He feels the blow as the rifle recoils into his shoulder. The air is white. The bullet strikes the nape of the child's neck. The child falls facedown. The others flee, leaving behind their sleds to run like scared rabbits. The sniper takes another look, circling with his lens, and casts an eye on the footprints that remain. He likes the silence as he checks over his work, when it's just him and his target. The hole in the nape of the child's neck is perfect. The little target, the *maleni cilj*, died on the spot and didn't even slide when he fell. The sniper won't have to waste any other shots to finish him off.

Now he's smiling with crumpled cheeks and motionless eyes because his heart is dead. He knows that it will be a while before they come to get the child. They'll wait until he leaves, until his shift is over. The child's face is turning blue in the snow. The cigarette butt that the sniper threw on the ground is still glowing. Every now and then a journalist climbs up and says, *Shoot so I can film you while you shoot*, and the sniper shoots for the journalist. Then he gives an interview, arms crossed, the cross hanging on his camouflage jacket, his black beret. *It's like firing at rabbits.* He smiles and then the crust of his face hardens. A wretched stupor remains, the stupor of the devil as he looks at himself.

The newborn baby cries through its clogged mucous membranes like a whining cat. Only Diego takes a step toward his child. Then he stops. He comes back to me and takes my hand.

The woman calls and beckons us over. She's showing us the child. It's a boy. None of us knew what he was, and yet here's Pietro.

"Pietro."

I look at him, but I don't see him right away. I'll see him later. Now I swallow him whole. I open my mouth in astonishment and he jumps into my throat. The midwife is cleaning him at the end of the stretcher. She turns him over and rubs him with a rag she dips in a metal bowl. It's freezing cold. His body is tiny and dark. He looks like a mollusk covered with seaweed. The woman works quickly. There's little poetry in the way she rubs at him. Pulling fish out of the sea is her job. We hear the wail of a siren. The light flickers and then there's an explosion, but no one pays it much attention. The woman curses the noise as one might curse noisy neighbors. The war is inside her, in her arms accustomed to extracting babies.

"*Odijeća . . . odijeća.*"

She wants clothes for the baby. She looks at us and asks if we've brought them.

I shake my head and open my mouth again. Nothing comes out but a sigh because I'm sorry. It hadn't crossed my mind. Diego tells her to wait. He opens his camera bag and pulls out a tiny garment, a little hand-knit woolen sleeper, white that's gone slightly yellow.

"Where'd you get that?"

He bought it at the market. I'm amazed he thought of it. The woman takes the sleeper and slips the baby into it. It's much bigger than he is. The sleeves cover his hands and the legs hang past his feet like empty socks. She hands him to Gojko, maybe because he's the only Sarajevan in the room, or maybe because she thinks he's the father. Gojko doesn't say a thing, just nods and moves his chin as if he were worried about intoxicating the baby with his brandy-smelling breath. He hasn't held a tiny baby since Sebina was small, and that happened in another world, another life, far from this rust, this cold, in a hospital that smelled of raspberry tea.

He moves closer with his nose and, careful to keep his mouth closed, breathes in.

"He smells good," he says.

Should I tell this to Pietro? Say, *Look at this Bosnian buffalo, this survivor, this tour guide you're not so sure you like because he doesn't have much patience and he plays rough at soccer. He was the first to hold you in his arms, the first to smell your newborn baby smell.*

I look at Diego but Diego's not looking at his son in his friend's arms.

Should I tell this to Pietro? *Your father wasn't looking at you, he was looking at the sheep, whose belly was gone, her red head limp on the pillow.*

His expression was so intense he didn't notice me or my embarrassment. The two of them were alone, this I remember, alone and immersed in the past.

She wasn't looking at the baby, either. She'd never looked at him.

And now it really felt like I was standing beside a bed that wasn't my own, spying on two lovers as they swore an oath to each other.

Everything had happened on the end of that bed: the changing of the baby, the makeshift bath. Aska's legs were curled up, perhaps in reaction to the pain. The midwife was getting ready to leave. She was patting Aska's folded legs. Aska was sitting on something, a metal container for the placenta.

The woman says she'll be back to check.

Finally Gojko hands me the baby. It's as if he's handing over a meteorite.

I smell him, too, the smell of an old soul being born again to hope among men. I still don't know if he's my child, if he'll be mine. I'll have to wait until

that day when he's in the third grade for him to baptize me. But in the meantime I hold him, and I'm already the wolf, the sniper who passes back across
the snowy field to look at the hole in the nape of the child's neck.

The midwife takes the white curtain down and drags the shadow screen away
and all that's left is this newborn baby, wrinkly as an old apple, dressed in a
sleeper that reminds me of a worn sock.

I study him in the dim light as the sand rises back up through my body
and my organs return to their places. I feel my heart now, like a tongue of
flame and pain beneath my ribs.

Should I tell Pietro that he's given me back my heart, that I no longer felt
it and now it's pounding?

The woman comes back, pushes on Aska's belly and sticks her hands
beneath the covers. The sheep spits out the placenta.

As the midwife removes the metal container from beneath Aska's body,
I see for a moment her bloody leg and her sex, a bloody hole like the hole in
Gojko's mouth. It doesn't shock me particularly. Life is the same color as war,
snow and blood, trenches like intestines in the mud.

When the woman passes by me, I see for just a moment the gray package
of the placenta. Now I no longer need the sheep. She's served her purpose,
like that inner membrane that kept the child alive and is now just something
to throw away.

I should feel sorry for her, but I'm consumed with the fear that she'll
change her mind, start screaming, retract her consent.

She lost her family. Maybe she'll want to keep her baby.

I'm afraid she'll put up a fight. I'm looking for signs of restlessness because
I don't trust her. I've smelled the baby, the smell of Diego's blood.

I hear Velida's words. They fall from her wild eyes, which I dream of every
night. *Don't be like me. Don't bow down to Death. You've got to fight, Gemma.
Seize life.*

The money. I have to give her the money, all those deutschmarks in small bills
as she requested, just like the prize the snipers get for every successful hit.
She'll buy a car, too, a convertible BMW to drive off in.

I'm myself again. For me the war has ended. The blue child is buried.

Diego's child is alive. This sheep, this lesser creature, must be banished from view like the dirty sack of her placenta.

There are no laws, there is no justice. Courage is all there is.

Gojko hollers that he'll write a poem when he gets back home. It's been ages since he wrote, but he'll write one now to celebrate the birth of this child. He declaims drunkenly:

> *I have the feet of a pig and the tail of a mouse*
> *life drags me upwards like an elephant in flight*
> *Adieu, ghosts. Today I'm not with you . . .*

"Who are you with?"

He takes another sip.

"I'm here with my friends."

But the truth is that we are ghosts looking at our reflections in a metal pit and mourning life.

I went to the bathroom and took off the backpack. I sat on the toilet and gave Gojko a bundle containing a thousand marks.

"What do you need it for?"

He took our passports, too.

"I'll be back soon."

I emptied the backpack into a pillowcase and went to Aska in the bed.

"Here."

With a tired gesture she pulled the pillowcase swollen with marks to her side and hid it under the covers.

The newborn lay in a metal bed, far from his mother. The midwife had folded a piece of cloth, set him on top of it, and left him there. He hadn't moved. Outside, the explosions were starting up, closer and closer, along with random bursts from the Katyusha rockets. The baby was used to those noises. Aska was sleeping, too, her head under the covers. She woke just a couple of times to ask for something to drink.

Another woman came in, younger than the first, and explained how to take care of the baby, how to change him. She pulled his tiny little legs out of his sleeper and showed us what to do. But they didn't have diapers, so she gave us some gauze and pieces of cotton. The baby didn't need to eat yet. He let her shake him like a bundle of rags. He hadn't cried yet. Now he was alone again in that stretcher, the roll of cloth behind his back. The girl asked if the mother planned on breast-feeding. I shook my head. She didn't say anything, just looked at Aska's body on the bed. She was used to exhausted women. She apologized and asked us for a hundred marks. She was sorry to make us pay but she definitely was not the one who would pocket the money. She came back with a can of formula that had already been opened and a glass bottle that had already been used. It was the first intact piece of glass I'd seen in ages. I put everything in my backpack.

Now the war was coming to our aid. No one asked us any questions. No one seemed interested in keeping that newborn baby in the hospital so near the line of fire. The two of us were foreigners and we could leave the city no one could leave. The girl asked us how the child would be traveling.

"By plane. We're waiting."

"Are you journalists?"

"Yes."

She gave us a letter for her sister, who was in a center for refugees in Milan.

The explosions were under way again, and so were the desperate journeys of the ambulances and the makeshift cars that picked up the wounded. It was daylight, but the child did not wake.

Finally Diego looked at him.

And it's this gaze I should tell Pietro about, leave out the rest and tell him about Diego's eyes, the eyes of a dog as it looks at another dog. Here's our little manger scene, wild eyes, trembling hands, thoughts in flight.

Gojko comes back with the man who's helped us, a drugged-out survivor face like the people who sell news to the journalists at the Holiday Inn. There's a humanitarian flight due to return to Italy in the afternoon. They've been to the UN Headquarters and got our names on the list. He gives us our passports and the baby's birth certificate, which is all we'll need to get through. I read. Their language, our names, Diego's name next to the word *otac*, father, mine beside *majka*, mother.

This odorless miracle hardly seems possible.

I hug Gojko.

"How'd you manage?"

No one bothered filling anything out when we entered the hospital because they don't have any forms anymore. Our passports and the money did the trick.

Gojko lets me shake him like a bag.

"Nowadays certain things are easy."

He wouldn't have done it for anything in the world. He's the type who would beat up the black marketeers, the profiteers getting fat off the war. But he did it for me. Now, I imagine, he'll never want to see me again.

Aska is sitting on the bed. She clutches the pillowcase full of deutschmarks. She's feeling better, although there's a yellow, anemic tinge to her skin.

Thank you, I told her.

She nodded. It looked like maybe she finally wanted to cry, but there was no time.

We go. The sheep has been excluded from the documents, from history. On his stomach, hidden beneath the rough wool, there's a knotted bit of cord where this baby no bigger than a hand was connected to the flesh of the sheep. The bit of cord will dry up and fall off and leave behind a seashell from a distant sea. The baby won't stay in the valley of the wolves. He won't ever be a rabbit, a *maleni cilj*.

This time the soldiers on duty are from Ukraine. They help us into a white armored vehicle. I turn toward Gojko. I don't know it, but it will be sixteen years before we meet again. As always in Sarajevo, it's as if I were saying good-bye to a dead man,

"*Čuvaj se.*" Take care of yourself.

He's the one who spoke with the soldiers and used the rest of the money to convince them. The UN shuttle to the airport has its price. Now we're inside the white turtle as it sets out on its journey. There's an infernal racket. The baby bobs like a doll to the trembling of the armored vehicle but doesn't wake up. Who is this baby who lets himself be carried along weightlessly, soullessly, like a foot in a sock? He's everything I wanted, the reason we crossed this hell, and now I'm so exhausted I could drop him. We can feel the armored vehicle climbing over wreckage beneath our feet. One of the Ukrainian soldiers laughs and asks us in English about our baby. He reaches over to move the coverlet so he can see the baby's face.

We stop at a checkpoint. The soldier leans out the window to talk with a militiaman. This friendly exchange between a Serbian aggressor and a Ukrainian from the UN ends with the Serbian three-fingered salute.

We climb out of the vehicle and go into the dark box of the airport. Diego tells me what to say, what to do. We're nearing the checkpoints. A thin woman dressed in camouflage looks at me. She's got cheekbones like a horse. I'm afraid of her gaze. I lower my eyes. I huddle close to the little group of civilians traveling with us. They all wear bulletproof vests over their parkas. No one feels safe. This is the last and perhaps most frightening gateway of the siege. All these soldiers seem to hate us. They're the sharks of war. They know the mental state of their prisoners. The silence is tense as they smell our fear and maybe even have fun toying with us. It feels like they could start shooting at us at any moment. We move warily, avoiding sudden movements. All of us are scared something will happen. The Serbs often bomb the airport even though it's in their hands. In the broken glass of a mirror, I see the little houses of Butmir, their roofs flopping over frameworks of beams. Now all of a sudden everyone is yelling. There's fighting on the Dobrinja front. The air is freezing. I bend over the baby. His little nose, the size of one of my fingernails, is cold as ice. I breathe onto him. Diego rubs my back, an exhausted, mechanical caress. Then he bends over to look at the baby.

"You have nothing to be afraid of."

And I don't know if these words are meant for his son or for me. Or for himself.

All of a sudden they tell us to get up and run. A gigantic UN soldier escorts us to the tarmac. A police officer beside a door without glass checks for our names on the list before letting us out. It's a rapid operation. We move forward, heads lowered like livestock. I hand over my passport with the certificate from the hospital. The police officer hasn't noticed the bundle in my arms. His gaze is set on a group of soldiers running below the control tower. Maybe he's waiting for a signal. I'm waiting for the red stamp, just like an animal. My heart has stopped. The police officer barely lifts his chin to look at the baby wrapped in the coverlet. It's five in the afternoon. It's already dark. The police officer's face is rough with cold. He has a wide red nose. I can't even feel my arms. I worry again that I'll drop the baby. The man moves a hand toward the coverlet and widens the opening where the little face is hidden.

A strange expression crosses his face, surprise and bitter dismay. He withdraws his hand and lets me go. I take a few steps in the chill. Bursts of wind come down from Mount Igman and raise snow that whitens the runway. I turn because I feel the emptiness, an emptiness I recognize because I've been carrying it around for months like an omen though I crushed it deep down inside. Diego is no longer behind me. I've lost him. I turn, but I know that looking back is useless because I already lost him a long time ago. I know now that earlier he was bidding us farewell.

You have nothing to be afraid of.

And perhaps I should tell his son about the way that emptiness felt, the sensation of life in free fall. Orphans, we take our first steps, the uncertain steps of some long-legged beast who's just been born and must stand up right away in order to survive.

I look back at the barely illuminated hole of the airport, already distant in the darkness dirtied by swirling sleet. I see nothing but silhouettes, shadows. I don't understand what's happening. Diego is next to the police officer. They're making him wait. In the meantime they let the others pass, two journalists who run past me. Diego waves both his arms and yells. He's telling me to run, to get away from there.

I glide forward with my head turned behind me, toward him. They're firing to the east. There's a glare of tracer bullets.

I climb up and throw myself into that metal belly. I wait, gripping the door, my face stiff with cold and wind that cuts like a blade. I've set the baby on a bench next to a military backpack. Maybe I could leave him there. He'd get to Italy no matter what. Someone would take care of him. I could put his birth certificate in his coverlet and call Dad from a satellite phone at the Holiday Inn. Yes. I could throw myself off this plane, which never even turned off its engines, and go back to that glass door without glass, go back to the body of my love.

Should I tell all this to Pietro as well? Tell him I thought about abandoning him as I stood with my body hanging in the freezing wind of the runway?

"Why did they stop my husband?"

"He lost his passport."

The soldier is a tall boy with a helmet and a Venetian accent. He apologizes and says there's nothing they can do. They unloaded the humanitarian aid packages and now they have to go back. Those are their orders. They didn't even know they'd be taking on passengers. I look at Mount Igman, petrified in the cold.

I'm a lucky guy.

Oh, really?

Very lucky.

Years earlier, his luck fell out of the sky along with a heavy snowfall that blocked all the departing planes and I wanted to slap him because he'd won. That slap is still stuck in my frozen hand as it grips the ladder while the soldiers tell me to move because they have to close the door.

I didn't manage to do it. I didn't manage to go back down that ladder, to leave Pietro, choose another destiny.

The wind throws me backward. The runway is immense and black. A bullet could get me. I collapse into the plane. I want to be alive when the plane climbs into the sky.

The truth is that I made my choice and Diego knows it. I would never have left empty-handed, but now I have this bundle to consign to the world. I'm taking the best part of him, this new life unsullied by any pain, and I can almost see his smile. I press up against the only opening to the outside. The plane is moving. I look at the boy from Genoa for the last time.

He's standing there beside the policeman, his thin body black and distant against the weak bubble of light let off by the airport with no glass, no personnel, no flights. His young face, haggard like an old man's, looks up at this C-130 as its wheels move along through the sleet. He looks at us, at what he's losing.

He stayed on the ground, on that dirty ground, and I'll never know whether or not his passport really fell in the snow.

I'm a lucky guy.

Oh, really?

Very lucky.

The plane goes straight for the sky. They put a belt around my body and order me to hold the baby tight. No circling around. When planes take off from this siege they aim straight for the sky, because a missile could still strike. The engines are flaming mouths. The plane moves upward vertically.

Our heads whip backward. Bags roll toward the back. You feel the climb, the violent effort to cut gravity. It's a difficult, wartime levitation. My eardrums are burning. I hang from my seat and clutch my bundle.

Then comes the truce. We've reached an altitude of nine thousand meters. Now not even the most sophisticated missile could reach the humanitarian plane flying over Mount Igman. My neck returns to its place. My bones still hurt from being contracted. The roar of the engines abates and that's when I hear the voice. The bundle is crying. So he's alive. He hasn't died of cold or fright. I hold him in my arms like a loaf of bread. I push the coverlet aside. His face is red with life. His mouth is wide open in a violent, toothless howl. *Who are you*, I ask him, *a sheep or a wolf?*

The newborn's wide-open mouth with its bare gums is like an old man's or a bird's.

He was quiet until takeoff, quiet for as long as he was down in the womb of war, quiet and immobile as if he'd never been born, as if he knew that a mere whimper could cost him his life. Now, at an altitude of nine thousand meters, he can finally be born, up in the sky where the missiles can't reach us. He cries, makes himself heard, demands attention.

In sixteen years, when a friend asks him why he was born in Sarajevo, he'll say, *It was by chance, like babies born on airplanes.*

And I'll stop still, breathless, and lean against the wall. Once again I'll hear his cries as he came to life when the C-130 reached nine thousand meters.

I look out through the opening. I can't see anything, just blackness and the white glow of the moon in its midst. I remember something Diego used to do. He'd take my pinky finger into his mouth and hold it there, sucking on it every now and then until he fell asleep, and then I was the one who kept it there. My hands are filthy. I wash my pinky with my saliva, suck on it to clean it, then stick it in his wailing mouth. He sucks on it a little bit and then falls asleep, exactly like his father. And I kiss him for the first time, resting my lips on that tiny forehead.

That night we crossed the velvet carpet of the Adriatic and then we were there. When I got off the plane my hair was glued to my head. I was wearing a torn and filthy parka and carrying a limp backpack and a baby in a coverlet.

I found a restroom and looked at myself in the mirror, an entire, intact terrible wall. The woman looking back at me with her bony face and her wide, absent pupils was a wild animal. I stank, the stink of Sarajevo, of war, of confinement. I hadn't noticed the smell before but I smelled it now in that clean bathroom. I didn't know what to do. There were two sinks. I put the baby in one of them. I left him in that ceramic cradle and washed myself in the other sink, slowly taking off my jacket and lifting my T-shirt. I rinsed my face. There was a fresh scab on my cheek and a dark mustache on my forehead. There was something else, as well, an opaque patina like pottery that's lost its glaze and holds the signs of time and dirt.

The door opened, and a man came in. He glanced at me in the fluorescent light. I was standing there in my bra, the bones of my rib cage sticking out of my skin. He was wearing a dark uniform. He smiled.

"This is the little boys' room."

I clutched my T-shirt in front of me to cover myself. He closed one of the doors behind me. I heard him urinate. He came out. I hadn't moved, hadn't even put on my T-shirt.

The man goes to the other sink. He's tall, with heavy footsteps and wide shoulders. He's wearing a uniform with a big leather belt around his waist. He raises his eyes and meets mine in the mirror. He's just a man who's taken a piss and has to wash his hands, but I don't know that. Wolves piss and wash their hands, too. I'm afraid of men in uniform. I'm looking for my boy, who's as thin as I am and has long unkempt hair like mine and my same story in his eyes.

The man looks at me in the bathroom mirror.

"Whose child is this?"

Giuliano's whole life is right there, in that bathroom he's come into by chance. Until just a moment earlier, he'd planned to stop for a piss when he got on the highway. He was in a hurry to get away from a day full of humanitarian aid packages and refugees to be sent to welcome centers. He made sure warm meals were distributed along with snacks for the children. He held the smallest ones in his arms and filled out and stamped bureaucratic paperwork. He looks in the mirror at the newborn baby in the sink and at this woman clutching a rag to herself. Her shoulder blades are bluish under the fluorescent lights. Maybe she's a refugee who for some reason did not board the bus and came instead to hide in this restroom with her baby. She has eyes like an animal on the edge of a cliff.

"Whose child is this?"

Now he notices that the woman is crying without moving, without even blinking an eye, huge tears that fall like pearls. Instinctively he would like to gather them up like pieces of a broken necklace and give them back to her. He knows the gaze of refugees, of people who seek in his eyes confirmation of their own existence, as if it were up to him to let them live. It's difficult to maintain eye contact with them.

The man looks at me. He has a broad face, compact and Italian, and a shiny, bald forehead.

"Whose child is this?"

Giuliano doesn't know that the child will belong to him, that he'll be the one to bring him to school and to the pediatrician's. He doesn't know that he will live for this child. We endure a long moment of placid consternation in that restroom where destiny casts its net.

The baby is dirty, a ball of confused flesh, abandoned in a sink, the sky in a hole.

"He's mine."

I race to grab my bundle.

"Excuse me."

I lower my head in self-defense.

The man smiles. He has nice teeth. I see them float beneath my eyes, which are sticky with old tears that descend abruptly like pieces of ice falling off rocks.

"I take it you're Italian?"

"Yes, I'm Italian."

I leave the bathroom in a hurry and walk through the dark hangar. I don't know where to go. I have to get myself to the train station and find a train to Rome. Or find a hotel. Call my father. I have to change the baby. He stinks. I stink, too. He must be hungry. Fuck, he must be hungry. If I don't feed him, I might kill him. Fuck. Where's the war? Where are the sandbags? Where's the ice? Where's Mount Trebević? Where are the snipers hiding? The truth is, I can't handle peace. I can't even handle my own footsteps. They're going to figure out that the baby isn't mine. Here there's no war. Here there are no bombed-out hospitals to protect me. Here we're in the legality of peacetime. I have to get out of here. They'll arrest me. They'll do tests and discover that the baby isn't mine, that the birth certificate is fake, that I bought it. I won't go far away, I'll just take a few steps in the dark and stop to die out in the open against a wall with the baby hidden like a dog, like a dead puppy. Where is the boy with long hair? Where is my favorite orphan? Where is the baby's father? Only he can save me, because the baby has his genes. He was supposed to be the pass that would get me through, but he didn't come with us. He lost his passport in the snow. He lied. I'm cold. My back is bare. My parka's falling off. I set it over my shoulders to get out of that restroom as quickly as possible, to get away from the man in uniform who's probably following me because he must have understood there's something strange going on. A mother doesn't leave her own child in a sink just to rinse her face in the next sink over, just to look at herself in the mirror and cry.

I see a bench and sit down. I set the baby down next to me and slowly put my clothes back on, my sweater, my parka.

A boy comes over to me. He can't be more than twenty. He looks like Sandro, a boy I was friends with in high school. He has the same too-red, too-full lips and the same round eyes like two hazelnuts. Who is he? What does he want? Why is Sandro coming toward me from the high school desk he covered with graffiti: LONG LIVE CHE GUEVARA, LONG LIVE PUSSY?

"Excuse me, ma'am. Where are you going?"

Slightly inclined in my direction, he stands there looking at me. He isn't Sandro, not with this southern accent and this uniform.

"I don't know."

The boy points toward the silhouette standing near the door. The man from the restroom is waiting on the threshold.

"The captain wants to know if you need a ride somewhere."

"To prison?"

The boy laughs and reveals teeth that are too small for his big lips. He likes my joke.

"I'm taking the captain to Rome, to the military hospital."

We run together to the car with CARABINIERI and a red stripe on the side. Inside there's an incomparable peace. The seats smell good, like new leather. The black perfumed spoon of this powerful sedan welcomes me and takes me toward home along a road paved with normal asphalt, without holes, without barricades. It's smooth as a satin ribbon. For a moment I feel like a poor little creature, a deer hit by a kindhearted driver who's now taking me to the veterinarian's. The fake Sandro is driving with his cap on. The captain is sitting bareheaded next to him, reading a newspaper beneath the interior light.

Before I got into the car he said, "We should have a car seat for your baby, one of those egg-shaped ones for newborns. It's illegal to carry him like that."

I smiled a stupid, shaky smile.

"You're right," I said. I waited. "What should I do?"

He said, "There's nothing we can do about it now. Please, have a seat."

I felt a bitter crazy laugh crackling inside me. It was full of black humor, like the jokes of the Sarajevans. The baby I'm carrying is some sort of prehistoric crab who's just escaped a war, and yet the moment he lands on these smooth roads he already needs an egg-shaped car seat to survive. How idiotic peacetime life is.

The captain must not have appreciated the look in my eyes. He heard something, the tail of that ugly laughter. He turned on the light, set his cap with its golden flame on the dashboard and started reading. Maybe he regrets having his generosity. Maybe now that we're in this closed space he smells my odor, which has to be something like that of the gypsy women he probably arrests every now and then, women who scream and lob curses.

I look out at freedom, the industrial apartment blocks on the outskirts, the villas with perfect roofs, the street signs without bullet holes.

Then the baby I'm holding, the little crab, starts squirming around. How many claws does he have? How many nerves?

I try to stick my pinky in his mouth again but this time it doesn't work. The captain turns.

"Maybe he's hungry."

We stop at a highway pit stop. Fake Sandro slides the car into a parking space and stays behind to guard it. The captain gets out with me, and we walk together through the dark to the restaurant. I go into the bathroom. There's a changing table, a white plastic shelf hanging off the wall. I set the bundle down and rummage through my backpack for the cotton wool and the bandages they gave me at the hospital. I open the coverlet and look for the buttons on the little sleeper made of wool as hard as cardboard. I pull out his tiny legs. I've never seen anything so small. I unwrap the gauze. The cotton wool is completely wet, and the excrement is yellow as if he'd drunk saffron, but it doesn't smell bad. It's the first time I see the child's body so close up in my own hands. He's got a swollen belly like a chicken's. He cries and draws his legs in, holding them close against his body like paws. I take a deep breath. If I don't manage to change him I'll just wrap the coverlet back around him and we'll be off. The gauze around his umbilical cord has fallen off. I see the little black bit of hanging cord. I bend over to check if it smells bad, but it still smells of alcohol. I mustn't think. I've got to move my hands. I turn on the faucet, wet a piece of cotton wool and rub it between the baby's legs. I wrap the remaining cotton wool around him and use the gauze, which I have to tear off the roll with my teeth, to hold it in place. The baby keeps crying. I have to get his formula ready. I bend over to pick up the sleeper, which has fallen to the ground. There's a dry sound. I'd bent abruptly, my open backpack hanging from my shoulder. When I look, it's just as I'd thought. Sarajevo glass, glass with no future.

I throw the remains of the bottle into the garbage. There's a knock at the door.

"Do you need help?"

I pick up the bundle and open the door. There's the captain with his sparse hair.

"I broke the bottle."

We leave the highway to find a pharmacy that's open at night.

The captain has taken to heart the case of the hungry little crab, in part because Pietro has a voice like an alarm siren that punctures your eardrums.

"Take the next exit," he tells the orderly. "We have to find a bottle and a rubber nipple."

Fake Sandro doesn't say a word. He puts on the right-turn signal and heads into the darkness. What exit is it? There aren't any houses, just fields.

The captain is no longer reading his newspaper. He doesn't even seem to mind. He turns toward me and looks at me for longer than necessary.

I smile, my eyes wide like a captive deer's.

"You don't have milk?"

I point to the backpack. "Yes, I have some. Half a container."

He doesn't turn back around. His eyes stay on me.

"Breast milk, I mean. You don't have milk of your own?"

Instinctively I cover my empty bosom with the bundle and hug the baby to me tightly.

"No, I don't."

"Too bad," he says, and turns back to look at the road. "It would have been easier."

We find a pharmacy in a little town cut in two by the rural route. The neon sign is not lit up. The captain approaches some men playing cards in a café. They take him to the building where the pharmacist lives and he rings the doorbell. The pharmacist dresses and comes down. He's a thin man with dyed hair. He must be a small-town bon vivant. We move among the darkened shelves that light up all of a sudden to allow the uniform in, the cap with the flame. The captain suggests I get a plastic bottle.

"It might be better," he says.

The pharmacist asks what kind of formula I want.

"For newborns."

"What brand?"

I look at the captain, look around, look at the pharmacist.

"Whichever. A good one."

The captain steps toward the counter.

"Let's see what you have."

The pharmacist piles jars up on the counter. The captain puts on his glasses because the writing is very small. He reads.

"Let's get this one. It's hypoallergenic." He seeks my opinion. "What do you think?" He speaks familiarly. I nod.

"Good."

I don't have a lira to pay with. "I lost my wallet," I whisper, and in the meantime I put away the diapers I'd grabbed earlier. Maybe the crab will refrain from crapping out saffron until we're in Rome.

The captain grabs the diapers and sets them on the counter along with the rest. He looks at the pharmacist with dyed hair like an old-fashioned crooner's.

"Do you have a whatchamacallit?"

The pharmacist looks at him and waits.

"Those thingies that make noise. A rattle."

It's not really a rattle. It's a plastic toy that plays music. As we climb into the car he says, "Excuse me for taking the liberty."

He's speaking more formally again. Maybe before he was just trying to make it look like I was someone from his family, his sister, his wife.

He opens the toy, extracting it from the plastic with some difficulty. He shakes it alongside the baby's red face. The baby doesn't stop crying. He may not even hear the rattle. He's made of hard stuff. He's used to the sound of bombs. The captain sighs. "You can tell I don't have children, can't you?"

We stop again at another rest stop with fringed lampshades and red booths like in a fast-food restaurant.

"Are you hungry?"

"Thank you. I'll have something after I feed the baby."

He goes ahead and bites into a *piadina*. He turns toward me and talks through his mouthful.

"How warm should the water be?"

"A little."

He nods and looks at the boy behind the counter. "A little."

You don't want to contradict a man in uniform. The boy thinks for a moment before throwing in his two cents. "Actually, the water needs to be boiled and then left to cool."

The captain steps over to the counter and interrogates the man.

"How do you know?"

"I have a little baby."

"How old are you?"

"Twenty."

"You got an early start."

"My girlfriend got an early start."

The captain and the boy behind the counter share a laugh. The captain points to the milk steamer nozzle. "Proceed," he says.

He comes back to the table with the water and two little plates with more food. His hands are capable. It's one of the first things I notice about him, these thick hands that you'd expect would be awkward, and instead they manage to carry a bunch of things in perfect balance without dropping them. His feet are flat, firmly set on the ground, like a professional waiter's. I look at him for the first time in this second rest stop, and he strikes me as a nice man. All of a sudden I miss my father.

Giuliano sets the things on the table and pushes the bottle toward me.

"Did you know you have to boil the water first and then let it cool?"

"No."

He laughs and studies me.

Maybe he realizes that I'm hiding something. It doesn't matter. I lean against the back of the booth. He puts his glasses back on. He reads the side of the formula jar to see how much powder to use. He asks if it's too much water. And now while he waits for an answer he looks at me over the top of the glasses that have begun inching their way down his nose.

I don't answer. One day he'll tell me it was obvious I wasn't the birth mother. I seemed so utterly alone in front of that jar of formula.

"He'll eat until he's full," he says.

I don't have any idea whether or not I'm pushing the nipple too far in. The baby gazes up into my eyes, wraps his entire mouth around the nipple and eats without breathing. He reminds me of a jellyfish in the water. Then his eyes go limp. He closes his eyelids slowly, releases his mouth and whimpers a bit as he falls asleep. It must have been very hard work. He's all sweaty now in his wool sleeper from Sarajevo.

The captain goes back to the counter to get a bottle of sparkling water. He fills two glasses.

"He needs to burp."

He pushes a glass of water to me across the table.

"I remember from when my nieces and nephews were small."

He tells me about how his sister, when her kids were small, passed them to him after they had their milk so he could pat softly on their backs. He would put a handkerchief over his shoulder so as not to stain his uniform.

He does the same thing now in this self-service rest stop with its pseudo-country décor. He pulls an old-fashioned, immaculate white handkerchief made of light cotton batiste out of the pocket of his uniform pants and spreads it over his shoulders, covering his medals and rank.

"May I?"

"By all means."

My eyes don't stray from the plate as I eat the remaining sandwiches. It's only after a while that I notice the captain is observing me. I'm wearing this filthy parka, my hair is dirty, I'm clearly ravenous. I don't have a penny to my name, just a baby a few hours old whom I've just stuffed full of formula.

One day he'll tell me that he didn't even notice that my parka and my hair were so dirty. He'll say he thought I was a beautiful woman, audacious and extravagant, and that he appreciated my appetite more than all the rest because he'd been married to a woman with a green and acid heart who let nothing but salad pass her lips.

The baby is leaning against his uniform. The captain takes a few steps toward the newspaper rack and then comes back. He's massive, imposing but graceful as well, with calm, restful steps.

Fake Sandro drank a Coca-Cola and crumpled the can and now he's waiting for us. When the captain moves past him, he jumps to his feet, ready for an order that doesn't come.

The captain holds the baby with one hand and pats lightly on the tiny little back with the other. The bundle lets out a huge, sharp burp like the sudden noise of a sink drain.

"See?"

Even fake Sandro says wow.

The baby's face nestles on the big shoulder. The burp shook him but did not wake him. I've finished the sandwiches and drunk my water. I let out a little burp myself. Now I'm as sated and tranquil as the baby.

I look at this man as he holds the baby from Sarajevo. All of a sudden I feel the sorrow that will get me every time and that has its very own way of assailing me. It clutches the nape of my neck. My whole neck stiffens. It's Diego, holding me from behind. I recognize his hands, his breath, but I can't turn. He should be the one holding the baby. He'd have been a wonderful father, a saint, a jester. He's the one who's holding me by the nape of the neck and whispering that I should look at what lies ahead, scenes from my life without him. He's the one who won't let me look back, won't let me embrace Death.

The captain takes a seat across from me.

"Are you tired?"

"A little bit."

"Did you give birth in Sarajevo?"

"Yes."

"That certainly took a lot of courage."

We chat. I tell him my husband, a photographer, is still there. Giuliano nods. I talk about Diego, about how we met, about his photographs.

The yearning I feel in this moment is atrocious, an overflowing river. I see Diego's legs at the airport, thin and cold like metal tubes. I see him as he stays behind. I stop, my chest swells, I breathe and go on. Giuliano lowers his eyes and remains silent.

One day he'll tell me that he, too, was moved because he'd never seen a woman so in love. He'd had a wife, a girlfriend, the odd relationship here and there. But listening to me that night, he felt yearning for a love that he'd never fully grasped.

He tells me he didn't go to the military academy, that he was in the Special Forces, that he served in Lebanon. He tells me about a parachute that didn't open properly. That's why he's got an office job now. He makes me laugh. He says he's so full of metal plates that it's always a nightmare when he goes through the metal detector at the airport.

He stands, goes to the register and buys some chocolates. He offers me one and uses one of his big capable hands to open the box without ever taking the other off the baby, who never stirs.

He tells me he's an amateur photographer and asks if I have any of Diego's photographs to show him.

I tell him I didn't travel with anything except the baby.

"I didn't make it back to the hotel."

"And your husband?"

"He lost his passport."

He hands me his card. "If I can help in any way . . ."

The city with its signs and its shuttered buildings appears through the quiet winter dark. It's five in the morning. Soon the lives around us will get up out of bed, assume a vertical position, clog the streets and resume the stupid running around of peacetime life. A garbage truck blocks our way. We stop. I watch the metallic arm as it hooks onto the dumpsters and lifts them into the air. Once again I feel like I've lost everything.

When the car pulls up below my building, the captain gets out to help me with the baby. He opens his mouth as if to say something but then he doesn't say it. He puts his uniform cap back on. Maybe this trip was his way of keeping an eye on me, his kindness a way of lulling me into a sense of false security. His face looks like that of a bird dog, the ones who seem to wander aimlessly around the countryside and then come back with the prey in their mouths. He's aware that there's something strange about my situation. Maybe he thinks I kidnapped the baby. He turned to tell me so, but then he thought again.

One day he'll tell me that for the entire trip he was torn between his uniform and his instinct to trust me. One day he'll say, *The law can go take a hike; love should be left undisturbed.*

Chapter 16

The door opens onto silence and the carpeting in the hall. The blinds are drawn and there's a musty smell. The radiators are lukewarm. I don't have anything to unpack. All I have is the baby. Diego's corduroy jacket with the elbow patches is hanging on the coat rack. His tie's there, too, the thin red one he wears to parties. A strip of blood.

Without even bending over I use my heels to take off my boots. They're still dirty with mud from Sarajevo. I haven't set down the baby yet. It's not exactly your typical homecoming with a newborn. I don't know where to put him. No freshly decorated room awaits him, no crib or changing table. There's just his father's piano, the white couch that could do with a washing, the smell of a house frozen in the silence of a previous life.

As I pass the line of feet waiting for the subway I remember that Diego no longer liked these photos and wanted to take them down. In the bedroom I open the window a crack to let in some air. Then I set the baby beside me on the bedspread without even taking off his coverlet or my parka and immediately fall asleep beside him, leaving everything else for later. I slip into a black dreamless tunnel of sleep like a mole into the earth.

When I open my eyes again I have trouble moving. I feel broken. Every one of my bones hurts as they struggle to wake. Maybe it's because my body abandoned all its defenses when it surrendered to sleep. Light is coming in through the blinds and the baby is awake. Without a sound he's looking up at the ceiling with his nearly sightless eyes.

I kept the door open when I took my shower and turned the water off constantly so I'd be sure to hear if the baby started crying. The grime came off and slid down the drain. I called Dad. I was back in my old bathrobe.

"Hello . . ." It was the hoarse whisper of an old man, a mouth stagnant with silence.

"It's me, Dad."

He yelled my name twice as if he were yelling into a ravine.

I didn't say anything about the baby. I told him I was back and had just finished showering.

I went into the kitchen, boiled water and filled the bottle. It was easy. The baby couldn't move, so it was okay to leave him. Now he started crying. I rushed to count the spoonfuls of formula into the bottle. It was our first day just the two of us, alone.

"Were you wounded?"

"I'm still standing. See?"

He hugs me with hands I don't recognize.

"How much weight have you lost?"

He's lost weight, too. He's skin and bones. It's been ages since my last call.

"That was really unacceptable."

"I'm sorry, Dad."

He stands in the doorway. It's hard for him to come in.

"No. It's unacceptable."

He says you don't treat a father that way. You don't even treat a dog that way. It's not the way he brought me up.

"You're selfish. You and Diego both."

Bread, standing next to him, barks hello. He'd like to slip into the apartment to sniff around.

"Dad, Diego didn't come back."

All of a sudden his eyes darken and his Adam's apple bobs up and down. He looks around the darkness of the landing as if he were looking for a shadow.

"What's that supposed to mean, *he didn't come back*?"

"He stayed there."

He drops the leash. Bread seizes the opportunity and comes in.

"What's that supposed to mean, *he stayed there*?"

Dad comes in behind the dog to call him back. He comes in because there's no shadow out there. The boy from Genoa hasn't left any tracks. As he walks in he brushes against the jacket with the elbow patches and the thin red tie. His eyes move around through the silence.

"Bread, come here. Bread!"

But Bread heads in the other direction and goes into the bedroom. Dad follows him.

"Watch out!" I yell.

Dad takes a step back, toward me.

"What's wrong?"

"The . . ."

I don't say any more. I let him find out for himself. We're standing in the doorway to the bedroom. The dog's nose is on the bedspread, sniffing the baby's poo, the dirty diaper I left there. Dad whispers, *Down, get down*. He sees Pietro on the bed. He doesn't move toward him, doesn't say a word. Then he asks a version of the question the captain asked in the airport restroom.

"Whose is this?"

"He's ours, Dad."

He steps toward the bed and bends slightly.

"Is it a real baby?"

"Of course he's real!"

He rummages in his jacket for his glasses. He studies the baby with the same attention he used to give to his students' work.

"How old is he?"

"A day."

"Did the two of you adopt him?"

"No. I hired a surrogate mother, Dad."

He looks at me with the face of a man who's been hanged, all the blood drained from his face.

I could have lied. I could have said Diego had an affair and that I paid the girl not to abort in order to save the child. I could have painted myself in a different light. But I don't want to lie to my father, even if it means his opinion of me might change.

He raises his eyes and wobbles on his feet.

"I have to think about this. I have to think."

He crosses the hall and the living room to the door. He calls the dog, but Bread won't budge. He's standing guard over the unknown baby who's pierced the solitude of this apartment.

Dad comes back and looks at his dog, still and noble as a statue, like a greyhound standing before his king.

My father bends to hug me. I'm sitting on the bed and he's standing. He's tall and I'm short, like when I was a child.

"Good Christ, how can I leave you alone? How can I?"

Pietro opens his blind eyes to the silhouette of the Italian grandfather who sold the house he'd planned to inhabit in his old age so that this baby could be born. His money ended up in the pockets of a punk Madonna, a trumpet player in love with Nirvana. A ramshackle nativity scene.

My father smiles at Pietro and says softly, "Darling, darling."

I see why it was worth it, the spark of life it supplies. I imagine my father bending over me when I was a newborn and calling me darling.

My father has no more questions.

Wherever this child came from, he's here on this bed now in his heavy sleeper made of rough, dirty wool. Dad goes down to a baby-clothes store on the boulevard. When he comes back his eyes are shiny, like his dog's.

"I got size zero."

We open the package, remove the tags and slip the baby from Sarajevo into the brand-new size-zero outfit. Now he's a little prince in his eyelet lace and the softest of wool. The stink of the stable, of death, has disappeared.

My father doesn't leave me alone again. I suspect that his arrival in the morning long precedes the moment when he rings the bell. He goes to the market, walks the dog in the streets below my house. It's almost impossible for him to tear himself away. At night he doesn't so much sleep as dream about the baby. His face is pink and new, as if his skin had gone back in time. His eyes are slices of pure water. When he knocks on the door he breathes hard, like a dog scared of being chased away.

"Is this a bad time?"

"Come in, Dad."

He brings fruit, newspapers, bread, because I live barricaded inside the house just like during the siege. He always finds me in my dressing gown, worn out after those nights, the feedings that disrupt my sleep so it doesn't come back. Instead, it's the blue child who comes back, and Diego, and all those people waiting in line beneath the snipers. At night everything is amplified. When the baby cries I become immediately discouraged. I'm scared he'll get the shakes, like a drug addict's baby. I'm afraid his nerves will explode, like mine, a delayed reaction in this silence. I hug him and ask him to help me. Befuddled, I rock him, and walk him up and down the hall alongside the feet waiting for the subway. I stop in front of the window, walk back, deposit the bundle in his bed, let him cry. I close myself in the bathroom and rock back and forth on the edge of the tub. I'm yellowish and losing hope, like the women who slide into depression after a difficult birth.

Calm returns with daylight.

Dad has a book about the first few months. He leafs through it and says that the most desperate crying, when the baby draws in his legs, is due to colic. Pietro eats too quickly. Now, after a feeding, Dad holds him belly-down and gives him a calming massage.

In just a week Armando becomes more of an expert than a seasoned nanny. He smells of formula and spit-up and almond oil. When he's not with us he's at the drugstore, studying the shelves with products for newborns. He consults the girls in their uniform white lab coats with gold crosses pinned on the lapels. He's become friendly with them all and calls them by name. They talk about poo and hiccups and rashes. His eyes are languid, like someone who's just fallen in love. He's lost his head.

Bread is depressed, like me. His tongue hangs limp from his mouth. He's dying of jealousy, like a neglected older brother.

Our first outing is to see the pediatrician.

Dad goes to get the car and parks it on the sidewalk in front of the door to my building. He doesn't care if he gets a ticket. He's charged with escorting Pietro, the oracle, the future of humanity. I'm wearing dark glasses and a black overcoat. I'm thin and pale, like a sad princess, mother of the heir to the throne. It's cold. Dad's draped a cloth over the car seat. The doorman, a neighbor and the lady from the café come over to see.

There's no reasoning with Dad. He moves the cloth aside for no more than a second.

The woman from the café smiles at me.

"I didn't know you were expecting, ma'am."

"My son-in-law is a photographer. They travel around the world. They're a modern couple, not house pigeons like you and me. They don't let anything scare them. They have their children wherever they happen to be."

The woman compliments me. She lowers her gaze to my stomach and says it doesn't even look like I've been pregnant. She says I'm lucky to have the kind of physique that springs right back into shape.

In the car, Dad's cross. He keeps checking the rearview mirror. I worry he may be getting senile. He rails against the woman from the café.

"She makes skimpy cappuccinos to save on milk."

Growling like a guard dog, he turns toward the back and checks the car seat. Now he's the one who's scared someone might take away the crab. I'm just scared I won't make it.

Over time the baby and I get used to each other. I learn to recognize his voices. I know when he's crying because he wants to be picked up and when he's crying because he's hungry or because of colic. There are spit-up stains on the shoulders of all my T-shirts, where he rests his mouth.

I carry him around the house. I'm not so worried anymore that I'll hurt him. I stand in front of Diego's photographs and tell the baby about his father. I try to trick him, saying, *When Daddy comes back* we'll do this, we'll do that.

The stump of his umbilical cord fell off. I smelled it. Then I opened the piano and put it in there among the keys.

By now I do just fine with the practical side. I know how to wash the baby, how to change him, how to feed him. The rest, I don't know. I live in suspension, waiting for news. Even my gestures are suspended. I do everything but it's as if I were going through the motions, like an efficient babysitter, as if this child had been entrusted to me and all I have to do is take good care of him until it's time to give him back. I should love him already. It would be normal. But it's as if all my love had died in Sarajevo, in those passageways through the filthy snow.

When I wake up at night, I don't know how to leave my heavy sleep and take care of him. When I get up to make his formula, I burn my hands and make a mess in the kitchen. This baby from Sarajevo is hungry all the time, the hunger of his miserable origins.

It's true, he smells good. I breathe it in through my nose. He's still part sky and at the same time he's already lake. But what am I to do with him? His too-good smell hurts. It slides into me like a pain. It could be the same smell his father had when he was born. His father should be here to smell it.

I take care of the baby without any real love, as if he were a car. I put in fuel, keep him clean, park him in the crib. Sometimes I go back to look at him in his sleep but it's only because I'm looking for his father. Is there any resemblance? This baby will only really become mine when Diego returns and Pietro becomes ours.

I see Diego in my sleep. He's carrying the baby in a baby carrier. He supports the baby's head with one hand and holds me tight with the other. We walk along the river, down below, and it's very peaceful. This peace is tangible in the dream. We're no longer struggling against ourselves or against the things around us. Destiny is kind to us, almost as if it somehow needed us. It's the first time we've felt useful to the flow. We understand what peace is, the meaning of this motion—this forward motion without hesitation into the world like the river water that pulls itself along its own course toward the culmination of its journey. We walk to the barge that has been waiting for us right where we left it, waiting to see how our story would end. Diego says, *Thank you for the baby*, because only now does he know what it means. Only now does he know that he's safe.

For my entire life I'll think that Diego might have managed to live if he'd held the baby even for just one night, if he'd held the breathing baby near him.

He doesn't call, and I don't wait by the phone. My dreams vanish by day. I have the photographs—the puddles, the feet, the wild-eyed faces of the Marassi ultras.

Then he does call, and his voice, tormented by the pain of life, is very far from the peace of the dream.

"What's going on? Why don't you come home? Is it because of your passport?"

He doesn't even seem to remember.

"Oh, yeah. My passport. I found it."

"Where was it?"

He says it fell out of a torn pocket into his boot.

He doesn't ask about the baby. I'm the one who brings him up. I tell him Pietro's doing fine.

It's still really cold in Sarajevo, he says. Everything is exactly like before. The worst doesn't even exist anymore because they've already experienced it and there's nothing else, just the monotony of pain, like a lament being repeated over and over again.

The line drops and we've already said enough. It's practically a miracle. But we haven't given each other anything. There's been no comfort.

I hang up the phone and smell Sarajevo: nettles, burning shoes, people standing in line to die. *You're not there, Gemma*, I tell myself. *It's over. You're out.* I breathe in and choke. Dad brings me a glass of water.

"Drink, darling. Drink."

But I know why I'm upset. It's because now I know there's no reason on earth I would want to be there to face that suffering.

My father will rock the baby tonight. He'll sleep on the couch beside the piano.

"It's no bother," he says.

He sings a lullaby. His voice heals the wounds of the dark. He loves the baby. All he needed to do was look at him to love him. I, on the other hand, have my doubts. Every time I look into his eyes I think of his father's wounded eyes, which no one is tending. It seems that this newborn is stealing life away in mouthfuls off Diego's back. This is what I think and cannot say.

Dad doesn't ask me anything. He's afraid of my thoughts.

As he sings I think of the sheep's belly and the look in her eyes as I left. Maybe they'd decided it all in advance. She knew he'd come back to her and her listless gaze concealed a swarm of underground thoughts. She knew she'd won. Maybe Diego convinced her to give me the baby to get rid of me, to send me off with something. They could have other children and I wouldn't come away empty-handed from that ordeal.

He'd given me what I wanted. The child was the price of his freedom. I didn't just pay deutschmarks. I exchanged one human being for another. Aska took the flesh of my love.

I start drinking a whole bottle of grappa. Dad says, *That's enough*, and I say, *I want more*. Drinking saves me from hell by taking me back to hell. Back with them. I yell that I don't want this baby anymore, that a Bosniak whore stole my husband, that she took advantage of my weakness to worm her way into our blood.

The eyes of the blue child come to mind. Why wasn't he saved, rather than the child of those two wretches?

The baby cries. Dad picks him up and brandishes him like a cross, like an exorcist trying to repel evil.

Because tonight the devil is in our house, in this little Roman apartment with the white piano. I look in the crib and all I see are those two snakes still swallowing each other in the misery of that city. This starving piece of flesh is their brat. I should have left him there. His father and his mother could have taken him for a walk in his baby carrier through that ice-covered fire.

The dog barks. The baby cries like a stuck pig. Dad brutally thrusts him into my arms. Until this moment he's protected him. Now he's abandoning him to me.

"He's your son. Do what you want."

Why does he risk it? He isn't usually so brave.

I take a few steps backward and fall onto the couch. I let the baby slide down next to me. If he were a snake he'd bite me and slide away. Instead he stays put, his cries muffled by the pillows. He's incapable of moving, like a beetle on its back.

I stand up and move away. I go to the bathroom and throw up grappa. Because it now seems to me that there's no difference between life and death, between motion and silence.

Dad's gone. He dragged the dog with him. When he slammed the door it was as if the wall would come down, or the whole world. He went away in dismay.

I pick up the baby, raise my arms over my head and hold him suspended in the air. He seems to like the height. He stops crying. Every now and then a sob shakes him. He doesn't seem to notice, just like when he spits up. For a while we play airplane. When he comes back down to earth he's calmed down. He stretches his mouth in a way that's reminiscent of a smile. I don't put him in the crib. I stretch him out on top of me, belly to belly. It's the first time I've done this. I don't know which of us falls asleep first. I dream there's a city resting on my belly. When I open my eyes it's already daytime. It's a Monday and Pietro slept the night through. He didn't even wake up for a bottle.

Chapter 17

Dad was the one who got the call.

The Dubrovnik police found a folded scrap of paper with a few telephone numbers on it in Diego's wallet and simply dialed the first number on the list. It was my father's number, next to the word *DAD*, so they assumed the number belonged to the boy's father. The official spoke Italian and so it all went relatively smoothly. Dad didn't ask any questions. Right then he couldn't have strung two thoughts together. He just said, *I understand . . . I understand . . . I understand.* Three times, like a robot.

Just what he'd understood he couldn't have said. Those were the only words that came to mind, and he pronounced them loud and clear in order to deal with the situation with dignity, in order to stanch a hemorrhage that couldn't be stanched.

My father was a dignified man, reserved, even shy. He wasn't used to letting go, and so his body reacted to the pain by imprisoning it within.

When he knocked on my door a couple of hours later, his mouth hung crookedly, as if his chin had dragged it down, and one of his eyes was partially closed.

"What happened?"

He hadn't even noticed his face was paralyzed. The dog came in behind him. I brought Dad to the bathroom mirror. He looked at himself without seeming to see, or at least without any interest. He nodded.

I was scared by his deformed face, his slurred voice, the listlessness of his one open eye. He needed to see a doctor, go for some tests. It might just be an ear infection, but it could be a stroke.

He had a paper bag of loquats with him. He'd been clutching it since he came in.

It was very early for loquats. Spring had just begun.

We went into the kitchen and sat at the table.

"Pietro?"

"He's sleeping."

Usually he ran to see the baby the minute he came into the house.

He washes the loquats. He takes one and polishes it with a kitchen towel, then removes the stem. I look at his hands for other symptoms. His gestures are very slow, but he seems to be moving all his fingers.

Dad breaks open the loquat and slowly extracts the shiny pit, which is divided into two parts.

He offers me half of the fruit. I bite into it and look at him. He's brought the grainy orange flesh to his mouth but he can't get it past his paralyzed lip.

Dad has a thick head of hair, a gentle face with clean lines, a classic nose. He'd be described as a handsome man. Every so often, though, he can look stupid, for example when he opens his round eyes a bit too wide and raises his eyebrows or when he wriggles his ears and nose on purpose—things he only does occasionally, to entertain children. There's something austere about his face, so it's surprising to discover it's so mobile. When I was little my friends were crazy about my father's eyebrows and ears.

This morning there's that same stupid look on his off-kilter face, which appears to be frozen in a grimace that could be one of his party tricks except that it doesn't go away.

Dad can't swallow his loquat.

Tears well up in his open eye. One spills out and runs down his cheek.

I think it must be because of the paralysis. It seems ridiculous to be sitting here eating loquats when we should be racing to the hospital.

I stand and tell him I'm going to get the car keys.

He says, "Sit down, darling."

The weak chirp that comes out of his mouth is as alarming as his maimed face.

He breaks open another loquat and offers it to me.

"Here. Eat this."

I can't swallow it. It sticks in my throat. This all seems so absurd, so implausible. Because now I realize that there's a terrible secret concealed behind his miserably crooked face. It's as if it were stuck in a scream suspended over a river, like in Munch's painting.

I drop the loquat and remove the unswallowed pieces from my mouth.

I look at Dad's one open weeping eye.

"Dad? Do you know something I don't know?"

Now I remember that loquats are Diego's favorite fruit. Dad always brought them for him.

"What's going on?"

And I don't understand why Dad decided to bring them today, when he probably had to go all the way to the city center to find them, seeing as they're not in season yet, seeing as I don't like them all that much, as he well knows.

There were a thousand ways he could have told me, or maybe just this one. He's brought me the flavor of Diego when he was alive and that's already something. It's all we'll have from now on.

Silently, we'll eat loquats in memory of the photographer from Genoa, who scribbled Armando's number next to the word that represented what he'd missed most. *Dad.*

Now I'm ready. The old memory is inside me, the refrain I learned in Sarajevo.

You have to let the sand pass through, let it slide down into the depths of your body. That's the thing that keeps us on our feet no matter what, like the cement base of a deck umbrella.

"He's dead. Am I right?"

Dad sits looking at me. Now I understand that his lopsided face has its origins in a place that's as far away as the scream in the painting.

He doesn't nod. He keeps staring at me out of the one open eye and the crack of the other. His head bobs like an inmate's in a mental asylum.

He lets out a soft lament. *Oh ... oh ... oh.* Three times.

I wait for the collapse, my eyes on his distraught face.

Then, slowly, he nods, but ever so slightly, as if he weren't really convinced. He sits there with his crooked chin, hesitating as if he were asking me—or those stupid loquats—to tell him that there's been a mistake, that the dead man they found was not Diego but someone else.

I wait for his face to regain its composure, to rewind. But I know that can't happen.

I lower my eyes and look away from this face devoid of itself, devoid of its sweetness. A face without peace. It feels like a last farewell from Sarajevo. My entire future is captive within it. From now on my life will contain nothing but this lopsided expression, this terrorized grimace.

Maybe my face, too, will be locked into a voiceless scream. My father and I will be a pair of cripples.

I fear for the old man. I'm afraid he'll die, too. Now, in my kitchen. That he'll collapse on the table among the loquats.

He looks at me to see if I'm losing it.

He's scared. I smell his fear. It comes off his agitated hands as they fiddle with the fruits.

"Is he dead?"

"Yes."

I'm not going to lose it. I've already learned everything I need to know. The lesson was part of the trip, part of the package. Everything was included in the deal.

I've already lived through this moment. In the Koševo morgue, between Jovan and the blue child, there was a naked metal stretcher. It was empty.

Now the stretcher—which I saw and forgot—has returned. Now I know that it was waiting for a third body between the old man and the child. Like a crucifixion scene awaiting completion. The boy from Genoa, the boy I married, had long ago announced to me his destiny. The rest of it—the passport that fell into his boot, Aska herself—they were just events. Everything had been foretold. We don't decide on life and death. In between we can embark on a more difficult route, challenge destiny, but all we're doing is teasing it.

I'm a widow.

I know I should react. Instead, I look at the loquats on the table. Even as I stand still I know I shouldn't, because later it will hurt. I know I should cry, break down. It's dangerous to retain your balance while everything collapses around you, to stay exactly where you are without moving an inch. It's a pointless sort of heroism, as pointless as dignity.

"Was he hit by a shell?"

It's normal to talk.

Saliva falls out of the crooked furrow of Dad's mouth as he says, "It was an accident. He fell off a cliff . . . on the beach."

What's he talking about? Sarajevo is hours from the sea.

"Dubrovnik. An island off Dubrovnik."

"What was he doing there?"

Dad doesn't know. He didn't ask any questions.

It doesn't matter. I'm not the least bit curious.

I'm seeing something I've already seen, something that's been waiting for me for a long time.

I stand without knowing why. I take three steps like a chicken whose neck has been wrung—nerve spasms, muscles remembering motion. I sit back down and look at the loquats again.

Hearts of pale orange flesh. Diego could eat a mountain of them. He'd laugh and see if he could spit the pits into the garbage.

Diego.

When it comes down to it, this is something I've always known. There's nothing new, just destiny revealing itself.

I was always afraid I'd lose him.

I move two pits together on the table and look at them. We were never so perfect together. There was always something that didn't quite fit, like a corner that sticks out, a bit of a dress that always hangs out of the armoire and bothers you at night so you say, *Now I'll get up and move that piece of cloth.* Then you stay in bed and say, *I'll do it tomorrow.* Now I know what it was. It was this day, these loquats, this death. He had the upper hand.

I smiled because he died falling, near the sea like his father.

I smiled because I wasn't surprised, like when you suddenly find the solution to a riddle that's been driving you crazy, a riddle that's tormented you and instead it turned out you couldn't solve it because it was so easy, too easy, and you were looking everywhere but in your own pocket.

I smiled because I didn't know whether or not I would survive, but I wasn't worried.

So. I won't see him again.

I'll never again see his antelope legs, never again breathe in the smell of his neck. He's taken away the eyes that watched me. I won't be able to ask, *How am I?* He won't be able to answer, *You're you.* His voice is stuck in a dead throat that they'll bury.

So. That's that.

I smile because I'm enfolded in the sensation of a pleasant breeze. Diego turns toward me. We're at the station. He's brought his green plastic chair from Genoa because he wants to show it to me, because he used it as a child. Now he sits on it at Termini Station to show me he still fits into it. Because he's thin as a mosquito. *Like real poor people*, I say. Day laborers from the olden days. People in Africa. I laugh. He wants to know if I love him. He's come to show himself to me, to sell himself like a slave, because he loves me so much he can't live without me. He says he knows he's making a mistake, because there's nothing appealing in this lack of compunction about coming across as so foolish, so in love. *But that's how I am*, he says. I smile. I turn my back on him in the station. I think he's stupid, out of it, on drugs. I think his back's too narrow and his legs are too long. I turn. He's standing now but his ass is still stuck in the little green chair. He follows me like that. When I stop, he sits again and crosses his legs. He doesn't have a cigarette but he pretends to be happily smoking. *I'm waiting*, he says.

For what?

Life. I'm waiting for life.

So. We clear the pits off the table and throw them in the garbage.

Dad says, "What do we need to do? What are we supposed to do?"

Diego was like a son to him. Now he wants to know how you bring back your dead son's body.

"We need to call the Foreign Ministry."

"Oh. Okay."

I stand and put on my glasses but then I don't do anything.

"I'll go to Dubrovnik if you can't."

Where can he go with a face like that?

"Dad, you have to go to the hospital."

He nods, but he can't believe it's so easy, so normal.

The baby wakes, and he's hungry. I make his formula. When Dad picks him up, Pietro cries because he doesn't recognize him. He's frightened by Dad's grimace. That's how we learn that he can see clearly now. Once he recognizes his grandfather's smell he accepts a bottle from him despite the lopsided face. For a moment I watch Dad sobbing and feeding the baby and wetting him with his tears.

I say, "Be careful, Dad."

He lowers his head. He's ashamed that I'm strong and he's weak. The dog sleeps, his muzzle resting on one of Dad's feet.

I flip through the phone book for the number at the Foreign Ministry. They've received the news, the official says, but adds, "We don't know the details yet, ma'am."

The sky's clouded over. I move aside a blind to bring in the drying rack with the baby clothes and bibs. I change the baby and hold him awake for a while between Dad and me. In the shadowy light Dad's face looks even more sinister, like an elderly man with mental problems. His open eye is wide open.

He loved the boy from Genoa from the start.

"He doesn't have a job, he sneaks onto trains without a ticket and he's penniless!"

At first, I'd taken it as a reprimand. I had just gotten out of my ridiculous marriage to Fabio. Dad looked irritated. Then he wiggled his ears and nose.

"But he has everything else! Hurry up. What on earth are you waiting for?"

Later he'd become Diego's assistant, and Diego would take him around on his motorcycle. Never again would he be so happy.

The minutes ticked by. The sand descended through my body. I thought about the sea and about Diego covered with sand. I didn't think about the corpse. I was in no hurry to hurl myself into the reality of phone calls and foreign voices. I felt slow and dull-witted, like a pregnant woman. Diego was no longer of this world but I felt that he was still inside life, floating in the liquid roots of a big cosmic placenta. I rested my hand on the baby's belly. I had him to thank for the calm I felt. He sat there quietly gurgling. He was used to this house that he now recognized. He was used to this life. He would not suffer because of this tragedy. He didn't even know it existed. He'd never met Diego. The little eyes he could now move back and forth did not seek Diego out. Pietro was fatherless, just as his father had been. All of a sudden his destiny had shifted but he didn't know it. He sat there saying, *Ga ga*.

Pietro's lack of awareness was a shield against the pain, but it was also the real death of Diego.

Dad didn't want to leave me. He was afraid. He told me so, mumbling through his crooked mouth. I had called his doctor, who was waiting at the hospital. The taxi was downstairs.

"You're too calm. It worries me."

But I wanted to be alone.

I called the Foreign Ministry again but they still didn't have any news for me.

We're waiting, the voice said.

I fell asleep with the baby on my belly.

I had gone to the window and opened it and leaned out as if to jump with the baby in my arms. It was a good test. I discovered I didn't have any intention of doing it. Besides, the second floor's not high enough up to die. There were some people on the street. I watched a young couple leaning up against a moped, kissing.

I dreamt of Sarajevo. The city recomposed itself like a film on rewind. The ruins lifted themselves off the ground. The broken glass became windows in houses and stores. The metal shutters of the shops in the Baščaršija opened. The arches of the National Library soared once again skyward and the thin girl resumed carrying books through the orderly rooms. The lament of the muezzins came out of intact minarets. There was summer and then snow and fires burning in the hearths and then the parade for Tito with all the majorettes in turquoise outfits. There was the mountain hut at Jahorina and Diego's gaze the first time he looked at me.

In my sleep I clutched him tight like a knife, like a lily. It was a white bloodless wound.

When dawn came I thought I'd never make it.

But I did. I put Pietro in the baby carrier and went out. I'd found the business card from the captain of the carabinieri.

I waited for a while. Then they let me in.

I sat down. He smiled and said the baby had grown.

"What can I do for you?"

I asked for a drink of water.

He had someone bring him a bottle. I drank.

He drank, too. He smiled.

"You make me thirsty."

And only then, in front of this slightly overweight, slightly balding man in a uniform, did I start to weep. I wept for a long time. He waited, wordless.

Later he would tell me that he fell in love with me that day, because he, too, had been waiting for a destiny he'd never seen. Now, all of a sudden, he saw it.

He was the one who helped me bring Diego's body back to Italy.

I decided not to go to Dubrovnik. I no longer had any desire to cross that sea. I had the baby to take care of, and Dad wasn't well. He was recovering from the paralysis but he wasn't the same as before. We were like artificial people from a science fiction film, mutants emptied of ourselves and inhabited by automatons.

There was a different sound when we kissed each other hello, the pain of one colliding with the pain of the other. We found it difficult to meet each other's eyes. It was easier to look at strangers, people who didn't know.

The apartment was sick but it continued to feel alive because the cleaning lady came and Dad kept bringing flowers and fresh fruit and tried to do everything more or less like before. He went shopping, tended to the baby, gave water to the dog, tidied my fridge. But then, as soon as he could, when Pietro was sleeping, he'd plant himself in front of Diego's photographs and stare at them for a long time, all else forgotten. He'd sit on the couch and look as if entranced at a puddle or a line of feet. When he noticed my presence he'd lower his gaze. His eye was beginning to open again but it was still different from the other one and unsettling to look at.

I was floating on pain. A subtle membrane kept me on the surface. Like those insects that live on the leaves of water plants, I never really touched the ground. Little paralyses were exploding inside of me, too. I'd suddenly lose the feeling in a breast, a foot, a part of my shoulder—the parts of my body Diego had touched. It was the thought of his hand resting on me. I was anesthetizing those parts.

I was reading a book about insects. I liked it. It wasn't a distraction. It simply spoke to me of myself through other life-forms, insects that froze on the bark of trees, that adjusted to fear by transforming themselves, changing color, stopping dead in their tracks.

The medical report arrived from Dubrovnik. Diego had died from the fall. He had a fractured skull, fractures all over his body. His hands and forearms were covered with abrasions as if he'd tried to grab hold of the rocks and bushes on his way down.

I asked the captain if it was possible someone had pushed him.

The police in Dubrovnik had excluded the possibility. A number of witnesses had seen Diego walk along the dock at Korčula and then climb up the cliff.

"He was . . . confused."

Giuliano lowered his head, opened a drawer and pulled out a pack of mints.

Now he was looking at me. I felt his pity envelop me.

All of a sudden the baby moved in the baby carrier, pushing his feet against my legs and pulling himself up. I put a hand on his head. I was worried he'd turn toward the captain, irrationally worried—now that he could pull himself up—that he'd suddenly start talking and tell the captain he wasn't my son.

Stalling, the captain opened the mints and offered me one.

"Did your husband use drugs?"

They'd found a syringe behind a bush in the place where Diego had spent the night and there were traces of heroin in his blood.

I lowered my head. I wanted to bang it against the table. But the baby's head was in the way. I wanted to bang it slowly a hundred times, say *no* a hundred times. The boy from the alleyways had chosen his end.

The captain nodded, his eyes as still as glass.

"It's not easy to come back from a war."

There was a yellow envelope next to the medical report. I'd been eyeing it for a while. It was the most terrible part of all. Giuliano had set it to one side; now there was no choice but to open it. It held the photographs of the body.

Giuliano used a letter opener to pry open the reluctant envelope made of strong paper from the old Yugoslav bureaucracy and quickly flipped through the photographs.

I watched his face for a reaction. I kissed the baby's sweet-smelling head and suddenly found myself hoping for a miracle, hoping that the dead man—despite the documents that attested to his identity, the detailed descriptions of his clothes, the silver ring on his finger—would turn out not to be Diego.

The captain must have been accustomed to photographs of dead bodies. He didn't change expression. When he looked up his face was still gentle.

"One should be enough. It's necessary. You have to sign a certificate."

I looked at the photographs of the dead photographer. They passed before me as calmly as boats on a river.

"Yes. It's him."

While he was putting the photographs back into the envelope the captain said, "He looks like Che Guevara."

It was true. He was a beautiful dead man. His face was white, devoured by shadows. Yet it was possible to see the tension of his soul, his passion for life.

Days passed and I learned how much easier it was to take a newborn infant out of Sarajevo than to repatriate a corpse from Dubrovnik. At long last the coffin arrived.

It was a sunny day. The military plane sank into the soft asphalt of the runway in the absolute silence of a liquid sky that shimmered on the horizon. The captain, in perfect uniform, reached the plane with long strides. Unreal seconds went by, like before a birth. Then the hatch opened and the coffin slid out of the metallic belly.

I started sweating. My shirt was stuck to my body like a bathing suit.

A few years later, when Giuliano asked me to marry him, I would think back on this arrival, Diego's body in the box and the captain waiting for him under that hot shimmering sky. One destiny on its way out, one on its way in.

I stayed with the coffin for an entire day. They put it in a small room. There were some problems; the funeral was scheduled to take place the next morning and the airport had no intention of storing the body. Diego wasn't a war hero or anything remotely similar. He was an unknown photographer who fell off a cliff with heroin in his veins. The captain impassively witnessed my lack of organization, which by now came as no surprise. It should have been obvious that the coffin would be my responsibility once it reached Italian soil but the thought hadn't crossed my mind. I stood there like a lost tourist in my little cotton hat and sweaty shirt. A long back-and-forth of phone calls and discussions began.

In the end, four young soldiers lifted the coffin and carried it into a small, airy room that reminded me of a house at the seaside. There was a door with a greenish shutter. I asked them to leave it open. It looked out onto a service area with a metallic hangar and a length of barbed-wire fence.

I stayed until sunset.

It was wood. It was nothing but wood bathed in the half-light of that isolated room. I was constantly distracted. I looked outside, drawn to the light like a restless fly. I looked at the reeds that had grown up along the edges of the runway, breaking the asphalt. I tried to concentrate, like when I received the host in church as a child and shut myself in prayer, but despite all my efforts I floated along, thinking about whatever came to mind. I was just waiting for time to pass. I felt slightly uneasy, like when you start off on a trip and have the feeling you've left something behind. You go over a list in your mind, rummage through your pockets, open your purse, but you can't figure out what you've forgotten.

Then two things happened.

The first was that Diego came into the room and spoke to me. The sun was starting to go down. It was a time of day we'd always liked, when we'd open up a bottle of wine and sit chatting. So it didn't surprise me that he'd chosen this moment to visit. He didn't come out of the coffin. He came in from the outside, bending so as not to bang into the shutter.

Hello, baby.

He'd come to keep me company in the vigil, like when we used to wait together at the fertility clinics. His face was smooth, devoid of his Sarajevo beard. He was wearing his old white collarless shirt and his explorer pants. He'd just showered and his damp hair smelled of shampoo.

I asked him if he'd suffered.

He smiled and nodded. *A little.*

I asked him, *What is death, Diego?*

He didn't have to think. *It's a river flowing upward.*

The coffin sat between us. He rested his feet on it. It was like a wake for a man dead many years before, his father, perhaps. Now he was playing the guitar. I looked at the worn soles of his boots, the soles of a man who's done plenty of walking. A little military plane with a propeller stood outside the hanger.

Do you want to leave, my love? I asked him.

He looked at me for a long time out of ancient damp eyes that held the force of life and the fragility of the sky.

No. I'd like to stay.

Only now did he ask me about the baby.

I told him about that morning, when Pietro peed in my face while I was changing his diaper.

He laughed and said he peed on his mother, too, that it was something all little boys did. He spread the fingers of one hand over his face and sat there for a while beneath the cage they made.

When he left he placed a roll of film on the coffin.

The second thing that happened was that I really did find a roll of film. Someone who maybe hadn't known how to unload it had pulled out the film and crumpled it up and forgotten it there on the floor beside the green shutter. I put the roll of sun-ruined film in my pocket and felt better. It was as if I now held the thing I'd been vainly seeking before. I left the room.

At the funeral the next day there are a lot of young faces, the kids from the photography school. Viola's hair is growing back in. She beat the cancer but she can't control the little Afghan, who wriggles away and takes a few solitary steps toward the coffin. The priest is an old schoolmate of my father's. He's solidly built and speaks in a singsong voice. Every time he says *Diego* I start. *Why is he calling him?* I wonder.

A skinny guy hardly taller than a child comes up to me.

"Are you his wife?"

He has the same alleyway accent as Diego, with its wide-open vowels and the consonants that melt like the sea.

"I'm Pino."

He hugs me tight.

A boxer's face, dark glasses, slicked-back hair like an undertaker's.

I've seen his photograph many times. He was the head of the Marassi ultras. I can't believe he's so small. In Diego's photographs he looks like a giant.

He introduces me to the others, the group from Genoa with their bony, drug-addict faces. He asks whether they can drape the flag over the coffin.

It's an ancient relic, filthy and tattered and covered with players' autographs. They spread it over the coffin like a shroud.

The flag is your father, your mother, the job you don't have. It's heroin, the good stuff.

Diego's mother came by car with her boyfriend, seven hundred kilometers to this neighborhood church with no particular distinguishing features.

She sits next to me, riveted to the pew. Afraid. Poor Rosa. She's a withered flower that will never bloom again. But it's clear she's been to the hairdresser's. Her head is covered with motionless, lilac-colored curls. I hold her hand and she squeezes mine as if to ask my forgiveness.

One day she said to me, "I couldn't keep him at home. I had to send him away to an institute. If I could go back in time . . ."

You can't go back in time, Rosa.

Now she may be thinking about those years when Diego was little, *as thin as my pinky finger*, when he'd toss and turn in his sleep and fall out of the bunk bed and they'd call her from the infirmary because the little boy was asking for her. But Rosa couldn't go all the way to Nervi, to the institute—*a fine institute, don't get me wrong*—because she had her shifts at the cafeteria. They spoke by phone. She told him to *be a good boy*. Now she lives in Nice with her boyfriend. They have a little house. It's too bad her hands are so shaky.

She kisses her grandson on the forehead but she's scared to take him in her arms. She seems preoccupied, at the mercy of ghosts even more miserable than she is. Silently she breathes in the odor of her mouth that was closed in the car for all those hours.

I ask her if Pietro looks like Diego when he was a baby.

"He looks just like a picture I have. I'll show it to you. I'll send it."

She smiles absently, dazed.

"She's full of Valium," Pino will say later.

The girl who reads the Gospel is mildly retarded. She looks like a seal in a wig. Diego would have chosen her as a model.

I've got a tape recorder with me. I stand and push play.

There aren't any flowers on the coffin, just his battered Leica and the Genoa soccer flag. "I Wanna Marry You" floats out over that meagerness.

Oh, darlin', there's something happy and there's something sad . . . Duccio stands the entire time beneath the lateral arch, his back against a column, his arms crossed and his legs spread wide, as if he were a bouncer.

The students from the photography school hoist the coffin bearing their young professor's body and carry it out.

The little Afghan is calm now. He's blowing bubbles. They're like flying puddles. Diego would have liked them. For a moment they seem like his eyes falling through the air.

There's the usual burst of applause.

With the baby as his excuse, Armando spends the entire time wandering around the back of the church. He's unshaven. His blue eyes are lost in his dark skin. His face is almost back to normal. Every so often we hear a whimper as he lulls Pietro to sleep in the baby carriage. Now he stands in front of the coffin and stretches out a hand but doesn't touch it right away. He waits, as if there were a thought in progress or a prayer being transmitted from his hand to the wood. He's an old man. It's the first time I've seen him this old. He lowers his head and practically leans against the coffin as if he were asking the motionless boy inside it for help, the boy who by now is nothing but a mummy.

Cheeks slap against mine one after the other, air kisses, death kisses. My skin hurts. I don't take my sunglasses off because I don't want to meet all these eyes that would like to meet mine. Black fish.

I hear Rosa's boyfriend ask, "Was it cold inside the church?"

They load the coffin onto the photography school van. No funeral director, no hearses.

Duccio looks aghast at that wreck of a van. He hugs me, his mirrored glasses sticking to his thin face, and bites his lip between his big, predator teeth.

"He was a great photographer, the best."

He presses the button on his key chain and shuffles toward his Jaguar.

"He didn't really think so," Viola says. "People always speak well of the dead." She sucks on her sodden cigarette. "After all, who really gives a shit about them anymore?"

I rip the cigarette out of her hand and crush it beneath my shoe. "Stop smoking, you imbecile."

The light's changed. The sky is gray and it looks like rain. Pietro is dressed in white. He's awake now. He's kicked aside his covers. He lies there with his little bald head and stares out of his enormous eyes at the toy bee wobbling from the hood of the baby carriage. *Dad*, he's saying, *what are we supposed to do?*

Yes, what are we supposed do to? It's not a wedding. There's no reception. It's not a normal funeral, either. There's no hearse, no grave. Diego didn't want one. He'd always said, *In the wind.* In the wind it will be.

"Dad, bring the baby home."

We cross the city to the crematorium. We go through a gate and drive down a dusty boulevard. It's a good shelter. There's something light about it. It reminds me of a plant nursery. The waiting coffins look like boxes of seeds. Pino carefully folds the Genoa Soccer flag. He doesn't want it to be cremated.

We stop at a little café. In the square in front of it there's a fountain, with spurts that soar, water flowing upward instead of falling.

Diego's mother gets in the car. Her boyfriend closes the door. A piece of her dress hangs out. I watch it flutter.

Pino and I are the last ones left. We share a sandwich.

"What was his father like?"

He grimaces with all the pain of his failed life. In the end, Diego was the one who made it.

"He was a bastard. He beat them up, really whaled on them."

"Diego talked about him as if he were a hero."

Pino sits there with his black leather jacket and his battered face. He does a little leap and smiles like De Niro in *Raging Bull.*

"What the fuck! You know how Diego was."

"No, I don't. You tell me, Pino."

"He didn't want to see the bad things. All he ever wanted to see was the beautiful thing."

I look at the fountain. The water flowing upward. *The beautiful thing . . .*

Chapter 18

Our luggage is packed and waiting on the bed. Wet towels are strewn about the room. Pietro is wearing a clean T-shirt and polishing his Ray-Bans.

"What should we steal, Mom?"

I look at him, confused.

"Why do you need to steal something?"

"You have to steal something when you go to a hotel. Otherwise it means you weren't satisfied."

"Who said so?"

"Dad."

I can't counter this, because the man he calls *Dad* was promoted to the rank of colonel in the carabinieri a month ago.

Pietro grabs the piece of plastic hanging from the door handle.

"I know. I'll take the DO NOT DISTURB sign. What do you think?"

"So, are you satisfied?"

He frowns and shrugs and tucks the sign into his backpack.

We drag our bags down the hall. The wheels struggle over the lumpy carpet.

"Are you sorry to leave, Mom?"

"A little."

"Me, too. A little."

I look at him because I can't believe he minds leaving this poor gray city.

Maybe he minds leaving Danka, the hotel maid with the pierced belly button. But they don't look at each other very much when they say goodbye. They hug for a second, as stiff as two insects.

Out on the street we wait while Gojko turns the car around. Pietro says, "Before, I didn't know where I was born. Now I know."

"And are you glad?"

"I don't know."

As we pass the reconstructed buildings around the train station, I look at his face leaning against the window and understand his *I don't know*. For years, Pietro had imagined the place where he was born—*by chance*, as he always said to his teachers and friends. He must have thought a lot more than I'd ever suspected about the *chance* this city represented. It may be that he's been looking for it over the last few days as he's walked around, eyes downward, without seeming to look at much of anything.

Last night in bed he asked, "Was Diego better than me at the guitar?"

"No, you're better. You've had lessons. Dad played by ear."

He turned. Then he tossed a million times, making it impossible for me to settle into sleep.

"Do you mind telling me what's wrong?"

He reared up like a tiger.

"I don't like it when you call him Dad."

"But he's your father."

"So why didn't he come back to Rome with us?"

"Because he was working."

"No. He left us."

He tugged at my arm.

"Is it true?"

I waited for him to fall asleep. Maybe something within this city has spoken to him, whispering a truth that's now dead but that nonetheless once existed, a truth that has been registered somewhere just like the names on the plaques attached to the walls of these wounded and mended buildings.

The Lion Cemetery lies beside the stadium complex, next to the cement buildings that house the locker rooms. The tombs ascend a slope that resembles a terraced vineyard.

The Muslim headstones all face toward Mecca and look like they've been buffeted by the wind.

Gojko asks me if I want to stop.

I've wanted to come here since we arrived, but I haven't felt strong enough. I don't feel strong enough this morning, either, but because we're leaving, I touched his shoulder when he asked and said, *Yes, please stop*. Offhandedly, Gojko hit the turn indicator and pulled over with the same expression on his face as if we were stopping for a coffee.

Now he's walking ahead of us, his sweaty T-shirt stuck to his back. He doesn't bother looking at the graves. He knows the way.

He looks like a farmer taking us on a tour of his vineyard.

Half of Sarajevo is buried here. The dates of birth vary but the dates of death are repeated. Destiny worked indiscriminately. Death made an incredible harvest during those three years.

Death is solitude, but when they were forced to die in bunches like insects they were deprived even of death's privacy. Being robbed of life seemed almost acceptable in the end. Being robbed of death was something else altogether . . . to end up in a jumble, all mixed up like dirty laundry or rotten fruit.

Gojko translates some of the inscriptions on the graves. He does it for Pietro, who won't leave him in peace. Gojko doesn't try to worm his way out of it. He treats Pietro to the most macabre anecdotes.

"They ran out of black numbers for the graves, and so after a while they didn't have any more twos for 1992. Everyone was looking forward to the start of 1993, but then the threes ran out, too." He laughs. "A real tragedy."

He's stopped. He pauses, then bends over and pulls at a bit of ugly weed.

We're in the field with the Catholic crosses. I walk forward, though I'd like not to. He looks at me.

Things had already started to fall apart, but everything ended that day. All of it died—the yo-yos and the Levi's 501 jeans, Bruce Springsteen's songs and Gojko's poems.

By the time that day arrived I had been away from Sarajevo for some time. I learned about what happened by chance, many years later, in the lobby of an art-house cinema. I see a girl looking at me through her glasses. She's dressed in baggy jeans and a worn black satin jacket. She recognizes me before I recognize her. I kiss her hello, hug her and look at her again. This embrace, mute and dense, takes place every time I meet one of them. It's pain returning to retrace the mark it's left. She was Mirna and Sebina's neighbor, not much more than a child. She always climbed the stairs in the same way, head lowered and an arm dragging limply behind her to trail against the wall like a tail. I kiss her hard because she's alive, even though I didn't know her well and have never thought about her, nor wondered what happened to her. She translates novels from Serbo-Croatian. There was a moment, she says, after the war, when they were in fashion. She doesn't have much money. That much is clear from her opaque evening jacket. She had an Italian boyfriend but now it's over. She's waiting. She has tiny, extremely white hands and the placid proud face of her city. Her voice is so thin I have a hard time hearing her. We're sitting on a red couch. The carpet smells of damp.

She has a high forehead and dull, frizzy hair. We sit beneath a strong white light. She left Sarajevo during the last year of the siege. Some of the trams had started running again. She boarded one and sat in the back. She didn't bother ducking down, not even when the tram passed through open areas. She rode that way from Baščaršija to Ilidža. The tram was handsome; so were its intact windows. She saw the destruction of her city as if from a seat in a movie theater and decided not to stay. She couldn't bear the idea of living there. The scars seemed worse than the wounds.

"They didn't make it," she says.

The glaring light erases a part of her brown hair and makes it look white, like an old woman's. She shores me up with her gaze.

Perhaps I shouldn't be suffering like this because it happened so many years ago. It's no longer an open wound, it's already white scar tissue disappearing into the skin of time. And yet the pain is precisely the fact that so much time has passed without my having realized it.

I catch up with Gojko and look down at the ground. There are two twin graves marked by a companion headstone just slightly bigger than a single stone. It reminds me of the narrow double bed where they slept together, where Diego and I made love for the first time.

Sebina and Mirna are resting here.

I make the sign of the cross.

There's a long inscription on the stone. Gojko translates it for Pietro without once stumbling over the words. There is no change in the tone of his voice or the expression on his face.

Hold your end of the rope,
and I'll run through the world
with the other end in hand.

And if I happen to get lost,
you pull me back, mother dear.

Pietro asks, "Is that one of your poems?"

Gojko nods reluctantly. It's part of a ballad he wrote for Sebina's last birthday, February 13, 1993. They managed to have a proper party despite the snow and the bombs.

"It's one of my worst, but they liked it."

Pietro says, "I don't think it's bad."

I sob in my belly, in my shoulders. Pietro looks at me. I'd like to collapse and drown in my tears. But I feel like I have to hold on to my dignity for Pietro's sake and for Gojko, who lost everything yet stands here without batting an eyelash. I have to hold on to my dignity for the sake of my pathetic age. They call it middle age but right now it feels like I'm a lot further along.

"How did it happen?"

The tone of the girl's voice never varied as she spoke. I grabbed hold of that thin thread, which I now recognize as the voice of the survivors, those who carried on living, like loose strands. The monotonous drone of her Italian worked a bit like an anesthetic. This is how it happened.

The alarm sirens have already been ringing for a while. Sebina has to go down to the cellar. She still doesn't like to go but she doesn't complain about it anymore. It's become a habit. The cellar is equipped with a car battery that they manage to recharge every so often, so sometimes they can listen to the radio. There's a pot where they cook a common meal. A curtain hides the bucket that serves as their toilet. There are books, blankets and lounge chairs for the night.

Sebina's busy feeding her fish. Mirna tells her to hurry. Sebina grates a bit of the black lump that comes in the humanitarian packages, supposedly some sort of meat. It smells like fish food, and the fish love it. Sebina would like to take the fish down to the shelter with her in a jar that once held cherry preserves. Sometimes Mirna lets her do it but today she gets angry. Today the shells sound like rocks falling in an endless landslide.

Sebina brings her geography book with her. She likes New Zealand. She told her brother she'd like to go there and Gojko has promised that the first thing they'll do afterward is board a plane and make the twenty-four-hour journey. She goes down the stairs along with their neighbors, along with the older girl who trails her arm along the wall.

The radio is working today. First come the appeals, the breathless voices of distant relatives asking for news. Then, at last, there's music.

Sebina dances and jumps around. The woman who's making the soup tells her to stop. Sebina opens her geography book. Then she closes it and tells a joke she's learned from her brother. She makes funny faces and plants her fists on her hips. They all laugh, even the grumpy woman stirring the soup.

Mirna hasn't come down yet. She's up on the rooftop terrace hanging the laundry. It's the first real sunny day after months of cold. That's why the artillery squads on the mountains are so euphoric.

The terrace is in a relatively safe position because their building is lower than the others around it and set slightly apart.

Mirna's blond hair masks the white streaks. She's wearing clothes from her girlhood, a close-fitting skirt and a turtleneck sweater that fit her perfectly once again.

I see her on the terrace and wave to her. These are the last moments of her life. The second year of the siege has just started. More than once we've sat chatting on this roof with its chimneys and television antennae. Sometimes I'd go up to help her get the laundry and we'd end up staying to smoke a cigarette and look at the world below. I was fond of her and she was fond of me, in her own way, though there was no real intimacy, because of her shyness, because I always seemed a little remote. I could have been her son's wife. I was her daughter's godmother. But we never got to know each other very well. In a few minutes, after her shell falls, we'll never have the chance.

I go back down to Sebina. She's leafing through her geography book again. She's used to the darkness. By day a little window set at street level lets in a ray of pearly light and nothing more, enough to see each other and let some of the smoke out. Down here those who have cigarettes smoke them. The smoke bothers Sebina, even though she hardly notices it anymore except when they leave the cellar and she smells it on her clothes. She thinks of her mother. Sometimes Mirna lets her go up to the terrace with her, and she can finally stretch her legs, do splits and cartwheels and roundoffs and walk on her hands among the chimney tops and antennae.

Her legs are squat and strong. They used to be stronger. Now she's out of shape, but it won't take her long to get it back. She's lucky to be a little athlete. The war won't steal the Olympics away from her.

The moment has arrived.

I see Sebina as if I could reach out and touch her. We share a greater intimacy. I held her in my arms when she was a few hours old. I baptized her.

I'm sitting in the lobby of this art-house cinema where they're showing a movie I'll never see. I stepped in here by accident on a rainy day and now this is the movie I'm seeing: Sarajevo, May '93. The deaths of Sebina and of her mother, Mirna.

I sit and the girl talks. She remembers everything down to the smallest detail. I ask her if she only translates or if she's also a writer. She says, *How did you know?*

I know from the details. They're the details someone with a writer's memory would recall. A knife that separates and chooses.

My details are: a dirty handkerchief I once used to clean Sebina's mouth after she ate an ice cream cone. Now, absurdly, I wonder where I put that handkerchief with the imprint of her lips.

My details are: her fishy smell.

She's standing. Her head comes up to my stomach. I bend to kiss her and smell the mackerel from the humanitarian aid packages.

My details are: her fish flapping around in the dust.

The first shell lands close by. The pan falls from the burner and the soup ends up on the ground. Cursing the war, the woman yells and burns herself as she gathers up what she can with her hands.

Sebina watches the broth slide toward her. It's full of pieces of winter vegetables and misery. She raises her head and says she wants to go out. She wants to find her mother.

In the cinema lobby, the girl pauses and says, *No one stopped her. That's the most absurd thing of all. We shouldn't have let a little girl go out.* She stops.

Sebina runs up the stairs.

The girl didn't stop her. She was playing chess with a friend. Their home-made cork chess pieces had fallen on the ground and they were arguing because it wasn't clear anymore where they were in their game.

Now she thinks she could have used the arm she was always dragging behind her on the stairs to stop the little neighbor girl from embarking on that black journey.

The girl stops. She's a writer. She knows that destiny flows like ink and that there's no way to stop a little girl who's fated to die.

Sebina goes up the stairs because that's what's written. Where is it written? In what fucking book?

Sebina, with her funny face, her hair as straight as oil, her slightly square head, her jutting ears like pink strings of transparent skin and the mouth that it's impossible to describe because you have to have seen it at least once to understand how a mouth could be entirely inhabited by the joy of living.

She isn't beautiful. She never has been. She's the ugliest member of her family. She's short and her arms are too long. Her face looks like the character on the package of orange cookies.

And yet she's the most beautiful little girl in the world. She's my god-daughter. She's life in its purest state. She shines with all the light that isn't visible anywhere else, like a precious stone that's been dug out from the surrounding rock.

She's the one who took my hand and guided me toward motherhood. Every time I hugged her I said this creature has something for me. Somewhere she has a present for me.

I recall how incredibly exposed the knot of her elbow bone was. I remember her eyeballs and the downy hairs growing in on her forehead like a little curtain.

She rises. Like water parting from a sloping riverbed to flow upward like a flame.

Mirna has stopped hanging the clothes. Up here, the shock waves of the shell that made the cellar shake felt as strong as an earthquake. They threw her off her feet against one of the antennae that are about as useful as scrap metal now that there's no electricity. She thinks of Sebina. She could be buried down there. There's smoke coming up off the street. She has to run to make sure they're all okay, to make sure nothing's collapsed. She's never trusted these basement shelters. They weren't made for this purpose. They're built like any cellar, places to store lard and old sewing machines.

And so she goes down.

Yes, that's how it happened.

The Bosnian girl with the sad forehead and the luminous hair says that anyway she'll never write this story because it's too stupid, because sometimes death is too stupid and pat.

But that's exactly what happened.

Mother and daughter met halfway. They were running along the same stairwell, looking for each other, one going up, the other going down.

If they'd stayed exactly where they were they would have eaten some dust and had a scare but nothing more.

They'd finally decided to leave the siege. They were due to go any day now with a journalist friend of Gojko's from Belgrade.

But instead they'd stepped off the chessboard of life without realizing it. They moved along, dragged by the cord that bound them.

Hold your end of the rope,
and I'll run through the world
with the other end in hand.
And if I happen to get lost,
you pull me back, mother dear.

Death did the pulling for them. It pulled hard. A shell entered and crossed the sheltered building. In that very moment they'd reached each other. Mother and daughter. The womb and its fruit.

Gojko is sitting on an earthen step. Pietro is next to him. They're watching a soccer game, kids running after each other, their T-shirts and flesh.

The kids are about Pietro's age. The postwar generation.

White flowers of reconciliation.

Gojko says, "You know, she didn't die right away."

He lights a cigarette, spits smoke and raises an arm to holler foul. Soccer and the cemetery.

We get up and leave the burial ground.

Gojko needs a beer.

He sits on a bench beside the cemetery kiosk and drinks one after the other, straight from the bottle.

Mirna was blown to bits. They gathered the pieces together under a sheet so he wouldn't find her that way. This was his mother, the body that had made him, but he ran to his sister in a flash.

Sebina had lost her legs. The upper part of her body was intact. He found her lying composedly in a white bed in a space beneath a stairway in the Koševo Hospital. There were tubes in her hands. Her eyes were still as glass. He saw the emptiness beneath the sheet and wondered if she knew.

His little sister had dreamt of winning the Olympics. She was the shortest on her team, the closest to the ground. Gojko closed his eyes two times, the first because he didn't want to believe it, the second to thank God she was alive.

The doctors had said there was hope for this desperate case so similar to many others they'd seen. And Gojko, sitting in shock next to his sister, started imagining how it would be, the way he did back when he sold yo-yos and cheated the Montenegrins. He imagined shiny artificial limbs, the latest in reconstructive orthopedics. He would get her the most beautiful prosthetics ever made. He'd spend all the money he had and take journalists out into the trenches even by night to earn more if he had to.

He remembers that there was a shoe on the metal table beside the bed, an unnerving detail he can't shake. He brings his hands together to show me how small that shoe was, to show me that it's here in his hands. Poor Gojko. Poor brother. Now his voice is trembling, like an ogre tortured by a tiny mouse that's incredibly strong and cruel. He wanted to get rid of that shoe. Some helpful soul must have gathered it up on the stairs and, too shell-shocked to recognize the dark irony of it all, thrown it into the car alongside the gravely wounded little girl. But Gojko didn't dare move it. Sebina was awake. Her eyes were like marbles of light in the night, like diamonds. Gojko wasn't sure if she could feel her body, wasn't sure if she knew. The part of her that was visible was unscathed. There wasn't a single scratch on her face. When he spoke to her she seemed to be listening.

She asked after her mother, called out for her.

Gojko told her Mirna was okay, that they'd put her in another ward.

Sebina listened to his lie. She didn't want anything to drink. She didn't want anything.

She never moved her hands. The shoe sat there beside them.

And now I see that plane, the exit light, the unknown woman as she showed me those light-up shoes.

Gojko says something must have jammed in the blast because the light in the rubber sole stayed on.

It was a tongue of pale light on the metal table. Sebina could see it. Gojko let it sit where it was. He thought, *If this shoe can survive, so can she.* It was one of his games, the worst one.

Sebina died at dawn. The shoe survived her by a few hours.

"After that I left."

He went to fight, first in Dobrinja, then on Mount Žuć. He was a poet, a traveling salesman, a radio operator, a tour guide, a fool who'd never even shot at a pigeon. But he learned quickly, because you learn hatred overnight.

Months in the mud, his cartridge belt slung over his back.

"But I could have fought with my knife, or with my bare hands."

He stops. They set fire to a village full of Serbian peasants, civilians who'd never hurt anyone. He didn't take part, but he didn't say anything. He sat on top of a hill, smoking.

Pietro listens. He's no longer looking at the kids playing soccer. He's looking at a hero from this filthy war, someone who came back at the end weighed down with medals like a laden donkey.

"How many did you kill?"

Gojko smiles and pats Pietro's head because there's something new now in Pietro's eyes as he looks at him, something shining and scared.

"They're horrible things, things to forget."

"Tell me one story."

I say, "Cut it out, Pietro. Drop it."

Gojko points to the kids playing soccer.

"One day I found myself just like them, in a field, playing soccer with the guys from my brigade. But instead of a ball we were using a head, the head we'd cut off a Chetnik. We kicked it around and sent it rolling through a green field full of little yellow and blue flowers. We were sweating and laughing. It was a game. It was normal. The only thing we were sorry about was that we were getting blood all over our pants, so we rolled them up."

Pietro says, "Is that true?"

Gojko stands up and throws his beer bottle into the plastic recycling bin.

"It's true. The other day when we played with those kids was the first time I've played soccer since."

Chapter 19

We're leaving Sarajevo. I look at Gojko's back as he walks toward the car. Your back is the part you can't see, the most vulnerable part. Your back is weighed down by thoughts and by all the times you've made the decision to leave.

Gojko carries his back along with him. It's lower on one side than on the other, where life struck him when it changed course. His past sits there, motionless as a hawk on a falconer's shoulder.

I look at the pink swollen flesh of his hand before taking it in my own. It's the hand of a peace-loving man who exhorted his radio listeners to never, for any reason, give in to hate. It's the hand of a poor fool who ended up killing, who followed the law of war and left his own law behind.

I ask him how he managed afterward, when the deluge ended and he had to face the stagnant pool. What state did life find him in when he stripped off his camouflage uniform and his cartridge belt and washed the mud off his body in the knowledge that he could never again be the same man as before? He said he locked himself into a hotel room for a week to drink and doze in front of the television.

Only his poems spoke to him of himself, of his soul before he met evil.

That's why he hates them. That's why he stopped writing them, because his soul was dirty, and a poet cannot fool himself. Bosnia saw him as a hero, while in his own eyes he was a failure, a eunuch.

I reach for his hand and he lets me take it, entrusting it to me like a child. We walk like that for a while, like in the old days when the people we loved were alive. Pietro is watching us and probably thinks we're two fools. Before we get in the car Gojko asks, "Do you think I'm disgusting?"

I shake my head no.

He kisses my hand before giving it back to me: *Thank you.*

It's not exactly a highway but I'd been expecting worse. The car climbs through the somber green woods. It's been so hot; it would be nice to stop and enjoy some of the coolness. The trees bear no wounds. There was fighting here. The ground is still full of mines. But nature is intact, and these woods bring to mind mushrooms and blackberries and the damp we'd be sure to find beneath the pine trees.

Pietro is sitting in front. He likes to look at the road and at the cars coming from the other direction. I told him to take my seat.

"That way I can lie down," I said.

But it's not the real reason. I'm not tired.

Diego traveled this same road on his last journey and I want to be able to think about him in peace, to picture him with me as I go around the curves. It's a calm summer morning. We're like the tourists who, weary of the inland sights, head out to the coast because they'd like to take a swim.

We race southward along the Neretva River.

For a long time, Pietro stays quiet and looks attentively out at the road. He knows he's next to a warrior, a veteran. Now he's imagining the ghosts that could emerge from these woods.

He's got his iPod headphones in his ears and an open map of Bosnia-Herzegovina on his lap. Gojko drives with one arm hanging out the window and repeatedly takes the other off the wheel to plunge it into Pietro's bag of cheese snacks or to point something out on the map.

"What are you listening to?"

Pietro takes off one of the headphones and puts it in Gojko's ear.

"Vasco Rossi."

A truck coming from the other direction brushes dangerously close to us. The car is filled with its stink. Gojko doesn't even seem to notice. He's looking at Pietro.

"And who's he?"

Pietro's shocked. "You don't know him?"

"No."

"He's a poet."

Gojko removes the headphone. "He sounds like someone who's sitting on the toilet and having a hard time moving stuff out of his asshole."

"He fills stadiums."

The former Bosnian poet shrugs. "Fuck you. Poets don't fill stadiums."

"Fuck you! Vasco does!"

"What is a poet, in your opinion?"

Pietro laughs and says, "I don't know." Then he turns toward me. "What, are we in school all of a sudden?"

Gojko insists.

"What does a real poem talk about?"

Struggling, Pietro mumbles an answer.

"Things that hurt you . . . but that when you hear them they do you good, too . . . they leave you feeling hungry . . ."

Gojko shouts with joy. "Good!"

Then, abruptly, he asks, "Hungry for what?"

He looks at Pietro, waiting for an answer, and maybe his eyes wear the same expression as when, his finger poised for a silent moment over the trigger, he prepared to kill.

"I don't know . . . a sandwich . . . a girl?"

Pietro laughs a brusque laugh. He'd like to get away from this conversation, which is getting as serious as Gojko's face.

"Forget about the sandwich. Keep the girl."

Pietro nods and I'm sure he's blushing. Gojko waits a bit longer. Then he fires.

"Hungry for love," he says, and now he's the one struggling.

Pietro nods. He knew the answer, but the fact that I'm here made him embarrassed to say it.

"A good poet leaves you hungry for love."

Gojko takes his hand off the wheel to punch Pietro in the stomach.

"Right here. Don't you forget it!"

"Vasco Rossi makes you hungry for love."

Gojko collapses over the steering wheel and mockingly bites at it.

"Jerking off is more like it. He makes you hungry for a hand job!"

I get mad. Another truck brushes near us. The road is narrow now and the rocks beside it plunge into a gorge. Gojko suggests I calm down because he's an excellent driver and that's how you drive on these roads, with your imagination. I tell him I don't give a damn about his Bosnian imagination, I don't want to fall into one of these mountain gorges. I'm scared something might happen to Pietro, some stupid accident like what happened to Diego.

Gojko seeks my eyes in the mirror.

"I already saved the two of you once. Relax."

He winks, and for a moment it seems he still bears some of the malice of war. There's a gleam of spite in his eyes.

The Neretva widens and opens out. Now, instead of a river, it looks like a big crystalline lake. We stop. Cool steam rises up from below.

We're leaning against the railing of a long metal bridge that cuts across the lake. Pietro takes my picture with his cell phone. He asks me to move twice. First there's too much light. Then you can't see the river.

"Where do you want me?"

He makes me back up a few steps but he still doesn't seem satisfied.

His father never asked me to change position. He would take my picture all of a sudden, catching me off guard. He hated for me to pose. His photographs were a slap in the face, a surprise. Now and then I'd simply appear in one of his rolls of film. *I can't leave you alone, I need to come back to you*, he'd say. A thousand times afterward, after he'd left me on my own, in the moments when I felt ugliest and most deprived, I'd think that he would have snapped my picture in that precise moment of inadequacy and then handed me back to myself on a shiny piece of paper, revealing my thoughts: *Look what you're like, Gemma, how you torture yourself, how silly you are.*

We walk for a while along the river. The smell of grilling meat comes from a picnic area full of families with small children. Pietro asks if he can take a picture. A woman offers him a piece of lamb. He shakes his head, then accepts.

"*Hvala!*"

"*Dobar dan!*"

As we get back into the car, Gojko asks Pietro how the lamb is. Pietro licks his fingers. It's good, he says. He holds the piece of meat out to Gojko by the bone.

"Here, try it."

Gojko takes an enormous bite. Pietro gets mad. The two of them bicker for a while like two teenagers, like two hungry growing boys.

Then Gojko lets out a loud fart. Pietro yells, "Sick!"

Unperturbed, Gojko says, "It's a short composition I've been working on."

Pietro laughs like a maniac. Then he concentrates and lets out a terrible fart of his own, even more Bosnian than Gojko's.

"Listen to my sonnet!"

Gojko is red with happiness. "Loose verse!" he cackles as soon as he catches his breath. I yell that I want out of this car, away from these two pigs.

More curves, more silvery gorges like white beards among the trees.

Now my son and my friend are sharing the iPod and Gojko is singing the refrain along with the Italian poet who fills stadiums.

Vivere . . . vivere . . . vivere.

The trees are so tall they close out the sky like curtains closing over this road too narrow for two lanes, where vehicles brush past each other but, in the end, survive.

A dog, a clothesline, a field of lettuce, a country mosque. Landscapes from ordinary life.

The war passed through here, eagles and tigers and former Belgrade Red Star ultras with hooded faces like executioners.

They came along and burned villages, killing the men and raping the women. Nothing but thin ranks of survivors remained to flee along roads leading to other villages that had met the same end. That's the way death moved through here, like a sea breeze. You wonder how they manage to cultivate this land, to plant these rows of tomatoes and cabbages. You wonder whether the hoopoes come out of the woods at night to carry back the cries of dead souls. Dead bodies loaded onto trucks and dumped out like garbage.

Gojko tells us that in the intervening years, the survivors have waited their turn to be called in to identify the remains. Then they've lined up to look at pieces of bones, broken glasses, Adidas sneakers, bits of Rifle and Levi's jeans and Swatch watches.

"These are the dead of our times. They were wearing our brands."

Pietro stops taking pictures.

How long will it take to clean a land where the radiation of evil has penetrated so deeply?

A mere sixteen years have passed. The age of my son, the age of the youthful nape of the neck there in the seat in front of me.

His father used to say that the nape of the neck retains the smell of our birth and of the wind that carried the seed, like a furrow in the ground.

· · ·

We stop in Mostar. Pietro wants to take a picture of the famous bridge. We walk through the alleyways over cobblestones embedded in clay. There's a holiday air, tourists walking along in flip-flops, little boutiques selling knickknacks.

The city is this bridge. They called it The Old Bridge and thought of it as an old friend, a backbone of light-colored stone uniting the two parts of the city, the Christian side and the Muslim side. The Old Bridge lived for five centuries before it was brought down in a handful of minutes.

Pietro doesn't understand why Christians and Muslims fought.

"Weren't they united against the Serbs before that?"

Gojko explains that hatred expands easily, like a hole in a pocket.

"In the end even Muslims fought against Muslims."

We're eating boiled eggs and a tomato-and-cucumber salad at a restaurant with a view of the bridge.

Pietro is telling us about the adventure park he and his friends go to once in a while. They dress in helmets and uniforms to play war with paintballs.

"Do you play on teams?"

"Yes, or sometimes everyone against everyone."

"Just like us, in the end."

Pietro laughs.

The bridge is a masterpiece of UNESCO reconstruction. It has the same single span as the old bridge and they used the same rocks to build it. But it doesn't have the same intention.

Bridges unite men's steps and their thoughts. Lovers meet halfway. But the only people to cross this new bridge are tourists. The citizens of this divided city stay on their separate sides. The bridge is the white skeleton of an illusion of peace.

The muezzin's lament crosses the sky and dark little birds chase after each other. Gojko stands up to go, leaving some money on the table.

"Now they'll start in with the church bells on the other side. They compete to see who can make the most noise."

Pietro wants to watch the boy who jumps for the tourists. He looks a bit like Pietro, thin, with thick hair. He climbs on the balustrade and opens his arms wide like an angel. He concentrates, hamming it up a bit for the public. He wasn't here back then, or if he was, he was a very small child. For him, the bridge is a piece of luck. He jumps off, legs tucked close to his body, and flies nearly thirty meters through the air before entering the waters of the Neretva. For an empty moment the river remains still and dark. Then up pops his head and there's the boy holding his arms high in a V for victory. We applaud along with the other tourists. A little accomplice passes through the crowd with a plate.

Pietro asks if he can try, too. He says he understands the technique. He's already taking off his shoes. That's just what we need. *Get in the car*, I say. *Move it.*

The sun is setting. There's something more painful now about the silhouettes of the trees.

It may have already been night when the boy from Genoa drove through here on his motorcycle with the lights off—easy enough for him because he was used to the dark of Sarajevo. He might have taken paths through the woods. Aska could have been with him, pointing out the shortcuts. For a moment I see them, the sheep hanging on to Diego's body, the body that had made her a mother without a child.

Where were they going? They may have simply been fleeing, without plans, except in their dreams.

Maybe they thought they'd earn money as street musicians. Yes, they'd have lived like refugees in the subway tunnels of the world. Aska would have sung one of her *sevdalinke* full of melancholy and love and blown all her Bosniak pain through her trumpet for passersby and lines of legs on line for tickets. He'd have accompanied her on the guitar and taken her picture every so often to tell her something about herself. Bit by bit, he'd have healed her with his breath.

The house and the life I'd enclosed him in weren't his house and his life. He tried, but he just couldn't do it. One day he'd said to me, "I feel like a dog waiting in a store window for someone to buy me."

Once again she'd have worn her faded Kurt Cobain T-shirt. They'd have traveled by motorcycle and stopped to sleep in campgrounds or in fields or under a portico near a closed cinema, like those wandering artist couples you see on the street selling what they know how to do, throwing juggling pins in the air.

In the summer you come across them and stop to watch while you eat your ice cream. Wandering eyes stare at them out of the random huddle of the crowd . . . a loneliness in the multitude, a song, a caress. That's how Diego and Aska would have lived, without violence, as they chased away the after-taste of hell through a life devoted to the contemplation of itself and through their music.

That was the life he'd have liked, constantly traveling, his only home the lens of his Leica.

They would have stopped in Amsterdam. Aska had musician friends there. They'd have lived in a barge on the river, like we did at first. Yes, they'd have started from a river.

They'd have left a flower beneath the window of the Hotel Prins Hendrik, where Chet Baker fell out of, high on heroin.

Dad said to me, "I didn't think you'd be so strong."

I told him I had to be strong for the baby.

But what I really felt was that Diego's death hadn't actually robbed me of any future. And even now, looking at this road, I don't feel any real emotion apart from a muffled pounding in the pit of my stomach, an annoyance.

They went off without me, hanging on to the motorcycle in the watery darkness of this land that had been crossed by a massacre, like a red sea of slaughtered tuna.

I was the whale, the strong back he'd rested on, like a bird waiting for the wind to return so he could resume his voyage. And before he left, to repay me, he brought me a fish in his beak, a fish he'd gathered for me from the sea.

Now the fish is drowsing with one foot hanging out the window, the other on the dashboard. Gojko tells me to leave him alone, not to be such a pain-in-the-ass of a mother. I ask him, *How much longer?* He replies, *Not much.*

Now the Neretva is descending and the mountains begin to look scorched. The vegetation changes. We see dense clusters of maquis shrubs, sheaves of broom, wild geraniums. The rock is brighter, almost white.

After a few more curves we see the sea.

Blue and boundless like every sea, water flooding your sight, a submerged sky below us. The islands look like rocks and shapes from a broken necklace that came apart without ever really separating from the neck of the earth. The sea—the azure blood of these rocks, these forests.

Pietro is elated. He wants to stop to take pictures. We get out of the car at an overlook.

The salt breeze blows my hair into my face. It's so strong I have to close my eyes. The sun is a perfect ball barely clouded by a bit of haze. Because it's setting, it sits a bit lower in the sky than where we are.

The boy from Genoa probably looked out onto this very bay. At long last he could get off his motorcycle and walk without hiding, without moving in zigzags, without worrying he'd fall.

They won't shoot from the sea, he'd have thought as he hugged his red-haired sheep.

It's over, Aska. You're free.

"Come on, Mom. Let's go!"

Pietro is in a hurry now. He wants a chance to swim before the sun goes down altogether. He stops next to me and observes me as I look down.

He's restless. He recognizes the look on my face.

How many times have the two of us wordlessly observed our life together? The first time, he must have been three years old. We were in the park. A swing hit him and cut his forehead. I dragged him kicking and crying to a fountain. I had to hold him so tight that it hurt. When he managed to free himself, the blood kept flowing. It covered his wet face like a pink mask. He called me *Bitch*. He said *I hate you.*

I let go. *You'll have to apologize.*

He went to sit on a slope next to the bench where I sat. He stayed there a long time, digging into the ground with his shoe. I pretended to read.

In the end I went to him first. *Hurry up. It's late.* It was what he'd been waiting for. He'd been alone in the world until that moment, but his pride had prevented him from coming to me. *Say you're sorry. Sorry.* He was so alone. It was the first time we looked together at the world, at what had been taken from us and what remained.

Diego didn't witness his son's voyage, the ascent through the years of his child growing up. He climbed up a cliff instead. What was he trying to see?

His camera was dented, like his head. It wasn't loaded. He didn't bother loading it anymore. The gesture was enough. His last photograph must have been the river flowing upward as he flew down.

The town down below is ugly, full of cement and traffic. Between the mainland and the Pelješac Peninsula the sea is bordered by the red buoys of oyster farms.

Now the sun is falling. We travel along the coastal road. Every so often it moves inland through fig trees and rosemary bushes. We go through little villages of small white houses inhabited by fishermen, salt-worn church towers like lighthouses, stores selling shoes for the cliffs. We're forced to slow down. There's a line of cars. People stop and greet each other. It's Saturday. Tomorrow is a holiday. We even see a bride and groom. The hoots of the wedding party follow us all the way to the ferry boarding point at the other end of the peninsula.

The last ferry for Korčula has weighed anchor. We see it moving away over the metallic evening sea.

Gojko and I stand on the dock. He's wearing his mirrored sunglasses even though they're pointless now. He even wears them at night. He stands with his sturdy arms akimbo.

It's sad, but only for a moment, to see this ship leaving without us. It moves off without our being able to stop it. All we can do is bid it farewell from afar. Maybe there's something about this ship with the sea in its wake that frees us after all this time, restoring the happiness of something we've lost. Of a mistake. We laugh like two fools. Gojko makes an eloquent gesture as if to say, *Go ahead, ship. Stick it up your ass. Go ahead, life. Stick it up your ass.*

Pietro's taken off his T-shirt. He drops his towel from around his waist. He dives into the sea and comes back out. The white beach beside the dock smells of rosemary. Too bad it's almost dark and the water is full of shadows.

Pietro brings us a crab he's caught. He says it's big enough, we could eat it if we wanted to. But then he turns around and throws it back into the sea.

My son is thin, and he looks even thinner in the evening light.

We sit on the beach and watch him while he swims and for a moment we're a family. Maybe that's because this last night will change destinies. Unexpectedly.

"The two of us could have gotten married," says Gojko, "but you didn't want me." He still hasn't taken off his mirrored glasses.

I laugh and elbow him in the ribs.

"Are you happy with your wife?"

He nods. They have a wonderful daughter and a little restaurant by the sea. The cultural association they founded fills their lives.

"And you?"

I tell him I'm happy with Giuliano.

"I love him," I say.

But it's difficult to say it. I swallow. It seems like an empty phrase, and I barely hear it, maybe because the trip was so long, such a long crossing. Pietro calls to us from the water. "Hey! Aren't you going to come in?"

Gojko leaps to his feet like an athletic bear. He's all sweaty from driving. But who knows, maybe what makes him want to jump into the cold water is the fact that he's sitting beside me tonight, beside this missed ferry that should have brought him back to his wife and his life. Maybe he wants to chase away the torpor of our nostalgia.

And then I jump in, too.

Giuliano would be shocked, because swimming at night is not something I would usually do. I'm afraid of sea urchins and the dark water, afraid a hand will come up and grab me from below. I'm afraid that afterward I'll catch a cold because of my wet hair.

But I'm afraid in Rome. I'm afraid in the life that sailed away with that missed boat. Tonight I'm not afraid. Tonight I want reunion. Pietro climbs up on Gojko's shoulders. He dives with a yell and lands on his belly. Then I climb up, too, and Gojko holds on to my fragile white ankles. I'm old, past fifty. I've never laughed so much.

We find a little restaurant. A string of lights flutters over the bamboo walls of the veranda. We squeeze lemon juice over sea urchins and oysters. Even Pietro eats them. It's the first time he's sucked raw mollusks. Tonight he wants to try everything, the wine, too. It's a dense, dark yellow wine with the flavor of grapes grown beside the sea. Next come little salads and goat cheese covered with paprika. Pietro's mouth is on fire. He goes to get an ice cream from the freezer chugging away like a tractor beside us. Gojko moves the bottle aside to look at me.

"I'm old," I say. "I'm not worth looking at."

"You'll never be old. It's just time unearthing beauty."

The erstwhile poet pours a last drop of wine into my glass, shakes the empty bottle and asks them to bring a dessert wine this time, the *passito* they make on the islands.

We go back to the dock and hang out in the dark. Pietro wanders around like a dog without a leash. He's exhausted but now he says he wants to stay. We can change our tickets. He likes the sea here. He wants to go fishing and rent a windsurf board.

He stands beside the men fishing off the rocks. Their fishing lines stretch tautly into the sea that moves in hard waves. The sea is strong tonight. It looks like a lunar landscape, metallic mud.

There's no talk of finding a hotel. We'll sleep in the car. Pietro gets in and lies down on the backseat. He falls asleep right away, like when he was little, though his legs are too long for the seat. His hands lie folded beneath one cheek. His mouth is open, the upper lip jutting out past the lower one.

Gojko says, "He's a pure boy."

He runs a hand over my salty hair.

"You've done a good job."

"I didn't do anything. It's his nature."

We walk to where the sea begins at the end of the dock and lie down on the rock still warm from the sun. We look at the firmament of stars traveling through a phosphorescent sky.

The ferry departed hours ago and left us here to drink in this sky in peace. Gojko, my brother, Diego's brother, a Christian Croat, a crazy Saint Joseph, Pietro's putative father. Tonight we are the foolish children of the *passito*. We're warm algae, specters of flesh, visions from the past.

But to make love now would be like making love to finished lives and spurned hopes. To make love now would require a courage we don't have. Not with that pure son sleeping just a few yards away.

We fall asleep on the front seats of the car with our feet hanging out. My Gojko snores with his mouth open. I take his glasses off for him and kiss his red, sweaty forehead.

My dear, I say. *My dear. My dear*, because one day life will be taken from us all.

Chapter 20

The next day the sky is so bright it's like a slap in the face. Pietro keeps to himself on the ferry. He sits barefoot on a bench slippery with salt, his Ray-Bans shielding his face and one arm resting on a bent leg. It's an unusual position for him, a man looking out at the sea.

The port is a whirl of recently built red-roofed houses, noisy traffic, tourist traps flanked by racks of flip-flops and bathing suits, neon signs for bars and restaurants and other signs advertising Sobe, rooms for rent. We drive up out of the village on the panoramic route, with its curves that cut through the rocks and descend on the other side of the island.

The cultural association is housed in a big Venetian-style villa that feels like an old family home. It has light-colored walls, chipping here and there to reveal a pink undercoat as pale as flesh. There are fragile window frames, a tall doorway with a pointed arch and a French window that opens out onto a veranda with a wrought-iron railing. We walk over a mix of sand and gravel through a cheerful yard cluttered with children's toys and wooden easels bearing photographs and drawings. The air is festive, like at a village fair. A group of women work over a big table, pulling the threads of an enormous set of bobbins. They smile at me as I draw near, and then move aside so I can see the endless piece of lace they're working on.

Gojko introduces me. "This is my friend Gemma. She's here from Rome. And this is her son, Pietro."

Pietro allows all these mothers to kiss him and asks questions about their work, how long it's taken them to make the giant peace symbol. A girl explains that there's a lily for every child killed by the war. They weren't the ones to decide how big this sheet of flowers would be.

A woman clad in chic sunglasses and black linen moves toward me. She's talking on her cell phone. When she finishes her conversation she pats me on the shoulder.

"How are you?"

It's Ana. She asks if I recognize her and I say no, I wouldn't have known

her. She looks like an actress. But then we hug and I look at her again and realize that of course I recognize her.

She's married to a dentist. She works as his receptionist. They weren't able
to have children because of the treatments she had to undergo—*rays*, she
says, *but not from the sun*. Because Ana had a problem *afterwards*. Like many
women. *Afterwards*.

She and Gojko always stayed in touch. There are a lot of women from
Sarajevo here. Ana introduces them. I recognize some, aging faces from my
generation, the old girls from Sarajevo, from the communal house, girls who
before the war wore black miniskirts and listened to R.E.M. and Bosnian rock
and swapped boyfriends because it made them feel like they were part of
Europe.

Pitchers of homemade drinks have been set out on a table. Ana and I sit
together on a swing chair and drink blueberry juice like two vacationers from
another era.

Ana tells me about the association. After the war, women of different eth-
nicities joined forces to help other women. In the summer they organize film
screenings, photo exhibits, concerts and readings. In the winter they offer
vocational training courses—computer literacy, languages. There are dance
and music lessons.

She points to a beautiful girl with long black hair and extraordinarily
white skin. Her name is Vesna.

"One day she recognized her father in a film clip on TV. He was one of the
butchers of Srebrenica. Vesna didn't speak for six years after that. Her mother
left her father and came to us with her mute daughter. The day Vesna began
speaking again we all cried. We were on the beach. The first word she said was
sidro, which in our language means 'anchor.' And so Sidro became the name
of the association."

Gojko points out a building set close to the beach. It's made up of white
cubes with red shutters and flat roofs with drains for rainwater. The terrace is
rimmed with low flower boxes full of geraniums twisted by the wind.

"Here is where I live."

An unlit sign bearing the word RESTORAN hangs from the wall that
encloses the yard. We enter through a little wooden gate in the back that

looks like it's always open. We walk along a cement lane. Beneath a green cor-
rugated roof I see a little bicycle and a sun-faded Piaggio moped with stuffing
coming out of its seat. There are jars of preserves, cases of mineral water and
beer and a big keg made of blackened metal.

A little girl's bathing suit and a limp air mattress hang on the laundry line.
A few steps farther along we see a pile of empty flowerpots and a plaster Snow
White, her arms held wide in welcome.

Pietro asks where the seven dwarves are.

Gojko says his daughter didn't want them. She hates them. She calls them
old kids.

On the terrace, a barefoot young woman wearing a gauzy shirt over her
bathing suit and pigtails in her hair is fastening clips to the iron tables to hold
down the tablecloths.

"*Zdravo*, Gojko."

"*Zdravo*, Nina."

He kisses her hello, pulls on one of her pigtails and asks her to bring us
something to drink.

We sit outside beneath the roof of reed mats. Below us the sea is a blue
strip infused with light. A mild breeze comes up off the dunes behind us. The
girl returns with a tray and sets out a carafe of wine and a can of Coca-Cola
for Pietro as well as bowls of olives, little green peppers and sunflower seeds.

Gojko comes back with a little girl wrapped around him like an octopus.

All I can see as she hides against her father are her two legs, a pair of
striped terry-cloth shorts and a head of curls so blond they're almost white.

"This is Sebina."

Gojko doesn't look at me and I don't look at him. I look at the table, at an
ant walking across the waxed tablecloth. The pain is sharp and brusque, like
when you hit your elbow.

"Hello . . . Sebina."

I rub her leg. It's thin, too thin. I think of those stocky legs full of little
muscles.

Pietro tries to tickle her. She wriggles and kicks her legs but she doesn't
show her face.

"She was sleeping." Gojko sits down with his daughter in his arms and
refills our wine glasses.

We drink with this faceless little girl between us.

"It's beautiful here."

"It's simple."

Gojko tells me about the menu, the mixed grills they do in the evening. He does the fishing himself. Pietro can go with him to catch squid tonight if he wants. They have a few rooms to rent to tourists looking for a quiet place to stay.

The whole time he's talking he's rubbing his daughter's head. It's hard for me to watch his heavy hand as it passes hungrily through the blond curls.

A curtain flaps in the breeze at one of the open windows, a white curtain that swells and breathes like a little sail.

I watch that peaceful, reassuring white breathing. It bears the message that time has passed and remade itself, leaving seeds and new hair.

Summery music wafts out from inside.

The little girl is no longer hiding her face. She's looking at Pietro.

She doesn't look anything like Sebina. She's beautiful, with clear eyes and a light tan. She has full lips and the fixed gaze dolls sometimes wear. Sebina's eyes were the color of lead. Her lips were crooked as a fishhook. Her ears jutted out through her hair.

Pietro sticks out his tongue and wriggles his eyebrows and ears, just like his grandfather Armando.

The little girl laughs. She's missing a front tooth. She lost it the night before. She shows us the hole. She doesn't speak Italian but she knows a bit of English. She tells us she's sad because she can't find the tooth anymore. Pietro says that if she wants they can go look for it together.

The little girl slides away from her father's body and gives Pietro her hand. I watch them as they move away, my son and this second Sebina who doesn't look like a child from Sarajevo. She could be Dutch or German, a little tourist.

How old would my Bijeli Biber be today? Would she be wearing an Olympic medal around her neck or would she have become a chain-smoker like her brother?

I should feel some tenderness for this new child. I thought I'd be moved, but instead I feel defeated, even angry. Maybe the wine has gone straight to my head. Maybe it's beating hard against my hard heart. But I'm not convinced that this child, this second Sebina, has anything to do with rebirth. She's another child. It's another life. I'm not interested in this vapid and beautiful little girl. I want that crooked snout, the thoughts and the wretched courage it concealed. Today I feel fond of all that I've lost, all that I'll never see again.

"She's beautiful, isn't she?"

She's too beautiful. There's something about her that strikes a false note, just like the rest of this *afterwards* life.

Inside there's a smell I recognize, the smell of a simple seaside home, a smell of oregano, clean laundry and almonds.

A few of the child's drawings hang on the wall, with her signature, *SEBINA*, traced out in her still-novice hand.

I brush past the cool wall in the corridor and then the blue-edged back of a chair.

Now it seems like Gojko's pushing me forward.

I stumble over a low step and enter a little den furnished with two peeling leather armchairs, a magazine rack and the old portrait of Tito on the wall.

"It's the only thing that stayed in one piece." He laughs. "Everything caught fire, but the old marshal made it through, so I brought him along with us."

His eyes look red. His shirt, open to the waist, is damp.

"I have to tell you something."

Behind him, on a low bamboo table, there's a picture of him on a little boat and beside it a photo Diego took of Mirna and Sebina. I turn. A glass door separates this little den from another room. I see a window, a curtain moving in the breeze. It's the pale gauze curtain I saw from outside.

Gojko is smoking. He inhales and then studies the little embers that fall off his cigarette as he rubs it back and forth along the edge of the ashtray he's holding.

I sense something, a presence, I couldn't say what, something warm and slightly oppressive.

"What, Gojko?"

There's something strange in his expression; I back up, but he grabs me and holds me from behind, cutting off my breath with an arm. Maybe that's what he used to do when he held a terrified body with one arm and with the other broke its neck.

I feel his breath in my ear.

"Forgive me. I wanted to tell you the first night."

What do you have to tell me, you fool? What do you have to tell me that life hasn't told me already?

I step into the room. I see a pair of espadrilles thrown to one side and then the feet of the woman who's been waiting for me.

She's wearing a white shirt and a pair of jeans. Her hair is held up with a pencil. She's much taller than I remember, or maybe I've shrunk. She's not wearing makeup. She hasn't aged a bit. The years have simply granted her a composure she lacked before.

"Hi, Gemma."

"Hi, Aska."

I raise my arm in a slow, heavy movement that parts the air, divides the world. I let my hand sit in hers.

Go ahead and hold my hand. I don't know what to do with it. I think to myself that this may be the last movement I'll ever make. This tall woman with red hair and green eyes is beautiful, like a model just beginning to age. She's held on to the essence of beauty and no longer wears the silly patina of youth. I feel like an animal that has fallen into a trap to await death, motionless but alert.

The woman is inviting me to sit down beside her.

I don't hear her. It's as if the sound had been switched off. The movement of the curtain is all that remains.

Aska opens her mouth. She has beautiful teeth. My eyes take them in along with the rest of her beauty.

There's no longer any trace of her old, untidy look. What did I remember? A person who no longer exists, a girl disfigured by makeup who played the trumpet and whose laugh was just a little too loud.

I've imagined her dead so many times.

I've also imagined her alive, but not like this. The confused imaginings of a suffering and superficial woman.

So she and Gojko are married. Aska's telling me about how they met in Paris after the war, at the house of mutual friends, in one of those clusters of Bosnian refugees. They helped each other. Love came later.

"Do you still listen to Nirvana?"

"Sometimes."

"Kurt Cobain died."

"Yes. It was a while ago."

"He shot himself. It takes a lot of courage to shoot yourself."

"Not if you're high."

Diego's dead, too. He was high, too. Yes, the foolish wolf dies while the cunning sheep saves herself by dancing.

Nirvana's last album was called *In Utero*. I remember buying it. Life is absurd. It leads you on and fucks with you.

The curtain moves. I'm not listening to anything. Something's cracking inside me. A clean bloodless wound splits me in two.

It was a trick, the whole trip, everything: the photo exhibit, the walks through Sarajevo, the missed ferry.

This woman is simple and elegant and bears herself like a woman of today.

Now she'll tell me she never stopped thinking about her son, that she has a right to embrace him, to tell him the truth.

And I won't be able to say no. There's nothing I can do. I don't know the laws of this country. I'm far from home. I don't even remember the name of this little village. I boarded a ferry, lethargic with nostalgia. I followed a stranger, a man I know nothing about, a poet who became a warrior, a killer. I needed friends and memories. My life wasn't enough for me. I needed someone to force me to suffer, a witness, someone else who was there. I came back here on my own, of my own free will.

Gojko smiles at her and holds her hand. Beside her he's handsomer and less awkward. He seems more sensual, calmer.

They didn't come to look for me in Italy. They made me come all the way here. She must have said, *I want my boy. I want to see him. I want to see the son of the man I loved, the man who died. I can't stand it anymore. I've thought about this a long time. Now I want to hug him and tell him the truth, come what may.*

I need to call Giuliano. I need him to come. I have to protect Pietro. I have to stay whole.

"You don't trust me?"

"What do you want?"

"To see him."

"Look out the window and you'll see him."

"I saw him talking with Sebina . . . with his sister."

"Shut up. Shut up."

She cries, but now I could kill her because I catch a glimpse of something, a muddy foundation, the smell of a misery I recognize.

"You need money. Is that what this is all about?"

She opens her mouth and shakes her head, hard. She seems desperate.

"Don't insult me."

The curtain moves in the window. Only a gecko looks at us, its ancient transparent body motionless on the wall.

"Why weren't you the one to die?"

She looks at me without any surprise.

"I don't know."

I stand and pull my skirt away from my ass. Where's my jacket, my crumpled jacket? Where's my purse full of rubbish, passports, plane tickets, the lipstick that runs into the little wrinkles around my mouth? She asks me if I want some grapes, if I want to take a shower. Pietro and I can sleep here. We can eat fish on the beach. Gojko does a wonderful job with the grill.

All of a sudden I feel an unspeakable hatred, a distance that is immediately hatred. *Fuck you. You ate my life, you whore. You ate the best part of me. You took away Pietro's father. He's dead and you're here. You've been here all along.* I gather up my purse, my glasses, my petty old age. A year ago when I went into menopause I couldn't have cared less. My cycle never did me any good. The end of the blood was the end of my anger toward myself.

When I left this woman during the siege, she was counting marks on a hospital bed. Early on, I was terrified she'd reappear. I gave money to all the beggar women in the world, every refugee from the East at every intersection. It became an automatic reflex to turn around to find my purse on the backseat. To keep paying. I imagined her dead. I imagined her in one of those photographs of coffins, of fields sewn with tombstones. Instead, this woman in this white shirt is beautiful. She's still young, still able to have children.

"Pietro is Italian. He's my son. In a moment I'm going to leave. I'm going to take him by the hand and leave. Don't try to touch me. Don't try to touch us."

Aska lowers her head. I look at the nape of her neck, her upswept hair, a few wayward tendrils, and see something. A mark. I want to leave, like that other time. Instead I linger over that mark. It's a tattoo, some kind of flower, reddish and clumsy.

Then Diego's photograph comes to mind, the one tucked into the back of the show, above the umbrella stand. That strange rose on that strange wall. Now I know it wasn't a wall.

Aska covers the nape of her neck with her hand and rocks back and forth a bit.

A bee comes in the window. It flies away from us and comes back. You'd think we'd brush it away, but instead we stay right where we are.

So this is the story, and maybe one day I'll have the courage to tell it to my son, like a fable.

The two of them are there in that inn that overlooks the woods. They climbed the stairs hand in hand. Aska is wearing a shiny black dress. He said, *Don't come wearing all those spikes, they make you look like a cactus.* She obeyed. She's wearing the dress she wears for concerts. As they climb the stairs he looks at the lightweight fabric resting on her skin.

Hers is a beauty from that part of the world: thick copper-colored hair, green eyes like two leaves, wide cheekbones, a straight and slightly squashed nose. She's like her city, which is part Istanbul and part mountain village. She looks like a white Arab woman with the profile of a Kashmir goat.

Diego doesn't know what will become of them.

He's agitated, though he pretends not to be. He likes this pathetic, provincial girl. She's a little off her head, what with her overwhelming desire to see herself as someone important, a Janis Joplin. She reminds him of himself. He knows the feeling, the pathetic thrill . . . the Leica he bought at the thieves' market . . . he used to feel like Robert Capa when he was a kid.

She's struck a chord in him with her makeup-smeared face, the postmodern holes in her tights, her safety-pin earrings. He doesn't like punks, but she's struck a chord. He started to observe her, saw her stuff herself with sweets down to the last crumb and then lick her fingers clean. He saw her laugh. They've talked, and he knows she's not stupid. Her head is full of nonsense but there's a light shining in there, a battery that's always charged. She's got something he no longer has.

When they get to the room Aska looks at the bed and laughs. She dives onto it, raises her arms and takes a deep breath. She brazenly seeks his admiring gaze. She likes this game. Diego doesn't feel quite so relaxed. He says they'll start with their shoes and takes off his boots. Then he sits on the edge of the bed without lying down. He's still incredulous she even came, incredulous that this story is moving forward.

Over the last few days they've begun to look at each other differently. They've gone through a sort of courtship. Now that they're in this room where practically the only piece of furniture is a bed, they feel a little shy. She sits cross-legged. She's brought her trumpet and she starts to play "My Funny Valentine." He listens to her and thinks, *How much air is there in those lungs, little girl?* He says, *You have a future.* She pulls the trumpet away from her mouth, licks her lips and says, *I'd like to have it with you.*

He smiles. *Cut it out. Don't kid around.*

I'm not kidding around. Couldn't we pretend we have a future for just this night?

There's too much air in her lungs. This girl is too bold. He looks at her. *Don't forget your place.*

She's never remembered her place. She's always been a rebel. That's why she's here.

They lie down next to each other and talk for a while. He shows her how the camera works, how to use the focus knob. He stretches out his arm to take a picture of their faces sunk into the pillow. Aska pulls her legs up like a monkey's. She wants to foot-wrestle. She's tired of the sadness of these days. She went to the peace march. There's a peace symbol on her forehead. Her friend Haira drew it for her. She hollers that tonight she wants to have a crazy fun time. Diego gives in, raises his long legs, bends them and puts his feet against Aska's. They wrestle for a while on the bed. Then they stop. He looks at her eyes, her mouth, the rise and fall of her chest.

Up close she's incredibly beautiful, incredibly young. Before he kisses her he smiles. Then he stays inside her lips for a long time. Aska's mouth is fresh as a spring. He feels her breath change, tastes the first time he ever kissed a woman. Now he's a grown man and that memory is overwhelming and full of self-consciousness.

A bit sad, he pulls away from her. He's the shyer one and the older of the two. She's got the upper hand. He'd like to give her some fatherly or brotherly advice, the way he does with his students at the photo school. Instead he's here to make love to her. She's a free-spirited girl. She's the one who offered to rent her body. Now he's both excited and a little humiliated by this extravagant and erotic situation.

He packed too much passion, too much longing, into that kiss. He looks at her, caresses her head, sighs, thinks a bit.

She's a mischievous little Sarajevan. *Don't you like me?* she whispers.

You know I like you. And maybe I'd like another life. Maybe I'd like to grab my backpack and run away like when I was a kid. Hold another body tight against me in the dark, welcome a chance gift as if it were destiny.

He's tried so hard, but tonight Diego's tired of the flatness of his life, tired of all the hard work and nothing to show for it.

He looks at the dark window and thinks of me and of our pact. He wonders how we've managed to move so far away from ourselves, to slide into this motionless, reasoned folly.

So are we going to make this baby or what? Aska teases him. She's taken her dress off. She's wearing striped tights and a heavy black bra like a little corset. His eyes linger over her white stomach.

She shares a name with a crazy sheep from a story he's never read. As a joke she says, *Baaa baaa*. He answers, *Baaa*.

Let's smoke a joint.

They smoke in silence, passing the wet paper back and forth. The smoke loosens them up. She touches his face, his sparse, spiky little beard like a parched field. He says, *I know, my beard is ugly*. She says, *I like it*. Her hand is like a little rake running through the hairs.

He studies her from up close, her high white forehead. Now she reminds him of a painting of the Madonna he saw in church when he was a child and of a junkie in Piazza Corvetto who looked like a Madonna. He has no idea where taste in women comes from. Maybe it's because you're reminded of someone, a more beautiful mother.

He remembers, too, all the fucking candles his mother made him light for his father beneath that Madonna who was too beautiful and too dead to look at.

Aska sucks on one of his earlobes. He laughs. He doesn't have a technique for being with a woman. He knows how to be with me, knows to snuggle his fist into my armpit because I like to sleep that way.

She once said to him, *When your wife looks at me it's like a farmer choosing a cow for his bull.* He looked at her. *I'm not a bull.*

It's irritating to have a love-struck girl fluttering around you. He's given her advice, told her not to throw herself away, to concentrate on her music, on her future, to give up on all those *maudit* legends and junkie musicians. One day he took her picture in an empty cage at the zoo and a wave of longing assailed him, an open hunger. He didn't take any more pictures. He said, *Get out of the cage. Move it.*

I love my wife.

She laughed. *You make it sound like a life sentence. You seem sad.*

She's got all of Bosnia in her eyes—its melancholy, its crazy humor, even its rivers, which sound as they fall through their natural valleys as if someone were being slapped by God.

They've finished the joint. It leaves a strong taste in their mouths. Diego smiles and stands and drinks directly from the sink. He thinks of me, alone on those dark streets. He follows my footsteps, my back. He'd like to tap me on the shoulder. He'd like to have his tight torero pants and the little green chair from his childhood so he could sit down in the middle of the road and say to me, *I'm here. Do you want me?*

Did you fuck her?

No, I couldn't do it.

It doesn't matter.

I'm not a bull.

I know.

You're the bull. I'm the dust.

There's a lot of commotion down in the street, like a bunch of boxes falling. A good smell wafts up the stairs. They're frying *krofne* for the next morning's breakfast. She says, *Go downstairs and get me some. I'm hungry.*

Diego hops barefoot down the stairs, his shirt open over his tingling chest. He's stoned. He feels lighter. He can feel his body. It's been a long time since he felt it. He's down the two flights of stairs in a handful of seconds.

He doesn't even have time to realize what's happening. The cups in the breakfast room are all on the ground, the tables overturned. Shadows move through the dark, kicking things and yelling. It's just a glance, just one trip around the room with his eyes. The door to the outside is open. He hears other shouts outdoors and then the deaf noise of a machine gun blast, so close he thinks they've seen him, thinks they're about to shoot at him. A hole of silence, then more shouts and gun blasts and the sudden clucking of the frightened chickens and another noise like cans falling and rolling.

Diego is there in the semidarkness. Attracted by the sweet smell, he's come downstairs to get some *krofne*. He'd been about to make love. What he now sees through the dark is too far from the softness of his body, too hard. He doesn't understand what's happening. He thinks they're thieves. He takes two steps toward the kitchen. There's a shotgun pressing against the innkeeper's belly and a puddle of still-frying oil moving across the black floor. Now he sees the camouflage uniforms and the ski masks. *It's the war. It's here.* It's the last clear thought to pass through his mind.

After that it's as if a dike had broken, water as hard as metal submerging everything. He's nothing but instinct from that point on. If they were to ask him his name and why he's there he wouldn't be able to answer. He retraces his steps without turning and trips on the stairs. His eyes cut through the dark like a night visor. Like a crab left out in the open, he touches the wall as he climbs. He sinks into the first hole he finds, the broom closet covered by a plastic curtain.

For the moment, that plastic feels like a lifesaver, because he's already seen the first dead body. There's a man sprawled on the stairs now, an old man in wool pants. Diego saw the boy shoot him in the neck. The boy had pushed up his ski mask to eat one of the warm *krofne*. The old man raised his arms and said, *My son, my son.*

The broom closet is on the landing, just a few steps below the hallway. From the crack in the curtain, Diego can see the half-closed door to their room. It would take just a few steps to reach Aska, but he can't move. The bridge is broken. Those few steps are hard water, a flood that holds him back.

Aska is waiting for the *krofne*. She may not have heard anything. He sees her come to the door. She's put her dress back on, her shiny black concert dress. He can't see all of her, just her legs and a bit of cloth. He'd like to yell to her to close the door, to hide, to escape through the window overlooking the woods. He tries to open his mouth to speak and swallows salt. He has no voice. His vocal cords are hard strips, iron wires that don't vibrate. It's instinct that tells him to be quiet, to hold his breath, because in the meantime a black herd passes by on its way up the stairs along with the smell of frying from the oil spilled on the floor.

Mountain boots with heavy rubber soles devour the stairs. A passing hand momentarily sinks into the plastic of the curtain where he's hiding.

Everything happens too quickly to be able to say, *That's what happened.* He'll retain fragments, bits of images that won't go away, bits that will stay on him like his skin. Fear is an anesthetic that freezes and dilates.

Everything happens for him through that crack, that opening between the curtain and the wall. He sees the men split up in the hallway, hears them knocking on the doors, hears gun bursts and falling glass. They've reached Aska now. He sees something of her, her feet in her striped tights. He hears her yell.

Aska's seeing the wolves for the first time. She moves backward toward the window. She wonders where they came from, if they came down from the woods. They look like death in their ski masks. They speak her language and ask for her ID. They fill the room with their bodies, made bulkier by double cartridge belts crisscrossed over their chests. One of them kicks the only chair in the room, then sits legs wide on the table. She assumes he's the commander. On his chest there's a badge with a skull. He lights a cigarette and smokes it through the mouth slit in his ski mask as he looks at her. Aska is a rebel sheep and her fear makes her aggressive. She asks who they are and why their faces are covered. She says she wants to speak to the police.

The commander raises his ski mask to reveal a young, square-jawed face and light-colored eyes like glass. He turns to laugh with the chubby man beside him.

All Diego can see are their moving feet, their shoes below the camouflage pants. He sees things falling, a drawer, the chair where his jacket was hanging. They're hitting her. He can hear her yell and try to defend herself. Now she's whimpering. She's fallen on the ground. He sees a hand slide across the floor, then a mountain boot crushing it. He hears a voice ordering her to stand back up.

Diego has to leave his hiding place, has to defend her. He has to say, *I'm an*

Italian photographer and this is my girlfriend. Leave us in peace. It might be enough to threaten them with the press card in his jacket pocket. He has to get to that jacket. He imagines himself stepping out of the closet, taking Aska by the arm and brandishing his press card like a cross.

They're asking her why she's at the inn. They've taken her ID and now they're calling her a Muslim whore.

Stand up, Muslim whore.

Aska stands up. It feels like nails are going through her hand. She can't close it all the way. She understands that there are no police anymore. There is no order. This is war—the shots from the street, the noises from the other rooms, the shouts. She realizes there are no lights outside the windows. They must have cut the electric wires. She hears the cries of other people trapped like her, surprised out of their sleep in the normality of that outlying neighborhood. She has no way of knowing if it's just an isolated attack or if the whole city has been occupied. She can't know if the same thing is happening to everyone, like in a blackout. If it's happening to her friend Haira, her grandmother, her little brother. She can feel her perceptions widening, dilating, traveling across kilometers like an animal's. She has to sense the world around her so as not to remain isolated in this room, in this confused and dirty nightmare. The sweet smell of the *krofne* mingles with the smell of the men. They stink of earth, sweat, alcohol. They must be afraid, too. They're agitated. They come and go, kicking in the doors. She can hear a woman's hoarse cries like the mewling of a cat. Maybe it's one of the students from Zenica she heard joking in the hallway a few minutes earlier. They'd come by train for the peace demonstration. She sees something moving along the hallway, a body dragged along by the hair. She doesn't let herself wonder about it, just lets these images that seem to come from another world flow by her. She knows she will not yell. She still believes speaking to them will be enough to calm them. They're a bunch of boys. They can't be much older than she is.

She wonders where Diego is. Maybe they've stopped him. She waits for him to appear. He's a foreign photographer. These imbeciles are afraid of the foreign press.

The commander is looking at something, perhaps a map of the city. He's plotting with the chubby guy. He looks at her and asks her to play the trumpet. Aska tries, though she can't feel her fingers. She pushes what little breath is left in her chest through that brass beak.

Diego hears the trumpet and imagines Aska's cheeks swelling up like a fish's.

She forces herself to play something happy, a little symphony punctuated with high notes like in an old silent film. Here she is before the wolf, just like the sheep in Andrić's story. She, too, is a rebel, far from the flock. She truly hopes that her trumpet-playing will keep the wolf at bay. But she knows she's not that good.

She sees her future, the future she'd imagined, a stage invaded with light bubbles and smoke rising up like steam, just like in a Nirvana concert.

The Italian photographer looks like Kurt Cobain. She pictures his neck. It's the sweetest image that comes to mind, the kiss from a few minutes ago, his face so near her own, smiling at her. Afterward he traced over her mouth with his thumb as if to mark her lips. Maybe he feels something for her, too.

The commander tells her to cut it out with that screeching trumpet. It's true, fear has devoured all her breath and all she can produce are spitting sounds. He orders her to take off her clothes.

Diego is behind the crack. He sees the trumpet fall. He sees Aska in her striped tights jump, then trip. He sees them pull her up.

There's a gun on the bed—a Kalashnikov, a bazooka, who knows? She wonders where she is and whether this is really happening. They planted the gun between her breasts, they fired against the wall to make her obey and she stood immobile, watching them. She'd like to be able to take off her clothes, to obey them, but she no longer knows where her arms are, her hands. They're like the oars of a boat that has been left to rot. She has to reach back to open the hooks. The cloth is stuck to her with the same sweat that blurs her vision. Two hands tear her bra. Aska sees a nipple through the broken cloth and can't say whether it belongs to her or to another woman, her mother, a friend.

She realizes that there's no salvation. Death is there with her, hovering over the guns as they point at her. She has no intention of rebelling. She wants to live. She's still present, though she can no longer move, though she hasn't even raised an arm to defend herself. She senses that this thing has happened before, that it's not random, that it's something these men have already done.

They don't even seem aroused. There's no confusion. The gestures seem too practiced. They insult her and slap her without much conviction, as if they were already tired.

As if it were a rite repeating itself, a satanic rite, a sad meal for devils.

As a child in the country, Aska saw the castrator, the man who came to remove animals' testicles. He was short and carried a little folding stool and a briefcase. He wore a vest like a doctor's. He bent below the animals and mutilated them. Awe-inspiring bellows emerged from the depths of their shaken bodies. The castrator never changed expression. At day's end he took his pay and left with his sad face, the nape of his neck sweaty and dirty and his mouth still greasy from the testicle fricassee the woman had cooked and shared with him.

These men have the same ferocious composure. Their gestures have the same ineluctable sadness. Where did they get their training? On what bodies?

She feels something wet on her legs and imagines herself falling to the ground, melting along with her urine. This is what she wishes for, to leave, to become liquid, to slide beneath the bed, to disappear beneath the wooden floor. Moments earlier she was free. There's a peace symbol on her forehead. One of the men spat on it and the spit dripped into her eyes. She wonders what's become of peace. Moments earlier she was more courageous than many girls and now she's a hole, a crater inhabited only by fear. How can this be happening to her? Her panic bears the burnt flavor of her gastric juices. It's as if all her organs had shifted upward toward her throat as a defense against the ambush. She doesn't feel a thing down below, as if they'd given her an anesthetic, as if the hands grabbing her and the fingers pressing into her skin were touching a distant body.

They dump her on the bed where moments earlier she and Diego were foot-wrestling. The cartridge belts fall on top of her along with the smell of metal and death.

Diego no longer hears Aska playing the trumpet. He's crushed among the brooms. An old-fashioned one made of twigs scratches his cheek. He smells mildew and worn and dirty straw. He sees her stumble as she limps in her striped tights that hang around her legs like a bag. He has to leave that den of brooms, throw himself upon the men in camouflage, rip their ski masks off their heads. But by now he knows he won't leave the broom closet. He may never get out of the inn alive, but there's no way he'll manage to drag himself out of this hole in the wall. He wonders whether this hole will be his coffin, whether they'll shoot him without even opening the curtains, like in a film.

He's used to hiding.

When his father hit his mother he managed to disappear. He'd slide into some crevice and cover his ears. He was calm. He'd pee his pants without even noticing and look at all the little yellow puddles forming on the floor. He'd remove himself by thinking of a *beautiful thing*. He wouldn't come out again until everything was back in its place and his mother was in the kitchen beating eggs. He'd smile at her so she would understand that there was no reason for her to suffer or feel ashamed, because he hadn't seen anything, just the beautiful thing.

Now he knows what the beautiful thing is. It's Aska's mouth moments earlier when he kissed it, fresh and cool like a mountain spring. He pulled away out of shyness. He'd spied the bit of white flesh where her breasts rose with the cleft in between them like on a loaf of bread and he'd felt the way he used to feel as a child when, finding himself in a lovely dream, he'd pull the covers over his head to move more deeply into it.

He sees a hiking boot on the bed and a white leg open like a chicken wing. He turns it into a photograph. He sees the shot, the white leg and the black boot. The sheep and the wolf. Now he knows he can't come out. He's a witness. They wouldn't let him go.

His heart beats like a fist banging vainly on a door. The door of courage refuses to open for him tonight.

They drag her off the bed and onto the floor. Diego sees that body being dragged around like a wheelbarrow and burrows deeper into the hole. At the beginning the curtain seemed like a shelter. Now he knows it would have been better to die on the stairs. He closes his eyes and hears the blows, again and again, and the wheelbarrow banging against the wall.

Aska is thinking about her mother and the last time she saw her alive, when she made stuffed cabbage. Aska thinks about the smell that filled the kitchen. Her brother was watching MTV. She stayed to eat with them at the little table in front of the television. They laughed. Aska's mother had become more irritable since Aska left home, but she seemed happier that day. Aska left her some money, hugged her tight from behind, felt the flesh around her waist.

Aska tastes the flavor of that sweetness. She's removed herself in self-defense. She hears the distant noise of childhood memories. The bridge she crossed to get to the music school. A plow furrowing a field, its blades dividing the clods. She knows that field is her body, the noise of her head as it bangs against the wall when they shove against her.

Her father stopped speaking to her after she showed up at home dressed like a punk. She found a job so she could support herself. Then, some good luck: the opportunity to rent out her womb for a mountain of deutschmarks. She looks at her trumpet on the ground and wonders where the sparse beard of the sad young husband is, where his eyes are and whether they're watching her.

Diego was a junkie years before. Now he sees depressing images of drool-covered bodies sprawled on the ground. It happened to him once, too. He was saved by a miracle. The ambulance arrived just in time to administer an injection straight to his heart. He huddles among the brooms. It feels like he's never left that sidewalk in Brignole.

In the distance he sees the white foot squirm.

Aska's on the floor between the bed and the window. She wasn't even granted the consolation of fainting. She remained lucid to take in all that pain without reprieve. He didn't lift a finger to defend her. It didn't make sense to let them kill him, shoot him in the head, in the mouth. He presses back as far as he can among the dusty brooms so as not to see. He covers his ears so as not to hear her cries.

It's nearly morning when the wolves leave. They go back to the hills with their jeeps and their cartridge belts. As they go they fire parting shots at the dawn.

Diego saw the shadows go down the stairs. Aska was standing. She passed by him as they pushed her along. He thought he saw her velour dress and her trumpet. Maybe none of what he saw had really happened.

Diego lets time pass. He waits until the silence becomes hard and still, waits for it to swallow up the cries, the evil that's just exploded out of the ground. He feels the rape in his bones, his anus, his spleen. All of his organs are out of place, flesh beating inside his brain.

He didn't lift a finger. When Aska passed by him it was as if he were made of stone.

He leaves his hiding place, the curtain that hid him but did not separate him from the evil. He's not dead, but he's not completely alive. His legs are stiff. His eyes are about to fall from his head. They capture images that slide into his stomach as if into a cesspit. He looks into the room, smells the odor they've left behind, a furnace of organic emanations and nicotine. The sheets with the boot prints, the overturned chair, the bits of mud. He gathers up his jacket and his camera and goes downstairs.

He hears someone singing. It's Anela, downstairs, the owner of this inn for students and traveling salesmen that's been transformed overnight into a whorehouse for devils. The woman is crouching to gather the remains of the cups from beneath the tables that she's already returned to their places. She doesn't throw the fragments away. She rubs them against her apron and lines them up on the breakfast bar like archaeological remains.

Diego observes with shock this harvest of shards. As accompaniment to her madness the woman sings a peaceful harvest song.

She barely raises her eyes to look at this boy, bare-chested beneath his shirt. She takes a step backward. For a moment she thinks he's one of the devils.

Diego asks her what happened to the girls, where they've been taken.

The woman shakes her head. She doesn't know. She has a husband to bury, the old man dead on the stairs. She covers her head with a scarf and the two of them go out to the yard. The chickens are all dead, their bodies scattered over the grass. The devils shot at them for fun, to try out their new weapons. Diego watches the wind move through the feathers.

He wanders off through the bluish, underwater light and steps into the first open building he comes across. He's not sure whether it's a movie theater or a church. He simply sees the dark benches, lies down and falls asleep. He dreams of the heroin rush, of that climax when his blood melted and his nerves became docile wires. The thorns left his body, the pores of his skin expanded and a warm sea flooded the channels. It was the *beautiful thing*, his escape.

Aska traveled on a truck. Then they unloaded her. She doesn't know what this place is, maybe an abandoned factory. In her town when she was little they called her *mrkva*, carrot, because of her hair. Hair of that color is a sort of destiny. It draws the attention of birds, like a pumpkin lying open in the middle of a field.

She touches her legs to still them but her muscles are sizzling like sausages in a pan.

She doesn't feel pain. Something liquid is flowing from somewhere, down from her head over the back of her neck. She'd like to be able to see more than what she sees, but her eyelids are like two mice moving in a trap.

The other women make suffering noises. She doesn't. The men push them along with their guns to make them walk. She sees a warehouse and a tangle of metal and machines.

The women are closed into a long room with a strip of windows up near the ceiling. Drained of all energy, they slide along the wall and fall asleep crouched over their own feet, like chickens.

Aska wonders where the world is. Where is the music school and the kafana where she liked to get her breakfast? The next day, when they take the first woman away, she hopes they'll call her. She wants to yell, denounce what's been done to her. She wants to speak with the soldier who greeted them when they arrived, the one with the impeccable uniform who made sure they received crackers and soup.

When the woman comes back many hours later, blood flows from her nose and she trips along in her shoes as if they were full of oil. No one dares approach her, to ask her what's out there. Before, they were united like a herd of sheep in the dark, but over the coming days they'll slowly draw apart. They look for hiding places in the room, though there's nowhere they can hide without crossing through the wall, and to do that they'd have to be without bodies.

Aska has her trumpet. She hugs it to her chest like a heart. She plays with all the breath she doesn't have. She wants to console the other women. She wants to remove herself.

They tell her to shut up and throw things at her.

The soldiers dump a heap of brown blankets on the floor. There's a bathroom at the end of the room. Aska waits her turn to wash herself. Water is the only thing she desires. It fills her with a foolish childish joy, like when she used to throw herself into the river with her friends. She'd jump into a freezing swimming hole and watch her transparent white skin through the green of the current.

A dusty light comes in through the slits at the top of the wall. There are no city noises, no sounds of cars. She talks with the other women. Many are farm folk, but there are many with college degrees. No one can believe this thing can be possible, that this place is really a prison camp.

Aska takes her turn in the kitchen along with the others. When she plays her trumpet the men pay her compliments. They are glad for a bit of music, a bit of happiness in that sad room full of scared sheep who are starting to smell.

They come at night. Aska hides. They take two or three women at a time. When the women are brought back at dawn no one looks at them. Now they know they have to forget as quickly as they can. When the women are brought back they limp to the bathroom. They don't want the others to look at them. The men take Aska away, too. They notice her hair. She's a goldfish, easy to catch. Their eyes settle on her in the dark. She hears their laughter.

Aska manages to survive. They come for the little girl, too, a twelve-year-old. She doesn't come back.

Aska keeps playing, certain her music will save her. No longer does she wonder where her life is, where the Italian boy is, where the kafana is where she used to meet her friends to laugh and play jazz. Her lips are dry as salt. She wonders where the little girl is. When the masked men came for her she jumped up and followed them as obediently as if her teacher had called her to the blackboard.

Once in a while they make her play without any clothes on. She blows her fear into the trumpet. The one who seemed the most polite, the one with the dark birthmark below his eye, fills her mouth like a bedpan and stubs out his cigarette on her neck as if it were a barroom floor.

They come back for her more than once.

She understands why the little girl didn't survive. It was her body.

It's as if Aska's body were numb. The pain is deaf, captive in some other place, as if it were going through a body next to her own, like when a lightning bolt strikes the ground and shakes through you after passing through other things.

The problem comes later, after each rape, when she realizes it's impossible to get back into her body.

Ever since the little girl failed to come back, all Aska sees is a closing light like the little door on the wood cookstove where she'd hide as a child. It was a good hiding place but scary as well. She was afraid that she'd get trapped in there and that her mother would light it without noticing. She looks at the fire climbing up her skin and entering her like a fuse.

The musical notes always come at her while the men rape her, falling out of the sky like hair falling from a brush.

Aska no longer hears their voices. The words are always the same. *Muslim bitch, Turkish whore. Call Izetbegović. Call your president. Ask him where he is.* They laugh among themselves.

Why do they keep calling her *Muslim whore*? It's been years since the last time she was in a mosque. She's a modern, secular girl. She's studied solfeggio. She knows how to compose music. She speaks Italian, English, German. She was taking birth control pills.

They're monotonous. Everything is monotonous. The crescendo of the rapes is always more or less the same. Some of them move hastily. There's a new boy who maybe doesn't want to do it, can barely look at her but is afraid of the others. Because they have to stick together, in the same barn, in the same sheep. Some are too drunk and there are a couple who only want to kill her, Aska can feel it. They pull her neck back as far as it will go. But maybe they're following precise orders.

One of the women saw the little girl, the shell of her that remained. She heard one of the commanders yelling. He was angry that his boys had let themselves go like that. Then he forgave them and ordered them to throw the shell in the river.

At night Aska dreams of long gray latex noses like the ones they used to make in art class at school and that they'd wear at end-of-year parties. The noses come away from the wire and fly like bats. Then they settle on the men's shoulders like cloaks or overcoats. They're pale men. They may already be dead. They may be death. These cloaks are all they wear, along with black knee socks, shiny shoes and nothing else. It's dawn. There's an icy, duel-time light. The men are so many judges. They form a circle like bats embracing. She's in the center, like at the parties at school, when the boys in their nose costumes pretended to be a train around the girl they'd chosen and yelled, *Next station, next station.*

Aska knows where the next station is. She tries in vain to hang herself. The rope isn't really a rope, it's a pair of ruined tights.

She doesn't play the trumpet anymore. A boy used it in her body, the boy who always complimented her, the one with blue eyes like glass.

Now she could die like the little girl.

Her body. Her body is a bag that's been turned inside out and left to dry like when they make a wineskin. Her body is a long chain of suffering bodies. She asks herself what's happened to her mother's cabbage leaves and to her brother's glasses.

Then they leave her alone. They stop coming for her and leave her to wander the kitchens.

Diego tried but he couldn't do it anymore. He'd always managed, but after that night he was no longer able to find the *beautiful thing*. He returned to Italy. He looked for it on every piece of glass he touched. One day he spent hours photographing a can of tuna. He saw that fish dripping with oil, that pink flesh. He thought about the fish's life, before. That night, on his way back home from the airport, he stopped in Ostia. His old knack for sniffing out the life had come back and he knew which eyes to look for. He shot up heroin standing on his feet, his back against a salt-faded Campari poster.

He went back to hell. Every so often someone from the International Red Cross would visit the camps and the tormentors would put everything in order and hide the women in worst shape. The camera operators filmed human livestock as malnourished as the occupants of the concentration camps during World War II. Now Diego knows she's there. He's managed to get into the camp. He's made friends with one of the jailers, a boy with a dark birthmark below his eye. Diego has brought along his Polaroid. It was a good idea to take those big square cartridges with him back to Sarajevo. He brought them for the children. They love the shiny tongue that slides out of the camera as if it were a mouth. He couldn't have imagined that the Chetniks in the camp would also adore it. Now they all want a Polaroid portrait. They pose in their uniforms, the ski masks pulled up off their faces to show their long black beards. They examine the photo that comes out right away and write something for their girlfriends or their mothers on the white strip below the image. Diego snaps quick pictures with the Leica, as well. The Chetniks trust him. As they pose, they tell him about the difficulties of life in the mountains. They're vain, proud. They like the lens. They like to be looked at. And Diego is looking at them. Even the commander poses. He's a big man with a gentle face and blue eyes like the sea. He has Diego photograph him alone and with his boys lined up behind him, their guns planted in the ground. He asks if the light is okay. Diego takes his time, tries to frame the image in just the right way. The commander wants the photograph to show his best profile. He stretches his neck because he's self-conscious that it's a little short. They're mild-mannered with Diego. They stand there with their knives and their solitude, the solitude of killers. Diego photographs the devils and jokes and laughs with them and captures their faces on film.

They invite him to dinner. The women move like jellyfish around the table with soup and lamb stew. Then he sees her. He recognizes her, thanks to her hair. He doesn't turn. He stays bent over his plate. He retains the sensation of a turning motion, of her moving her head like a lost planet.

After dinner the commander pulls some good powder out of a drawer and they sniff it together.

The commander likes the Polaroid. It's ultramodern, full-color. Diego slides his wristwatch off as well, a chronograph watch that shows the time all over the world. He sets it on the table in front of the commander with blue eyes like the sea. Then he asks that favor, asks for that exchange: the carrot, the red-haired prisoner. They know her. Do they ever. The boy from Genoa nods as they laugh and make gestures. He opens his backpack and pulls out ten thousand deutschmarks bound up in postal wrap. He sets the money down next to the Polaroid and the watch and he smiles.

They bring Aska into the room. The exchange takes place right there. She's wearing a baggy parka. Diego barely raises his eyes and nods. Yes, it's her.

Aska doesn't recognize him right away. For a fleeting moment she even thinks he's another tormentor. He's changed, too. He no longer has his goat beard. Now he has long spiky strings that look like a burnt bush.

They leave the concentration camp as if it were the most normal thing on earth. They cross the silvery clearing of the field and go out through the gate. She can't even hold herself up on the motorcycle. She faints more than once despite the brisk wind blowing against her.

The Muslim doctor is short, with a ruddy complexion. He's wearing a strangely comic shirt with sleeves that are too short, as if he'd outgrown it, like a child. The veins that crisscross his bald head swell when he speaks. They look like captive snakes. He nods and tugs at the cuffs of his shirt. Aska has a few calcified fractures and a perforated eardrum, but there are no internal lesions. Even her spleen is in fine shape. She's a strong woman. The doctor lowers his gaze. The orifices will gradually recover. It will take time, like after childbirth.

He won't accept payment. He brushes Diego's hand aside and bows his head. A thin veil of sweat shines on his dark veiny skull. He says, *God will spare no one.* He says he's ashamed to belong to the human race. Diego doesn't immediately understand him when he says Aska is pregnant. He has to repeat himself.

The roll of film sits in Diego's pocket. He seeks it out with his fingers and strangles it in his sweaty hand.

Unlike Diego, the doctor already knows about women being used as trenches for rifles. Planting the fields with bad seeds is a wartime practice.

Aska's five months pregnant. It's too late to abort.

The Muslim doctor says, *Not even the children will be spared.*

He's an old Muslim. There's a pointy symbol on his jacket. He tends to the sheep. Every so often he unrolls his little prayer rug and lowers himself to the ground. It's as if he wanted to be swallowed up by God.

Diego looks at that elderly genuflected body and wonders where his own faith is. He'd like to have a similar source of comfort.

He rolls a joint. He's been thinking about the story of Herod. It was one of the stories the children liked best at catechism. He liked it, too. It terrified him. The doctor has those swelling veins on his bald head. Now Diego pictures them slithering down like snakes and, attracted by the smell of milk, climbing up a crib, where they wrap themselves around a newborn's neck and strangle it before slowly returning, sated and silent, to the doctor's head.

Aska doesn't move in the bed. Every so often she feels hands that disinfect her wounds, hands that tend to her, distant hands like flies on rotten fruit. Her body no longer belongs to her. It's no longer hers. It's simply something that dozes alongside her.

Her body is like a planet wandering through the cosmos, sinking into one vacuum after another. Her body is like a bucket abandoned to gather rusty water draining off a roof. Her body is like the hole left behind by a rocket— a shuttle, a Sputnik—that entered her vagina and came out her head, leaving behind a tail of fire like the Eternal Flame. Her body is a tangle of itchy stitches and cells engaged in combat against one another.

The doctor gives her calming shots that relieve the pain but she doesn't really need them. She'd be calm regardless. She doesn't even wonder why they're keeping her there, why they won't just let her die in peace like an animal in a nest of leaves.

She's in the womb that bore her, motionless in the same way. There's something about the pain that compresses, just like an amniotic sac.

Diego makes some broth. It dribbles down Aska's chin like water from a fountain.

Diego plays the guitar as day becomes night. Maybe music will help her.

Apart from the occasional tremor, as light as a leaf about to fall, Aska's body barely moves.

It's torture to be alive. Witnessing her pain strikes Diego as even worse than the pain itself. The candle on the floor stirs shadows and illuminates ghosts. He didn't lift a finger to defend her. He moved backward so as not to see and covered his ears to block out her cries.

Now he can't tear himself away from her. He slowly blinks his eyes in the dark. The body on the bed is black. It looks like Mount Igman by night. Aska's torn skin tingles and pulls as it tries to close over her wounds. Flaps of skin unite.

It's terrible to feel your body reawaken like dawn, like grass. The mice have left her eyes. The swelling is going down, the black bruises are beginning to turn yellow. Aska sees Diego's jeans, hears his breathing.

She manages to swallow a first cup of broth. Diego holds her head. She can't look him in the eyes. She doesn't want to. She's ashamed of herself, of what they did. She keeps her eyes lowered all the time.

She has a scab on her mouth. Diego waits for it to fall. He looks at the tuft of orange hair sticking out from the cocoon of sheets. He waits for the day when she'll ask, *Where did you hide?*

Diego has that full roll of film. He has her tormentors in his pocket.

He knows that evil moves in herds because it's too cowardly to act on its own. It has to have witnesses, and he witnessed. He, too, committed rape.

There's a mark, a cigarette crater, on Aska's neck. It's the eye of her tormentor observing her, a gift that won't have to be eternal because, thank goodness, the body does not endure.

She hadn't noticed she was pregnant because she's frequently bled. Now she'd like to abort. It's the only thing she wants, to vomit out the devil's sputum.

The Muslim doctor said, *Not even the children will be spared.*

She'll spit it out. It's written. It's a necessary destiny. It's written in the old doctor's veins and in the law of the body, an ancient law, like the law of the Koran.

She stops in front of the mosque. She moves toward the washing trough and washes her hands and the nape of her neck where the black mark is. That hole. She thinks of something the imam said back when she used to go to the little mosque with her parents and siblings.

On judgment day the woman who was buried alive will have to explain why such a terrible destiny befell her.

Now the punk trumpet player, uncertain about the laws of the earth, clings to a sky inhabited by prophets. She asks God to rid her of the devils' clot. In unprotected areas she slows her pace because she hopes a sniper will strike her belly, hopes a Chetnik will free her of that infected blood.

Diego brings her a cream-colored Turkish tunic that she wears buttoned up to the very top. It gives her a virginal look.

He's frightened, too. Men are often unaware of what goes on inside women's bodies, but he knows all about it. He's spent hours in fertility clinics. He knows the exact details of the process of fertilization. He's seen it under a microscope. He pictures the gamete sliding through the bubble of the ova and the bubble folding over on itself and then swallowing up the gamete like a jellyfish. He sees the separation of cells, like a heart, like the double pits of a loquat.

He looks at Aska as she rests and senses the multiplication taking place inside her body. It's such a long way from the cold clarity of the test tube. He pictures a sea urchin, an ova pierced by a thousand black spikes. He pictures the sea urchin detaching from the rock and fluttering at the bottom of the sea.

He sees that dark conception, insects one atop the next in the same hole.

He looks at Aska's tormented body, flowering as it dies.

He's tempted to give in to the mute destiny of Aska's pain and believe, as she does, as the Muslim doctor does, that the being forming inside her is unworthy of the amniotic fluid of life.

He photographed puddles without really knowing why, probably because he was born in a seaside city full of rain and of potholes that filled and emptied. He was always attracted to those little wells of drowsing water. They could be sullen or radiant as they swallowed the moods of the light and the alleys and swelled from within like a liquid heart. He would bend, attracted to these eyes that observed him and that he observed. The puddles taught him. They were a slate tablet like a nighttime sky soaked in ancient luminescence.

He's never thought of himself as a diviner. He was just a photographer of little urban swamps. He's just a boy. He doesn't believe in depth. He's always held on to an image of himself as a bit of a fool.

It's a rainy night. The mortar blasts mingle with the thunder.

When he looks out the window, it's daytime and the rain has stopped. He sees two rainbows. He's never seen two together before. One of them is incredibly close, as if it had its origin right there, a fountain of color-streaked light arcing impeccably across the sky. The other is smaller, less intense—a lesser rainbow, like him. Its colors are faded, as if it were a pallid reflection of the other.

This lesser rainbow, with its destiny of an imminent demise, touches something inside him.

His thoughts turn to the child. To the child we hadn't been able to have in the best of ways—through love. He thinks of the child in Aska's womb, forced into her in the worst of ways, and of the brazenness of life. Now the two misfortunes no longer seem so distant. He understands that this is simply the plan.

He did not enter that room by chance. He knows he was caught, like a fish, like the tuna in the can.

He's not happy, but it doesn't matter. He saw the small, faded rainbow, the lesser truth, where God revealed himself.

The boy is uncertain. Who knows? Perhaps even horror without meaning has its place in the mushy geometry of the world. Perhaps the child due soon to arrive through a black gate is the meaning. He, too, is afraid that the child will have three heads, five tails, an evil heart. He, too, is afraid that evil may only generate further evil. But he's willing to take the risk.

Maybe the child will be the compensation.

He'll give her the amount they agreed to, even twice that much. He'll tell his wife the child is his and she can start dreaming again.

Aska is doing better. One morning she's sitting on the bed. He's brought her some of Armando's peaches, the ones I brought from Rome. She takes a bite and the juice runs down her chin. The flavor, so sweet, so unexpected, is worse than everything else. It sparks a yearning she no longer wants to have.

He says, *You have to start playing again, and singing.* She could put so much courage into her new voice. She could gather together the cries of women like her—the women in the butcher room, the little girl who never came back—and make them into a white thread that divides the darkness from the dawn.

The new life inside her stagnates like manure in a stable, so quietly that she forgets she's inhabited. She doesn't want to leave her city. She'd always wanted to leave but now she wants to stay. She likes the prison of obligatory routes, the people facing a destiny reduced to nothing now but sheer madness.

Another image from the Koran: Satan cursed by God for refusing to bow down before a man made of mud.

One day she's sitting on a bench, drowsing in the sun. Things aren't quite so bad. An agitated camera operator picks his way through the rubble. She doesn't even notice the microphone thrust near her mouth.

The journalist asks her, *What are your hopes for your future and for the future of your country?*

Aska asks him whether the microphone is real, whether it really works.

The journalist is disconcerted. Of course it works.

Aska knows she's without hope. Her body is a nest of serpents. She's begun to feel them moving.

She considers the microphone, which works but is useless because no one will hear her voice.

The only sound that comes to her is the noise of a lost sheep. *Baaa, baaa.*

Diego doesn't know if the desperation that binds them is love. When he was younger he might have chosen another route. *There's just one route*, he thinks, *the one we've taken*. Human life is a rag that wipes the same surface clean over and over again.

He takes her hand. Now that some time has passed it's okay to touch her.

He doesn't look at her belly. He doesn't dare. He looks at the nape of her neck. He's brought ink and needles. A few nights later he pushes the needle beneath her skin. She asks him to. She can't stand the site of that grainy scar, like an orifice, the poorly healed cigarette hole on the nape of her neck.

His hand shakes. He's afraid of hurting her. Aska is immobile. How much can a little needle hurt? Her body has been drugged with pain. These little twinges moving beneath her skin are almost a pleasure. There's a rock around her neck that pulls her down onto all fours in that room.

Diego is clever with his hands. First he makes a drawing with a pen. Then he goes back over it with the needle. One stitch, then the next. There wasn't a single dockworker in Genoa without a tattoo. It was easy to learn.

Tattoos are new signs that you choose for yourself. You put something courageous between your skin and destiny.

Aska has chosen a rose, Diego's suggestion. The petals will look real on her wrinkly scar. A flower will bury the horror.

Aska touches the rose when it emerges after the scabs fall off. It's the first time she's willingly touched the nape of her neck. She can't see it, so Diego holds her hair up and takes a shot from very close up.

He takes it to be developed in a little photo shop that's managed to stay open. When he gives it to her, she says, *It's like a flower on a tomb*, and that's already something.

It's a Sarajevo rose.

They're sitting in a café without a door. They hear shots outside. The little Turkish coffee cups shake and so do the coffee grounds that are supposed to predict the future.

He's dirty. He's a wartime photographer. He's finally become what he always wanted to be. He says, *Think about it. You'd be throwing away a fortune. You just have to hang in there awhile. It will be like aborting, just in a few months. You won't even have to see it.*

She turns her head to look at the dirty tables and the people waiting for a pause in the shelling so they can leave. She can't stand the thought of keeping that living thing inside her, of giving birth to her torturers, of extending their lives in the world. It strikes her as absurd that the violence she experienced could yield so much money.

This child will be rotten for certain. It's impossible to find a good word for him.

Diego rests his chin on his hands and watches her. He remembers the first time he heard her play. A war ago. A lifetime ago.

She says, *Okay.* She'll keep it in there for a few more months. He's right. It's a good deal. Seeing as it's already started, it would be too bad to throw it away.

But Aska shudders whenever the baby moves. She moves her arms away from her body and hollers. She dreams of giving birth to children who rape her.

She dreams she's playing the trumpet and turning to liquid along with her instrument. Even her hair weeps.

Diego would like to tell me the truth, but it's too late for that now. He'd like to sit beside me on his green chair, tickle me, fall over together. He watches my back, the silence. He rests his hand on that silence. The truth is hidden in the folds of this war, in the images caught on the burning roll of film in his pocket.

He's never managed to keep a secret in his life. There's no mystery or secret charm about him. He's a simpleton. Now he's got to keep this horrible secret. He can't tell me the child is the son of the devils, something that's climbed up out of hell. He doesn't want to scare me. He doesn't want to mark the child's destiny.

There's no water in the washing trough in front of the mosque. Aska washes herself with snow that burns her skin. These ablutions will never be enough to clean her. She wants to pull her flesh off. The filth is deep inside.

When she bends to the ground, she feels her stomach, the demon. She prays with the intention of suffocating it. While she was dying, he latched on to her from the inside, and for this reason she hates him and always will. Diego gave her a long, dark, furry coat. She likes to look like a wolf. He won't leave her alone. He's always there, right behind her. Every so often she turns and tries to chase him away. Every so often she lets him embrace her beside a nighttime fire.

When the labor pains start, Diego's the one who sweats. She doesn't want anyone to touch her. She pants and holds herself up against the wall by the strength of her head. Once again she feels those blows. Giving birth is like experiencing the rapes all over again, her innards cut through by a plow.

Once her mother spoke to her about giving birth and left her with an intense image: it's like a wild beast that tears you to shreds from the inside and then dies when the baby surrenders itself to life and slides through the birth canal. And in the end, in the last phase of expulsion, the baby covers the pain with its weight, and then there's nothing left but the huge weight of future responsibility.

Her mother said giving birth contained a lesson.

Aska wonders what the lesson is in rape.

She thinks about the fields where she played as a child. She crossed through them on her bicycle on her way to school. In the spring they were full of yellow and purple flowers.

She thinks about the little girl. When the Chetniks took her away, she bowed her head and obediently followed them.

She wonders why God didn't stop at least that moment, why he didn't save at least that little girl. She was really too young. One little girl saved for all the women raped.

That little virgin child, left intact, would have been enough. The door opens and off she goes, calmly, with her uncertain smile. It seems to Aska that the little girl is helping her to give birth. The girl bounces her ball off the wall and counts. When the ball drops to the ground, the baby is born. Aska feels better right away. She turns her head so as never to know which devil the child most resembles—the one with the blue eyes, the one with the wide nose, the one with the dark birthmark beneath one eye.

Diego doesn't look right away, either, when the devils' sputum is born, when it comes to light in the completeness of flesh. All he sees is a gray cord like the rope on a ship.

His life has moved away from him during these months. Now it seems unattainable. He caresses the sheep and whispers, *He's born, it's over.*

Then Diego looks at the newborn's thin screaming red body. He doesn't look like a devil. He looks like a little chicken turning on a spit and not yet cooked. Maybe he'll have his father's evil heart, but who can say? His voice sounds like a lonely lamb stuck in a bush.

Aska hears him. She thinks of the little girl's voice, that docile singsong.

She thinks it's not fair that the little girl disappeared from earth to be restored to the sky as an empty shell. And instead the Chetnik's baby has come into the world. Tonight the devil will open a bottle of champagne.

Diego says, *Don't you want to see him?*

She says, *I know where he came from. Take him away.*

Before I leave I look at her. I step toward the bed. If I were to ask her now she'd tell me the truth. She has nothing to lose. She'd say, *You know, the photographer and I never made love. The little chicken is the son of the Holy Spirit of this war, the spit of the devils.* But I don't go to her. I don't want to know anything. The child will maintain his virginity.

A rainbow in a lesser sky.

Aska is empty. Her belly is pendulous. Milk ducts begin to swell in her breasts. Between her legs, she still has the sensation of the cord that, once cut, separated her from the child of rape. She's no longer inhabited. She's herself once more.

She has the money. She counts it on her bed. She can try to leave, to hide in the trunk of a car by night. But she won't do any of that. Now she knows that it was the child who kept her alive. She understands that she wanted to save him even though she hated him. She pretends to play the trumpet, whistling, eyes closed, her fingers bending in the air.

Now she knows that the opposite journey is possible. A devil can turn back into an angel. This, perhaps, is the lesson.

Diego doesn't even notice that we've reached the airport. He's looking at something flickering before his veiled eyes.

He doesn't board the plane. He turns and goes back toward himself.

This time Aska really cannot understand why the photographer is still there. He's come back for the afterbirth.

He stays at her side, plays the guitar, looks for food at the Markale Market. Until the day when she says that she's healed, that she really will try to live. She plans to open a music school with the money.

They spend their last night together on the island of Korčula. He climbs up on that cliff. He sees something he wants to photograph, a child catching fish, an Ante. It's the heroin entering his bloodstream, the *beautiful thing*. If a hand were to interrupt his flight to ask him how his life had gone, he'd smile and make an okay sign with his fingers. It went just fine.

He sits on the wood of his coffin, stretches his legs and looks at me. That roll of film is still in his pocket. It contains the faces of the devils. One of them killed the blue child. One of them is Pietro's father. The foolish young photographer never got his scoop. He drags the film out of the canister and burns it in the light. He takes Pietro out of History and puts him into the world.

Chapter 21

I walk through the sand and feel it rise up around my steps. Aska's tale was a lost song, a *sevdalinka*. When she finished, I got up like a robot and left the room.

As she spoke she looked at the white curtain swelling in the window. She didn't shed a tear. Far from its genesis, atrocity is reduced to ash on the wind. The smell of her house remained, the smell of the small peace she'd won for herself.

When her daughter called her, she moved her head abruptly. She'd never regained the hearing in her right ear. There's a constant noise in it like the sea dragging over rocks. She smiled and called it *the ear of History*.

I walk. I'd like to trip and fall, but I don't. I'd like to lie down on the sand, embrace it and thank someone, something—a passing insect, the infinite path of all lives.

I squint against the light and see my son jumping and sparring with the waves. The child is struggling against the young man and begging to be allowed to play for one more day.

He comes out of the sea and throws himself onto the sand. Then he gets back up and runs again toward the waves.

"How's the water?" I yell.

"It's even better than Sardinia!"

He asks me to take a few pictures with his cell phone. He wants to show the turquoise sea to his friends. *They'll be so jealous*, he says.

He stands with his hands on his hips and smiles, his nose crinkled, his eyes buried in the folds that shield them from the sun.

I wade in up to my knees and take his picture as he jumps. His body in the air, splashes of white foam.

He throws himself back down onto his towel. His curls are full of sand. He turns and says, "Mom, do you have a Band-Aid? I hurt my foot."

I rummage frantically through my purse. The wind blows my hair in my eyes. I open my wallet and find the Band-Aid I always carry around, stuck between bits of paper.

I carry it for him because he's always hurting himself. It's an old habit, as old as our habit of being mother and son, of walking along side by side.

Pietro waits, his eyes following my messy gestures. When I find the Band-Aid it feels like I've found who knows what treasure. He smiles, too, and sticks out his sandy foot. He stubbed his toe against a rock. It's bleeding and there's a piece of nail hanging off.

"Go rinse it off."

He doesn't want to get up. It really hurts.

I lower my head and suck up the blood and sand in my mouth. Then I dry his foot with a corner of my skirt.

The Band-Aid doesn't stick very well because his toe is still a little damp, and I can't really see what I'm doing because I don't know where my glasses are. But Pietro doesn't complain. He even says, *Thank you.*

Who are you? How many times will I ask myself that question? How many times will I look at you with suspicion? You laugh like Diego used to laugh, like boys laugh. You're at once foolish and intelligent, harmless and dangerous. You're one of millions of possibilities. A boy from the year 2008, born in Sarajevo at the end of December 1992. You're one of the first children of the ethnic rapes.

I see his back rise and fall as he breathes.

He's lying on one side, motionless as a boat pulled up on the beach, his bony butt inside his Australian surfer trunks. He turns. I see his broken tooth and his too-thin cheeks.

How many parts are there in a body? The fold where an ear attaches and hangs. The shape of a fist. An eye with its moving lashes. The knee bone. Little hairs like faded grass.

I look at the pieces of my son. The truth is that maybe I've always known. And I've never wanted to know it. *You're free,* I could tell him. *You're not his son. You're the son of a bunch of devils drunk on hate.*

He hops along on one foot and leans on me for support.

"You know I can't hold you up all the way."

"Yes, you can."

I recognize things here and there. The fish shop with its plastic curtain to keep out the flies looks just like it did all those years ago. So does the wild geranium bush as tall as a tree.

Pietro said, *I want to go there. I want to see where Dad died.* All of a sudden he's calling him *Dad.* It all seems so absurd.

I follow along behind this lie. Pietro climbs in silence.

Aska pointed the spot out to me. It's easy. It's the only big rock that looks like the head of a dinosaur with its mouth open. Diego climbed into that mouth.

Aska said, *He was coming back to you. He was ready.*

Then he started to climb.

It was just before sunset and the light was right, the light from all his best photos.

Pietro is faster than me and he's already reached the top. He looks around.

"Be careful!"

I'm scared, so scared.

"There's nothing up here!" he yells.

When I catch up to him, he says softly, "Mom, there's nothing here."

What was he expecting? A gravestone? A sanctuary? A camera buried in the rocks?

I'm sweaty and old and he's as young as one of these flying seagulls. We sit down and watch the sea, which looks truly infinite. Pietro rests a protective hand on my shoulder for perhaps the first time in our life together. Then he shoves something into my hand. My chin trembles.

"The wrapping kind of sucks," he says.

I unwrap the crumpled red paper he's been carrying in his pocket since who knows when, since that night beside the fountain. It's a pin, the silver filigree rose from the window display in the Baščaršija.

"Do you like it?"

"Yes."

"I knew you would."

He gets up to rummage around in the brushwood and comes back with a couple of sticks. He makes a cross and tries to hold it together with a few pieces of grass but it falls apart. So he takes his bandanna out of his pocket and ties it around the sticks. Then he plants this cross in the ground.

"How long will it last?"

It's so windy up here . . .

Pietro hands me his phone and asks me to take his picture beside the cross.

We talk awhile longer.

"Mom, what do you think I should do when I grow up?"

"What do you want to do?"

"I don't know."

"You like to play your guitar. Maybe you'll become a musician."

He says he'd like to open a chain of seven-star hotels. He'll design the biggest suite in the world, with an eighteen-hole golf course.

Then he looks at me.

"I know why Dad climbed up here."

He points at the sea.

"You can see Italy."

He smiles.

"He missed us, Mom."

Aska's standing beneath the trellis. She doesn't dare come closer. She's washed her hair and now it's drying in the sun. I saw her move around as she set the table and bent to pick up one of her daughter's toys. A woman like me.

Now she's watching us come toward her.

In the countryside many women killed these children. Mothers helped their daughters get rid of them. Gentle women became desperate killers. It was only after Aska's daughter was born—when her body opened up for the second time and she and Gojko held on to each other and cried for hours—that she went to a center for women lacerated by the war. Only then did she feel hatred detaching itself from her like the useless sac of a spent placenta.

Aska's eyes are on the ground. She brushes her damp hair back with one hand.

She repeats the gesture as we near her. I see her face crumple, see her mouth open and close.

Pietro is busy with his cell phone. I pat him on the shoulder.

"This is Aska. Gojko's wife."

He raises his indigo eyes and smiles and extends a hand.

"Nice to meet you. I'm Pietro."

Aska holds his hand. She isn't able to let go of it.

So Pietro leans forward and kisses Aska on each cheek. And she opens her arms wide and hugs him.

I watch as this circle closes.

She turns and says she has to get the glasses.

I find her leaning against the wall in the kitchen. She's crying, motionless. She smiles when she sees me.

She's holding one hand pressed tight over her mouth and nose. She's breathing into this hand.

Gojko moves toward her and enfolds her in his noisy body.

They were friends for a long time before they became a couple.

They went to the movies together and chatted in cafés about the films they'd seen and about other stupid things. It was easy not to talk about the rest of it. They already knew everything. The silence spoke for them and served in a way as a balm.

Gojko busies himself at the grill as the sea breeze rises. We eat fish with charred skin that falls away like bark to reveal aromatic white flesh, damp with flavor. Tonight we're eating sea.

Pietro asks me if he can have a little wine. Gojko fills his glass before I have a chance to say yes. Pietro laughs and says, *I'd be glad to never leave.*

Aska observes him. She consumed her meal slowly, like a serving woman or a nun, and never stopped looking at Pietro, though she barely raised her eyes. She kept them on the glasses, on the plates, on her life, almost as if she were worried she'd disturb mine.

Maybe she's ashamed. Shame persecuted her for years. These may be its dying breaths. She looks lost, like an intruder, like a thief.

It's a small sorrow in this sweet evening, but there's nothing I can do about it. We all carry it within us. Fighting losing battles is the soul's foolish agonism.

The wind keeps blowing on the embers that look the whole time as if they were about to go out but never do. Pietro talks with Sebina. They write words together on the paper tablecloth and play with the bread.

Gojko joins their game. He asks, *What is the most beautiful word in the world?*

Sebina says, *Sea.*

Pietro is undecided between *freedom* and *tennis.*

The sky is full of stars, the usual stars, the near ones and the far ones. The stars that make us surrender.

Gojko's eyes are those of a vanquished warrior, of a drunken poet. He looks at Pietro and says, "For me, the most beautiful words in the world are *thank you.*"

He raises his glass, clinks it against the bottle, then raises it to the sky, toward a star, and says, "Thank you."

Tonight, evil is dead.

Aska and I say goodbye on the dock like friends who'll see each other again. Pietro and I are wearing flip-flops and backpacks like tourists. Bodies move around us. Who could imagine a story like ours mixed in with all this random flesh saying farewell at dawn? The sea is silent, busy digesting a last bit of night.

Gojko drives us back. The return voyage is incredibly brief. At the Sarajevo Airport we lean up against the horseshoe-shaped bar among all the smokers to have a last coffee together.

"Now what will you do?"

"The Sarajevo Film Festival starts in two weeks. Kevin Spacey's coming this year. Maybe I'll take him around. I can show him where the snipers stood when they shot at us, give him the *war tour.*"

He laughs and then he's sad. He's like Pietro.

I have to go because they're calling our flight, because we've been sad and happy too many times. I punch my Gojko on the shoulder. He nods, like a big beast, like a boar.

We mustn't cry. That's the deal. I feel his rough beard against my face.

We're sea that ebbs and flows. Will there be another time?

I tear off the last bit of smell, of this Bosnia, this love.

On the plane Pietro says that takeoff is the worst part. The plane could crash, the engines are stretched to the limit. He's nervous. He sticks his chewing gum beneath the tray table. Business as usual.

I'm wearing my sunglasses. I nod in silence and think, *Calm down, son. You're never quiet. You're never still. How much life is there in your body?*

Mount Igman is small, like a cat's back. The houses are small, too, like Monopoly houses.

After a while Pietro dozes off with his head against the window and one leg tucked under him on the seat. All his thoughts and boyish chaos are at rest. Clouds discolored by the rays of the setting sun move by.

I look out at the wing of the plane. It doesn't seem to be moving, just like always. I think about my father. Maybe Diego told him his secret back in the seaside garage. Maybe Armando knew all along and kept it to himself. He died two years ago. We were on the way to a checkup for his pacemaker. I double-parked in front of the supermarket so I could run in and pick up a few things. I was in a rush, as usual. I left the keys with him. *Move the car if someone honks their horn.* When I came out with the bags of groceries, there were horns honking all over the place and Dad was sitting right there where I'd left him, his head bent forward. I dropped the bags on the ground. My arms were numb. It was surreal. People kept swearing at me because I was double-parked. I had to wait for the police to come before I could move the car. It was raining. I sat behind the fogged windows next to my father's body in this city without patience.

There's the airport below us with its lights and lines of planes waiting to take off. When we land Pietro walks up the aisle with long happy strides. We're back in the city where he grew up, the city he roams around on his scooter.

He looks at me. "What's wrong?"

"I'm out of it."

"Dad's right. You should take papaya supplements."

Roman air. A sea breeze. On the shuttle Pietro turns his cell phone back on and looks at his messages. I glance over at the screen and see the picture of Danka's pierced belly button.

Giuliano's waiting for us alongside the drivers holding up pieces of paper with names. He gives an excited little start when he sees us. He hugs Pietro. He holds him a long time and breathes in his smell.

"Hi, Pietro."

"Hi, Dad."

He's shyer with me, the way my father was. He gives me a kiss and avoids meeting my eyes. He glances toward me repeatedly as he gets our bags. He's wondering what kind of mood I'm in.

"Everything all right?"

"Everything's all right."

Now that we're back he's in a hurry. He wants to leave the airport, get away from this place where people say goodbye to each other.

"What about you? Did you eat out every night?"

"Have you come back angry?"

I smile. We know each other so well.

The first time he came in civilian clothes to take me out to dinner, we ran out of gas on the ring road around Rome. It was freezing cold. There were no cars, just a truck every now and then. *I'm sorry. This is always taken care of at work.* We set off on foot, hugging the guardrail. The headlights shone right in our faces. Giuliano spread his arms. *Follow me.* Later I discovered that there was practically nothing in his life outside of his work. He lived in an anonymous apartment in what was basically a residential hotel. I remember a bunch of forks and spoons that were still in their boxes. I rinsed them for him and put them away in the drawer. There's always been something a little ridiculous about the two of us together. I think that's what makes us such a good couple. Life is a hole that slides into another hole and, oddly enough, fills it up.

In the car Pietro talks incessantly about everything he's seen. He remembers names and dates. He speaks with Gojko's words. *Europe didn't lift a finger. They only arrested Karadžić now because they made a deal.*

He's sitting in the back but he keeps sticking his head up between us. He pats Giuliano's shoulder and shows him the pictures he took with his cell phone. He skips over the one on the cliff. I'm just as calm as that cross on the rock, it seems.

Giuliano turns the key in the lock. The door opens. The light goes on. There are our books, our couch.

Pietro watches tennis on TV. I take off my makeup and throw the dirty cotton ball in the garbage. I check that the kitchen gas is switched off and turn off the lights. There's nothing in the refrigerator, just the things I left, a limp head of lettuce and a couple of yogurts.

I go out onto the balcony and lean against the railing. Giuliano comes out to join me. He lays a hand on mine. We look at the bar down below and the kids leaning against their microcars.

"What did you do today?"

They moved at dawn to dismantle an unauthorized encampment of human refuse from Eastern Europe.

It's how he'll spend the entire summer. Depressing work. He increasingly dislikes this world where gypsy children's fingerprints are taken and put on file.

I tell him everything. Giuliano listens, his arms folded, military-style. His throat moves as he swallows. He's the one who drags me to Pietro's room. He needs to see him, to see the rise and fall of his breathing.

The door is closed and the DO NOT DISTURB sign is hanging from the knob. We go in anyway. The Chetnik is sleeping on his extendable IKEA bed that can't be extended anymore. His guitar lies on the ground beside his cell phone and his crumpled jeans. Giuliano crouches down and lingers with his nose against the nape of Pietro's neck. Like the last dog, the last father. He picks up the guitar and leans it against the wall, plugs the phone in so it can recharge, picks up and folds the jeans. He moves around the room. So do I. I watch us as this circle closes. Circles of us together.

Acknowledgments

Thank you to Renata Colorni, the sentry who guards over my work.

Thank you to Antonio Franchini, silent agitator.

To Giulia Ichino for the passion with which she reads.

To Moira Mazzantini because she's always there.

To Gloria Piccioni, who's covered plenty of ground in her life.

To Mario Boccia, whose photographs made me see.

Thank you to Asja, for her soul.